the
CATALYST

the CATALYST

KAY CAMDEN

the
ALIGNMENT
SERIES

The Alignment
The Two
The Oak and the Moon
The Catalyst
The Warrior

VISIT KAYCAMDEN.COM FOR MORE

CHAPTER 1

TREY

THE SKIN OF my chest smolders with an imprint of Liv's hand, planted on me seconds before I left her. At my first stop for fuel, I lift my T-shirt and check my skin, expecting a burn, bruise, or mark of some kind. I see nothing. The imprint keeps me awake in a cheap motel that night and rouses me the next morning, its tingle like a damning proof. My magic is inside her. In our daughter. My heir. The one the Moores are determined to destroy. And now I'm two thousand miles away from them, hunting down a man I should've killed years ago.

I cut the Camaro's engine at the rural roadside behind the Moore estate and lift my shirt to check one last time.

Still invisible to my eye, the imprint's presence hasn't faded but grown. The further I travel from Liv and our home in Montana, the deeper into flesh it sinks. It knows where I belong, and it's not going to let me forget.

A pistol loaded and holstered. A slam of the trunk. A short walk through the woods. I stop before the towering wrought-iron fence, face to face with the breach my father showed me when I was twelve years old. Except we were on the other side. It's a random section of miles of fence—the only part unaffected by the Moores' boundary spell, unrecognizable without the trigger my father put in my mind that day.

I enclose a bar in each fist, right at the weld, plant my feet and pull heat from the air, the ground. The scorch of hot iron on my palms offers a welcome adrenaline burst, fuel for what I'm here to do. Releasing the red-hot metal, I strike it with the sledgehammer I grabbed from my trunk. It snaps loose, along with the other. I hammer until the metal bends away and I'm through.

The underwood of the forest is thick and littered with fallen trees coated in mushrooms and moss. All my old paths have long grown over. I make a new one, heading southeast toward the corner of the rear lawn with the most cover. My direction brings me straight to the cluster of old stone buildings where the Moores lock up prisoners. Or used to. The roofs have burned away, the walls charred black. Christian told me they burned after I left, but he never said why.

I step over debris in the doorway of the building where I spent seven days at age fifteen and yank the chain out of the broken wall. I'm sure I'll have a use for it. If not, it's a nice souvenir. A clap of thunder splits the sky right over-head, and I look up at the gathering storm. I leave the site and double my pace toward the main part of the property.

The house sits ahead of me, its wide, stone walls lit by an orange tinge—some play of light under the purple-black sky prepping to spill. My phone vibrates in my pocket again and for the first time today I take a look. A text from Christian: *Just got home. Your dad's here too. Where are you?*

He must've gotten the first flight home when he heard I was coming. Sounds like my father rushed home too. They think they can stop me. Not this time.

I cross the lawn and scale the corner of the house to the second floor balcony outside the room I used to share with Kate. An interior light flips on, as if I'm expected. I pause outside, watching Kate enter and hand the baby off to her maid, who puts him in a crib. I unholster my pistol and aim at Kate's heart.

There was a time when I would've defended her with my life. Would have killed for her. And she was playing me like she'd been born to. Through the pistol's sight, I watch her walk to her dresser then pause for her maid to unzip her dress. She steps out of it and slips her arms into a waiting silk robe. The maid moves away, giving me a perfect shot. Christian would kill me. And this isn't what I'm here to do.

I wrap the chain around my fist and punch through the glass as thunder cracks the sky.

She spins around, bumping her dresser hard enough to topple an antique lamp. The maid dashes to the crib. I aim my pistol at her. "Leave."

"Take the baby," Kate says quickly.

Like I'd do anything to a baby. I'll have to wait until he's older. I watch the maid leave, then I cross the room and close the door.

Kate ties the sash on her robe. "Can you give me a minute to get dressed?"

I kick her chair out from under her desk. "Sit down."

She doesn't move, so I help her sit. She rubs her arm, glaring up at me. I take the rolled-up papers out of my back pocket, smooth them out on her desk, and hand her a pen.

"I miss you, Trey. I know you miss me."

"Christian's the only reason I'm not killing you right now."

"Which is why I had his baby. It's good protection." She gives me the most vicious of smiles.

I take out my knife and stab it into the desk.

"I did love him, though. I still do."

"Stop talking."

She lays down the pen. I put it back in her hand.

"I'm not divorcing you, Trey."

I flatten her other hand against the desktop and position the blade of my knife over her pinky.

"You wouldn't dare," she says.

"You don't know me very well." I press down. It doesn't take much to sever a pinky.

She chokes on her breath then takes a big lungful and breathes herself through it. The fury in her eyes brings me back to my life here, with her wild temper and our countless fights in this very room.

"That convince you, or should I keep going?"

She starts signing when I move the knife to her next finger. I flip the pages for her since I still have her hand pinned, only releasing her when she's signed the final page. Just in time—the pool of blood is becoming hard to avoid. I roll up the papers and slide them into my back pocket.

"You don't really love her, you know." Her voice trembles. Tears swell in her eyes from the pain she's fighting. She's never allowed herself to show me a moment of weakness. Maybe I should move on to the next finger, see if she'll break. She swallows hard. "It's just a spell. It's not real. You'll see what a fool you are, Trey, when—"

Her words are silenced as I finish drawing my family's symbol for quiet in the spill of her blood. That will give the Moores something to do after I leave. A spell to undo a muted voice isn't as quick as this. Maybe next time she'll listen when I tell her to stop talking. I collect my chain and leave the room without a look back.

The hallways are calm. Voices carry up the main staircase, so I head toward the sounds and descend right into their midst. Jared front and center, like he's here to receive me. Like this is his damn house. Pierce grinning behind him. And the one I came to see, leaning against the door frame. Dillon.

Again, my attention is captured by that imprint of Liv's fingers on my chest. I see the text she sent an hour after I left her: *Please don't kill.* And the second one she sent when I didn't answer the first: *You're better than that.* The response I withheld: *You're wrong. I'm much worse.* Worse than she could imagine. And I'm not sure what will happen when she realizes just how vile I am.

Pierce raises a hand to call off the two armed guards stepping forward at my approach. They didn't have enough warning to gather an army. Two men are all I have to deal with. Maybe it's all they think they'll need. They should know better.

It's then that I notice my father standing in the doorway of the parlor with Christian. There's an odd slant to my father's frame, a tightness in his face. Christian comes forward into the room, and I notice something grossly wrong. My father, the oldest son, has had the upper hand since I was old enough to understand the concept. His subservient stance proves what I can sense: there's a new power structure in this family.

"We thought you were having a change of heart up there, cousin," Jared says. "You want to switch women with my brother again? I'm sure he's willing."

"Plenty willing." Dillon has cupped his hands around his mouth so the words hit me hard from across the expanse of the foyer.

My father dismisses the two guards from the room. Kate comes down the stairs, flanked by her maids. Her hand is wrapped in a white towel soaked with red. She goes straight out the front door while one maid hurries toward the kitchen.

"*Really*?" Christian says to me, not amused. He's positioned himself between me and Jared. I catch him glance at his own fingers before I return my attention to Jared, who's got a look on his face like some new level has been added to our game.

"Funny," Jared says. "You were just with her, weren't you?"

"It's not that funny," I say.

The maid rushes back through with a bucket of ice. Holding a severed finger, no doubt. An oversight. I should have flushed it down the toilet. Dillon opens the door for her then closes it and comes toward me, hands in his pockets like we're having a friendly conversation. "You know what is funny? She..." he tilts his head toward the door Kate just exited "...told us early on to not bother keeping Liv away from you. To just let her find you. That all we had to do was let you know we were aware of her and you'd take care of the problem yourself."

Somehow he knows to jab that spot. The memory of planning her death, making it look like an accident. The overdose of herbs, the bluffs. It's fuel to a sickness so profound it has me wrapping the chain around my fist to shut him down.

He and Jared exchange a look that leaves Jared nodding smugly and Dillon cackling like a clown. "You *did* try to kill her. Kate said you were that easy to play. Are you really that easy to play, Bevan? Did you try to kill Liv?"

He waits for an answer from me. As if I would give him the pleasure. Christian's arm shoots out to halt my step forward. I don't know why he's trying to stop me. He should have stayed in Vegas.

Squinting his eyes, Dillon says, "You piece of Bevan shit. You don't deserve her."

I lunge and grasp his head with both hands and slam his face against my knee. He shoulders against my legs upon recovering, and we fall together against the marble floor. I don't know how many times we roll before he ends up on top of me, holding me down by the neck. Blood from his broken nose splatters my face. I swing, landing a solid punch to his temple. Then he's slamming my head hard against the floor. My eyes roll back—a reaction I can't control. So I shake my head, clearing the haze of unconsciousness before it takes me down. I shove his chest, and he falls back. We rise to our feet together. He draws a gun and aims for my forehead.

"Coward," I say.

"You think?" he asks.

He pulls the trigger, but he's turned, and I follow the muzzle of the gun to where my father lies on the ground, grasping his chest. In my peripheral vision I see Christian move toward me, and we both shove Dillon to the far end of the room.

Christian grabs the gun and hurls it. It glides away, spinning on the floor. Jared and Pierce are no longer visible.

"Go check on him," I say to Christian. My father is old, but he's strong. And Dillon is trying, but failing, to distract me.

Christian nods. "Fuck him up." And then he's gone.

I don't know how many punches land before I stop. It's a noble feat, Dillon's ability to remain standing. I step away for a breath and assess the far end of the room. It's vacant, Christian and my father both missing. The open, bold silence of the house seems very wrong.

Dillon spits a glob of blood on the floor. "I used to go to your fights, you know. Won a lot of money on you. Until that Korean guy. Remember him? I lost a lot on that one but it was worth it to see you lose."

I look around for my chain, hoping he'll talk some more. It will only make what I'm about to do more satisfying.

"Liv used to say those fights made a widow of her. She thought I was working. Meeting with clients." He coughs and spits, due to the mess I made of his nose.

He's changed my mind, though. Any more of his talking and there won't be an end that could possibly satisfy me.

"Jared's probably killed your mother by now," he slurs through all the blood.

Two large paintings crash to the floor with the force of his body slamming against the wall. I've pinned him, my forearm against his throat. A reaction I didn't plan, but I can work with it. "You better hope not." I see my own bloody spittle land on his face, inches away. Killing him quickly isn't what I came here for. I need minutes—hours—watching him bleed before I'll be satisfied enough to return home. And if any of them touched Máthair, I'll need even longer.

I shove away from him and take the stairs two at a time. My plan was to get her out of here before this got out of hand. Somehow, that didn't happen. I elbow open her bedroom door. She's pulling the zipper on an overnight bag.

"Dillon shot my father."

She picks up her bag. "I know. It's not safe for me here anymore."

"I'm getting you out. I'll come back once you're safe."

Christian comes through the door. "Martin's—"

"Dead," Máthair says. "We need to leave."

Christian takes hold of her shoulder to stop her—for what, I don't know. He's staring past her with cold eyes, gripping hard as if passing strength to her. We both know she doesn't need it. He then turns his eyes on her. "We moved him to the library … if you need to see him."

She puts a hand over his. "I don't. We've already said goodbye."

Christian curses under his breath. He's stuck in the middle of this bullshit but it isn't my problem. I have too many other problems right now. I take Máthair's bag from her and lead the way downstairs. Everyone's cleared out and it's way too quiet. At the front door, Christian stops.

"You staying here?" I ask.

He gives me the thumbs-up.

"Don't kill him until I get back."

"I can't kill him," he says. "Your mother asked me not to."

I hurry her to the garage and find a Jag with the keys in the cupholder. Load her in the passenger seat, her luggage in the backseat. A shuffle of shoes on concrete has me whipping around to catch Pierce walking through the open garage door.

"Not so fast," he says.

I'm on him before he can draw. He's old and hasn't aged well. His pistol would've evened the odds with anyone but me. After disarming him, I lock an arm around his neck. I've waited so long for this. Dreamed of it more than I should admit. How anticlimactic it would be to make it so easy. So I knock him out with an elbow to the temple and throw him in the trunk, slamming the lid.

Máthair has a hand over her mouth when I take the driver's seat. Her unending quest for my conscience is the last thing I need right now.

"Don't," I say, flooring the car out of the garage.

Halfway down the driveway, she puts a hand on the steering wheel. "Let him out."

"Forget it."

"Don't lower yourself to their expectations. To what they see in you. What they think they've created."

I see Liv's text again: *You're better than that.*

"What are you, Fearghus? Bevans don't murder people. Not anymore."

We reach the gates. "Maybe they should."

I get out to break the mechanism and push one side open. Seems like I just did this, only I was on the other side. With Liv instead of my mother, minutes away from the arrow piercing her chest, a wound that should've been fatal.

When I get back in the car, I make the mistake of looking into my mother's eyes. Her wishes are as bad as Liv's. Once they get through, fighting is wasted effort. They always win. I jam the car into reverse and back up until I can turn around. I squeal to a stop in front of the house and tug my sick fuck of an uncle out of the trunk and drop him on the steps. In a moment we don't have, I stand there and look at him, the smug grin on his face even while knocked out. I remember all the things he did to my mother. To Christian. To his mother. And I take out my pistol and unload it into him.

Máthair is as still as death when I return to the driver's seat. I floor the car. "That's what they did to my father," I remind her. My real father. Decades ago, before they shot and killed my stepfather. I doubt she needs to be reminded, but I'll say it again if I have to—even though I'm forced to push away a rich pang of guilt for bringing it up on a day like this.

Her voice is a controlled kind of weak. "I hate to see you become them."

"It's inevitable."

We circle the property and leave the Jag on the side of the road behind my Camaro. I move her bag to my trunk then sprint into the woods for my sledgehammer. There's a frantic rustling near where I left it, so I follow the fence to the noise: a trapped doe. With her front end through, she's stuck between the iron bars at the hips with her back legs in the air just like every other deer I've freed from this damn fence. Putting a hand on her side to steady her thrashing, I can see her pulse in her neck. She calms enough for me to heat the fence and bend it. Once free she turns to study me. Her mind is older than it should be. Familiar, somehow. It's impossible. I haven't walked this forest for over fifteen years.

She springs away and it's enough to remind me Máthair's at the car, alone and unguarded. I emerge from the trees and find I'm wrong. She's not alone. The doe has found her. Máthair has extended her hand to close the distance between them. A handful of fat raindrops hit hard around us like incoming fire. The doe takes the cue to leave, and so do we.

"You freed her," Máthair says once we're speeding down the road.

I head toward the same route I took the last time I escaped the estate. Backroads, so they couldn't track us easily, with Liv bleeding to death beside me. "I've always hated that fence."

Máthair remains quiet for a long time before she says, "So have I." She takes my hand and wraps a handkerchief around my bloody knuckles. "Your grandmother walked into the woods a few months ago and no one's seen her since."

"She's dead." I don't blame her for not wanting to leave her body in that house.

"No, Fearghus. I think we just discovered she's not."

CHAPTER 2

LIV

THE LITTLE BLOWN-GLASS bluebird catches the sunlight in the kitchen windowsill. Two days ago I dug it from the moving boxes that came from my house in Chicago, and I still can't understand its draw … or its sudden memory that sent me tearing through boxes to find it. Or why just being in the same room with it will calm the night shakes that have worsened to an alarming degree. I've been tested for every possible cause and everything comes back normal. Joints and ligaments are supposed to loosen with pregnancy, not be overcome with tremor. And glass bird figurines are not beta-blockers to treat it.

What I've been missing has been found. And with it a hefty sense of closure, a calming of the restless feeling I've forgotten something important but don't know what. Now if only I could understand the need for that thing, understand why I've been desperate to have this glass bluebird unpacked from its box and in the same room as me. A reason is still out there, and I fear I won't know what it is until it's upon me. Whatever it is can't be good.

I'll leave the bluebird in the kitchen here tonight. I refuse to believe its presence on my nightstand at Tara's house has been the cure. The shakes went away on their own, and tonight I'll prove it. Then I'll hurl the bluebird into the river and try to forget the day Dillon put it into my hand, how he looked at me, what he said. I can't live with a gift from my ex-husband in the house I now share with Trey. Not when it has such a breathtaking hold on me.

River and Trib are staring at me through the sliding glass door, like they know exactly what I'm up to. I certainly wouldn't test their loyalty to Trey over me. I know his would win. I also know they've been told to protect me, and I'm currently sitting in the kitchen of the house I'm not supposed to be in.

I open the door. The air outside is mountain-warm, which should be cool but my overheated pregnant body says it's a thousand degrees. "Don't you two have something better to do?"

To my surprise, River pushes past me inside. Trib makes a try for it but rears away at the last minute before turning in a tight circle like he's going to give it another go. He just can't overcome his outdoor blood. I leave the door open for him and take River downstairs to repack. There's no reason Trey needs to see the mess I made in the boxes in the basement. He'd think I went crazy, and he'd be right.

I repack and restack all the boxes under River's watchful eye. My gigantic belly doesn't make the job any easier. Back upstairs, I drink a glass of water, shoo River outside, and leave out the front. They trail my Civic all the way up the driveway to the road. Ten minutes later when I ascend the driveway to Tara's cabin, they're already waiting for me. And so is Tara.

"Heard anything?" she asks.

I shake my head. After sending Trey two messages to which he didn't respond, I gave up. I'm not going to spend days worrying about a man who knowingly walked straight into a trap. Worrying about people who leave you does nothing but stretch the time they're gone.

"Me neither. The jerk." She scours me head to toe. "Why are you covered in cobwebs?"

I look down. Cobwebs and plenty of dust. I brush off my belly as Tara pulls a long cobweb off the end of my ponytail. "I was cleaning up some junk at the other house."

"Again?"

I shrug. I can't be irritated with her. She's his twin sister and too easy to blame for the quirks that belong to him. The overprotectiveness is his sickness, not hers. If only I could cut it out like the cancerous tumor it is.

"I can't shake the feeling that he's done something really bad," she says.

"You're probably right." Her shirt is the exact same colors as my glass bluebird—vibrant blue, with a thin ribbon of orange and black detail around the collar and sleeves. Dillon had placed the delicate bird in my hand like he couldn't wait to give it to me, couldn't even waste the time to wrap it. *Did you know bluebirds are monogamous?* he'd asked. When I told him I didn't, he said, *Well, mostly monogamous. Sometimes they sneak out and find a new mate to have a second nest. And the males, they spend most of their time guarding the females to prevent them from mating with other males.*

I feel a tourniquet-tight grip on my forearm and focus on Tara's face.

"Liv, you with me?"

"Yeah, sorry. I think I need to lie down."

She releases her grip right as the tremor runs down my arm. I go straight to my bedroom and close the door. The tremor has already taken over, settling in my hands. They tremble worse than they ever have—a kick in the stomach of my theory. It's useless to lie down, but I do anyway, watching the ceiling while my hands shake and I try to think about anything but that damn glass bird.

Tara taps on my door an hour later. I heard her calling the kids to the table for dinner, but I can't let her see me like this. If the shakes start coming during the day, I don't know how I'll hide it from her. Or if I even should. So I stay quiet, hoping she'll think I'm asleep, and I feel rotten for it, but I don't know what else to do.

After the kids brush their teeth and fight over who gets what side of the bed, I hear Tara flip off their light and close the door. She joins them for bed not much later. I allow enough time for her to doze off, then I tiptoe to the kitchen and gobble some food and down some chamomile tea. I sit at the table with my arms crossed, hands tucked tightly against me, grounding the tremor so it feels like something internal instead of something affecting an extremity. I think about Trey, wondering where he is, what he's doing. And how I'm going to explain my shaking hands and the glass bird that seems to cure it.

That night I dream I'm walking through the woods. I'm on a trail, heading for something and moving at a good pace. The night sky is lit through the pine trees—although I can't see the moon, its light is everywhere. My feet are bare and the trail is littered with limbs and pine needles that prick my heels. I stop to rub a scratch on my ankle, propping my palm against the trunk of a nearby tree. The tremor in my arm is so defined, I can't keep my hand on the tree.

An assault of waking sensations hit me all at once. My loose, messy hair clinging to my shoulders. My torn nightgown. My feet—seconds ago a slight discomfort, now stinging in a way that leaves me gasping. A breeze hisses through the pines, chilly against my bare skin. This is no dream.

I spin in a circle, searching for a landmark that might explain where I am but it's all the same—an unending pine forest that would be a sea of darkness without the generous light of a full moon. It could be a hundred feet back to Tara's house or it could be miles. Without any memory of walking to this point, I have no idea how far I traveled, no gauge of time or direction. I have no food, no water, no clothes. And even though it's summer, it gets cold at night in the mountains. I could turn around and go back the way I came, but I no longer know which way that was.

The wind blows again but when it dies down, I sense a movement to my left that continues on its own. I squat—a reflex that seems to be my only hope for safety. I have no weapons, and I won't be able to outrun anything out here. Another shadow slinks by my other side, closer than the first. I catch sight of two pointy ears, a fluffy tail. A tingle crawls my back; I take a glance over my shoulder into the black-rimmed eyes of a coyote.

It seems bigger than the ones who stand behind it. A male, most likely. The alpha, perhaps. He raises his head to sniff the air, and I can't decide if standing would be a good idea or a bad one. These coyotes have a comradery with Trey, but I'm not sure how they feel about me. When they helped me drag his unconscious body into his cabin that was their allegiance to him, not me. I don't know how to communicate with them like he does, but I don't think they'd be gathered around me, watching me calmly if they meant me harm. I take a steadying breath and stand up.

The large male raises his snout and yips. It catches on, passing through the pack. I'm all at once aware of how many of them are hidden in the shadows as well as in front of me. When the yips turn to howls, I back against a tree, its welcome cover easing my drumming heart. The coyotes' voices are deafening, and frightening, and I'm not sure why they're calling until I see River crash through the underbrush, followed by Tara.

She sighs so deeply she practically falls down. Then she closes her eyes, a hand against her mouth. She's so still I'm afraid to speak, even if I knew what to say. The coyotes turn away and disappear into the pines. I take a few shaky steps to Tara; she's come forward to steady me.

"I'm so sorry—"

"It's okay, I'm just glad we found you. You're shaking like a leaf."

I open my mouth to tell her the shaking isn't from cold, but I decide against it. One thing at a time.

"We're much closer to your house. Let's go there to get you warmed up."

I take her offered hand, and she follows River through the trees.

"Where are the kids?"

"Sleeping at home. I had to call Shawn to come stay with them so I could find you."

"How did you know?"

"Trib woke me up. Shit, Liv, what were you thinking?" She stops to look at me, a mix of anger and relief that goes straight to the guilt I stowed away when I ignored her knock on the door for dinnertime. I can't lie to her anymore. I have to tell her. I have to tell someone.

"I think I need your help."

"Let's get inside first. If you die of hypothermia, my brother is going to cut my throat."

If only it were as simple as hypothermia.

Once inside the cabin, I go straight to the kitchen and pick up the bluebird from the window sill. My hands stop shaking the moment they close around the figurine and a rush of tranquility travels from my head to my toes. The cessation of the tremor brings such relief tears sting my eyes. The tears continue for another reason: the indisputable proof that Dillon's gift offers such a perfect cure, such satisfaction to a wicked craving.

"This is what I was after." I hand the bird to Tara, who's glaring at the thing like it's about to come alive and peck her eyes out. "I have some strange addiction to this bird, and I don't know what to do."

She stares it down, holding it perched between her thumb and index finger right in front of her face. "Where did you—"

"Dillon," I say. "He gave it to me the night I fell in love with him."

CHAPTER 3

TREY

Once we've covered enough distance without a tail, I pull off the road onto the lot of an abandoned gas station. Cutting the engine, I get out of the car for some air to help me think. The unreleased rain has made the open air stagnant and confining on top of hot. I wipe the sweat off my brow with my sleeve then place both hands on the Camaro's trunk and bow my head, closing my eyes, trying to gather some oxygen in the sauna.

I have to go back there. Dillon's still alive. And I wouldn't mind taking Jared with him—I could kill one in front of the other. But now I have Máthair with me, a complication I overlooked when I planned my visit here. I'm all she has now. My father is dead.

Every time I go back to that house, my plan seems so simple in my head. Then I arrive and it all goes to shit. If I could find somewhere to stash Máthair, for once I'll be there with no liabilities. For once nothing can go wrong. We'll drive until the next hotel. I'll just have to take the risk in leaving her alone. I get back in the car.

She speaks before I start the engine. "You can't defeat them alone, Fearghus. It isn't meant for you."

"It's worth a try."

"Have you not tried enough?"

I glance over at her, unable to remember a time in my life when she discouraged me.

"It's your job to raise your daughter. In doing that, you'll defeat them."

What she doesn't understand is I can do both. There's plenty of time to raise my daughter. I can end them now. I was unprepared the first time. The second time, I was distracted. My third time is still in progress, if I can drop Máthair somewhere safe. It's set up for me now and impossible not to win.

"More violence will only continue the cycle until every Bevan and Moore is dead."

"Not unless I kill them all first."

"You know that's impossible. Someone has to stop."

My phone vibrates in my pocket. I've been ignoring it all day. Something could be wrong at home. I answer it.

"Come home," Tara says. "We need you—"

"No you don't. Liv's as good a shot as me. I'm hanging up."

"If you go back to that house, you die."

"You don't know what the fuck you're talking about."

"I've seen it. We all die. After they kill you, they come for the rest of us. Liv, your baby, me and the kids. Ask Máthair. She's seen it too."

"Have you seen it?" I ask Máthair.

"I know you'll listen to your sister," she answers to the windshield. "I *have* seen that."

"I'm going back," I tell Tara into the phone.

"Fearghus. Everything rides on this one decision. You hold all our lives in your hands. Máthair is safe. Going back there serves no one but you. Your selfishness kills us all. That's all there is to it, and I'm not arguing with you. It's on you."

She pauses for me to speak, but all I know is to go home, to give in. It's such an ill-fitting idea that it rattles around in my brain with no slot to fit into. Not that it matters. She's already hung up.

I push out of the car and place my hands on my head, imagining how it would feel to go home and put all this behind me without some kind of fulfillment. With no end to the anger I've carried for so long. The anger I must carry back with me, to harbor for another impossible length of time. How long? The rest of my life? Will I never have my day?

"Liv misses you," Máthair says, standing in her open car door.

"They killed your husband. They killed both of your husbands." How can she not hunger for their end like I do? She's had more taken from her than I have.

"Fearghus knew the risks of what he was doing. And Martin was already dying. He was suffering with bone cancer. He had little time left." She makes no effort to soften the news. Another thing I should've been told, yet I find out after it's too late to do anything about it.

"Get in the fucking car." I've never spoken so viciously to my mother. I get in the car myself before I have to witness her reaction.

As soon as her door closes, my foot slams the gas and doesn't let up until we've put a considerable number of miles between me and the Moore estate. The only thought keeping me from turning around is my plan to return at some other time, by myself, with no phone and no contact with anyone who can talk me out of it. No one who can be hurt in place of me.

"He didn't want anyone to know," she says after hours of driving with the hum of the engine and tires on the pavement as our only company.

"No one tells me shit. I've learned to accept it."

"It was withheld from everyone, not just you. His illness was private to him. You know how he is."

"Was," I correct. My sharp tone sends a jolt of guilt through me that strengthens with every minute of her silence.

Night closes in, but I keep driving because now my goal is home. For the first time in days, I allow myself to think of being back with Liv. The distance between us can't be closed fast enough. When I notice Máthair dozing off, I pull off at the next nice hotel. I'm not putting her in the type of dump I'd stay in myself.

I prop open the door between our rooms, then I shove a chest in front of her door to the hall. I wash the sweat off my face and stare at myself in the bathroom mirror. Too much happened today, but not enough. My mother is lying in there by herself, a widow all over again. And the last thing I said to her was hours ago, the outburst from an asshole taking anger out on someone who didn't deserve it. Before I can talk myself out of it, I go in her room and sit beside her on the edge of her bed.

"What I said before—"

"Fearghus, there's no need to apologize to me."

I stare at my hands. "They killed him because of me."

"No, they killed him because he stood in their way. He always stood in their way. And he was finally weak enough to overpower."

"He wasn't weak."

"He was very sick, and very tired. Don't worry about me. I've been ready for this day for a long time. But I know you weren't. You lost a father today, and I hope you can peacefully come to terms with that."

She pats my hand in her gesture of releasing me from a conversation she knows I'm trying to escape, but I'm not done.

"He was sick when I saw him in Chicago. I knew he was sick. I just didn't …"

"You've had a lot on your mind. He'd never expect anything of you."

"No excuse." I was so caught up in my own business the day I went to see my father after Mamó's funeral, I didn't see his obvious failing health, his suffering, until it was explained to me almost a year later.

"You gave him more that day than you know. He finally felt he earned your respect. He said it took forty-five years, but it was worth it." She gives me a sad smile. "He also said there will never be another person on earth more hardheaded than you. Go to bed, *a chroí.*"

As if on command, I stand. But we both know there's more to say. If I hadn't come, my father would still be alive right now. Bone cancer or not, I got him killed. Everything I do has some tragic effect on the few people on my side. No matter how many times I learn this, I keep walking right into it.

Máthair reaches for me, and I kiss her hand, her cheek. I shouldn't have killed Pierce in front of her like that. I should've left him for Christian—shit, what am I going to say to Christian? *Sorry for blowing your dad's brains out.*

Máthair must be feeling it too. Her eyes are wet, and she looks too damn old. "Fearghus, sometimes I think I went about it all wrong. I should have stepped aside, not taught you anything. I should've let the Moores raise you as one of them. Maybe then you wouldn't be so tormented."

"I'm fine," I say. She's wrong. If she'd let them raise me, I'd be killing the wrong people. I return to my room and open the minibar. Soda, beer, bottled water. I go for the cheap gin. I peel off the bedspread and sit on the sheets. Closing my eyes only gives it more clarity. I see the bullets blast holes in my uncle, the blood ooze out. It haunts me like a bad dream. Like a mistake.

I take an unending gulp from the bottle. It's the only thing that makes sense anymore.

I wake with a start in a tank of blinding sunlight. Opening my eyes pounds it into my brain. Stupid. I didn't close the curtains. There's a tap at the door, so I answer it: Máthair and a tray of breakfast.

"It's not safe to leave."

"Don't be silly."

Rubbing my face isn't helping me wake up.

"You shouldn't drink like that."

I look at the empty bottles on my nightstand. Has to be all the liquor in my minibar, and I don't remember doing it.

"You remind me of someone, Fearghus."

I go in the bathroom for a shower then get out and devour what she left of the food. Then we're back on the road. When I take the turn for Roanoke, I tell her we need to make a short detour. She nods, her eyes on a rogue foothill of the Appalachians.

"Someone I need to see," I say. Someone I should have visited a long time ago.

My phone buzzes in the cupholder, and she answers it. Tara's voice is going on and on about something until Máthair tells her we're heading home and we'll deal with it then. "Keep her settled, keep an eye on her. It will be fine."

I take the phone away from her, but Tara's already hung up.

"Nothing to worry about," she says. "Liv just needs you home. The baby is fine," she adds when she sees what must be written on my face.

The house is a tiny thing on a quiet residential street with deep yards and long driveways. I park in the street and get out. Máthair stays in the car. It's still early enough to catch someone before they've left for work. Or maybe not, and I've timed this wrong. Another failure to add to the list.

I knock and wait. A kid answers the door, eating a toaster strudel.

"Bethany here?" I say.

He tightens his grip on the door. I haven't checked out my face lately, but I know it's still marked by a recent fight. He's old enough to want to protect his mother from a guy like me, young enough for his fear to overpower the urge. Forcing my way inside probably isn't the best way to do this but it's starting to look like my only option. Then a woman comes up behind him and opens the door wider. "Can I help you?"

It's her eyes that give her away. Christian would never shut up about her eyes and now I know why. A blue so light it seems supernatural. And she doesn't darken her eyelashes like most women, which makes it appear more exotic. She looks nothing like I remember—or maybe I never saw her. I was drunk all day back then. It's hard to remember anything. But whatever woman I imagined Christian to be in love with, this woman wasn't her. She's too pretty in an effortless way. Nothing like the supermodels he's normally with.

"I'm Christian Moore's cousin." I extend a hand. "Trey."

"Brother," she corrects, like I'm lying. She looks at my hand until I withdraw it.

"I need to talk to you."

"I'd rather not." She gets the door a few inches closed before I block it with my arm.

"Christian didn't do it. Our family brainwashed you."

"Get off my porch."

"They can do things."

She focuses past me, at my car on the street. "Things like what?"

"Magic. Spells to brainwash people. Push a pregnant woman down stairs and then make that woman think an innocent man did it."

A flush rises from her neck to her cheeks and her eyes tear up. "You expect me to believe that?"

"Do you believe this?" I release the door and jab a finger into a pot of half-dead petunias. Brown leaves turn green, drooping stems straighten, and the yellow blooms open. She puts a hand to her mouth, her eyes wide. I send more power through, and the flowers rise six inches out of the pot. If that doesn't convince her of what our family can do, it's hopeless. I brush the soil off my hand. She still looks unwilling to talk.

"Christian wouldn't do a thing to hurt you. I should've told you that a long time ago." I step off the porch and get halfway down the driveway before she calls my name. I turn around.

"I believe you," she says.

"Call him." I rattle off his number. The look on her face tells me she'll remember it like it was tattooed on her arm. It also tells me whatever spell they used has worn off, and all she needed was a little nudge toward the truth. "And water your flowers."

Back in the car Máthair covers my hand with hers. "You're a good brother."

"I'm not, but it's a start."

Two hours later I get a text from Christian: *Dude.*

And for once, I know what it feels like to do something right. It gives me about five minutes of peace before my thoughts return to killing Dillon and Jared. They're the only two left. Once I get them, I can rest. It will finally be enough.

It has to be enough.

CHAPTER 4

LIV

BRINGING THE BLUEBIRD back to Tara's was supposed to help me sleep. And it would—if calming the shakes was enough. What Tara and I didn't count on was my preoccupation with it, how I'd lie awake at night, not wanting sleep to sever my connection to it. She has some ideas to fix me, but her inexperience with "sadistic Moore magic" has made our decision. We can't take any risks without Sloane's input or Trey's help. As if Trey will be capable of helping once he finds out what's going on.

At least I now have something to keep me occupied. The clinic is understaffed and Dr. Wu called to offer me hours. I accepted, grateful for something to take my mind off spells and glass bluebird addictions and waiting for the sound of Trey's tires on the gravel driveway. Cutting my work schedule back to transition to maternity leave has left a void in my life I'm glad to refill while I can. But since a nurse with trembling hands doesn't bring much comfort to a patient, I've got the glass bluebird in my pocket all day with me. Its close contact only intensifies my addiction.

It's temporary—that's become my mantra. Sloane will fix me. She's got a major in Bevan magic with a minor in Moore. She knows all their tricks and how to counteract them.

On my way to an exam room, Shawn passes me in the hall. "That jerk boyfriend of yours home yet?"

"Not yet. Should be soon—maybe tomorrow?"

He parks his dolly against the wall. "Any more midnight sleepwalks through the woods?"

"Thanks for watching the kids for Tara that night."

"Any time. I'd just rather not do it because you're wandering the woods, ya know?"

I slide my hand into my scrubs pocket to make sure the bird's still tucked inside. "It won't happen again."

He nods slowly, pondering something he doesn't seem too apt to speak aloud. He tilts his dolly and turns. "I think you might be as weird as them. You're just better at hiding it."

"Weird as who?"

"Your jerk boyfriend and his hot sister."

I watch him walk away. Someone needs to tell him the truth about us. A guy who hops out of bed in the middle of the night to babysit so his girlfriend can track down a sleepwalker in the mountains deserves to know exactly what he's getting involved in. We can't continue to keep him in the dark.

No appointments remain. The waiting room is empty. I check with Anne, and she tells me it's slowed down enough for the full-timers to handle, so I clock out early.

On my drive home I set the bluebird in the passenger seat so it doesn't get crushed by my seatbelt. The space between me and it becomes a physical pain, a deprivation so pronounced I can barely keep my hands on the wheel. Lightheaded and nauseated, I pull onto the shoulder just to catch my breath. I can't let it go on like this. I don't know what effect Dillon put on this bird, but I don't want it around me anymore. I don't want it around my baby. I'll have to quit it cold turkey like I quit the sleeping pills. Like I quit my old life. Like I quit Dillon himself.

I turn around and drive straight to my house to pack that bird away where it belongs. I don't care how bad the tremor returns. I'll take it double-strength rather than allow an inanimate object to have any more control over me. And I can't admit—I won't admit—that this constant reminder of Dillon's gift has reminded me of my life with him. I don't need the memories. I don't need the feelings that come with them. I did love him, but I don't anymore, and the more I need to remind myself of that, the more it unnerves me.

When I park in front of the house, I have an even scarier thought. I asked Trey not to kill because I believe Trey's a better person than that. But the whole truth? I didn't want him to hurt Dillon.

I stomp from the car to the house with an urgency I don't understand. My light head has gone heavy and pounding and my pulse is off the charts. I go inside, slam the door, and pace. Something has to give; something's going to blow. The bluebird is in my fist. I open my hand slowly, feeling an onslaught of vibrations that resound in my head. Tara told me not to break it until we know what we're dealing with but why not? I read in Trey's ancient texts that all love spells require constant recharging, that something must be used to revive the spell regularly or it dies out. A charm would be just that thing. And if that's all this is, crushing it will end it.

Trey's family's books taught me how these charms work. They might explain what happens when the charm is destroyed. I go downstairs and pull them from the shelves, trying to remember which one holds the love spells. One slips from my hand, knocking another book off the shelf that falls open against the floor. I squat, cursing my pregnant body and its insistence on making me drop every damn thing I pick up. When I lift the book there's something underneath it that must have fallen out. A baby sock? I haven't yet bought socks, and I doubt Trey—

I notice then, the yellow letter S embroidered on the side. I remember the day I returned to the house Dillon and I shared in Chicago, with our baby and her one remaining sock. And how I went back outside and retraced my steps, hoping to find the missing sock that was a gift from the sweet old woman next door who embroidered them herself with an S for Sloane, the name I gave her from a grandmother I didn't know she should have. That was the last time I walked down that street with my baby in my arms.

I jump to the ring of my phone. Tara.

"Heading there now," I answer.

"I'm getting a bad vibe. The birds are going crazy around the house. Where are you?"

"At my house."

"Are the dogs there?"

I go upstairs to the kitchen. Both dogs are watching me through the back door. This is exactly why I shouldn't be here by myself. The Moores have lured Trey away so they can send one of their guys to Black River to kill us all. I'm the only person who can protect Tara and the kids, and I'm too far away. I open the door and tell the dogs to go to Tara but all they do is wag their tails. I can't communicate with them like Trey can. But if I get in the car they'll get the hint.

"I'm on my way and so are the dogs," I say into the phone. "Get that shotgun—do you remember where I hid it?"

"The only person I'll shoot is my brother for taking their bait and leaving us alone. I have some tricks I can use, but it won't hold them off for long. And if they send as many as they sent to my house in Chicago—"

"If they do that, we're better off fleeing. Put Winnie and Will's shoes on and get ready to run." I trample down the stairs and grab a rifle and some ammo. The baby sock is still on the floor, a mystery I stop to stare at when there's no time to waste. Maybe Trey found it in my stuff, realized its significance and tucked it into a book. But I didn't bring that sock with me from Chicago. It's still in the baby's room with everything else, in the house awarded to Dillon in our divorce at my request. And I never found the missing one. The dogs bark upstairs, urging me to go. I put the sock in my pocket and leave the bluebird on the kitchen windowsill because screw that thing. I'm done. I don't realize what a mistake it is until I'm crossing the bridge over the river. Trembling hands aren't going to help my aim.

When Tara's house comes into view, I see what she left out. It's not just the hundreds of chattering birds filling the branches of the pine trees—the whole coyote pack has taken over the front yard. From the number, it must be several packs working together. They part to make room for my car. I park as close to the door as I can. Then I take a quick glance around and make a run for it. Tara's right inside. She makes a sarcastic display of locking the door. We both know locks aren't going to stop them.

I hand her the rifle and grab the shotgun I've stashed safely away from the kids. It seems like a better choice for my shaking hands. Tara gets shells from the top of the fridge, and I load the shotgun and wait by the door. "Where are Winnie and Will?"

"Bedroom. Haven't woken from their afternoon nap. I did sneak in and put on their shoes. Why don't we just get in the car and leave?"

"Because we'll have to come back sometime, and it's better to deal with this now than not know what we're walking into." I pull an inch of curtain away and peek outside just in time to see the coyotes darting into the woods. The birds have fled the trees, leaving silence in their wake.

"You're shaking again."

I can't acknowledge it. Acknowledgment only gives it power. "Do you hear that?"

She moves to the window. "Sounds like a car."

I hear the same hope in her voice that has just bloomed in me, even though I know it can't possibly be Trey this soon. I go out the back door from the kitchen and circle the house, stopping at the farthest corner from the driveway. I watch the curve in the gravel where I'll get the first glimpse of the approaching car. The woods seem unusually quiet now that all those birds have fled. Trey is the only one who'd know why every nearby animal has gone mute.

Shawn's truck crawls up the driveway. I release all my held breath. It doesn't explain Tara's bad vibe, though, or the gathering of coyotes. Something falls through the branches of the trees to my left. I readjust my position, rounding the corner so I'm now against the front face of the house. More noises from the woods have me aiming high in the trees. It sounds like a busy squirrel but there's no way to be sure. It wasn't too long ago Trey had to take out one of their guys in the large pine that looms over our house. And not too long before that, they broke into this house through the skylight. Climbing the nearby trees would make that type of attack easy.

I hear Shawn turn off his engine and get out of his truck. Tara calls him to the front door, and I start backing toward it, covering the woods until I'm across the threshold.

"I feel like I shouldn't ask," Shawn says to me.

"Probably shouldn't." I lock the door. I know he deserves the truth. I have no idea what to tell him.

"You don't strike me as the Mossberg type."

I lean the shotgun against the wall. "I'm not."

He scratches his head and looks at Tara. She shrugs. We all turn toward a child's footsteps in the hall. Winnie shuffles into view, rubbing her eyes, her rainbow-colored teddy bear tucked under one arm. "Those three bad guys aren't gonna get us. The coyotes got 'em first."

The tremor worsens while I'm helping Tara put the kids to bed. It's too intense to hide, and I have no desire to hide it from her anyway. With a sympathetic frown at me in the bathroom mirror, she takes my position brushing Will's teeth. I wander into the kitchen and become overrun by memories that should no longer have any hold on me. Memories of my life with Dillon, now flavored by a warmth that Trey and Christian purged once before. I went through too much to kill the false love attached to those memories, and I don't want it back.

But there they are, the same old memories, with that affection added back in like it had never been removed. The way Dillon would smile when he'd tease me. How he'd tuck my leg over his hip in bed and bury his face against my neck, breathing me in. The broken look on his face when our baby Sloane's first short life had faded out. He loved her. He loved me. And I loved him. It feels too real for it all to have been a sham.

I jump—Tara's hand on my arm. "Liv, you're really starting to freak me out."

"I'm quitting it," I tell her. "Being so near it all day is making the attachment worse. I left it at my house and that's where it stays. I'll lock myself in my room tonight."

"No way. You stay here and I'll go get it for you. It's only a couple more days—"

"It's making me love him again. I can't ..." I hate the quiver in my voice. "I can't allow that."

She takes my hands and watches them shake, as if trying to analyze a condition that I've already determined makes no medical sense. But if she has any ideas, I'm more than open to them.

"I can mix something up for you that might help you sleep without the bluebird charm tonight, but it's not something you should do more than once, especially if you get this attached to whatever Dillon used."

That's when it hits me. It's withdrawal, plain and simple. It even shares symptoms with alcohol withdrawal. Since I don't exactly know what I'm withdrawing from, it's impossible to know what else is in store for me, but I'm willing to take it on. If I can quit sleeping pills cold turkey, I can do this.

The tea she brews for me reminds me of the one Trey made on my first night captive in his house, only hers has a floral sweetness his didn't. She doesn't offer sugar to ease the taste, and it's perfectly palatable without it. Tara sits across the table from me while I drink it, saying nothing because it's all already been said. Hoping Trey does the right thing is a waste of brain function. Counting on him to return with clean hands is pointless. For the past six months the Moores have lowered their offense to practically nothing, but he's going to reignite it to satisfy a need that has no recompense powerful enough to fulfill it. All we can do now is wait for him to return and assess the damage he's done. And start the countdown for when they're going to strike back.

The next morning I wake to the sound of dogs barking in my ear. The songs of birds close, clear, unmuffled by walls. And Tara screaming my name.

When my eyes open, I see my naked toes. The edge of a cliff. Open air beyond. I'm tugged backward and stumble into someone's arms. Someone who's cursing worse than Trey and Christian put together.

I start apologizing because I don't know what else to do. I can't think about what just happened, what could've happened, what I almost did.

"—and you're getting that piece of shit bluebird and putting it back in your pocket until Máthair and Fearghus get home," Tara is saying. "Holy oak, Liv. Holy fucking oak."

She sits in the grass, flushed and breathing hard, looking like she's going to pass out.

"Deep breaths," I tell her.

"Don't 'deep breaths' me. All calm and collected like you weren't just about to jump off a cliff." She twists her leg, exposing a deep gash running the length of her calf. "I don't even know what that's from. Maybe an early morning sprint through the forest to find you?"

I shield my eyes from the morning sun and peer around to get my bearings. We're on the bluffs behind Tara's house, the ones that overlook the river that separates Trey's and my house from hers. Across the gorge is an identical bluff that's visible from Tara's back porch. It was the bluff I spotted Trey on that night many months ago when Tara's house was mine and Trey was the asshole I couldn't get away from.

Our house is beyond that bluff, in the direction I'd been facing when Tara found me.

Tara's right. I need to stop being stubborn. That bluebird is evil but it's keeping me alive. I need it with me until we can figure out how to break the spell.

Tara goes to check on the kids in their beds once we reach her house. I head straight to my car. Knowing the bluebird is minutes away has deepened the tremor so much I can barely drive. At the house I fling open the front door and go straight to it. I pick it up. It slips through my fingers and hits the edge of the countertop. Blue glass shatters on the floor.

A fragrant stalk of fog rises from the mess—spearmint, pine, something else that burns my nose and eyes. I fall to my knees in the glass, sickeningly aware of one crucial thing: Trey went to Virginia to kill Dillon. It might be too late but I have to try. I have to stop him.

CHAPTER 5

TREY

"IT'S A HOUSE from a fairytale," Máthair says when I park in front of Tara's house. "I can't wait to see yours."

"Don't get your hopes up. Mine's not as nice." I take her luggage out of the trunk and carry it to the door.

I pause at the sound of tires on the road below to determine if they're getting closer. They are. I return to the trunk for my rifle and aim it at the curve in the driveway. Tara's CR-V drives into view, kicking gravel with more speed than usual. I swing the rifle toward the woods, the house, the bluffs, checking for threats. If she's racing here, she might be trying to warn us about something near the house.

She skids to a halt and hops out, leaving the door open. "Liv's gone. She broke that bluebird charm—I don't know where she went but she's gone."

"What do mean she's—"

"Come—your house. I'll explain on the way." She rushes toward Máthair and gives her a hug. "The kids are in my car. Can you—"

"I'll get them inside," Máthair says.

Tara and I get in the Camaro, and I drive in the grass around her CR-V. She twists completely in the seat to look out the back window. "I hope they're not freaked out."

"Put on your seat belt." We're about to break some speed limits.

She does, then she buries her face in her hands and takes several steady breaths. "So, Liv found this glass bluebird figurine. Some kind of charm from Dillon. It's been making her crazy. It calms her shakes—"

"What shakes?"

"Her tremor. She used to get it only at night, but it started coming during the day until she found this charm that calmed it down. But she was worried she was becoming too attached to it, so she left it at your house … Well, she went back to get it today and must've broken it. Then she took off."

I leave some rubber on the road on a tight turn. Tara curses, grabbing the door handle. If Liv took off, then we're traveling in the wrong direction.

"I need you to identify the magic from that bluebird. I don't know Moore spells. If you can figure out what it is, maybe it can tell us—"

"Where she's headed."

She points in agreement at me before she's thrown against the door for a hairpin turn. She fights with her locked seat belt all the way down my driveway. It releases once we stop. We sprint to the door. I sense the spent magic before we're even inside. She pulls me into the kitchen. It's ripe with the bloat of it, Moore magic overpowered beyond reason.

Tara points to shards of blue glass that litter the floor.

"It's Moore," I say. "And really fucking potent."

"It was strong while contained in that bluebird. When it released on her, the concentration of it must have been too much, must have sent her running to …"

She expects me to confirm her guess, to say his name, but I won't. I refuse to speak his name until I have a knife plunged into his throat.

I go in the other room for my riding jacket. I toss her the key to the Camaro. Then I go to the garage and start up the Ninja. She follows me out, screams over the sound of the engine to be careful. I nod at her before putting on my helmet and tear the hell out of there. I try to do the math in my head—Liv traveling at the speed limit, me doubling it. How many miles until I reach her? The missing variable is when she left, the current distance between us. So I turn it off and think about the road, the mountain curves I know so well, and the tiniest miscalculation of throttle or steering that could send me flying over the guardrail to be of no help to Liv at all.

I get on Route 2. It's the way she knows. The one she took on her move out here. The one we took with Christian on our trip to Chicago. My visibility will be better once I reach the plains. My speed will also be better. But I hope to catch her before then. I check my fuel gauge when I pass the town marker for Casper. Half a tank. I'm already shooting past the gas station so that decision has been made. I'll just have to count on catching her before I run out of gas.

Coming out of a tight curve, I spot an abandoned car ahead on the only span of shoulder on this road for miles. And damned if it isn't a red Civic like Liv's, just to fuck with me. I ease off the gas, shift down a gear. That's when I notice the driver standing on the other side of the car, studying the front wheel. A very pregnant driver. Waves of osprey-brown hair in a ponytail and a yellow dress just like Liv's favorite. When she looks up at me I lose my place for a moment, I feel a missed heartbeat, a lethal shot of relief. I steady my hands on the handlebars so I don't kill myself, easing up on my speed. Since I've already passed her, I make a U-turn and then another, slowing to a stop behind her.

She's looking at me like she doesn't recognize me. I shouldn't have to take off my helmet—she's seen me ride enough to know it's me—but I take it off anyway. Her eyes are red with big tears. She brushes her bangs to the side and gets another good look. Still nothing. I'm reminded of the day I gave her the capsule designed to make her forget Dillon, but she forgot me too. Funny that his magic makes her forget me and so does mine.

I set my helmet on the seat, grab her by the arm, and drag her down the embankment into the pine forest.

"Trey!" She tries to pull away. "I'm okay … it's okay."

Now engulfed by conifers and too far in to see the road, I stop on a level spot and force her to her knees. I drop to face her. I can't be relieved she knows my name. All of Dillon has to come out of her head now. "It's not okay."

She tries to get up, but I force her down again. It's an easier feat with her so pregnant and not as lithe and balanced as she was before. I'm such an asshole for taking advantage of that.

I grind my knees against earth and take a pull from the elements, her head sandwiched between my hands. When it fills me I know it's too much, but my anger has once again undermined my control. I pause, long enough for her to knock my hands away and lean back.

"It *is* okay. That flat tire reminded me of the day I moved here, the first day I saw you. I don't need him. I don't need anyone but you."

The magic is rising in me, straining for release. It's a secondary pulse in my core that's syncing to me fast. Becoming mine. I try to get a grip, control my breath enough to speak. "That magic is potent … not that easy to shake."

She hugs me hard, her belly tight between us. "I just thought I was dreaming, seeing you so unexpectedly like that. Why couldn't you have called at least once?"

It's when she pulls away that she notices the change in me. The inquiring upturn of her brows falls. Eyes go vigilant. Guarded. Distrustful. She shoves back, giving herself some space away from whatever it was she said I looked like the last time this much energy tingled in my blood. To temper it, I plant my palms against the layer of pine needles covering the ground and return some of it to the earth.

She sucks in a quick breath at the static discharge in the air. "What are you going to do?"

"Purge all thoughts of Dillon. Make him dead to you."

Her eyes fill again. Her voice, normally so calm, trembles. "You killed him?"

I want to say yes, I killed that piece of shit. I carved him up one organ at a time until he begged me to end it. I made him apologize for what he's done to you, then I jammed my knife into his jugular and twisted it while he screamed, while I watched him choke and die. It's that fantasy of his slow death that cost me. If I had just killed him quickly before going for Máthair he'd be dead, and it would be over. I wouldn't be kneeling here, watching the tears stream down Liv's cheeks for a man who still has his hold on her, a hold Christian and I already purged, a hold that returned as any good spell would through a charm designed to compel its victim to return to *it*. So the spell could repower itself. It's something I should've thought of then. Something new to haunt me like everything else. I'm fighting the same battles over and over and I can't figure out what I'm doing wrong. Why I can't just fucking win.

But right now I have only one problem to solve. This might be the rough way, the wrong way, the way that has consequences, but I don't care. It has to happen now.

She's crumpled, crying into her hands. I peel them away and make her look at me. She ducks away, twisting on her knees. I push closer, take her head, and force her eyes to meet mine.

"What are you doing?" she says.

"Look at me."

"Not until you tell me what you're doing!"

She tries to escape; I hold her tighter. She closes her eyes.

"Open your eyes!"

A tiny shake of the head is all she can manage in my grip. I release pressure, sink back on my heels. Too many times I have to remember to treat her like the woman I love and not an opponent. She opens her eyes, but she's not the Liv I know. She's closed something off. "Just tell me."

"I told you. Rid you of Dillon. He's not dead, but he will be the next time I see him."

She turns to stare off into the trees.

"Liv, that spell you released is too powerful to live with."

"I know. But I can."

"You can't. So keep your eyes on mine and—"

"I know it can't be that easy, Trey." She knows too much about what I do. About the price of things that are forced.

"It can be. I survived the last time."

"What was the last time?"

It's a flash of high-definition imagery. Driving through the forest, underbrush and saplings snapping under and around the Camaro. Liv bleeding to death beside me. Then me on hands and knees, erasing a car-sized hole in the woods that would lead the Moores straight to us. It's hard to decide which catastrophe that set off, but I'm putting my money on their best work. "I got my ass kicked by ten guys at once and had to spend days in bed."

"That was the Moores' doing, not some force of nature trying to balance out—"

"We're all connected."

"And what did you do to cause that?"

"I covered our tracks so I could save your life."

She clasps her hands in her lap, studying them a moment as if to digest what I just said. "Well it's not worth it this time. Those ten guys almost killed you. My life isn't in danger right now, not any more than it normally is." She stands, brushes herself off, and heads toward the road.

I watch her climb the incline. This decision is not hers. It was my family who affected her; it's my job to remove it. She's compromised, incapable of making the decision herself. And she's walking away from a fix I could perform in the blink of an eye. The risk is mine to take, not hers to deny.

I go after her. When I take hold of her arm, she loses her footing on the slope but when I reach to right her, she's throwing elbows instead of taking my help. Avoiding her blows, I manage to keep us from falling, but we've both slid a good way down the slope when I can release her. And then she's sent a good jab into my ribs. I raise both hands. I'll be damned if I'm going to fight her back.

"Trey, I swear if you touch me one more time …"

"We're doing this now, whether you want to or not."

She straightens, an angry flush spreading to her cheeks in a way I've never seen. "Get away from me."

Her second attempt at the hill is slower going now that she has a hostile eye kept on me. I'd help her but she clearly doesn't want it. Any of it. I send the unused magic back into earth with a hard punch that has her turning around to study me, eyes more cautious and distrustful as ever. I feel a part of me strip away like the magic stripped away moments before. Her fault, not mine. But it fits so snugly with all my other screw-ups perhaps it is mine.

She's hauling her spare out of the trunk when I reach her on the road. I take it from her. She complies, her expression as hard as ever. Then she plants herself at the front of the car to watch me, like I'm some prick who can't be trusted to change a damn tire. When I drop the wheel and the jack in her trunk, she gets in the driver's seat. I slam the lid and she's pulling away. She makes a U-turn, heading home. I get on the Ninja and catch up fast, riding her tail all the way back to Black River.

At home, I pull up beside where she's parked. I dismount and stab my knife into the sidewall of her back tire. One is enough to immobilize her with her spare already in use. Then I take the keys out of my truck while she glowers at me from the driveway. When I pass her to go inside, she gives me the finger. She's still holding it up when I open the door to our cabin. Ah, it's going to be a fun night. "Get inside."

She keeps the finger up all the way in the door and once we're closed into the house together, I wonder if it's a good idea to contain two bodies so volatile, and so suddenly incompatible, in such a tight space.

I help myself to a big gulp of scotch in the kitchen partially because I know she hates it, mostly because it's the only way to lower the explosive charge before something detonates. She goes in the bedroom and slams the door hard enough to rattle the kitchen window. It's so fucking good to be home.

CHAPTER 6

LIV

I LOCK THE DOOR and shove the dresser in front of it. Not that it would keep him out, but maybe it will keep me in. Although he's gotten so much better in the past few months, now I see it doesn't matter how he improves. The bully is still in there, getting more pissed the more he tries to subdue it. The alcoholic? Even worse. And I'm captive in his house all over again with no escape from either of them. He must get off on this.

When I hear the shower turn on, I toss some of his clean clothes out of the room and barricade the door again. I don't care where he sleeps, but it's not going to be with me. He doesn't scare me, but he should—he just dragged me into the woods—not once, but twice, the second time nearly knocking me down the slope. I still feel his grip on my arms, the vise of his hands on my head. He's lost it. And he's crazy to think I'll let him anywhere near our daughter if he's going to act like that.

Suddenly breathless, I lie down on the bed, feeling the pressure of her legs against my diaphragm. I can't think about what a gentle father Dillon was. What a sweet husband he was. I can't think about him—not now, not ever, unless it's to remember he was a cheater. Conning me, lying to me, abandoning me. What I feel for him now is a continuation of that con. I know that and I remember it. I don't need Trey to take a risk to suck it out of my head before we have a chance to fix it the right way. He's doing that for him, not for me.

I pick up my phone and send a quick text to Tara because I know Trey won't.

I'm home. Trey's home. All is fine.

All is not fine but there's no need to worry her now. She's well aware of the main problem: Trey's an asshole. That problem seems to be largely unfixable, a pathetic lost cause. And we can think about fixing me another day when I haven't been manhandled by the man I love—the man I *really* love.

The room is hot in the morning, with the door still closed and the sun streaming through the window. I push the dresser back to where it belongs and take a long look at my perfectly tremor-free hands. It's nice to have my steady hands back. It's not nice to be in love with Dillon again. To be dreaming of him all night. To wake up remembering how grabby and angry Trey was, knowing he'll never learn.

He has problems that can't be fixed. Dillon was nothing but an actor, but he was a gentleman. He never laid an angry hand on me.

I sneak out of the house past Trey sleeping on the couch beside a shocking collection of empty bottles. He's the type of alcoholic who will sober up long enough to trick you into thinking he's well, only to fall back down in it harder the next time. This is no household for a child.

River and Trib catch up to me on the path to Tara's, thumping across the footbridge to wait for me on the other side. I stop to catch my breath. The baby stretches out, compressing my lungs. I wish she could reach my heart. Press it back together with her powerful legs. It's so broken.

Trey's Camaro is in Tara's driveway as I suspected. Her front door is unlocked, not due to carelessness but because they probably knew I'd be coming. I enter to the smell of eggs and toast and coffee. Sloane pulls out a chair at the table for me, and I drop into it, my face wet with tears I don't remember shedding. Winnie gives me her rainbow teddy bear.

"We should have the fix for you this afternoon," Tara says. "No more crying."

"I'm not crying."

Sloane hands me a tissue. I blow my nose. Will puts his ear against my belly. I hold him against me, the sweetness of his silky hair the most powerful mood enhancer I could ask for.

After breakfast I ask Tara for the key to Trey's Camaro so I can go to work. She and Sloane both try to talk me out of going, but I've already promised Dr. Wu; they're still short-staffed. If I don't go, it means good friends will have to work double shifts. And time away to tend to other people is a way for me to heal and feel right again.

Tara follows me to the door. "What if Dillon's spell causes you to have one of those walking episodes—"

"It won't. It's already re-affected me. He's back in my head, which is what it wanted. I'm fine."

"Fine with Dillon Moore back in your head?"

"He's twenty-three hundred miles away. Stop worrying."

"Only if you stop crying."

I smile at her. "Done."

She squeezes my arm, and I flinch from the raw pain. The look that crosses her face turns my stomach cold. Then she's yanking up my sleeve and drawing a shocked breath. "That hypocrite asshole."

I follow her gaze. Purple finger-shaped bruises from my scuffle with Trey on the side of the road yesterday.

"He might have a few himself, Tara."

"Oh my god, do not make excuses." She straightens my arm to look it up and down. "And your wrist. Did you see this?" She turns it toward me so I can see.

It's like a shuttle to the past, to the first time I found bruises on my wrists from Trey. Just before The Alignment, when our hatred rose to its most heated. When I thought he was going to kill me but somehow I talked him down.

She grabs her keys from the table by the front door. "He's about to have a few more. And when I'm done with him, I'm calling Christian. Have a good day at work."

After what Sloane told me, Christian has enough to deal with right now. He's burying his father. He's hopefully reuniting with Bethany. And besides his son, he's the only remaining direct heir to that estate and whatever power comes with it, but she and Tara aren't convinced he will take it. With the murder of Christian's father, Trey has made Christian king. Intentionally or not, he's killed off every single one of their direct line but him.

I get in the Camaro and move the seat forward. Something hard rolls against my ankles. I reach down to find half a bottle of whiskey. It's a last straw so big it has broken my world clean through.

Take the love out of it. Strip away the magic. Forget he's my destined mate, our connection invoked by the stars. I'm an idiot for staying with him. I should buy a plane ticket for anywhere, take some time away from Trey, from the Moores. I need to decide if staying with him is the right place for me and for my child who's been given a second chance at a new life. She won't get a third.

My phone rings as soon as I park at the clinic, and I know it's him and the apology he owes me. Tara's doing, for sure. I can't give him the credit.

"Drinking in the car," I answer. "Classy. And selfish."

Silence. I must be overwhelming him. He only thought he'd have to apologize for his roughness yesterday.

"Are you just trying to kill yourself or your mother too?"

"Liv, I …"

I hold my tongue, trying hard to give him an opportunity it looks very much like he's about to blow. And with his continuing silence, he does. "You what? You're about to lose me, so you better figure it out soon."

He says nothing. Before I say more, I hang up. I press clammy hands to hot cheeks. My pulse is racing so fast the heartbeats are practically on top of one another. There's no time in my life I can remember being so livid. I'm shaking now in a new way, a brittle, teeth-shattering way that might just break me apart.

I snatch my bag and go inside, desperate for the clinic's order and routine like most people crave the end to their workday. The morning passes in a blissful series of vitals, vaccinations, and small talk. For lunch I join an order for carryout and eat with two other nurses in the break room, sharing pregnancy stories. We disperse, and I head for my first patient of the afternoon.

I give the chart a quick glance and enter the exam room. Shock collides with joy in the most nauseating way—I've stepped backward into the door handle, its cold hard edge sending a jolt up my spine.

He pushes the door closed behind me. His thick arm stretches over my head. "Sweetheart."

He leans down and kisses me. It's so familiar I almost kiss him back. He hesitates, expecting me to pull away. I won't even give him that. The bliss of seeing him, of being close to him, mixes with fear and regret. It's a sickening combination.

He ends the kiss but doesn't pull away, his gaze shifting to the amulet around my neck and lingering there. His hair is buzzed shorter than I'm used to, and it's a darker blond because of that. I remember how the light of the hospital picked up the gray of his eyes the day we met in Chicago. The same lighting must be in here.

"You're using a fake name now? That's pathetic, even for you, Dillon."

"How else was I going to get you alone? He trails you like a dog." He drops his arm. Two healing black eyes, a broken nose, and cuts all over his face. He certainly does look like he needs medical treatment.

"I can't imagine why he'd need to do that."

He laughs. "God, I miss you."

He's much too close, but I won't back away. It takes effort to look away from him. I know it's the spell, but in this moment, alone with him, my need to be with him feels dangerously real. He's supposed to be twenty-three hundred miles away. That's the only way I was going to survive this spell until Sloane and Tara could remove it. I wipe my mouth with my sleeve, trying to remove the taste of his spearmint gum that has taken me back to our first date.

"What do you want?"

He snags the rolling stool with his foot and rolls it to me. I walk over to the sink and set the chart on the counter. It's obvious he'll be guarding the door for a while. If I can get him comfortable, maybe I can make a break for it without creating a scene.

"Just to chat. Let's go somewhere we won't be bothered."

I cross my arms and rest them on my belly. "I can't leave work right now. Why don't you come over tonight for dinner?"

"And get your poor boyfriend upset again? He's not good with stress."

"Stress, huh? At least he's man enough to stick around."

His eyes narrow. He clenches his jaw, exhales hard through his nose. The reference hit him where it should, but it's probably a bad idea to engage him. It would be giving him what he wants.

"It wasn't my idea to leave. I wanted to stay with you."

"I know it was your idea. I meant nothing to you. They had me where they wanted me—with you. You left on your own because you couldn't handle what happened. You ruined their plan. Don't lie to me. We're done with that."

He leans back against the door. "Their plans change."

I turn to the chart. "So do you want me to fake this? What do you want? A concussion? Strep? Ringworm? Do you want to see the doctor?" I jot down some fake vitals.

"I want you to come away with me."

My hand freezes. I stare at the new patient record with the fake name and fake vitals. It should not be this hard to say no to him.

"Liv, what they have planned for you and your baby … it's worse than you could imagine. Stuff of nightmares. Come with me. I'll take care of you. You can have anything you want. No one would condemn you for wanting to save your baby, especially after what happened to her the first time. The Bevans killed her, you know."

He's lying. It can't be true. I look into his eyes. The anger that's there, the grief, it looks so real. It looks too much like my own before it fled, before I found out I'm getting her back. But she's not his anymore, so he'll never have her back. His grief is still a solid part of him that will never fade.

"I have a car outside. We can go anywhere you want. Remember Aruba? We could go there. It could be like that, all the time."

He couldn't have faked Aruba. He may have married me out of arrangement, but he did not fake the time we shared in Aruba. That was his genuine self, holding my hand on the beach, dancing with me in the discotheque all night, laughing so hard on our way back to the villa we could barely walk. There's a real person inside him, if I look hard enough. If he stays away from them, maybe that real person will come out.

"Liv, I won't see you suffer over the loss of another child. And this time, it won't be quick. It won't be easy. They have plans to do things to her …"

I can't leave Trey. He's crazy to think I would, even though I considered it on my own. A temporary time apart to reevaluate what to do about the seriously flawed father of my child. The man I love. The physically aggressive bully. The alcoholic. The man who, days ago, murdered his uncle and maimed his estranged wife's hand. And that's only what Christian told me—there could be worse things he withheld.

"I know everything about them, and I could keep you safe from them. Trust me. You can't fight them and win. It's suicide."

I trusted him before. He was doing a job. Filling a role. Playing a game. He's still playing a game, but the remaining parts of the effect he put on me are trying to tell me otherwise. Or am I overestimating their power? "You tricked me into loving you. You put a spell on me."

"And so did Trey. His family did. The difference is you and I actually *made* something out of that. Trey doesn't understand love. He's not human."

My defense of Trey halts behind reality. Dillon's right. My connection to Trey was arranged. There's something different about it, though, something set straight. I close my eyes and rub my temples, but Dillon's presence is too solid a distraction to follow the thought to its source.

And then his hand is on my arm, and I'm looking into his eyes.

"Give me another chance to take care of you. I failed the first time. I promise to make it right."

He needs closure. He never got it, and he's still reaching for our old life together, for our daughter. They are long gone, but he never moved on. Maybe if I can help him do that, he'll leave us alone. It's a small comfort for someone who used to mean so much to me.

"Liv, you stay here with him, she dies. They're building an army. I don't care who Trey is, he's only one man. They'll kill him and take her from you. If you come with me, I'll call them off, tell them not to kill him. And she can stay with you. You'll save them both if you come with me."

"Come—to Virginia? I won't go there."

"Not there. Anywhere. They won't care where we go as long as you're with me." He takes my hand in his, turns it over to run a finger along the crease in my palm, like it's some precious thing. "I'm done with them. All I need is you."

I close the chart. "No one can see me leave with you."

"I'll wait for you outside. It's the gray BMW M5. Come out in five minutes."

"Five minutes," I say.

CHAPTER 7

TREY

I'VE NEVER DRIVEN *drunk*. That's what I wanted to tell her. She won't back down, though, or believe me. I've seen the public service announcements: buzzed driving is drunk driving. I can't disagree—too many gravestones in this county alone would blow my argument. And I have no excuse, other than it's one of many things I've desensitized myself to. There was a time I understood it was wrong. When you do something wrong for decades, it stops being wrong and becomes normal. And at some point for me it became necessary to survive the life that was forced upon me, and the one I sought out. The high of violence, the low of a drink. Raise the intensity, repeat.

I park in front of the little white church in the shade of a ponderosa pine. The lot is vacant, and I have thirty minutes to kill. I watch the sun blaze in the blue sky above the church's bell tower, trying to think about anything but the things that have led me here. These memories, long buried, are coming back to drive my bad decisions home as if I'm still capable of learning from them.

It was the first night I'd gotten back into fighting for money after I left the estate. Kate and Aaron had just been killed—or I'd thought—and I was living with a brand of anger so potent nothing could subdue it. But I still tried.

I've forgotten what city it was but it doesn't matter. The venues were all the same. I stood on the entry just inside the door, looking over the heads of a packed crowd standing a level below me. Someone could've gotten killed in there and no one would've noticed. Cold air blasted from large ducts in the ceiling, meeting the vaporized sweat and cigarette smoke hanging around my head. Still standing at street level by the door, I was one of the few in there who could breathe fresh air.

Two guys were already going at it in the ring, and not very well. At least they were evenly matched. I knew I couldn't hope for that.

A hand came from nowhere to shake mine. "Trey Bevan, right? You're up next." He had to yell to be heard.

I shook his hand and watched him chew a straw while he looked me up and down.

"Bets ain't good on you, but you're new. It's your night to shine, my friend. Prove 'em wrong. Follow me."

He descended the stairs and cut through the crowd. Heads turned to me now that I was with him. Sizing me up. Fresh meat.

"I'm Davey. The guy to find if you win." He let us into a roped off section behind the ring. "No bag? Nothing to stash?" He looked at my empty hands.

Several other guys were warming up. I could've taken them all without breaking a sweat. I pulled my wallet from my jacket pocket and held it up.

"Lockers over there." He pointed.

"Rules?" I couldn't even hear myself.

He read my lips. "Anything goes."

My kind of place.

I left him and went to the lockers. Found an empty one and tossed in my wallet, my keys. Stripped off everything but my workout shorts. Then returned to the roped off area and took a seat on one of the benches. None of the others said a word to me. Good.

The room crawled with bodies. I didn't know how the place hadn't been shut down. Guess once you break one law, you may as well break them all. I knew it fronted as a gym, but the cops had to know what went on after hours. Somebody was getting paid off, that was for sure.

Two women on the other side of the rope tried to get my attention. I stared at them until they gave up. The ring shuddered and the crowd exploded. I looked up. We had a winner. Davey motioned to me from the other side of the ring, so I stood and climbed in. All the eyes were impossible to ignore up there. They fueled an excitement I'd never felt. I was a god. And one by one, I could've sent them all to hell.

The other guy had already taken his corner. I watched him wrapping his hands and tried my best not to smile because he wouldn't be needing that. He gave me the finger. The crowd roared.

This wasn't going to be fair. But it was going to be fun.

When the bell rang, he charged me. I let him shove me into the ropes to make him feel tough. The tougher he felt, the more devastating his takedown would be for him. The better my high would be when I was left standing. His elbow came for my face, and I fought the impulse to counter. I let him get in a few hits. My blood sprayed. The crowd ate it up. Gore is what they wanted. Gore is what they'd get.

One shove and he was back in the middle of the ring. He seemed surprised. If that surprised him, he was in for a treat. More like a fucking buffet. I spat blood. He took the opportunity, like I wasn't paying attention. I dodged, kicked him in the gut, and punched him in the ribs. He fell back against the ropes on the other side. Now he was pissed.

I stood still and waited for him. He didn't want it so bad this time. *How long do you want to drag this out? I have all night. I have eternity.* A few people in the crowd started to boo, and it caught on fast. The frequency of it deafened me, filled me with unrest, with a need to act. To make it stop.

He kicked for my groin, and I grabbed his leg, twisted it, then kicked his lower back. He fell to one knee. My arm circled his neck. A choke-out would end it now. A quick snap of his neck would end even more. That might've been pushing it, even if there were no rules.

The crowd was in my ears again, and he'd slipped from my hold, gotten around me. I turned and avoided a strike. He got a head butt from me. He didn't like it. My blood was all over him. So much that it looked like he was the one bleeding. He came at me again. I gave him a flying knee to the chin, and he dropped on his back. I circled, giving him a chance to get up. He crashed into me and the ropes dug into my back. I got my leg around him, and he was down again. My knee on his gut, my hand holding his neck against the mat, I punched his face until the sound in the room reached a volume so high I was enveloped in silence. Nirvana.

Shouts cut through, and I allowed their owners to pull me off. Several others surrounded him. He rolled to his side to breathe. On his back, he'd drown in his own blood. He lay there, his chest the only thing moving. In and out. The puddle around his head grew from a slow leak in his face now covered by a wadded white towel. I wished I could say I was done, but I wasn't.

The ref held my arm in the air. I could tell who in the crowd had lost a lot of money—they were the only ones not going insane. A few started stomping their feet. It traveled the crowd in a wave until the sound throbbed in my brain.

Previous fights were never like this. I'd found a new hobby.

And I wanted to kick my own ass for only signing up for one go.

I slipped under the ropes to the ground. The guys in the holding pen gaped at me like I'd just ruined their day. Someone tossed me a wet towel, so I wiped myself down and got dressed at my locker. Davey found me before I had to find him. This time he couldn't yell over the crowd. He shook my hand long and hard then handed me a wad of money and a flyer with dates of upcoming fights. He put an invisible phone to his ear and mouthed, "Call me." Slapped me on the back and pointed me toward a nearby door.

I pocketed the cash and ducked out the door. It opened to the back lot. It was good to see no one had swiped my motorcycle helmet. A woman stumbled over to me, swinging her purse and smiling widely. She was missing a shoe. I wondered if she knew that. She caught herself on the car parked next to me and told me she wanted to have my baby. She didn't know that was a sure way to get herself killed.

I put on my helmet and started my bike. There was no natural way to douse a high so fucked up I couldn't think straight. I needed to find somewhere I could drink myself to sleep. A liquor store OPEN sign blinked at me from the side of the road, so I pulled in and bought the first bottle of whiskey I saw. I drained a quarter of it in the parking lot before securing it for the ride. By the time I found a motel, my vision was long blurred, and I knew I'd cheated death one more time.

It was one fight of many I ended that way, city after city, year after year. I'm grateful I didn't say those words to Liv: *I've never driven drunk.* It would be a damn lie. *I don't get off on hurting people. It doesn't give me pleasure to kill.* All lies.

Cars have joined me in the little church's lot, parked close to the church doors like their drivers were eager to go inside. I can't think of anything I'd rather not do. I step on the clutch and go for the ignition, but then I remember Liv, what she last said to me.

I get out of the truck and present myself to the church's wooden doors, summoning a will I don't have. I check my phone, fully aware I'm stalling. I power it off. To my right is a sign:

AA Meeting

All Welcome

You have the power to help you!

Of everything I've lived through, I think I finally found something that might kill me.

I turn to the sound of footsteps behind me. An older woman balances a tray of cookies and a jug of orange juice. "Would you mind getting the door?"

I open it for her. She goes through, stopping in the doorway so I have to hold it open.

"Coming? As you can see, we have cookies. Homemade this time. And there's another door inside I wouldn't mind your help with."

I follow her in, through a propped open door and down a stairwell. Then we're stepping through another doorway, past another propped open door. The room we're now in is some kind of community room with about ten people standing around, a few sitting, the murmur of small talk. And I see what she's done. She hands me the orange juice so she can unwrap her tray and set it on a table. She trades me the orange juice for a paper plate of three cookies. "Please take a seat. Wait—don't forget some juice."

Then my hands are full and I have no choice but to sit down. A handful of people flock the table, leaving the circle of chairs as an empty and waiting hell. *For Liv,* I tell myself. And I sit the fuck down.

When it's over I'm the first to the door. On my way out I grab a flyer with the meeting schedule. I'm the chump who'll be here three times a week. In my truck I text Tara: *You better have figured something out for me.* Because I'm hitting it with everything I've got. And I'm not doing this any more times than I have to.

She texts back: *Did you get my message? Bad news. Get home now.*

I notice several missed messages from her before I toss the phone on the seat and floor it out of there. This is why I can't stop drinking. There isn't any time to stop.

CHAPTER 8

LIV

D ILLON'S BMW IS parked to the left of Trey's Camaro. It's clever on his part—anyone watching me would think I was headed to my own car. I open the door to Dillon's car and slide in casually. "Don't pull away yet," I tell him.

He takes his hands off the wheel. I can see the tension in how he places them on the armrests. He's humoring me, but I can tell he wants to get on the road. There's something he has to clear up for me, because I keep seeing that baby sock that should not have been in Trey's basement but was, and if what he said about the Bevans is true …

"I need you to tell me the truth. You said the Bevans killed our baby. If that's a lie …"

He heaves a breath. "It's just a guess. We don't have proof."

"Without proof, that's an awful thing to say."

"I wouldn't put it past them." He shifts the car into reverse and backs out of the spot. "So, Aruba?"

"Just drive."

He heads west, and I consider telling him not to go too far but my eyelids are heavy, and the seat is perfectly comfortable, so I rest my head back and close my eyes. I realize I'm nodding off, but I let it take over, all at once feeling my exhaustion like a heavy cloak. I reach for my amulet. It's missing—that's right, I stashed it in my bag so Dillon wouldn't see it, but now I'm not sure why I did that. And somewhere far away I hear my own voice screaming at me to run.

I wake to stillness. A muffled voice, cars whooshing by. I sit up in the seat that's been adjusted to lie flat and spot Dillon on the phone, pacing in front of the car. We're parked on the edge of a truck stop, semi-trucks clustered in a group closer to the quick shop. Dillon stops pacing to toe the gravel with his shoe, once polished leather now covered in gravel dust. He's been out there a while. A low afternoon sun burns above rolling foothills behind him. I go for my own phone. I owe Tara and Sloane a phone call. It's not fair to make them worry. When I don't find it in my bag, I pat down my pockets then search the seat and the floorboard of the car. I pull the handle for the door—it's locked. Dillon looks up, ends his call.

"Feel better?" he says, getting in.

"I can't find my phone."

He starts the car, unconcerned. "Adjust your seat."

I find the button. He reaches across me for my seat belt. When it clicks into position he smiles that exaggerated smile I remember, so big and wide it's a joke and he knows it. But he gets away with it because he's so painfully cute, even with the black eyes and abrasions on his face.

"Where are we?"

"Just crossed into Idaho."

"Dillon—"

"What do you think about Sacramento?"

"Way too far. How many hours are we from Black River?"

He pulls onto the highway heading into the sun. "Not many."

"Hand me your phone."

Once it's in my hand I realize I can't call anyone. All their numbers are stored in my phone, not in my brain. But there's one—the landline at Tara's house. It used to be my house, and the landline is still in my name, my own phone number dedicated to memory. I dial. She answers with a strained, demanding "hello."

"Tara, it's me, and I'm fine. I'll be back in a few—"

"Liv? Whose number is this?"

Dillon snatches the phone and ends the call. "The less they know, the less my family will find out. The safer we are."

"Hanging up on her is just going to make her worry."

"You told her you're fine."

"And what *about* your family? Kate? Your baby son?"

"Rex will be fine without me for a while." He's quiet a moment before he says, "You know, Rex will never learn to hate your daughter if they grow up together. If she grows up as a Moore."

Something hangs on the periphery of my thoughts. Wanting in, needing acknowledgment. I try to reach, but it slips behind the new sensation of Dillon's warm hand taking hold of mine. Lifting it. Pressing it against his lips.

"I know it seems like the most dangerous place for her, but if she's raised there, she could be one of us. They'll never have a reason to hate her. They'll treat her like royalty."

"Isn't that what they tried to do to Trey? It clearly didn't work."

"His mother corrupted him. You wouldn't do that to your daughter. You're not a Bevan."

"No, but my daughter is."

"She doesn't have to be."

I turn away to watch the foothills roll by. I needed an escape from the dysfunction of life with Trey so I could figure all this out. Somehow, it's getting more complicated.

"She was my daughter once," he says. "She was a Moore."

"She was never meant to be yours, Dillon."

"How are you so certain you're on the right side? The good side?"

I don't think I'm on any side right now. And there it is again, that peripheral awareness. I reach, but it's moving away. It's like walking into a room and forgetting what I went in there to do. The ghost of that forgotten task remains on the farthest edge and the more I try to recover it, the further it moves away. Only when I stop thinking about it is when it comes.

"We have the power right now to blow apart that prophecy. Raise my son and your daughter together, so they don't become rivals. So one doesn't have to kill the other off."

"Or here's something easier. How about the Moores find a way to forgive, and your son and my daughter will learn nothing about each other. Happily ever after for everyone."

"It's *our* job to forgive?" He turns to look at me, his eyes off the road for much too long for my comfort. "While your boyfriend runs around like a rabid dog, killing us off?"

There's a pulse in my head. A memory of Christian grabbing my hand after a conversation about Dillon. *He followed you and Trey that day when you left the estate. He wanted to kill you in front of him.*

"You wanted to kill me. Aaron shot me with the arrow, and you followed us to finish me off. Is that true?"

He slams the brakes. The seat belt locks against me as I brace for an impact from a car behind us. The side mirror shows vacant road. For now. Anyone could come around the curve and smack into us, now stopped in the driving lane of a highway.

He's faced me. "Tell me who told you that."

I press the button on my seat belt with one hand and pull the door release with the other. Locked. I scramble to unlock it as Dillon reaches for the button to lock it again. It's a fight for perfect timing, and then I'm shoving out of the door and stumbling into warm air.

The car blasts ahead of me and stops hard on the shoulder. He gets out. "Come on, babe."

"You just contradicted everything you said at the clinic. 'Let's run away to Aruba, hide from the Moores.' Now you're trying to convince me to move in with them?"

"We're talking. Finding the best solution."

"You wanted to kill me."

He puts his hands on his head and looks skyward, exhaling heavily. "I wanted to kill *him*."

"You wanted to kill *me* in front of him."

He takes a few steps toward me. "*Who* told you that?"

As if I'm going to rat out Christian. I back up. Dillon surges forward, but I stand my ground. A test to see if he's as gentle as he's always pretended to be. His hands are up but instead of grabbing me they've gone to my face. It's a gesture that could've been proof of the evil blood that runs through him if it wasn't so tender. If his eyes weren't so calm. If his thumb wasn't sweetly stroking my lip, his lips weren't so softly on mine.

And then we've parted, and I realize I kissed him back. The taste of his spearmint gum is on my tongue. There's a breathtaking burn in my chest, a roiling of some nameless emotion. He's smiling that brilliant smile again, and it somehow gets inside me. He offers his arm. I take it.

He leads me back to the car. "We need a destination."

"Do we?"

He opens my door. "I'll keep driving west until you tell me to stop."

After crossing another state line, I get an unsettled feeling so severe I tell him to stop at the next restroom. I don't vomit, but there's something in my eyes in the mirror that scares me enough to wish I had. Back on the road, each mile is another papercut on some unreachable part of my body. The more I reach for that ghost of a memory hanging out on the horizon, the more hopeless its retrieval becomes.

"Spokane."

"For the night? Sure. I'll find us somewhere nice."

The hotel is luxurious and historic and probably the most expensive one in the city. Dillon's shoes click across polished granite in the lobby next to my silent nurse sneakers. Our room is on an upper floor of the tower with a city view I lose myself in while Dillon orders food and tries to get me to do anything but sit and stare out the window.

"I don't even have a toothbrush," I tell him. He heads out to find one.

I change from my scrubs into the change of clothes I always carry in my bag: sundress and leggings. No clean underwear, unfortunately, or socks, so I'll be in the same ones for a while. Pleasant.

I could call Tara again, but I shouldn't—the number will show up and she'll know where I am. Then Trey will know. Maybe it's unfair, but I can't trust him to learn my whereabouts and stay parked in Black River to give me the time I need to work this out. It should make me sad to admit that, but it doesn't. It's nothing new. I know how he is.

Instead, I go through Dillon's luggage for my phone. I could call her on that. Dillon returns after I've exhausted my search—unsuccessfully—and returned to my staring.

He hands me a toothbrush, his eyes glued to his ransacked luggage. "Find what you needed?"

"Nope."

He untucks his shirt and sits heavily on the bed. "I wouldn't have killed you that day, Liv. It was all a show for them."

"That's encouraging."

"It's true."

"Well, the problem with that is how do I know what's true with you? Where does the show end?"

"It ended as soon as you walked into that exam room at the clinic."

"Bullshit. What happened to your face?"

He laughs. "Trey."

I get up from the chaise longue by the window and stand in front of him. "That's a lie. Trey went there to kill you. He wouldn't have stopped at two black eyes and a broken nose."

He shrugs, holding the position with a face so blank I know he's keeping something from me. "Our food is here."

A second later there's a knock at the door. He gives me that dazzling smile before heading toward the door. I have to sit on the bed for how it makes me melt inside. The baby shifts her position, crowding my lungs. The melty insides and shortness of breath are a combination I do not need. It's becoming harder to remember this infatuation I feel for Dillon is false. That I'm not reliving my old life. That this isn't the weekend trip Dillon and I took to Toronto during my first pregnancy. That this baby is not his.

Dillon pours himself a drink with dinner, and I restrain myself from throwing it across the room.

"You're the only good thing that ever happened to me," he says.

I want to roll my eyes so hard. More lies, after we just established it doesn't work on me anymore. "Yet you're the one who left me. You see how that doesn't quite add up, right?"

"I didn't want to leave you."

"You did, to go back to Kate. Because you were cheating the *whole time* we were married."

"Not the whole time."

"Oh, well, shit, you deserve a medal." I stab my food because god, even though I remember that crippling moment I discovered his cheating, I still love him with a power that's beyond me. It's turning this conversation into a lover's squabble that will be diffused like all disagreements in committed relationships. Through conversation, time, or whatever it is that puts a petty argument behind. We're together. And even though we're flailing at the surface, our commitment is the undercurrent that will drag us along to where the water is steady again.

His face is grim, his eyes far away. "I couldn't live in that house after she died."

"I couldn't either. But you left me there, to suffer it alone."

He puts down his fork and pushes away from the table. Bows his head, rubs his face down. When he faces me I see it again: that grief. It chambers the highest possible caliber of sympathy and love, and then it's shooting. Tearing through me with no exit wound. But it's not quick enough to stop the lightning-fast realization that strikes me before I go down.

He doesn't want me. He wants the baby. For the same reason I want her: to heal a wound so raw just one poke into it hurts bad enough to kill. I recognize then what a victim he is. How he was used by his family to fix a problem, but their fix backfired and he was the only one standing within range. They didn't even bother with damage control. They just brushed off their hands and let Dillon and me live with the pieces. I couldn't have expected them to care about me. They didn't know me. But Dillon was their flesh and blood.

I have to keep my daughter far away from the Moores. If only I can figure out the best place to do that. With Dillon, holding him to his oath to hide us from his family. With Trey, their enemy, who would fight them until his last breath. Or on my own.

Dillon pours himself another drink and takes a long gulp. "I'm not sure what to say to you, Liv."

"You need to stay away from your family."

He chuckles as if I've made some strange conversational jump.

"They're using you."

He looks down at his hands, letting his breath out. His shoulders slump, like the spark of life that was holding them up had just been extinguished. "You know what it's like growing up in that family? Has he told you anything?" He suddenly looks up at me, like he was surprised at what he just said aloud.

"I know enough." Christian told me enough. The worst things Trey could only tell me himself, and I know he never would.

He takes another drink, draining it. When he sets it down a change has come over him, like something he just remembered has charged the unstable mix of what's in his head. The re-exposed, unresolved grief over our dead child. The acknowledgment of how his family used him. The role he's locked into with a family that undoubtedly abused him. He turns his eyes back on me, and I see an unfamiliar man inhabiting him.

"So you know," he says. "And you think he's risen above all that. Well, you're wrong. He hasn't. He's as bad as me, as bad as all of them. No, he's worse. And has no remorse for the things he's done. Is he the kind of guy you want raising your child?"

"That's really none of your business."

He leans across the table toward me. "I'm going to let you in on a little something about the Bevans. They're animals. If left to themselves, they'd be living in the woods with the wolves. He has no human emotional attachment to you. You're confusing his love for a primal urge to protect his mate and his young. He doesn't love you. He's incapable."

The night I spent with Trey in the woods at Mamó's funeral flashes in my mind—the tiny leaves clinging to his hair, the moon reflected in his eyes. And me, sandwiched between the warmth of the ground and his solid body. If Trey is an animal, there is no harm in it. Only beauty. And I reach, grasping that ghost of a memory and yanking it from the edge of my thoughts into dead center. I see it now: my connection with Trey was no love spell. He explained what it was, and what we have is real, something we built. Something that can't be broken. Trey's flawed and angry and violent, but he's mine, and I'm going to help him. Maybe not now, but I won't give up until I can.

I pour Dillon another drink. While he sips and broods, I clean up and flip on the TV for background noise. He relocates to the bed, leaning against the plush pillows, legs crossed. I top him off with the remaining whiskey in the bottle. His eyes have gone sleepy, his frame loose. He pats the bed next to him, and I lie down beside him like I'd done so many times in our old life. Fifteen minutes later he's asleep. I power off the TV and wait thirty more.

Then I take the Glock from the bottom of his suitcase, the BMW key and valet ticket from the nightstand, and sneak out of the room. My back prickles on my walk down the hall, expecting him to storm through the door behind me. The elevator ding breaks the sound barrier. I stash the Glock in my bag and try to slow my pace so it looks like I'm heading out for a late dinner instead of a hasty getaway.

Night brought a chill, and I wish I had a jacket. I crank the heat in the BMW and head south, away from Dillon. Away from Trey. Dillon will expect me to go back to Black River. And Trey, I'm still not certain I want to return to him. The stars give the black of night texture above me. The road is my own. I stop at a gas station with bright lighting to search the car again for my phone. I find it in the place I knew it couldn't be but decided to look anyway: the trunk.

I'm crippled by my effort to ignore my need to return to Dillon. My grip on the wheel is fatiguing but necessary to keep me on course. If I didn't know it was Dillon's spell at work, I'd be turning around thinking that's what I wanted. Instead, I'm counting mile markers because it's the only thing that keeps me moving away from him. I wish it would get easier with each one, but it's the opposite.

Once another eighty miles stretch between Dillon and me, I make a turn off the interstate and follow a state road to the parking lot of a small-town hardware store. It's after hours, the vacant lot serenaded by nighttime insects. There's nothing discreet about a one-hundred-thousand-dollar BMW in an empty, well-lit parking lot in a small town on the border of Washington and Idaho. It looks as stolen as it should. Hopefully the cops have no reason to patrol here. The GPS is no doubt connected to Dillon's phone. I'll need to ditch this car as soon as I can.

I roll down the windows and turn off the engine. I take the amulet Trey gave me out of my bag. It's a concrete reminder of my life with Trey and the dire events we've shared that brought us close, taught us how to be together. Dillon's spell is powerful but it has a serious vulnerability. It only works on a person whose heart is uninhabited. Mine belongs to Trey, and no spell is powerful enough to compare. Trey, though, is a walking disaster. He's a magnet for the Moores' hatred, and instead of taking steps to temper it, he's throwing on fuel and adding flame.

My phone's battery is almost dead. I need to power it off to conserve the battery for emergencies. If I'm going to call, there's no time to stare at it.

Tara answers on the second ring. "Liv?"

"Sorry, did I wake you?"

"No. I'm too busy pacing a hole in the floor. Are you okay? Where are you?"

"About three hundred miles from Black River."

"Which direction?"

"I'd rather not say. Is there any way Sloane's still up?"

"She's right here. Hold on."

When I hear Sloane's voice I get a lump in my throat. It's her son I've left. Her granddaughter—her namesake—I've run off with. There's no reason she should want to help me, even though she's the one who knows the most about the Moores. She repeats my name in that calm, measured way of hers, and I hear an understanding in it so deep I know she's the person I need to speak to. "I'm sorry for leaving like that."

"Don't be. I don't blame you one bit. If you need time, you take all you need."

"I really don't know what I need."

"But you do know your options. This is your choice to make. Just know that no matter where you raise your daughter, if you raise her with love, she will be the victor in this war that has gone on far too long. That I know. I only wish I could share with you the part of my heart that knows it's true."

I watch the moths flittering in the parking lot light above me, flashes of white against the layers of stars beyond. I was committed to my place in that war. Many months ago, I was the one who persuaded Trey to stay and raise our daughter to win against them. It was an easy call to make with Trey by my side. It's much harder to accept now that I see Trey's priorities aren't so aligned with mine. Leaving me to even a score that will never be even, not calling even once while he was gone, drinking too much, self-destructing. The attack on the side of the road. The control issues. I need him with me, not working against me.

I ask the question that's been burning through me. "Did you kill my first baby?"

She takes a moment before she answers. "I took her away, gave her to earth to keep her safe until she could return. Had I not, they'd have taken her and made her one of them. And after watching them turn my son ..." She doesn't finish. She doesn't need to.

"Would the Moores ever kill a child?"

"No."

"How can you be certain?"

"Because they didn't kill you."

CHAPTER 9

TREY

If TARA HADN'T dumped every bottle of scotch and Irish whiskey down my kitchen sink, I'd be halfway through my stash right now. She didn't take the empties, now all lined up on my kitchen counter, each containing drips, maybe a whole shot if I combine them all. But that would be pathetic. And make my problem more fucked up, if that's even possible. They've filled the room with their smell. It's about to do me in. I have the power to help myself, right? I dump them all in a bag and take them outside.

The night air is cool, the breeze a much needed sedative. I go in the garage to look at the Ninja. What am I doing home when I should be on the road searching for

Liv? I take the receipt Shawn gave me out of my pocket. His handwriting on the back: *gray BMW M5*. Under that, the license plate number. It was blind luck he was sitting in his work van when Liv came out. Yeah, maybe he should've stopped her, followed her, done something before Dillon drove away with her. But shoving the guy halfway across Tara's kitchen is a bad way to get that across. I should be thanking him.

You're a danger to yourself and others, he'd said. No shit. I'm working on it.

My phone rings. Christian.

"Finally," I answer. "Where the hell have you been?"

"Taking care of the shit you started. You have five minutes."

"Is Dillon at the estate?"

"Haven't seen him. But how the fuck should I know? I don't follow that shithead around."

"Did he leave in an M5?"

"Probably. That's what he's been driving. You want me to check the garage?" I hear a door open and close, then a breeze hits his phone. "What's this about?"

I weigh the thought of telling him. He's cleaning up a mess I made in his house. Again. He doesn't need my problems adding to his load. "Just tell me if the car's there."

He greets the garage attendant. Late shift guy, probably wasn't around to see people coming and going during the day. Christian grills him anyway. I can only hear his side of the conversation but it's enough to know the car left days ago and Dillon hasn't been seen since. She's definitely with him.

"Ask the guy if he saw Jared."

"*I* can tell you that. He took a flight to Chicago after you left. I've already warned Tara so she could pass it along to your people. Anything else or can I go to bed?"

"Should be it. Thanks."

He mutters something I don't catch. Before I can say anything, he's laying into me. A bunch of crap about my bad timing, my outbursts, his role being stuck in the middle. Then, "I'm out here questioning the garage attendant because you've left me no source of information."

Meaning I killed his father. The only one left in our immediate family. *His* immediate family. "Your father couldn't be trusted to tell you shit."

"I had a way of getting it out of him."

"So take control. Hire people to bring you the information before you need it."

I hear him slam against something, probably the impact of his fist and a wall. "How many times do I have to tell you I'm not taking over for them?"

"That place is your—"

"Fuck you, Trey."

This is how he wants it to go? Okay, I'm game. I'm pissed off and far too sober and have no decent way to find Liv. "No, fuck you. You should've done something about Pierce twenty years ago. Don't give me shit for finally doing you the favor and pulling the trigger."

He chuckles, like I'm some stupid kid. "Hey, asshole, nobody asked you to do that."

"Shit happens."

"Sure does." He hangs up.

I restrain myself from throwing my phone against the wall of the garage. I go in the house and to the basement for my family's texts. The one we learn to never use, the one I've studied so hard I could recite it. *Dubhealaín.*

Black magic.

I've made enemies of Liv and Christian. May as well make Tara and Máthair hate me too.

I can already see the page before I find it. Of the many methods to locate a person, the one I have in mind will let me see through their eyes for as long as I can hold onto the connection. It's a sadistic invasion, something I'd never do to Liv. It requires freshly running blood of the target's close relative. Not something I could score for Liv since she was an orphan. That's two reasons I can't use it to find Liv. But for Dillon, there's a guy I could use as his close relative. And I'd love a good excuse to spill his blood.

After a couple hours in the car and a few in the air, I'm landing in Chicago. The airport glows orange from the rising sun. It's a big city in which to find one guy, but he's exactly where I expect him to be: the house Dillon bought for Liv, the one she wanted no part of in their divorce. The one where we found her and Winnie after an army attacked us in Tara's house in the middle of the night. A perfect place for Dillon's big brother to hole up while doing whatever business he was doing.

I climb the porch steps and try the door—unlocked. I let myself in. Try not to think about Liv here with Dillon, their normal life. There's a muffled TV somewhere, running water ahead. I pass a table in the hall, a framed wedding photo of the two of them. I slam it facedown before I realize it will ruin my advantage of surprise. The running water shuts off. Looks like ambush is out of the question.

Jared steps into the doorway in front of me. I pick up the framed photo and hurl it into his face. He turns; it hits him behind the ear. Glass shatters at our feet as my elbow smashes into his jaw. He wraps an arm around my neck. I counter with a twist that takes us both to the floor. Objects fall off walls and tables and splinter around us. We tangle against the kitchen chairs. Ducking a blow, I see a good sized shard of glass lying within reach. Then it's in my hand, cutting into my palm. I drag it down the side of his face. Payback, served decades cold.

The floor has gone slippery with blood. I'm not sure if it's mine or his. He knees me near the groin, too close for comfort. His strength is waning. He's no match for me. No one is. I get a solid hold on his neck. He goes for that arm which frees my other enough to land a punch that nearly knocks him out. Then his hands are up. Surrender.

I'm afraid that's not an option.

He stays like that, hands raised, like I'm just going to back off so we can have a fucking conversation. I clock him in the nose a few times to make the blood run. Then I knock him out. I get up, search my pocket for the bag of ash I've already affected. I streak my eyes in ash, then I streak his. I plant my hands in the puddle of blood around his head and as I recite the words I've memorized, I'm drawn into the floor and away.

Beige linoleum with gold flecks. A set of polished black shoes. The view lifts, filling with a man in a shirt with a logo—a rental car company. He speaks, we follow him out the door to a waiting Cadillac. We circle the car. Dillon Moore's face reflects in the window. We take the key. We watch a different man load a piece of luggage into the trunk.

The vision darkens at the edges. Flickers. I sense Jared coming around below me. I knee him hard in the ribs. Then I'm back, in the driver's seat, starting the car, turning to check the side mirror. The passenger seat is empty. No Liv.

I withdraw my hands from the blood soaked floor and sit back. Jared moans, rolling his head back and forth. His face is a horror movie. He splutters blood. I take hold of his collar. I could end it here. One more of them dead, one less I have to execute.

Please don't kill.

And one more thing to diminish me, to chip away at the tiny remaining portion of me that Liv can love. If there's anything even left.

I release him. His skull hits the floor and he groans.

"Mind if I use your sink?" I wash my hands and face. Glance at my shirt—a lost cause. I head upstairs and locate the master bedroom closet. Find a T-shirt and slip it on. There's another framed photo of Dillon and Liv on a beach. I bash the glass against the dresser and remove the photo. One close look is enough to pool enough anger for that black magic to rise before I even choose to conjure it. I wad the photo in my fist. A pop of fire and then it's soot falling between my fingers. The burn on my palm has cauterized the wound from the shard of glass. Bonus. When I get back downstairs he's still flat on the floor. I help myself to a glass of water.

"Dead," he says, choking on big wet coughs that don't sound healthy. He gets an elbow underneath him and points at me. "Every Bevan dead."

I toss him the kitchen towel from the counter. "There's something on your face."

On my way out, I dump my shirt in the trash can at the curb. Convenient that it's trash day. It saves me from having to explain a bloody shirt to airport security. I don't think about the vision until my ass is parked at the gate with hours to wait until I can board my return flight. What I know is Liv left the clinic in his M5. A couple days later, he's picking up a rental without her. If she ditched him and took his car, maybe she's overcome the spell. Maybe she's coming home.

Or maybe she's on her way somewhere else, somewhere I'll never find her.

The easy power of black magic hides what a tricky beast it is. The clue it's given me has only shown what little I know. To find out what I need to know to win this, I need to invoke more black magic. How much is uncertain. It's like any vice—a little pull might seem harmless until you realize it's not enough. I wonder if it was worth it.

I order a scotch from the flight attendant because I need it more today than I need to focus on quitting it. One can't do any harm. She also brings me two large bandages and points me toward the bathroom. I cover the worst of the wounds on my face so I don't scare the other passengers. After landing in Montana, I drive home, deciding I won't need more magic to find Liv. She's going to be there. That M5 is going to be parked in my driveway, and I'm going to enjoy setting it on fire.

All I see when I arrive is her red Civic sitting on its flat tire. I go inside to no trace of her. I open the cabinet in the kitchen—empty. My habit is too much a reflex to even require a thought in my head. I resign to giving Liv some time. A day, maybe two, for her to call. To return. To tell me it's over. I should sleep. I can't remember the last time I got any sleep that wasn't stolen while crunched up on a plane.

I go in the bedroom and sit on the bed. Look at her slippers on the floor. Her hairbrush on her nightstand. I go downstairs to my family's text and find the next location spell, the one I can use on her. I copy the wording onto a piece of paper then go upstairs for a drink.

Of course the damn cabinet's empty. I kick the kitchen chair into the wall. See the dent it made. Kick it again. I hear tires on the gravel outside and pause for a moment to make sure I'm not imagining it. It could be her. It's not.

"Where have you been?" Tara's saying as she gets out of her CR-V. Before I can answer, she stops abruptly, keeping a cautious distance and a narrowed set of eyes trained on me. "What did you do?"

Black magic doesn't wash off like blood. Its residue remains, as a warning to others. As a lure to some.

She closes the space between us and takes my hands, turning them palms-up. The gory wound on one of them isn't her concern. She sees the distortion in the air as clearly as I can, and she stays there, watching. Letting what I've done soak in, letting it scare her. Enrage her. She shoves my hands away. Turns her back to me. "Did you get what you wanted?" she asks quietly.

I don't answer because there is no answer. Yes, I got what I wanted. No, it wasn't enough.

I don't blame her for keeping her back to me like she can't stand to look at me. "I suppose you're not open to what Máthair and I came up with."

"Try me."

"You've been in her mind, Fearghus. You don't need to draw *dubhealaín* to help you find her. She's already in you. There are ways—good ways—to make that work for you."

When I don't answer she turns around to see me shaking my head. It's been too long. The signature of Liv's mind doesn't last long in my head among all the other sick shit. If it's still in there it's become covered in that shit. Unrecognizable. I knew Liv was too sweet for my bitter world. Maybe I should let her go. She and our baby will both be better off.

Until the Moores find them and execute them.

I whistle for River. Tara watches me, sad and defeated. Her attempts to steer me onto the path of good will continue to disappoint her until she learns the waste of her effort. I'm not the good guy. I took the fork in the road a long time ago and there's no route back.

River dashes from the woods. She stops short, as suspicious as Tara was, so I call her forward and rub her ears for reassurance. She rushes off to find her friends and fulfill my request.

"I'm busy," I tell Tara. She needs to go home.

"This..." she gestures around us "...is exactly the kind of thing that made her leave. And why she won't come back. And if she does come back, why she'll leave again. You don't have to do it. You choose to. And you can stop, Fearghus."

"Are you done?"

She turns away from me and walks back to her car. "You have to back off and let her choose. Let her come back to you. If you can't do that, you'll never get her back." She stands there, looking trampled and defeated, missing the

vigor that normally inhabits my sister. It's almost enough
for me to call it all off. To go inside and sit my ass down
and wait, just like she said.

She gives me one last pleading look and drives away.

I go inside to the kitchen—*fuck* that empty cabinet. I
tear through the house. I find a few strands of Liv's hair
under the bathroom sink. In the bedroom, I go through
a drawer of her clothes, sniffing one thing after another
before realizing they're all too clean. I go to her pillow on
the bed, take a deep inhale. It's saturated with her scent. I
yank the pillowcase off the pillow.

Black magic is greedy. It releases tentacles that glean
power from all life around its invoker—a neighbor, a com-
panion dog, a sycamore in the front yard, a thriving field of
crops. Its range and intensity vary depending on the power
called by the spell, but even a little life sucked here and
there from a circle around will leave you with a wiped-out
crop or a crippled dog. No herbs needed, no prep. It's fast
and direct, a shortcut. And extremely powerful. A person
has to be a real asshole to use black magic.

I might be an asshole, but I'm not going to suck the life
out of the innocent creatures around me. Black magic is
bold and tricky, but I can trick back.

With a proof of my worth, the black magic will grant
me a request: I'm tying the power source to my DNA. The
magic will use me as initial power source and send out its
tentacles in search of more, blind to all life but me. It will
drive into earth, through stone, circle the world looking for
the only thing that will satiate: me. It will find me again,
but there's no knowing when. And when it finally finds me,
it will be starving. And pissed. There's a fucked-up sen-

tience to black magic. Use it too much, and it will begin to use you. And before you know it, you've scorched the life out of everything around you. Unless you trick it into only wanting you.

I hike into the woods. River catches up to accompany me to the grounds by the rock formation where the Moores' ten men almost killed me. When we reach it, I see the coyotes hard at work, digging up bones they previously buried, retrieving the bones from other parts of the forest of all the men who've come here for me. They've made a pile. An altar. The dark magic rears inside me, around me. The lives I've taken. The power I've snuffed. A worthy sacrifice. An offering for the request I'm about to make.

I sit and watch the coyotes work.

At midnight under the stars, with Liv's hair in my fist, I call upon the sound of her voice. *Trey,* she says in my head, my name in a gentle scold. I hear her laugh. I imagine her skin against my bare chest. I see the little curl at the end of her ponytail, the depth of blue of her eyes. The worry in them. I taste her mouth. I press the pillowcase against my face and breathe. Her scent is thick and alive, like the grand finale. The unique recipe for Liv—my Liv—is present, and I release it like a beacon in the sky.

I'm on the ground, sprawled like I've been hit. I need to get up, to be ready to receive the response to my call and just when I've made it upright, I sense a rushing motion and I've been hit again by what feels like a silent blast of sound.

This time I can't get up. I don't even try. I watch the sky. One star pulses deeply. Then another. A third, a fourth. Fifth, sixth, seventh. Then everything's normal. I wait for it to happen again and it does. One. Two. Three, four. Five, six, seven. It's like one of those Vegas signs with the illuminated arrows pointing walkers-by into a club. And it's pointing to the southwest. All I have to do is start driving, and the magic will lead me straight to her.

Something new hits me from within. If the release of that spell and its return call were powerful enough to flatten me on my back on the ground, I can't imagine what it did to Liv when it found her.

CHAPTER 10
LIV

THE STARS ARE my only company again. From my view through the windshield of my new rental they appear stationary, stable, twinkling in their positions like they're meant to be there each and every night. I know the truth: they're in motion just like me, just like everything out there. It's my perspective that makes all the difference.

And my perspective has changed. I've made a life in Black River. I left the city I was born in to move there, to start over, to find my own stationary place far from the city where my heart was broken twice. I have a job I don't want to leave, people I care about. Tara and the kids and now Sloane, whom I'd love to get to know. Shawn and all my friends and patients at the clinic. I never had family like this before, and I won't allow Trey's bad decisions to take that away from me.

What's more motivating, though, is the truth I couldn't see with Dillon's promises clouding my thoughts. No matter where I go, the Moores will find me. Fighting them alone is a noble gesture, but a stupid one. I need Trey. Our baby needs both of us to grow up as herself. If the Moores take her, she'll carry their stamp just like Trey and Dillon and turn out as broken as they are.

I pull off the highway to get a room for the night. Under the humming lights in the motel parking lot, I power on my phone. I have one message from Shawn: *If you come home, you can stay at my place anytime.* I don't waste the battery life to tell him it's Trey who'll need a place to stay next time, so he'll have to extend that offer to him. Staying at Shawn's place would be such a perfect punishment for Trey, I'm going to kick him out as soon as I get home just to see it happen. Not that it ever would—Trey would opt for sleeping in the woods instead. I power off the phone to conserve the remaining battery for emergencies. I don't want to talk to anyone anyway.

After checking into the motel, I drive around back to my room. When I get out of the car the dome of stars catches my eye, like there's a motion at play that shouldn't be. Their steady points of light I'd just admired twinkle as they had been those hours on the highway, just me and them. A static charge tingles in my clothes. The hum of the parking lot light grows louder then pops, leaving me alone with the stars.

A high-pitched whine comes from far away, gaining volume. I take a few steps away from the car to look around. It's not so much in the space around me as it is directly in my ears. I cover them, but it only seems to keep the noise inside that's getting unbearably loud. A slam, a blast of light. A deafening pulse of sound splits through my head. My shoulders and spine crack against a hard surface. I slide down the wall I landed against into a squat. The car I was just standing beside is now fifty feet away.

I lower myself to sit on the sidewalk against the building, cradling my head. My ears ring like I've fired a shotgun without ear protection. I know I should be running, getting the hell away before whatever just happened happens again, but I'm just now feeling the impact of my back against the wall and the raw, bleeding tip of my tongue I hope I didn't just bite clean off.

A car starts up on the other side of the building, and I know I need to get inside. My bag is on the ground, its contents scattered between my new position and the place I was standing a moment ago. I hurry to collect my things—wallet, sunglasses, Chapstick, Glock. Then I see the amulet Trey gave me glowing red hot, a plume of smoke rising above it. I pick it up by the chain. Did it act as a shield against what just happened, or a lightning rod?

I let myself into my motel room and try not to wonder why the baby is so still.

The chain lock is broken. I wedge a chair against the door instead, knowing neither will keep Dillon out. If he's responsible for what just happened, he's already found me. I check myself in the bathroom mirror. A drying drip of blood under one nostril. Bloodshot eyes that may have existed before the impact. Two skinned elbows. And my tongue, still very much bleeding but thankfully intact. My ears still ring and my head is throbbing but it's not going to kill me.

With inventory taken on me, I place hands on my belly. I press on the side where her feet were last, hoping to annoy her into some kind of physical reaction. Nothing.

But it is past midnight. She could be sleeping. *I* should be sleeping. I crawl between the sheets, blocked from my view of the stars, so utterly alone.

Hours later I wake to a rolling baby pressing against my bladder. Relief is so acute it numbs me. Experienced alone, it carries a hopeless loneliness I don't expect.

The first thing I do in the morning is power up my phone and call Dillon. I've put enough miles between us to be safe, in the direction he wouldn't expect me to go. The long way home not only gives me ample time to think, but keeps him off my trail.

"Liv," he answers. "Tell me what you want from me. I'll do anything—"

"I left your car at the Lewiston airport. In the rental car lot. The attendant has the key. You owe him fifty bucks."

"Come on, babe. Anything."

I open my mouth to ask him what I called to ask: what was he doing at midnight last night? But something makes me hesitate, so he takes the floor to sweet-talk me while I consider my options. If he's responsible for what happened last night, he obviously hasn't found me yet. Confirmation of his work might help him. I can't give him that.

"—if that's what you want. Or we could just travel the world until we decide where to settle. Just tell me what, and I'll do it."

"Dillon, I've made up my mind. You need to take care of yourself and stay away from your family. They bring out the worst in you. I have to hang up. My cell—"

"Don't you dare hang up."

The change in tone sends a shiver through me that doesn't awaken fear, but anger. He just got my answer and he wants to push? He caught me on the wrong day. After that spectacle last night, my patience is wearing thin. "You speak to me like that, and—"

"And what? You'll leave me? Never speak to me again? Already did that, Liv. Think of something else."

A wave of adrenaline runs the length of me, along with a dose of Trey's unbridled rage that passed to me the last time he was in my head. It comes alive at the worst times, when I'm already struggling to keep my cool. "*You* left *me*. Don't ever forget that."

"Here's something you shouldn't forget. He's a loser. A violent drunk. He has you locked up in some shit house in a shit town in the middle of nowhere. I could give you a good life. And you're going to pass it up to be with— to *breed* with—a Bevan. Do you know what they were a century ago? The lowest of the low. In Ireland they were rats, only suited for cleaning shit off the street. They were run out of Wales. They were trash, and they still are. You could come with me. We could go anywhere. We could even go back to the Moore estate. They would welcome you, raise her as one of their own and she'd never have to know her low-bred origins. It would be the safest place for her. You're killing your own baby so you can continue to fuck Bevan trash."

I don't know why I let him finish. Or why I stay on the phone, waiting to hear more.

"His people started a war against us, and they refuse to end it because they crave the bloodshed. And he's the worst one of them. He's only happy when he's killing people. Is that what you want for her?"

Maybe it's the proof of his hatred that I crave. I take it all in and bundle it inside me, saving it for the day I'll be free of his love and can remember the man he truly is. Or maybe it's the spell, wanting me to believe him and go back to him. It might work on a person who's never experienced real love. But me, I've had it. In that moment I saw Trey unconscious on the ground that night he fell off the roof, it changed me. And every near tragedy, every victory, every shared moment since then has thickened the bond between us. I know real love, and nothing else compares.

I realize Dillon's end has gone silent, so I look at my phone and find it's dead. Great timing.

My only options for breakfast are fast food or fast food, so I pick one and go inside to eat. I find a packet of green tea in my bag and get a cup of hot water from the cashier who directs me back on my route. Black River is so small she hasn't heard of it, but she knew the way to Missoula so that's good enough for now. With no phone, no map, and after driving so far out of the way, the route home is a bit indirect. I've gotten myself as lost as I could.

From Missoula I head toward Kalispell, feeling exposed on the well-traveled highway. I remind myself Dillon doesn't know what car I'm in. Then I remember he sent a pulse from the sky to knock me across a parking lot. It wouldn't matter if I was flying a stealth aircraft. The jerk has magic blood. I find the rental car office in Kalispell and ask to use their phone.

Tara picks up her landline right away.

"It's me again," I say. "I'm in Kalispell."

"Staying? Or coming home?"

"Home. I need a ride."

Children's voices fill the background, then the sound of a closing door. "I feel like I should …" She sighs heavily. "Warn you. Talk you out of it."

There's nothing she can warn me about. I already know what a mess he is. But I'd rather not say any of this three feet away from the rental car agent. "It's okay."

"He's gotten worse."

"Impossible. There isn't anything worse."

"He's doing things he shouldn't be doing."

I laugh. I can't help it. She's talking as if he hasn't been murdering people for fifteen years. Also something I can't say within hearing range of strangers. "I can't—"

"Sorry—you probably can't talk. It'll take a few minutes to load everyone in the car and then we'll be on the road. Can you fit between two car seats?"

"No, Tara, that's too much trouble. Just tell Trey I'll be waiting here."

"Okay, but … I'll try, but I can't promise I'll reach him. You'll be at this number? I'll call you back."

I hand the phone back and take a seat in the waiting area. I browse the magazine selection but opt for staring at the wall, contemplating all the ways I could rip into Trey in the hours we'll be encapsulated in his car on the way home. And trying not to think about Dillon, and how he's been used his whole life. How I just left him again.

"Ma'am?" The agent holds the phone out to me.

I get up and take it. It's Tara. "Fearghus says he'll be right there."

"Driving from Black River?"

"No, driving from I don't know where. All he said was he'd be right there before he hung up on me. I'm telling you, Liv, he found a new low."

I return to the chair, her words adding a chilling haunt to the otherwise bright room. Yeah, he has problems that are largely due to his own selfish decisions. He's an addict and a substance abuser, but so was I. Sleeping pills are a drug as much as alcohol and every homemade potion he's abused in the past fifteen years. But the timing of this new low has spread a guilt through me, giving a new spin to those things I'd practiced to say to him moments ago. My eyes sting when I remember what he said to me not long ago: *You heal me in so many ways.*

I'd love to continue to heal him, if he'd let me. But there's another side to it: the person willing to *be* healed. The person who decides to stay home with his family instead of running across the country to rouse a war that's been calm for months. The person who calls his worried family after walking into that war and being gone for days. The person who will return home without resorting to old dangerous habits. The person who won't drink and drive.

I try to read a gossip magazine but I hear his words instead. *What would I do without you? I was lost without you. So lost.*

On the Montana backroads I got as lost as I could. And back at home, without me, Trey was becoming lost too. I don't know what Trey sees in me that helps him, and I don't know how to invoke it. Finding a lost Trey is not as easy as asking a stranger for directions. The route to him is a mirror maze, a trek through woods filled with brambles and land mines.

There's a surge of heat on my chest where the amulet lies against skin. After Dillon's assault from the sky, I figured it would be put to better use if I wore it like I was supposed to. I reach under my collar and take it out, its living warmth a pulse against my hand. Fearing whatever struck me behind the motel is about to make a second attempt, I stand and turn toward the windows. The amulet burns so hot I drop it. That's when I see Trey.

He's standing in the middle of the parking lot, staring at the building as if waiting for something to happen. His Camaro is several yards behind him, pulled in sideways like he came in fast and made no effort to park it. It's bright enough outside there's no way he'd be able to see me through windows that are surely reflecting the day back at him, but somehow our eyes meet. He must've stopped like that when he spotted me, but he's making no move toward the door. Just standing, arms straight against his sides, staring.

God, for a man who walks into any fight and relishes confrontation with any person willing to step up, he sure can be shy. I gather my bag and go outside. Halfway to him I stop. The amulet is heating again, threatening to burn me if I don't get it off. I lift it by the chain which has already started to absorb the warmth.

"I'm sorry," he says as I draw near. Spoken a moment before we've reached the range of normal conversation, it seems like he's either been dying to say that, or he wanted to get it out before I said anything.

"For what?" Yeah, it's a test. And he's going to fail because he couldn't possibly list everything.

"All of it. I'm sorry."

"Oh, spare me. And yourself. You might pull a tongue muscle using those foreign words twice in a row."

I'm close enough now that I can see his eyes. An unfamiliar element dwells there, something … not him. I get a rush of discomfort, like when meeting a stranger who gives you that gut feeling there's something not right about them. Something you can't trust. Although he's looking into my eyes, there's a strange lack of focus. I'm afraid to find out what has him so preoccupied.

He looks at the amulet which I'm still holding away from me. It has a slight orange glow now. It doesn't appear to be letting up. He goes around me to undo the clasp then opens the Camaro's trunk and tosses the amulet inside. Maybe it's acted up like this before. He's had it much longer than I have.

His fingers enclose my wrist and I yank away—reflex, remembering our little brawl beside the highway near home. Then I see he's not trying to grab, he's looking for something. Bruises that are long gone due to the quick healing that transferred from his body to mine to protect our daughter. Tara probably gave him hell about those bruises.

I get in the car because I'm not going to stand out here all afternoon while he repeats vague and insincere apologies.

He gets in beside me. I shouldn't look at him, but I do, and what I see on his face makes me regret it. "Trey, don't—"

"Where is he?"

I restrain my own arm, prepped to punch him. "Take us home, or I'm going back in there to get my own car and I can't promise you where I'll drive."

He starts the car and hits the gas hard, making the engine and exhaust roar even louder than it already did when starting up. It's almost offensive after spending so much time in the composed luxury of Dillon's BMW. I look out the window at the blue-gray outline of the mountains in the distance, trying not to think about that bullet list of damning evidence I have against Trey and all the things I'd love to tear into him about. It would just be another twist of the knife. Instead, I ask, "How'd you get here so fast?"

His gaze doesn't stray from its determined focus on the road ahead. "I was in the area."

"For what?"

He withholds the answer. If I'm reading him right, it's not because he doesn't want me to know, but because he knows it will make me mad. Time to own up.

"Looking for Dillon," I answer for him. I couldn't sound more disappointed, and yet it's not enough.

"Looking for you. Would be nice to find him though. Killing him would end his spell real quick."

I put a hand against his stubbly cheek when I see him grinding his teeth. I don't want to be affectionate; I just can't stand to see people hurting themselves because I spend so much time fixing people. Him especially. I've lost count of all the wounds I've cleaned, bandaged, and sutured for him in the past nine months. The broken ribs and concussion. The coma. And not going with Dillon has just bought countless more, maybe the one to end it all.

Other than relaxing his jaw, he makes no reaction to the contact. A new bruise covers most of his cheekbone. The split on his upper lip is also new. So is the gory gash on his brow and several other cuts. They're all in need of a good cleaning and bandaging; the brow gash could use a couple butterfly bandages. All the marks that returned with him from his drive to Virginia are still there too, looking very old compared to the new ones. And the knuckles, also torn up in Virginia, are freshly bloodied. I'd put the latest fight in the last day or two. I'm not sure I should ask who it was. Maybe that's my problem though, letting these things slide.

"Who'd you beat to death one to two days ago?"

"I didn't kill him."

I slow-clap. "Noble of you. You're a changed man. But it doesn't really answer my question."

He shifts in his seat. "Jared Moore."

That means Jared must have come out here too, either with Dillon, or soon after I escaped him. I can't be sure Dillon ever wanted to run away with me. Dragging me back to the Moore estate must have been the plan all along. I cover my face with my hands because there it is again, that blooming of sympathy for the Dillon Moore I love. The one I yearn to save from that family who's using him and corrupting him. It's all false.

False, false, false.

Trey looks over at me. "What?"

"Nothing." I'm not sure if I can live with Trey, but I can trust him, and I love him more than any spell could trick me into loving someone else.

I reach for his hand, and he willingly lets me take it. The knuckles are badly peeled but scabbing over. There's an unusual amount of blood caked under and around each nail. Jared's blood, most likely, and I worry for what Trey did, and how they'll retaliate. This bottomless pit of hate Trey has for them is the source of every one of his problems. The violence, the drinking, the fixation on revenge. I understand some of the drive behind that hate, but a lot of it is still a mystery. Trey has offered nothing but vagueness. Christian told me some detail—enough to convince me what he suffered. Then there are those few heartbreaking images that leaked from Trey's mind to mine. My understanding of what drives his hate isn't what's necessary to get past this. What's needed is Trey's understanding, his processing of it.

So I take a breath and ask the question I know he doesn't want to answer. "Will you tell me what they did to you when you were a child?"

His eyes remain on the road as if I hadn't spoken. I watch a mile marker pass by on the shoulder. Then another. Trey withdraws his hand from mine, places it back on the steering wheel. And then he starts to talk. His voice is flat as he tells me story after story of mental and physical abuse. A scared little boy who learned how to act tough but it still didn't keep them away. A boy who worried so much for his mother but was too young and weak to do anything to protect her. The loneliness and isolation when other children would visit and band together to abuse him. The things they'd say. The toys they'd break. His uncles, who knew how to hit so it wouldn't bruise. Who sometimes didn't care if it would bruise or break. The birth of

Christian, his only friend, taunted and abused because of his friendship with Trey. Used as bait just to incite Trey. The murder of Christian's mother.

And all of that was nothing compared to what they did to him once he grew big enough to fight back.

The sun is a blood-red ember half consumed by the horizon when he finally stops. The swell of my belly is damp from falling tears. We're silent when we arrive home and go inside. Then I sit him down in the kitchen to clean his wounds while he tells me more. Random stories throughout his childhood that he didn't mention in the car. The things he loved that were destroyed. The burden of secrets he carried, knowing if he told his mother she'd confront them, and then they'd target her, might even kill her like they killed Christian's mother. And when I'm putting the final butterfly bandage on his lacerated brow, he takes my hands and tells me what he did after they told him they killed Kate and Aaron. All the people he killed. And how much he enjoyed it. How if given the chance to go back in time, he'd do it all again. This is the only time his detached tone gains a little emotion, and it's not the emotion I was hoping for.

I stand to look out the window into the dying light. He gets up behind me, gathers the mess of bandage wrappers and alcohol pads. Instead of going for the liquor like I expect, he heads downstairs and stays there until night consumes the house. I take a shower and put on clean pajamas, a luxury after days on the road with no change of clothes. The basement is silent—no barbell dropping, no bag being punched. He must have left while the shower was on, probably went for a run. I grab a jacket and go outside to the back porch to wait for him. I watch the sliver of moon rise, listen to the breeze through the pines. River and Trib wander onto the porch. It's strange they're not with him.

Trib rests his muzzle in my lap for an ear scratch. I give him a good one. He's earned it many times over. He loses himself in it, leaning so hard against me he has to stumble to right himself before he falls over. "You should really be at Tara's," I tell him. But Tara's probably being guarded by every coyote in the forest.

I go inside and check the time. It's almost midnight. I pick up my phone where it's charging on the counter. No messages from Trey. Maybe I'm being unreasonable expecting him to, I don't know, stick his head in the bathroom and tell me he's leaving for a few hours. Leave a damn note on the counter. Write it in blood on the wall. *Went for a long jog. I'm not being murdered by my family. Don't wait up.*

I send him a quick *Where are you?* text. His phone dings in the other room. He didn't even take his phone with him. It makes me feel tired rather than annoyed.

When I flip off the kitchen light it brings the outline of light around the basement door to my attention. It's unlike Trey to leave a light on. I reach for the switch on the basement stairs, pausing to wonder if there's a chance he's still down there. I descend the steps. Halfway down I notice no other lights on but when I turn to go back up, I spot a figure out of the corner of my eye.

He's sitting on a stool at his workbench, completely still. I can't see his face, but I can feel his eyes on me.

"Trey?"

"Irreversible."

"What? Why are you—"

"I've done a bad thing."

I keep hold of the handrail as if it could spring me back upstairs, away from this strange man who's been sitting silent in the dark basement for hours. "Can you please come upstairs? You're freaking me out."

He lays his hands palms-up on his knees and stares at them. There's a glint of white in the shadow where his head is. A smile?

"Can I at least turn a light on so I can—"

"Go upstairs."

"Excuse me?" My skin prickles under my jacket, not because of cool basement air. The detachment in his voice, his stiff and unmoving posture, the command to go upstairs when he knows he's on probation for bossing me around—it's all causing alarms to ring in my head but I have no concrete reason why.

"Please, go upstairs."

And that doesn't sound like him at all.

For once with him I do as I'm told, because it doesn't feel like I'm following his order at all but an order coming from a creature that silently hunkers for hours in the dark. I get in bed, stick a cushion between my knees to help support the weight of my belly and fall asleep wondering if I should have stashed a weapon under my pillow.

I wake groggily to the bed creaking under his weight, the solid warmth of his body like a sleeve over mine. His hand goes around my belly, his lips against my hair, and when he whispers my name it's so full of hurt I know it was only released because he thought he was alone in his wakefulness. So I put my longing to help him to sleep and I follow, knowing if he needs me, he'll come for me when he's ready. If I can pick glass out of road rash and metal shrapnel out of an eye, I can fix Trey. It's my job to fix people; I've been doing it all my life. And there's no one in the world I'd rather fix than him.

CHAPTER 11

TREY

THE MORNING SUNLIGHT is harsh enough to send a shockwave through my head and make my eyes water. I walk the house closing curtains and blinds then find Liv in the kitchen on the phone. The flyer I picked up at the AA meeting has been tacked to the fridge. She catches me looking at it and gives me this smile that rewards me with hope she doesn't hate me. Hope she might stay. For once I did something right. I start coffee for me and put the tea kettle on for her green tea.

She ends her call. "That was Christian. He thinks you need to build some bedrooms onto the house."

Of course he does. Because any time he thinks I'm losing my shit he tries to get me involved in some pain-in-my-ass project.

"Look at this." She stands to show me a photo on her phone. Christian's son Aaron sitting on a couch next to the kid who opened Bethany's door. They're holding game controllers and so focused on the screen they're oblivious to who's taking the picture. Aaron's mouth is open, chatting away like any spawn of Christian would be. And damn, he looks like Christian. Along with someone else I'd rather not see: our uncle Paul.

"Nice." Because I have to say something.

"Nice? How about 'awesome'? He says they have all the same interests."

"What—video games and crappy music? They're teenage boys."

"You did a great thing. Take some credit, will you?"

I'm not going to take credit for something I should've done a decade ago. She reaches out and grips the counter, huffing out a breath. I get a cold jolt, a foreshock of the mindfuck of helplessness I'll no doubt experience while she's giving birth. I pull out a chair. She waves it away.

"She's just stretching out and pressing my lungs. If I sit it'll be worse." She straightens her back and takes a breath, holding the air as if in a fight for space inside her own body. "She's getting so big."

Liv will think I'm crazy for closing the blinds but screw it. This light is killing me. I cover the window and open the fridge to start breakfast. While I work she studies me like someone might analyze a stranger. Normally she'd be helping at my side in the harmony we've always fallen into. Her hesitation casts light on the cavern between us.

"There's something different about you," she says across the table once we're seated. Her hesitation has given way to wariness. "And your pupils … they're extremely dilated."

"It's nothing." Nothing but a little *dubhealaín* making me sensitive to light. Trying to make me nocturnal. The blackest magic requires the cover of night and the more hours I'm available, the more it can use me.

She leans forward to scrutinize my face. Now I understand her concern. She's worried I've mixed something up downstairs, a new substance to abuse instead of alcohol. The tea she and I almost overdosed on. The tablets I made to join our minds. Yeah, there's a lot of stuff downstairs that could keep me appeased in the absence of my scotch. I haven't touched any of it and don't plan to. I've started using something much worse.

She leans back, but she doesn't look satisfied. "Did you sleep last night?"

"Not much."

"You kind of scared me, sitting downstairs like that for so long. I thought you'd left. What were you doing?"

The dogs appear through the sliding glass door. River is not happy with me. Trib takes a step closer to the door to peer in, raises his lip, and growls. Liv looks at him and turns back to me like she doesn't know me again. Doesn't trust me. Is afraid of me.

Fully aware I haven't answered her question, I get up and rinse my plate. Start cleaning up. She wants answers. Logic. Reason. I don't have any to give her.

She joins me at the sink to start on the dishes. "I mean, if it's something I can help you with—"

"It isn't."

I notice the water has been running for a long time but Liv hasn't been moving. She's rinsing a plate that has long been clean. I take it from her and turn off the faucet. She looks up at me, her eyes wet. "I shouldn't have left you."

"You had every right to." I don't deserve her, never have. Her leaving should be a wake-up call but all it did was make me deserve her less. The things I did trying to find her can't be undone. I should've told her on our drive back. I told her everything else.

She doesn't flinch when I take her by the shoulders and it's sick that I expected it. What's even sicker is I'm obsessing about Dillon Moore still being in her head instead of thinking about what I can say to stop her tears. I've got nothing. So I pull her against me and hope to the fucking elements it's enough for now, that I'll come up with some valuable reason for her to want to stay with me real soon before she remembers what an angry and selfish piece of shit I am.

She hugs me hard, her belly tight between us. I have to find some way out of the black magic's hold before it eats away the only remaining good part of me—the part that loves her.

After dropping Liv off at work, I sit in the car, wearing sunglasses that aren't dark enough, waiting for Shawn to show.

Any normal person would give the guy a proper thank-you so that's what I'm going to do. I might even shake the asshole's hand. In the hour that passes, I think of all the things I didn't tell Liv. I couldn't spare her from my violent nature—she's already well aware of that—but I had to spare her from my stupidity. Looking back with all I know now, I don't know how I couldn't see it. I can't even claim denial. I was simply unaware I was being played by a family who had made a joke of trust. I was dumb to think any part of my life was my own. Any happiness I found not to be some game of theirs.

Too many stories to tell Liv, too many that prove how stupid I was. I've spared her, but I can't spare myself, not when new ones keep hounding me like I need to be reminded. Maybe what I need to process is my blame. The clues I shouldn't have overlooked. Like that time we all went to New York—Kate and Christian and me. They'd always drag me to the clubs so they could dance. I'd spend the time drinking. The music was crap, but it sounded better with each shot. Kate looked so hot on the dance floor I almost forgave her for bringing me there. I always felt like I owed Christian for entertaining her so I didn't have to. If I only knew how much entertaining he was doing.

I have a clear memory of leaning on the bar when the bartender came to take our empties. "She your wife?" He nodded toward the dance floor.

"Yeah." Nobody ever missed that ring I bought her. When she wore it.

"Then who's he?" He set three more shots in front of me.

"My brother."

"You're a braver man than me." He moved away before I could reply.

Kate and Christian joined me then, sweaty and laughing. They both threw back a shot and Christian leaned on the bar, shaking his head at her attempt to pull him out there again. She backed away, pointing at both of us, smiling big.

"I'm done!" he yelled over the music.

She headed to the dance floor alone. We put down a few more shots. When I turned back around, some asshole was dancing with Kate. His hand ran up her leg, under the edge of her skirt, and then I was shoving him halfway across the dance floor. It was amazing how quickly the bodies parted. The guy on the ground put his hands up in surrender. Probably not his fault. She'd started it. But it didn't shut down my need to kick his ass.

Another guy offered a hand to help the guy up. He brushed off his pants then ran the back of his hand across his mouth. A bloody lip. I don't know how that had happened.

Christian shoved me back a step. "It's over."

"Touch her again, you die," I said to the prick, but when I looked at Christian, he looked like he was the one who'd been punched.

Kate was already back at the bar, waiting for us. When she saw my face, she rolled her eyes. "I suppose I'm in trouble."

"We're going."

She pouted. Christian settled the tab. I took Kate by the arm, but she pulled away. "Give me your car key. You ride with Christian. I have a friend I want to meet up with."

I shook my head at her. She dug into my pocket for my keys. I don't know why I let her.

She widened her eyes. "Something wrong? It's almost like you don't trust me."

I jerked my chin toward the dance floor. "Can't imagine why."

"Oh, baby, I was about to make him stop. You always jump the gun. Come on. I'll meet you boys back at the hotel in a few hours. We only have one more day here. I want to see my friend."

I looked at Christian for his input. He could've already had plans and didn't want to tote me around. He shrugged. I didn't know why he was the one sulking. Nobody did shit to him.

Kate latched her arms around my neck, kissing me with tongue. I don't know why I let her do that either. She then kissed Christian on the cheek. He ended it before she did. Unlike him. He was usually such a sucker for attention.

We followed her out the door and walked her to my car. When I got in his car with him, he peeled out of the parking lot.

"What the hell is your problem?" I asked.

I'll never forget the way he clenched his jaw and looked right through me.

I wonder if he was fucking her then.

And this friend she wanted to visit? Can't be a coincidence Dillon Moore lived in New York at that time. Cheating on me with two of my cousins, and I didn't suspect a thing. I don't know how I'm supposed to put all this behind me if the memories keep springing from nowhere. It might help to get one thing through my head: I wasn't the only victim. Christian was mixed up in all that shit, and not many years later, so was Liv. And I was the only one who could've stopped it.

An hour is too long to sit alone with my thoughts in the glaring sun now that my spot of shade has moved. My apology to Shawn will have to wait. I head into town for a reason I can't admit until I'm parking in the back of the liquor store because parking in front might reward me with some witnesses in this damn small town. I can't get by with nothing to drink in the house. One bottle, to sit on the shelf just in case. A small drink now and then isn't going to hurt. It will help me get through the not drinking. I'll leave it out in the open so I don't have to lie to her. Cold turkey just doesn't work.

I'm still sitting in the Camaro when a tabby crosses the back of the building at a good clip considering how emaciated she is. She leaps onto a dumpster a few shops down but freezes in place when a nearby door opens. I get out of the car, spooking her off the edge and behind the dumpster.

"Les! Get me my .22. That cat's out here again."

I can't see the guy who opened the door, but he's put down the bag of trash. Cat eyes glint from underneath the dumpster. Aw hell.

The cat's probably feral and doesn't trust people. Normally not a problem for me, but with this black magic coursing through me I'm about as trustworthy as the guy who just came through that door. She comes to me when I summon her, although hissing and spitting. She'd probably rather take her chances with the .22. I open the car door, and she goes straight to the passenger floorboard, still hissing like it's going to scare me.

"You have any kittens out there?" I don't want to save one cat and orphan a litter.

I take a long look at the door of the liquor store. I can't leave a feral cat in my Camaro, especially when some idiot with a .22 is itching to kill a cat. When I start the engine it angers her further.

"You piss in here, I'll throw you in the river."

She releases a wail that has me laughing so hard I almost forget the bottle of scotch I won't be getting today. I stop for a bag of kibble on my way out of town, then I dump her on Tara's porch with a pile of food. You feed a stray cat once, you have a friend for life. In this case, it's Tara who has a friend. She just doesn't know it yet.

Back at home I try to work in the garden but the sun reflects off every surface in a billion different rays and each one is an icepick into my pupil. I go inside to the basement and keep busy working on the gentlest, most effective cleansing spell for Liv. Again. The first one was screwed up by me but did eventually work, of course until she released Dillon's magic and reinfected herself. The second one was tied specifically to Christian. I could redo that one and tie it to Dillon, but Tara and Máthair created it. I'll need their help, and I'm not going back outside until the sun has lowered itself to a less punishing angle.

Deciding to leave Liv's cleansing spell to the experts, I start on one for me. I expect that black magic to return for me at any time. And when it does, I'll need something prepared to counteract the draining of my energy. It will suck me dry, and I'll be hungrier than ever for another hit of that easy power.

I lie in bed that night listening to Liv breathe. The clock moves impossibly slow. I should be glad for the unhurried return of the sun but there's no liquor in the house, and I'm about to cut off my leg if it doesn't stop twitching. I need that bottle I tried to buy earlier. Not to drink. I just need to see it sitting on the counter.

Two hours later I go outside to walk. The nervous energy has reached a breaking point. Liv had started to stir from my tossing and jerking, and I couldn't stay in there. She needs her sleep. The chill of night air is intoxicating. I breathe it in, letting it cool me from the inside. Then I head for the woods. River and Trib won't come near me but that's not new—they've been avoiding me since that night we built the altar of bones. The coyotes have been keeping their distance too. Most animals don't trust black witches. They're too often used as fuel.

Here I am, at that altar. The bones stand out against the forest floor even though most disintegrated the last time I was here. The remaining bone pieces are scattered like sea shells on a beach made of gray dust. A wave of unstoppable weakness courses through me; I fall to hands and knees. I shouldn't have come out here. I'm painfully sober, and I need something, anything. If I don't get it fast, I'm going to separate on the inside. Muscle snapping away from bone, skin peeling away. My eyes roll up in my head. I feel my face smack dusty earth. The black magic is here now, in my ears, on my tongue, all around me. I get my palms under me and push myself up, into the most potent swirl of pure, bottomless energy I have to take just one taste.

I take a pull of *dubhealaín* so insignificant no one would notice. But that pull doesn't stop, and I feel it fill me from the bottoms of my feet to my shins, to my knees, my hips, my navel. I'm an empty glass and it's pouring in the top and it's not stopping. I can't stop it. It's going to take me over, and I'll have nothing good left. Nothing for Liv. Nothing for our daughter.

There's a barely human growl coming out of me, my voice being shoved out as I'm filled to the ribcage. *Liv, Liv, Liv. Stop this for Liv.* I drop and plant my hands against earth—a frantic attempt to get my bearings, to find the spirit of the trees, the rush of the wind, the call of rain. The elements, my companions, my source of true power. I sense nothing so I push further out and there it is, reaching back, into fingers, hands, arms, chest.

The collision of my magic meeting black magic inside me throws me backward. Flames erupt in the trees around me. I stagger to my feet, gather the wind and blast it at the ground, throwing my arm against my face as protection against the blast of earth and bone dust that's now raining down, extinguishing the flames.

The silence that follows is a jarring return to reality. To what I've done.

To how much further I've fallen into the trap of *dubhealaín* and how much smaller the escape hole is above me.

Liv wakes me in the morning and makes me move from the couch to the bed. She kisses my cheek and says she's going to work, and I fall back asleep pissed at myself for not getting up to drive her.

I wake up hours later. Eat breakfast in the basement because shit if the sun was bright yesterday, today it's blinding. I cover my eyes on the way to the garage. My motorcycle helmet's visor is tinted but not damn near enough. I put it on and stand in the driveway while my eyes adjust. It's a hammering in my skull so brutal I nearly go back inside. But no, I'm doing this.

Another AA meeting. I don't talk and the group doesn't push because they think they know why and they're trying to give me time. They're partially right. I did fall off the wagon; they're just wrong about which addiction I gave in to, and they wouldn't believe me if I told them.

On the way home I stop at a gas station and buy a bottle of scotch small enough to last only one day. If I reach a low again, I'll have something else to turn to besides another pull of *dubhealaín*. Seems like a solid plan, looks pathetic. *Is* pathetic—I'm on my way home from a fucking AA meeting. As I cross the lot I see another motorcycle parked directly beside the Ninja. Not a sport bike. Some kind of standard Honda with saddlebags. I'm guessing the woman in black leather leaning against a nearby tree might have something to do with that.

She pushes off the tree trunk with her boot heel as I near. I stash my bottle in the pocket of my riding jacket and pick up my helmet. She's almost made it to me by the time I mount my bike. Starting the engine doesn't deter her beeline toward me. I flip the kickstand and she reaches over and turns off my engine.

She lifts her sunglasses, propping them on top of her head. "*Máistir na nDúl?*"

I get a good look at her through my visor. Rust-brown hair, about my age, eyelids smoked dark. I know it's just makeup but it reminds me of the seeing spell I did to Jared

Moore. She reads unfamiliar. Definitely not a Bevan or a Moore. She could be hired by them. Could be someone else entirely. But anyone who calls me that has to be checked out. She's traveled too close to my family to not find out where her loyalties lie.

Grateful we're in the shade, I take off my helmet and get a whiff of the mint she's chewing. To my kind, it's a common way to enhance a background power, to ready a mind. Or maybe she's just into mint. She offers her pouch of leaves, retracts it when I shake my head.

"No one calls me that."

"They should. I felt your pull of power last night from the Canadian border."

"You need to go back to where you came from."

She laughs like I've told a joke.

Time to cut to the chase. "What's your family name?"

"O'Dowd." She takes a pinch of mint leaves.

"Ó Dubhda?"

She shrugs. "If you wish. Now tell me yours."

She doesn't know? She's the one who sought me out. "Bevan."

When she frowns and takes a step back to scan me head to toe, I realize I haven't gone back far enough in my bloodline.

"Farrelly."

That has her interest. She swallows her mint and straightens up. "A bit of a troublemaker, then?"

"I'll give you thirty minutes to get out of Black River. A day to get out of Montana." I go for the ignition. The key is missing. She dangles it by her face, smile friendly, eyes dangerous. Maybe the makeup is ash, to do seeing spells whenever she pleases.

I dismount, aiming to grab her arm, but then I remember Liv. My mishandling of her beside the road. Her bruised arms as described by Tara. Thank the elements I never had to see them.

The woman offers a handshake. "Inis O'Dowd. What's your first name, Farrelly?"

I'm not sure which name to give her so I decide to give her neither. I open my left palm, avoiding her handshake. "Key."

She returns it, using the excuse to grip my hand and send a spark up my arm that lights my brain with a taste of black magic so potent I feel my addiction fall harder into its quicksand depths.

I twist free from her grip. "There's no room in this town for a black witch."

"You mean no room for two? You dishonor the art. We're sworn to work together, even those not born to it."

"I don't follow the art."

"From what I sensed last night, you do, and quite well. There's nothing more powerful than the joining of male and female power. You know this?"

My *dubhealaín* text teaches of the power that can be established by a joining of minds—one male, one female. Teams built out of male-female pairs who've studied together since birth, like a brother and a sister, are mostly unstoppable. "Find someone else. I'm getting out."

She reaches to poke my jacket pocket. "I have something that can break that whiskey habit."

"I have no habit that needs breaking by you." Any method of hers would drag me further into the depths of *dubhealaín* I'm trying to kick free from.

"Anyone who buys those little bottles has a habit." She opens a billfold in front of her—my billfold. Slides out my driver's license. "Ah, you did say you're a Bevan now. Trey Fearghus Bevan."

When she hands it back she's taken another liberty with a grip on my arm. A stinging heat scatters across the inside of my forearm.

"Call me if you change your mind. And don't get any ideas, Farrelly. This is business. Platonic. I don't mix it with pleasure."

She straps on her helmet, fires up her bike, and rides away. I push my jacket sleeve up to find her phone number branded on my forearm. If it's the spell I know, it will only disappear if I stop thinking about her. Platonic? Well, that's great. I'll just mention that to Liv and she'll be so happy I found a friend, a female friend who's seared her number onto my skin. Especially since I've been treating her like shit and spending every daylight hour in the basement.

I take a long drink from my little bottle of scotch. So much for it lasting all day.

CHAPTER 12

LIV

TARA'S CR-V FOLLOWS me down the driveway to my house. I'm not sure if she's here to see me or Trey, but from the harsh set of her eyes, I suspect it's Trey. Truck, Camaro, and Ninja are all here, so unless he's wandering the woods again, he's inside.

She goes straight into the kitchen while I set down my things and take off my shoes, then she's thundering down the basement stairs. I can hear her voice but can't make out what she's saying until I go into the kitchen for a glass of water.

"—that's what I mean. What you're emitting, I'm not living next to it, not with my children. And what about Liv and the baby? If you think it won't affect them you're a fu—"

The barbell hits the ground with perfectly timed censorship. I wonder if he did that on purpose.

"You need to stop, or Máthair and I will find a way to do it for you, and you know it won't be pleasant. This is Liv, Fearghus. And your *baby*. You'll drag them down with you."

"I've already done worse to her," he says. It's the despair in his voice that freezes me in place. He used the same broken tone that night he spoke my name in bed when he thought I was sleeping.

She doesn't answer right away, probably because that tone has given her pause. Her voice turns gentle. "All the more reason to stop."

Now it feels like I'm eavesdropping. I go into the bedroom to change my clothes then the bed sheets, which are full of gray dust and dirt from whatever Trey was doing last night. Tara knocks a few minutes later, so I open the door. The agitation she arrived with is gone, replaced by a grim reserve that has me glad I stopped listening when I did. She takes the other side of the bed, and we strip it together. She folds it into itself to keep the dirt inside. She doesn't ask about the source of the dirt, and I have a feeling she knows more than me. "Do you want help talking to him about—"

"No, I've got it. It will be better coming just from me."

"Well, if you want to come over afterward and spend the night, or just talk, you're welcome at any hour."

"It'll be fine."

She grins at me, envious at my cool head when it comes to Trey. She's said it so much she doesn't need to anymore. "The jackass doesn't deserve you."

Trey comes upstairs as I'm walking her out. Their eyes meet, a silent acknowledgment of whatever they discussed that turned Tara almost as somber as Trey. I'm sweeping the floor around the couch when he gets out of the shower. He takes the broom away from me. "Sorry. I should've cleaned this up."

I stand and watch him, hoping he'll explain the mess without me having to question. He must get the hint, straightening to face me. "I went for a walk during the night. I—" He sets the broom aside and drops to the couch, his face in his hands. "Shit, Liv. It's too much."

I sit beside him but he remains like that, silent, covering his face. With whatever burden he has, it doesn't seem right to drop something else on him, but I see no way around it. "Nancy Carter showed me an apartment in town today."

He exhales into his hands.

"I want to help you, and I think you need your own space—"

He looks up at me. "I don't."

"You're overwhelmed."

"Not by you."

"It will be less pressure on you so you can focus on getting better. And when Sloane is born, we'll be close enough you can visit every day."

He stands abruptly, crosses the room like he's going to hit something. As quickly as the motion begins it ends, and he's left staring at the fireplace in an unnaturally stiff pose. "I'll build some bedrooms onto the house."

"No, Trey."

"Christian's right. If I keep busy—"

"The baby will be here any day. I don't want to live in a construction zone with a newborn."

"I'll hire a crew and have it done in no time." He has the intense look of someone on the edge, begging for his life. My defense is strong; I know this is what's good for both him and me. But then he's dropped to his knees before me and he says one more thing: "Please."

I shift on the couch to look away, to try to head it off before it goes through me but it's already too late. It pushes through my defenses and pulverizes me on the inside. Tough love isn't supposed to be this hard for the giver. It should feel like the right thing. The only thing.

"Move in with Tara."

He's compromising? This is new. "I'm not bringing our problems over there. An apartment—"

"I'll go crazy," he says.

"That's the problem though, don't you see?"

"No, the problem is they'll kill both of you while I sit around here, unaware of the whole thing until I go to this apartment of yours and find your corpses. I'm not crazy because of you. I'm crazy because of them." He stands and takes a few steps away, rubbing a hand down his face hard. "I went to my meeting today."

"That's gr—"

"I bought a bottle of scotch on my way home."

There's a delay before the disappointment hits, so hard I get a lurch in my chest. Even then I watch his face, sure that he's joking when it couldn't possibly be funny.

"A black witch is hunting me. She branded her number on my arm." He turns the inside of his forearm toward me.

Now there's a weakness in my knees. I want to get closer to read his arm, but I don't trust myself to walk. He looks shocked when I reach for him, like after all that, it's impossible I'd still want anything to do with him. But I don't withdraw my hand, so he returns to the couch beside me. I take his arm and turn it, reading the feminine scrawl of inflamed numbers on his arm.

"I didn't want it, but she gave me no choice," he says.

"Why is a black witch after *you*?"

"Too many pulls of black magic will lure them. She wants me to join her. The number won't disappear until I stop thinking about her." He pulls his arm away, exhaling, shaking his head. "So now you'll know exactly how long I'll be thinking about another woman."

I lean back on the couch. Thinking about another woman is okay … unless it's not okay. Trey and I have both been victims of cheaters. There's no way he'd do it to me. Ever. But that number will last as long as his anger does. Being involuntarily branded would irritate most people—I can only imagine what it's doing to Trey. And every time he looks at it, it will only incite him further.

"What did you do with the scotch?"

"Drained it dry."

The nonchalant choice of words would propel me to Tara's for the night if I'd taken them alone without a glimpse of his face. Disgust and defeat are so evident I can't do anything but take his hand and hold it against my lips. If I weren't so pregnant I'd get in his lap and put my arms around his neck and stay there forever. This is nothing like picking glass out of road rash—it's a foreign body I couldn't ever reach. It's not something I can fix with suture. It's so profoundly tangled inside everything that makes him who he is. The only person who can fix it is him. But I'm going to be beside him the whole way.

"I didn't know you could practice black magic."

"All of us can. But we don't. It's against everything we believe. I shouldn't have touched it." His attention moves down to his hands. Then he laces his fingers together and looks slowly back at me as if noticing me in the room for the first time. The otherness has returned, marked by such subtle changes in how his eyes meet mine, how he's with-drawn from the room in spirit, how his familiar body lan-guage and expression switch to something unrecognizable. If he wasn't the man I love, I'd be inching toward my bag, palming my pepper spray, preparing to mace him.

He stands and rubs both hands over his hair and face as if scrubbing something off. He takes the broom and dustpan full of dirt and dust to the kitchen, and I hear the back door open and close. Silence drags long enough for me to wonder what he's doing, so I go to the kitchen and peer outside. River and Trib are standing at the porch railing, looking across the yard. There's no sign of Trey.

I go outside, rubbing my arms against the chill that's accompanied dusk. I catch subtle movement well past the garden—Trey, carrying the dustpan. He crosses a narrow section of lawn, then he's stepping through the trees. I've unconsciously thrown my hands in the air. Where the hell is he going now? I gather a breath to call his name. Claws scratch wood as River and Trib peel out, tearing off the porch and down the hill. It's unusual they weren't on his heel when he walked down there, ears up and tongues lolling and eager for a job to do. They streak across the yard toward him, stopping just short of the woods where he entered. It's almost like they're suspicious of him, policing him. This whole situation isn't right.

Back in the house, I slip on shoes and a jacket and find a flashlight and my Ruger. Trey's phone dings on the counter. I glance at it—I shouldn't, but I do—a message from Christian: *Three Moore households to visit thanks to you. They want to feel me out. Won't come here because they're afraid you'll show up full-massacre mode. I'll try to find out how they plan to kill you.* Another one comes in right after it: *Wait, my bad. They won't need to. Cuz I'm gonna bring them your fucking head on a stick.*

I'll be sure to put Trey's head on ice for Christian after I kill him.

Halfway across the yard, something spooks the birds in the trees. They burst into the sky, a wild flapping mass that's so bizarre I stop to scan the land around me, my hand on the Ruger. A faraway thrum follows, gaining pitch. Fear of a known threat washes through me. It's Dillon's spell. It's too similar not to be. I reach for the amulet—it warms in my hand, grows too hot to hold. So I release it and run for the trees, my pace hindered by the weight of the baby.

Something streaks overhead as a pulse vibrates in the earth below my feet. I look up to nothing but the evening sky and the limbs of the first pines at the edge of the woods. I crash into the underbrush, scratching my arms on branches, calling for Trey.

Then I'm on my knees, catching my forward motion with both palms. Everything around me is in motion: the trees tremble, the air and earth vibrate. I felt a mild earthquake once in the Midwest, but this is different; there's no back and forth jerk. It's a humming, a buzzing, a dance of atoms. I sit back on my heels, my belly heavy on my thighs. I reach for the flashlight and pistol I dropped. And everything stops. Whatever it was wasn't after me.

I get to my feet and run toward the barking. River and Trib, saving Trey's ass yet again. They're circling something on the ground that's out of my view. A few more strides and I see Trey flat on his back. I'm at his side. Blood runs from his nose, mouth, and ears. He has a weak breath and an almost non-existent pulse. My god, I've done this before. I don't even know where to look for injury. What vital organs does a magic pulse from the sky target?

He starts seizing. I kick a rock away from his head, drag away a large branch. Blood bubbles from his mouth as the seizure goes on and on, and I cover my own mouth so I don't scream. River is barking like we're being attacked by some invisible creature. Trib snarls and snaps at the air. My amulet is a scorching point of feeling that doesn't register as pain. It's red hot, burning through my shirt. Trey's body goes still.

I go to his side. His breath a strain. Pulse erratic. I flip on the flashlight and check his pupils. They're all black and red, no green at all. Just pupil and burst blood vessels. I turn his head so the blood can run out of his mouth. It's not enough. I shove my hands underneath him, try to roll him on his side. He jerks, coughing up a fountain of blood, but I don't think it's him, it's just a bodily function, but then the coughing ends and he moves his lips like he's trying to talk.

"I'm here," I say, putting my ear to his lips, pushing away the thought these are his final words. I've saved his life before, and I will save him again. He's not going to die, not now, after all we've been through.

What comes out is so weak I can't make it out. I turn my face, press my forehead against his. Our minds were joined once, maybe he can will the words to me. His lips move again. I close my eyes, close off everything around me but him.

Your blood.

Yes—my blood. It's rich with immortality, the same effect that used to live in him now lives in me with our daughter. I need something sharp—a tree branch. I find a dry one and snap it to make a fresh break. I drag the sharp end across my palm, grateful the adrenaline is still coursing through me to mask the pain. Now where to cut him—over his heart. I tear off his shirt and stab, opening flesh more easily than I'd expect. Then I press my palm against the new wound. He shudders, his limbs spasm. But something's wrong. There's a prickly cold moving up my arm, and Sloane flips inside me so violently it takes a moment to catch my breath. And Trey's limbs aren't spasming anymore, they're shoving me away.

I remove my hand and look at my palm. The wound isn't bad enough to numb my arm. And that cold feeling is draining out with each drop of blood that falls. There's something inside Trey, something my blood can heal, but not if it gets inside me too. If only I had a shield …

The amulet. I rip the chain off my neck and grip the amulet with the fingers of my wounded hand. I press my opened palm against Trey's chest once more. This time he doesn't react. He's gone very still. My arm remains my own, so I flatten my hand and expose more surface against his skin. I check his pulse with my other hand. Rapid, but not erratic.

River and Trib have quieted. I keep my blood on Trey's chest wound as I raise my head to look around me. The dogs are pacing in front of a backdrop of coyotes who appear relaxed, almost as if they're here for moral support. Maybe they are. It's strangely calming, and I feel the adrenaline seeping away, shakes and fatigue taking its place.

Trey's heartbeat is steady and strong. His nose has stopped bleeding, but he's still out. I need to get him home. If the dogs' behavior is any indicator, the danger seems to have passed, but I have no idea if—or when—it will return. I need to get Trey indoors. I need to call Tara and Sloane. I'm moving branches and rocks to clear a path through the woods when I hear Trey rustling awake. I go back to his side. "Be still. You need to stay down."

His eyelids are slits, eyes watering bloody tears. He reaches for my face. I return his arm to the ground.

"You're injured, I have no idea how bad. Probably internally." My blood is healing him, but I don't know if it will heal him fast enough to save his life.

"Help me up," he whispers.

I actually consider it. I don't know how else to get him home. The coyotes helped me once, on a day that feels like decades ago. He rolls, attempting to get up himself. I stoop to get his arm around my neck and steady him as he gets to his knees, but he's too tall and I'm too short to be of any more help. His legs crumple. He hits the ground hard before I can even reach for him.

His eyes have rolled into his head. I straighten his neck and limbs and he starts coming around again. "Don't you dare try that again. I'll go get help—"

He catches my hand. "Stay."

On my knees, I check his pulse again. I look around, from River to Trib then from one coyote to the next. Time will allow the healing to work, and we have bodyguards while it's working. There's already a chill in the air, though, and I'm not dressed for a crisp mountain night. "It's too cold. I have to go back and get blankets."

Grunting, he digs his fingers into the earth. Warmth rises from the ground then his body goes slack, his breathing hitched. "Stay with me."

Again, I'm reeling from the thought those could be his last words. I won't release the sob that's in me, not while he's clinging to life and needs strength to survive. Even if I ran for the house and called an ambulance, they'd never make it in time if he's really dying. His injuries are a mystery, most likely untreatable out here. I wonder if they're even treatable by medical science. All we have right now is what's saved us before, what kept him alive after he was beaten nearly to death by those ten guys, whatever saved me from an arrow through the chest. All we have is each other.

"I'm here. I'm staying." And not just tonight. Forever.

When I settle beside him the coyotes get comfortable too, some lying down, some sitting. River and Trib have left, probably to check on Tara and Sloane and the kids. The pallet of earth Trey's magic heated beneath us warms me to my bones. It's a sedative too impossible to fight, especially while crashing from the type of adrenaline dump that happens when someone you love is dying before your eyes. I don't fall asleep until I've compulsively checked his breathing and pulse at least a hundred times. And either the moonlight is casting magic upon us or the wound I opened on his chest appears to have a day-old seal. My own wound already itches with its own healing.

These attempts on his life are starting to get old.

The moon is overhead when I finally allow my eyes to close, and Trey is beside me, grounding me to the only place I want to be.

CHAPTER 13

TREY

I WAKE ON HARD ground, dawn filling the forest with a hazy light around us. River comes to lick my hand. If that's not enough to know I'm clean, I also have the missing weight of black magic coursing through me, nagging me to pull more. It's all absent—the burning desire for more and the ready power itself. Sucking all that out must've been included with sucking out all my life.

I get my elbows underneath me and push up, my head swimming on storm-grade waves that turn my stomach. Choking it back, I turn my head, just in case. It wouldn't be good to throw up on Liv after she saved my life—again—then spent all night on the ground beside me.

She stirs. In the next second she's up and taking my pulse, checking my ears, feeling my skull, looking in my eyes, poking around on a gash on my chest. "You look like hell."

"Thanks."

"Do you have any idea what that was last night?"

I put all my effort into getting to my feet because I'm not sure I'm ready to answer that. I haven't figured out a way to explain what I did: call upon a mass of black magic, harness it, trick it, then wait around for it to come back and screw me up. All because I couldn't stand to give her time, couldn't wait for her to come back to me on her own. Couldn't trust her. I offer her a hand.

She shakes her head and rises on her own. "You can barely hold your own weight."

River leads the way back to the house. The coyotes trail us to the edge of the woods. I owe them again, and they know this. They're keeping track. Trib could be at Tara's but without knowing for sure, I send River off to check. Then Liv and I climb the slope to the house. I'm not going to make it without a rest but screw that, I'm not resting. I'm focusing on nothing but putting one foot in front of the other when Liv stops short beside me and I stop, falling to one knee, a hand on the ground to keep from face-planting in the grass.

"Who's that?"

I follow her gaze to the driveway. Black Honda motor-cycle. Saddlebags. There aren't enough curse words in the world. Trib is sitting at the edge of the woods on the other side of the house, watching something out of our sight. Liv helps me up, and we head toward the front door where Inis O'Dowd is sitting on the porch, filing her nails with a rock.

Liv takes in her leather jacket, black jeans, boots, and looks up at me without having to ask. I respond with the tiniest nod. Looks like a black witch, *is* a black witch. Inis doesn't stand when we draw near.

She tosses the rock, polishes her nails on her jeans, and smiles big. "Farrelly."

"Get the fuck off my porch."

"Now, I had the manners to leave the two of you snuggling sweetly down there, and you're going to repay me by being a prick? I've been playing damage control all night for whatever you unleashed last night. Calling that much power to one place? What are you thinking, Farrelly?"

She's upright now, blocking my doorway. And I can barely keep my legs under me.

"And doing that while I'm still in the area? It's almost like you're trying to pin it on me. You wouldn't do that, would you?"

"I didn't call that. It came for me." Why I'm explaining anything to her is beyond me. I need to get in the house and lie down.

"I'll admit I was surprised to see you all cuddled up next to one of my kind. That's something I think you should've mentioned when we met."

One of her kind? I don't know any of her kind except her. And since I'm about to collapse, I push forward, my eye on the door like it's my lifeline. Liv's hand slips from my grasp. I stop, look behind me. She's got her calm, professional face on, but the way she's staring at Inis …

Inis extends a hand to Liv. "Cousin."

Liv hasn't moved. "I don't have any cousins."

"Well, distant cousin. Technicalities. You're an O'Dowd, right?"

"She's not an O'Dowd," I say. This is complete bullshit. I try to catch Liv's eye, beckon her inside with me. We can slam the door and wait for this woman to leave. Or not. She can stay out there all day for all I care. She won't stay forever. Even black witches get hungry.

"She *is* an O'Dowd. I already tested to make sure. Bounced right off, just like it should. Then your coyotes started—"

"What bounced off?"

"My magic. Here, I'll show you."

My processing of her answer is interrupted by the ground below Liv bursting into flames. The fire laps against her knees. I have no strength to gather, nothing to extinguish it, but I don't need it. Liv steps away from the flames, unharmed. She takes her amulet out of her pocket and stares at it, incredulous as if still surprised by its power.

"Oh, another go without that," Inis says, snatching it from her. The fire flares up at Liv's feet and she steps out, untouched again. Inis tosses the amulet back, hissing and rubbing her hand where it burned her. "Black magic doesn't hurt my kind. I'm guessing your mother is an O'Dowd?"

"I didn't know my mother," Liv says.

The ground tilts. The corners of my vision turn dark. I stumble and catch myself against the house. I'm being deposited onto the couch by two women, and I don't remember the steps it took to get there. Liv is dragging the armchair from the corner to the middle of the room and offering it to Inis, and I'm hearing the last words Inis just spoke: *Black magic doesn't hurt my kind.*

I'm drowning in darkness. I force my eyes open. Passing out is not an option, with this woman in my house and Liv far too willing to welcome her. I lie down on my back, focus on the beams in the cabin's ceiling, and fight the building buzz in my head.

The next thing I sense is a soft kiss on my lips. Fingers against the pulse in my neck. I draw a breath and open my eyes and look straight into Liv's. I have no clue how much time I lost.

"Coffee?" She sets a mug on the coffee table.

Behind her, Inis sips from a mug with her eyes on me—calculating, silently laughing. She's enjoying this. Total sadist.

Liv shoves pillows underneath me. "I think you'll be okay propped up just a bit so you can drink. When's the last time you ate?" She hands me my coffee.

I drink, wishing it was something stronger.

"I remember now," Inis says. "The feud between the Farrellys and the Moores."

"Bevans," I correct.

"Right—Bevans. So, the Bevans joined one of their own with an O'Dowd to defeat the Moores? No wonder the Moores hate you so much."

"I'm not an O'Dowd," Liv says for the hundredth time.

"Fine. Child of an O'Dowd deserter, then. You still carry and pass on O'Dowd blood. It's an interesting combination, earth magic and black magic. You've created a little firebrand there." She gestures with her mug toward Liv's belly.

"She's a hero," Liv says.

"Depends on which side you're on, I think. She is certainly going to make waves though. A little catalyst. People with a double bloodline like hers are born to start wars."

"Or end them." Liv glances at me. Something's worrying her. Hard to tell if it's my latest near-death experience or our daughter's future. Probably both.

"I can't do what you and Trey can do," Liv says, returning her attention to Inis. "I knew nothing of this world until I met Trey. That was less than a year ago. If my mother was an O'Dowd like you, she didn't pass anything to me."

Inis shrugs out of her jacket, contemplating. "So then you're descended from the line who abandoned the arts. Training can awaken it, if started early on. It's too late for you, but not for your wee one."

Liv sets her mug down with a bang on the coffee table. "I'm sorry, I don't believe any of this. You can't tell me who I am just from setting a fire at my feet."

I don't want to catch Inis' eye, but I can't help it. We might be from different teachings and opposite beliefs, but the ring of common blood is a powerful thing, a concept she and I must share from the knowing look she's giving me. If all this is true, then Liv's lost that ability too. This doesn't matter, though. I need her to go back to something she said earlier, something far more important. "You said black magic doesn't hurt your kind. So if Liv is one of you it can't hurt her. Can't hurt our daughter. Right?"

"You saw her step out of my fire. Keep up. We're well beyond that."

I clarify, just to be sure. "*All* black magic."

"Not all. Only ours. Yours? Another story. It's not present in your blood like it is in ours, so it's completely erratic.

Knowing your kind, it's probably formulated just to punish us. But don't get any ideas. You're in no condition to target me right now."

Not the answer I was looking for.

Inis hooks her leg over the arm of the chair. "What's for breakfast?"

I point to her coffee mug. "You just had it. Time to leave." I lean forward to stand. Then the black shade is withdrawing from my eyes again, and Liv is helping me sit. Another lost moment. Hopefully this is exhaustion and not brain damage.

Liv tugs the pillows from under my shoulders, and I fall flat. The sudden brief movement blackens my vision yet again and lays a sheet of fatigue over me I can't fight off. My senses fall away, leaving only my hearing.

"Let's go in the kitchen so he can sleep."

Two sets of footsteps fade away to a tiny pinpoint of sound and then nothing.

When I wake, Liv is sitting beside me, copying the phone number from my arm into her phone. "*In-ish*. I-N-I-S, right?" She takes my silence as confirmation. "Feel better?"

I sit up. The room blurs but doesn't go dark. Progress. "Seems better. Is she gone?"

"She left about an hour ago. Said she'll be in the area for a while, and that you should call her if you change your mind."

There's a question in those words I shouldn't need to answer. I pick up the glass of water on the coffee table and gulp it down, ignoring the extended look Liv's giving me.

She takes the empty glass. "Now I know exactly what you've been up to, and I see why you didn't want to tell me. All the other things you do, you've done …" She looks away. "Strange to think this, but they seem justified. But this? It's not you."

"I'm through with it."

"It scares me."

"It's just magic."

"It's not your family's magic. It's bad."

"Funny you say that. If Inis is right about you, it's your family's magic."

"Inis says my line deserted it. She's actually … she thinks a distant O'Dowd went missing around the time I was born. She's going to find out. It could be my mother."

"You can't trust her."

"Of course not. She's far too interested in the baby. She wants to train her when she's born, to awaken the O'Dowd blood."

"She can go to hell." I clamp my head between both hands and press at the temples. Shit, I don't need this. If I hadn't drawn her here, she'd know nothing about our daughter.

"Dillon wants her too. And not for his family, for himself."

"Dillon can come try to get her. He won't—"

"And let's not forget the Moores want her. What are we going to do?"

"Nothing. Let them come. I'll kill them one by one." Inis included.

"Is there anything you need to tell me?"

Nothing I need to tell her, nothing she needs to know. Maybe things I should tell her, but why? It's behind me.

And she knows so much now; when I look at her, she's a mirror of all I've done. I have to be a better man for her.

Her question feels like a test, though, one I can't fail again. I've had all my chances. This is it. "I'm going to stop drinking. I swear."

"Don't swear. Promise. Tell me you promise to stop."

Oh, she's good. "I won't break a promise to you, Liv."

"Then don't. Say you promise and don't break it." She grips my arm with both hands, her eyes so blue and desperate it hurts to look at her.

"I promise to stop drinking every day," I offer. Her grip remains, demanding more out of me. And those eyes, they'll be my end. I wish I could tell her everything she wants to hear, but I can't lie to her. I won't. "I can't promise to stop for good."

"One drink a month."

Funny how I consider it, pinned down as I am. Her hair is still messy from our nap in the woods. She's round with my baby, and she's never been more gorgeous. And now she can tell I'm admiring her, and the hardball expression has gone soft, the worry in her eyes now almost a smile. I pry one of her hands off and kiss it. She watches me do it, half irritated, half won.

"One drink a week," she tries.

I don't even want to agree to that. I'm too much a loser. I'll never pull it off.

"Just say you'll make it a goal, and that's all I'll ask for now."

"Done." I offer a handshake. She kisses me instead. I lose myself in it. If she kisses me like this every day, I'll never need to drink again. I believe she's magic, whether it's true or not—but it's not O'Dowd black magic; it's a new type of magic so pure the effect is intoxicating. Healing. Removing all vice and reforming it into a strain of tranquility that could grow if I let it. I only wish I could.

Then I remember Dillon Moore—in her head. We still haven't fixed her. I break the kiss, sever the transmission of that tranquility.

"Sorry," she says, pulling away. "You must not feel totally well yet. I'll get dinner started. You rest."

She leaves the room, and I don't correct her. I listen to her moving around in the kitchen. She's carrying my baby, and I'm going to be a slob on the couch while she makes my dinner. Right. I get up and stretch, joints popping and creaking like I've been sleeping for days. In the kitchen I nudge her away from the stove. She relents, miraculously following my suggestion she rest on the couch. Minutes later she's back in the room, holding a little sock out to me like it's something I should know about.

"Where'd you get this?" she asks when I don't offer a comment on it.

"What is it?"

"A baby sock. *My* baby's sock, when she was first born. I found it smashed in the pages of one of your books."

No shit. I lower the heat on the skillet and take it from her. Turn it over in my hand. "I've never seen it before."

"You didn't put it there?"

"No. Never seen it."

She takes it from me, hesitating like she just arrived at some answer she doesn't want to share with me. "Where—who had those books before you did?"

"My mother packed them up and sent them with Christian on his visits here."

"What year?"

She would have to ask that. My life after leaving the estate and before I met her is one big monotonous haze. Drinking, fighting for money, killing the Moores' guys, more drinking. Some of the texts I did receive when I was living in Arizona, but I don't think it was all—no, it wasn't.

"I don't know what year. She sent the important ones right away. The others came a few at a time, I'm not sure when."

Something outside the back door captures her attention, so I go back to the stir-fry that's close to burning. She opens the door and squats down, extending a hand outside. I lean to look—there's a cat out there, hunkered low. Tabby. Skin and bones. Aw shit.

"Is it strange that a cat would be all the way out here?" she asks.

Not if it was dumped at a nearby house. "That's Tara's cat."

"Oh, yeah? Since when?"

The cat rushes inside to rub against my legs. I look down at her and tell her to go back to Tara's. I realize with cats it's more a suggestion than a command, and I don't have it in me to order her around like I did that day in the alley. We'll take her back to Tara's tomorrow when we go for the fix to remove Dillon from Liv's head. And hopefully they have something for me too, so I can quit those meetings and honor Liv's one drink a week request.

CHAPTER 14

LIV

TREY GOES TO his knees in Tara's living room to give Winnie a proper hug. She's been worried about him, been asking about him for days. She latches onto his neck, and Will wanders up, also looking worried until Trey scoops him into the group hug. No matter what trouble Trey causes, there's a good man inside him. I have to help dig him out. It took me leaving him to understand this, to never forget it. Now that good man is about to be tested. Tara and I have some news for him.

Sloane takes the kids outside to play, away from the furniture that's about to be thrown. She squeezes my arm on her way out, a gesture that tells me so much I wonder if she's transmitting words straight into my head. She's done that before.

Tara closes the door behind them. "Okay, Fearghus. Sit down. Intervention time."

He doesn't sit. I drag him to the couch by the arm and force him down. He's only compliant because he's not yet sure he's back on even terms with me.

"Liv, Máthair, and I have decided not to apply the fix to Liv until after the baby's born."

He looks at me. I nod.

"She'll be born any day," she continues. "We don't want to risk affecting the birth."

"No," he says.

"Actually, yes. So deal with it for a few more days, a week, maybe two. Then we'll get Dillon out once and for all."

He tries to stand up as I predicted. Which is why I'm anchored to his arm and not letting go. Tara frowns at me, disappointed. She was looking forward to smacking him out of it.

"Do you have the fix?" he asks.

"None of your business." She takes in his expression. The burst blood vessels in his eyes still haven't healed, adding a nightmarish element to the savage look he's casting her way. "You really want to push this?" She tilts her head toward me, a move so subtle she probably only meant for him to see.

Trey loses the rigid anger so fast I unconsciously release his arm. Then he's got a hand on my knee, pressing gently as if he's using the leverage to stand, but he's not getting up. He remains slightly bowed but lost to the conversation, reining in a thought that got away from him. I look at Tara, her surprise a copy of my own, proving it's not my imagination: Trey's making an effort to be calm, and it's actually working.

He turns to look at me. His voice is low with the control he's invoked. "This really what you want?"

I don't need to answer him. He exhales a slow, even breath, staring straight ahead at nothing. Resigned. I hug him so fast and hard I almost knock him over. He puts a reluctant arm around me, the fuse on his anger not yet extinguished but also not reaching its payload. He's extended it, giving time for it to go out before it explodes. I hug him harder, hoping to throw a bucket of water on that lit fuse. I kiss his cheek. When his arm tightens around me, I know I've reached that good man. And I'm not letting go.

"What about the effect for me?" he asks Tara.

I perk up. I wasn't aware they were working on a spell for him. There are too many things that need fixing in him for me to guess what it's for.

"No dice on that either," she says. "We think it's a bad idea."

"I didn't ask what you thought, I asked you to do it."

"Too bad. We're not doing it. A Band-Aid on a drinking habit is only going to push an addict toward something else. If you had no other vices, sure. But after you start pulling *dubhealaín*? Máthair and I are out. You're on your own. Beating the habit with nothing but your own unaided self is the only way you'll get better without moving onto something worse."

From the curses he's dropping, she must be right, and he knows it. He thought he was going to beat alcoholism with magic? If only he could. I'm glad I didn't know about this possibility before or I'd be sharing in his disappointment that has turned his brow severe and his gaze into an angry stare at the wall.

"*Tá brón orm, a Fhearghuis.* You know it's the only way."

He stands and goes to the front door, yanking it open to reveal Shawn on the porch, his fist raised to knock.

"Bad time?" Shawn does a double take at Trey's face, squinting as he gets a good look at his eyes. "Whoa, is that contagious?"

The sliding door opens and kids' voices spill in from the kitchen, along with Sloane's. Chairs scoot and the faucet turns on—it must be time for a snack. I head in there to help, but I'm stopped by Shawn saying my name.

"I have something to show you." He digs in his pocket, but then Trey is offering him a handshake. Tara and I exchange another look of surprise.

"I owe you a thank-you," Trey says.

Shawn backs up a step, clearly as surprised as Tara and me.

Trey hasn't withdrawn his hand. "For the info you took down. It helped."

Shawn gives the whole room the once-over. "Is this—"

"Thanks," Trey says. "I'm grateful."

Shawn accepts the handshake, his eyebrows just about meeting his hairline they're raised so high. When he gets his hand back, he checks his palm like he's the butt of a practical joke and expects to have a handful of slime. Then he walks around Trey, watching him closely. When he stops in front of me, he's looking like he forgot what he was going to say.

"Oh," he says, digging once again in his pocket. "I have to show you this. Don't you have one like this?"

Out comes a medallion dangling on a simple silver chain. I catch it, turn it over to see the front. On it is the same motif from my amulet—a concave triangle inside a circle. The metal isn't as worn as mine, and the engraving of the motif seems cleaner, like it was done in a more modern age. But it's not new either. If his is one hundred years old, mine is five hundred. I fish my amulet from under my shirt and hold them up side by side.

"See?" Shawn says. "Thought so."

Tara and Trey swoop in, both talking at once. *Where did you get that? Whose is that? How long have you— Why didn't you tell us—*

I've handed the necklace back to Shawn to put a hand against Trey's chest because he's way too close and Tara's continuing shower of questions seems to be making him worse, not better. Voices are rising and I glance at the kitchen where the kids are. Tara does the same. She jabs Trey in the arm and shushes him.

"Hand it over," she says to Shawn.

"Hell no. Not until you and your brother calm down. Jeez, it's not even mine."

"Whose is it?"

"My mother's. She used to wear it, hasn't for a long time. Then I saw Liv's—what, last year sometime. It reminded me."

"McCalister," Trey says, looking at Tara.

"Yeah?" Shawn says. "What's it to you?"

Tara's shaking her head at Trey, eyes glued on his like they're having a conversation we're not a part of. She suddenly looks at Shawn. "What's your mother's last name?"

"What do you think? McCalister."

"No, before she was married."

"What business is it of yours?" He looks between the two of them and seems to decide answering a harmless question is the better option than saying no to two equally intense and demanding twins who aren't going to back down. "Moore."

Trey shoves Shawn out the front door with Tara on his heels.

I'm slowed down by a Braxton Hicks contraction so strong I have to brace my hand against the wall and breathe through it. That's two in the last half hour. If I get another I need to time it, start keeping track. But first I have to go outside and stop Trey from killing Shawn.

Outside, Tara's doing the interrogation while Trey stands by, ready and waiting for a cue to attack. Shawn's saying nothing as the questions fire. He's simply standing there, arms crossed, waiting for her to finish. It's not fair, two against one. It saddens me how quickly Tara can turn on the guy who's done so much for her, for her kids. For all of us.

When I approach I have no idea what I'll do. No plan. All I know is nothing's going to be solved when Trey and Tara are out for blood. I'm not going to stand by and let Trey ruin the breakthrough he just had. Trey surges forward and takes Shawn by the collar—some aggressive move to get him to talk, but Shawn's still not talking. Not fighting back. Not doing anything. He knows it will frustrate both of them, and he's doing it on purpose.

"Back *off*," I say to Trey.

He releases Shawn fast. Steps back. Runs a hand over his hair to collect himself. He won't meet my eye. He knows he screwed up. I don't care if he couldn't help it. He should help it.

"Shawn, drive me home, please."

"And end this lovely visit?"

"Please." I hook my arm with his.

He shares one final look with Tara. Her face hasn't changed—narrowed eyes, tight mouth. Cold. Unforgiving. But what I see on Shawn is different. He's been betrayed by someone he loves. Oh, how I know that feeling. He and I are probably wearing the same expression, but I don't share it with Trey. All he gets is my back, walking away.

After Shawn closes me in the passenger side, I hear him muttering all the way around his truck. He gets in and starts the engine. Tara's gone inside but Trey remains, watching us leave with a look on his face so broken I have to close my eyes and remember what he just did. I won't make Shawn stop so I can run back to him.

"Damn, that guy's an asshole." He pats my knee. "No offense."

"None taken. Sorry about Tara. I can't believe she'd take his side so easily."

"Don't be sorry. That's my fault for liking her. I know she's hotheaded. Must be genetic." He snorts. "What was all that about, anyway? Did I miss something?"

He sure did. And not just something. He's living in a different world but hasn't been clued in on anything about it. I'm not sure how much I'm allowed to tell him, but at this point I don't really give a shit. If they wanted to control how much information he'd be given, they should have told him things a long time ago.

"Pull over somewhere."

He gives me a look that says *that bad*? I'm too busy trying to figure out where to begin.

We end up in an overgrown gravel lot just before the bridge over the river. It's a small descent from the road and behind a grove a pines, which gives us good cover should Trey decide to drive home. Hopefully he'll pass us right by and keep going.

"My old make-out spot," Shawn says, killing the engine.

I lift my amulet from under my shirt again, and he supplies his for comparison.

"I used to be a Moore," I say.

"No shit?"

"I married one. That BMW—that was him."

He forms an 'O' with his mouth but doesn't make a sound.

"I left that day with him … I just needed to settle some things."

"Are they settled?"

"Nothing will ever be settled with the Moores. They've been warring with Trey's family for a very long time and neither one of them has any intention to stop."

He pulls back, laughing. "Warring? What, like mafia type stuff?"

"Pretty damn close."

He rubs his face. "Okay, so, they think my mother …" He lowers his hands to look through the window. "That's just crazy."

"Yeah, I know. Her name could be a coincidence, except she had that amulet."

"Of course it's not a coincidence. If you're somehow related to my mother—or your ex-husband is, then there's nothing strange about having the same damn necklace."

"My amulet belongs to Trey's family. Not the Moores. It's very old, very important to them." Here's the part where I can tell him so much more. I hesitate, not because I don't want to but because I think it might make this way too complicated. It's complicated enough.

"Okay, so that's why Tara and Trey flipped out. My mother, their supposed enemy, has their precious family heirloom."

"Exactly. Do you know how your mother got it?"

"Not really. She might've brought it from her family's house, but I doubt it. I was always under the impression she took nothing when she left. She was young too. Sixteen."

"She ran away when she was sixteen?"

He nods, handing me her amulet. "You can have it. She said she doesn't need it anymore."

I fasten it around my neck with the other one. Maybe if Dillon sends another strike of magic from the sky, double protection will make a better shield, and I won't end up thrown across a parking lot. I cradle my belly, a reaction to the pit of worry I've been fighting since that day.

"You okay?" he asks.

"Yeah, I'm fine. I should be asking you."

"Nah." He looks out the window toward the road. "I don't know why I love that woman. She breathes fire."

"I think she and Trey make each other worse."

"Sounds solid. Twins, man."

"Hopefully her twins won't inherit that."

"Yeah, I kind of love her kids too. It's a problem."

I find his hand and squeeze it. There's so much more I could drop on him, but I don't think it's the time, and I don't think I'm the one who should do it. It will be more meaningful to him if it comes from Tara. "It's not a problem."

"It is. Because they're all so weird. Haven't you noticed all the weird—"

I'm not sure if he cuts off or if I've stopped listening because this Braxton Hicks feels like way more than a Braxton Hicks. And how long has it been since that last one?

"Hey, do I need to take you to the clinic or something?"

I wave my hand as its grip subsides. There was an edge to that one the others didn't have. And I have an immediate strong need to go home.

"Liv?"

"Drop me at home, will you?"

"Sure. I'm just dropping you though. I'm in no mood to get my nose bloodied today by someone I can't hit back."

"You can hit him back. Any time."

"Yeah, but then Tara would make me pay."

I laugh, knowing he's right.

"Their mother is so chill. How can that be?"

"She has to be, to put up with them." I want to include Shawn and myself in that statement, but it doesn't seem right. Sloane's infectious calm and bulletproof composure can't be compared to my barely sane handling of recent events. Fleeing with my ex, stealing his car, getting myself lost in order to find my way home. It was more than the revival of Dillon's spell over me—that was just one piece of the pickax chipping away at the ground below my feet. Despite all our problems with the Moores before, my feet were firmly planted. Trey's leaving was the first swing of the pickax. Then Dillon's arrival. Inis. More glaring problems with Trey. Now this. There's a fissure in the ground ready to swallow me up, and I think the calming pregnancy hormones are the only thing keeping me from losing my balance and falling deep inside.

At home I wave goodbye to Shawn and go in my house, running into Trey who's tying his boots just inside the door. "It happened to Tara."

"What?"

"The same thing that happened to me. I just got home when she called." He pauses, his hand on the doorknob. His eyes say *please come*, as if his behavior could've angered me enough to not help Tara. I follow him outside and get in his car.

She's on the couch when we arrive, a wet cloth over her eyes. Will is crying softly by her side as she strokes his hair. Her shirt has a large stain of blood near the collar. Trey picks up Will so I can check her out. He asks him where his sister and grandmother are; Will points to the basement stairs, smashes his face against Trey's shirt, and cries harder.

"Help me sit up," Tara says weakly, removing the cloth from her eyes. They're all red and black, burst vessels and dilated pupils, just like Trey's were that day he was attacked by that imaginary force in the woods.

Trey asks Will if he can be a helper for his mom, and Will nods, curbing his tears, desperate to help. Trey sends him on a hunt for pillows. Once Will's out of the room, Trey kneels beside Tara. "Who did this?"

She closes her eyes and shakes her head, so sad and drained she doesn't even look like herself. "It came straight for me. Whatever you did—" She stops with a hand against her mouth like she's afraid she'll cry. "If it takes from the kids what it took from me, it'll kill them."

"It won't come for the kids."

Will returns, his arms stuffed with pillows. We all work to prop Tara so she can sit while supported. She's so deflated she can barely keep her head up, but she manages to strengthen her voice. "Máthair's down there now working on a shield for them."

"For what? We need to find out who—"

"You, Fearghus. The black magic you called—"

"No—"

"Yes!" She sits forward.

I take her shoulders and shift her back against the pillows. If Trey's going to upset her, I'm going to have to kick him out of the room. And Will's staring at his mother and looking close to tears again, so I walk him to the doorway and send him downstairs to Sloane.

"It only came back for me," Trey says.

"And you know that, how?"

"I tied it to me. Only me. My DNA."

She moans into her hands, shaking her head over and over until I put a hand on her arm.

"Tara, you need to rest."

She points at Trey. "Your DNA? You share it with me. That black magic came for you, didn't get everything it wants, so it kept looking until it found the next closest match: me. Next it'll go for Máthair and my children. Then your daughter."

I know she's right by the way Trey's gone statue still and wild in the eyes. Caught, by something he never saw, never expected.

Tara's leaning off the couch toward him now, her red eyes wet with angry tears. "You never learn. The things you do, they don't just affect you. They affect all of us. Our mother. My children. Your daughter!"

A perfectly timed contraction hits as if this new danger she's in has taken hold of me to wring her out. To face it. A helpless newborn baby, targeted by a power that left Trey seizing on the ground and vomiting blood. Then came back and did the same to Tara. We'll never win against this.

"Go downstairs and help Máthair," Tara says, her voice trembling along with her shoulders and arms. "And send my kids up here. I don't want them around you."

I can't look at Trey and the hurt I'll surely see on his face. This oversight of his is unforgivable, another consequence of the steps he's taken away from us. Another mistake that could've been prevented if he'd only taken one brief moment to remember he's not alone anymore.

But he was alone. When he brought all this on, he was alone because I'd left him. We can only win against all this together, and if he forgot that, so did I. I won't forget it again.

I tell Tara to rest, to stop worrying, that we'll fix this. She only shakes her head, defeated in a way I've never seen. I get her a tissue for her tears and a clean shirt to replace the bloody one, then I go in the kitchen after Trey.

He's standing over the sink, gripping the countertop. For once I recognize the kitchen is his natural retreat—it's normally where the alcohol is kept. It's probably a haven to him even when there's nothing to drink, like a placebo.

"Let's go help Sloane."

He raises his head to look at me in the reflection of the window above the sink. "I'm incapable."

"You're the only one who truly knows what we're fighting."

He snorts and smiles, amused yet disgusted. "That's the truth."

"You need to try."

"I've been a fuckup my whole life, Liv. I don't know how to help. I only know how to kill, how to break, how to ruin. The things in my head…" he raises his hands to press at his temples hard, too hard "…it's all a mess. What I've seen, what I've done. It doesn't go away, it doesn't stop. It just goes on."

"I'm here to help you."

"No one can help me. It's a burden I won't share." He moves to the sliding door to look outside again.

It's what he does, what he's always done. The isolation, the push away from people to protect them. Maybe it's a mechanism learned as a child living in abuse, or maybe it's a symptom of post-traumatic stress after what he thought happened to Kate. And it's all tangled in the memories he carries of his old life. Some of those things have been remedied, yet he's still being haunted.

I moved here to Black River to start over, to close the door to my old life. He came here to dwell on the tragedies of his, to punish himself for things out of his control. I doubt a cross-country move would help him without the mindset to go along with it. Somehow I have to help him see the new road we're on, his past in the far off distance behind him, not hanging overhead.

"Those burdens formed you. They're a part of you that won't ever change. There's no reason to carry them in your heart too."

He stands there and breathes a few moments then goes outside. Closes the door. Closes me off. I watch him through the glass in another one of his forced isolations. An asshole, yes. But also very ill. It's a sickness that scares me more than the goriest of injuries. This can't be fixed with bandages and medicine. I can't clean him and suture him and wait for time to heal. All I can do is stand beside him while he struggles to find the tools to fix himself.

Then he's back in the room with me on a rush of sun-warmed air, catching me against him, holding me as tight as my belly will allow.

"I have no heart," he says, bowing over me, his face against my hair. "It's with you now. It's yours to refill."

CHAPTER 15

TREY

MÁTHAIR AND I work well into the night. I take a break to help Liv put the kids to bed and move Tara to her bedroom. Before heading back down, I take a short walk in the night air outside. Máthair refuses when I suggest she do the same. Her focus drives me. She's convinced of our success, and I ride on that, forcing down everything else.

This numbness—I've never felt it. For once there's nothing worthy of hitting. Nothing that could disperse the pressing mass of failure. Of what I did that's brought on this need for Máthair and me to be elbow-deep in herbs and books at one in the morning. My dysfunction feeds the

Moores' destruction of my family. It's so perfect, almost like they planned it.

When I hear Liv get up from the couch and creak across the floor above us, I wipe my hands and climb the stairs to check on her. She's coming back inside with a rifle when I reach the front door.

"It was nothing." Her eyes are puffy with sleep, her voice scratchy.

I take the rifle, draw the blanket over her on the couch. "We're almost done."

She yawns and settles in, readjusting the pillow between her knees. "Will it work?"

"Máthair says yes."

Her hand attached to my shirt, she drags me down for a kiss. I stay there a moment too long, just enough to remind me what a couch feels like after a day like I've had. If Máthair wasn't downstairs working by herself, it would win me over and that black magic would swoop in over-night and kill us all.

I trudge back downstairs. Máthair's bent over a book—another book—and I see the disaster we made of Tara's work table, the mess we still have to clean up.

"Don't look like that, Fearghus. We're still finished. I just found this one and wanted to make sure it wasn't a better option." She flips the book closed. "You'll be glad to know it's not. Let's just cap off these jars and clean the rest up tomorrow."

That I can do. I cover the fragile ingredients and dis-connect the Bunsen burner and make sure the gas is off. She pours our creation into a clean jar and screws on a lid. When I flip off the light, the darkness makes my eyelids close involuntarily, and I almost trip on the stairs. We wake Liv, Tara, and the kids for their sip of bitter liquid—exactly what most people love to be woken for in the middle of the night, especially two four-year-olds who only take it out of sleepy ignorance. Tomorrow they'll be wise to it, and it's going to be a long game of deliberation and bribery.

We finish the night in the kitchen, her taking a sip and offering the jar to me. I turn away and screw on the lid without dosing myself. I'll let the *dubhealaín* feed from me every day if it means it will never touch one of them. I'll let it kill me. If Máthair notices my refusal, she doesn't say a word. She's always been on my side, no matter how many times I mess up.

"Thank you," I tell her. I don't tell her enough. Maybe never have.

"It's a good effect. We did well." She takes the jar from me and stashes it in the cabinet.

The magic was simple once we figured it out. It's now a working agent in their bloodstreams, traveling through their bodies to mask their unique human signature with a protective enhancement. Anything looking for my brand of Bevan blood won't find it here in anyone but me.

"Now stow your worries and get some rest." Máthair lays a cool hand against my cheek before heading to her bedroom.

I go to Liv lying on the couch, her face so serene in sleep I can't will myself to wake her for a bumpy ride home. I look around the room at my options: one unoccupied cushion of the couch, armchair, floor. I lie down on the rug below Liv and fall hard into sleep.

I wake in one of the bedrooms, and I'm not sure how I got there. The room is full of sun, baking me in my sweat. The house is awake around me—voices, feet in the hall, running water. When I sit up my head swims. I lie back down. Food is what I need, but too much sleep in a hot room has left me groggy and more tired than I should be after sleeping past noon.

A little prodding finger wakes me a second time. I rub my eyes and take the cup of water from Winnie. The curly purple straw must've been her touch.

"Are you gonna sleep forever?"

I ruffle her hair and get up.

Tara gives me food in the kitchen, along with a death stare that tells me she did me a favor by not smothering me in my sleep. The red in her eyes has cleared up a little, and her frame is straighter, less frail.

"Where's Liv?"

"Went to the clinic for a check-up."

"Máthair?"

"The garden."

I try to help her clean up, but she latches onto my sleeve and hauls me to the front door.

"Nothing personal, but get the hell out of my house."

Liv took my car so I walk home through the woods. They're much too bright and alive for my mood, with the sunlight filtering through the pines to play on the ground and the birds calling across the forest. River matches my pace and licks my hand. I shoo her away but she does it again just to piss me off. She's glad I'm back to my old self, and that makes two of us.

When we reach the river Trib has joined us. They crash into the water to play-fight, raising their lips and growling and snapping at each other. I go to the water and splash my face, the shock of the coolness a welcome wake-up call. My knees have sunk in the mud. I extract myself, earning a nice smear of mud up my forearm that takes me straight into a scene from a memory so buried it feels like a new experience.

My mother in her dinner gown, dragging me into the woods when I was fifteen. The bare trees, the frozen ground. She taught me to thaw and warm the earth under our knees. Overzealous and aggressive, my first attempt failed, as it always did. I hear her voice: *Ease it back, Fearghus.* Gently correcting—always a welcome relief when corrections from others were far from gentle.

Magic is a balance, she'd said. *Draw too much and it will draw from you.*

It's a deep-seated truth I've always known, unaware how pointedly it came from her. And then it all comes rushing back, her words like the river's water running into my cupped hands.

Magic must not be wasted, must not be called upon carelessly. It's only for the most dire of situations, ones where normal human action won't suffice. Overuse and misuse will wear on you. You'll become its slave. You'll be used as a draw for other forces beyond your control. It's addictive. It can control you. Never use it as a substitute for good sense. Never use it to cheat in life. Every spell we know has a price, some higher than others. Seek out the ones where the benefit outweighs the risk.

Then she taught me to paint my arms with mud and inscribe them with the design of our family's warriors. She didn't tell me of our real family, but she didn't need to. I knew we were different from the Moores; I'd known all my short life. And on that day, she confirmed it. She gave me a new power against them, a new shield that lasted a long time.

These are the pieces of life I should keep in my heart. Liv's right—I actively carry the things I should bury and bury the things I need to live. All these things in my head that burden me, the memories of that house, the abuses against me, against Christian. Their lies about Kate and Aaron. The people I killed. Those things have buried the good. I could've used the good had it been on top. It might've saved me from the recent mistake that racked up a debt paid not only by me, but by everyone I work so hard to protect.

Instead of climbing the bank to the footbridge, I wade across the river. I emerge with water-filled boots and soaked jeans, but I don't feel the weight. More memories come. The layers are peeling without any work from me, and have been for some time now. That flashback of the first paid fight after I thought Kate was dead. The club with Christian and Kate. More I probably don't remember, unearthed as the shovel did its work in my subconscious. I relive them through new eyes, recognizing the difference between who I was then and who I am now. How my life has changed for the better. The memories power my legs, push me into a sprint toward home.

Liv's not home when I blast through the door, and I'm glad she doesn't have to see me so manic. Máthair quoted

Thoreau to me on that frozen day in the woods when I was fifteen. I thunder down the stairs and strip *Walden* off my shelf. It's been well used and has the browning decades-old tape holding it together to prove it. I should probably re-read the whole thing. But it opens straight to the end, a weak spot in the spine like it's broken there. And there's a dusty outline on the page in the shape of something I've recently seen. A baby sock, in Liv's hand.

I see the words: *The sun is but a morning star.*

Liv is my sun, my morning star. And finally I'm awake.

I set *Walden* back on the shelf and go outside on the back porch. The day breathes around me. Two coyotes wander out of the woods at the far end of the garden and point their noses my way. I give them a nod. The young male yips back at me; the other turns back toward the trees. I watch the pines quiver in the wind, their trunks spearing straight into the sky.

Let the *dubhealaín* come. I have more life in me now than it can handle.

Liv takes a nap when she gets home. I do some overdue work in the garden. Another pair of coyotes arrives to check on us—either I haven't noticed how often they've been coming around, or they've upped their surveillance. I'm too high on the day to be worried, but spotting a change in their behavior and not investigating it is a recipe for disaster.

I stand to call River, but I'm distracted by Liv crossing the yard and the thrill that lights me. It's intoxicating—all of it. The sun catching in her hair, her bright eyes. The fragrance of the lavender at my feet, the black soil clumped between my fingers. She's brought life back to me. The experience of it. The reality I've been missing for so long. I need to remember this, stop screwing it all up.

She halts halfway to me, her focus sliding away like she's lost her way. I drop my trowel into the earth and go to her.

"Walk with me?" She regains her composure, lays a hand on my arm.

"Where?"

"Doesn't matter. Anywhere. I just need to walk."

I go in the house for my SIG and my knife. When I get back outside, she's waiting for me at the edge of the woods with River and Trib beside her. I should tell her about this new insight, but I don't know what to say. It can't be summed up in a matter of sentences. It's a culmination of too much.

She points to her untied hiking boots—that's my job. I squat to tie them for her. Then she leads me into the trees, across the pine needle floor. I catch her hand because I want her to know—what? Something I can't wrestle from my head. But if I don't tell her now, I fear I'll lose my chance. I'll return to the same old shit, the same cycle of mistakes, the same failures, and she'll never hear it from me. When she notices I've got her hand she looks up at me, and it rolls off my tongue. "*Is tú mo chuisle.*"

She releases a breath, the curiosity on her face turning sad even with the smile. "I love you too."

But that's not it. Can't be it. It's not enough, when I keep doing what I do. I wish I could pledge to her I'll change, I'm not that guy anymore. I see the difference now, and I'm working hard to make myself worthy of her. But I can't trust I won't fall into it again.

"What, Trey?" She has a hand on my chest, looking worried, like she expects me to drop some dire news.

The breeze catches her hair. I trail my finger across her brow to brush her bangs out of her eyes. "I just want you to know."

"I do know."

"I'm trying."

"I know you are."

I'm not sure why I'm surprised she's still looking at me like she is. Probably because this blip in my head tells me I can't be trusted. And that's exactly what's in her eyes: trust. If I break it, that's all I'll get. There'll be no more chances.

She stands on tiptoes and wraps both arms around my neck. I bend to kiss her, to pour into her what I can't say in words. She droops, going heavier in my arms until she's pulled me down to her level. I gather her tighter, closer, the kiss lengthening from words to sentences. Paragraphs. A whole book of what I need her to know. If we were any closer, I'd be slipping into her mind, passing a whole lifetime of understanding on one brain wave.

She breaks the kiss and pulls away, her hands on my cheeks. "God, Trey."

I straighten up, removing her hands but keeping my hold of them. I'll break my own bones if I ever lay an aggressive hand on her again. That's a pledge I will make.

The soft crunch of footfall on pine needles has me turning around. More coyotes. And they're not just here to check on us—they want to tag along. They'll get rowdy if we don't start walking. I extend a hand before us to tell her to lead the way. She takes us to the river and along the bank. I go to the water and plunge my hands in, cleaning off the garden soil. River takes a loud, messy drink beside me. I send a splash her way that she ignores. But when I stand, her wet nose goes straight into the hand I just washed. I try to swat her, but she's too fast, running toward Liv and Trib, her head low, paws pounding earth.

When I return to Liv's trail, she's made it far ahead, past the curve in the river, Trib at her side. An entourage of coyotes move along with her like a river on her other side, flowing around the trunks of the pines and under low-hanging branches. She stops, bowing a little at the waist, her hand propped against a tree trunk. I increase my pace. When I reach her I see her eyes are closed, and she seems abnormally short of breath she's attempting to lengthen through some serious concentration.

I watch Trib dart away and keep going until he disappears in the distance. Probably going to check on Tara's house. "Should we go back?"

She shakes her head, a slight motion that's more reflex than conscious response. Her fingers knead against bark, like she's working hard at controlling something that's about to overtake—wait. "Liv."

The grip over her washes away like it was never there. She takes her hand off the tree and says, "I'm okay." Then she's hiking up the incline like that strange intermission didn't just happen.

I follow. If she's in labor, she'd be heading toward the clinic, not dragging me deeper into the woods. Another cold nose jabs into my hand. This time my swat makes contact with her tail before she can scoot away. She wheels on me, a game-on if I want it, but I'm too distracted by Liv to be a good opponent. I climb the hill after her. Reaching the top, I see she's turned direction. I let her get a bit further before I speak up.

"Do you realize where you're going?"

My unanswered words hang in the air. And sure enough, she keeps plowing forward to the place she refused to visit the last time Christian was here, when I wanted to retrieve my SIG from the battleground where I'd dropped it but she didn't want to see the ten corpses we'd left littering the earth. She didn't know those corpses had already been taken care of. And she doesn't know the more recent event that took place there, the altar I built, the black magic I summoned. Now it's me who doesn't want to go there. I've stopped walking to think, to try to come up with a way to stop her without having to explain why the place is covered with fragments of human bone. River sprints back to me, telling me to come, it will be okay. I need a dog who isn't so blindly optimistic.

My long pause has caused Liv to move out of view. I rush to catch up, spotting the top of the rock formation before I spot her. It's glistening wet from the spring higher on the hill, a mini waterfall in the dimming early evening light. Liv's stopped at the base where the water trickles off into a shallow pool that feeds a crevice in the ground, water returning to its home below the earth. And River was right. There's no sign of foul play. No bones, no evidence of my altar, no gray dust. Only the memories I have, the ones I'd rather forget.

Liv has flattened both her palms on the lower rock. She leans forward, her forehead against stone. In labor for sure, and only getting more comfortable out here.

"I hope you're kidding," I say.

She looks up at me, breathing hard. I turn away from her. We're out here at this site she refused to visit because she and I killed ten men here. We're a long walk from a car, a phone. The middle of nowhere. And she thinks she's going to give birth to our daughter.

"This isn't fair," I say. She can't expect me to help her. I don't know what the hell I'm doing. We should be heading back.

Her eyes are on me when I face her again, but she's focused inward, and too far away. I don't think she can understand me at all. I'm talking to myself. Well, she's just going to have to walk back. There's no other way.

I almost grab her arm before I correct it and take her hand instead, giving a slight tug that would incite most people to walk. She goes to her knees instead, resting her round belly on her thighs, and I get a full-body flush at the thought of what's about to happen. It's not some far off event anymore—our daughter is coming, and whether it's minutes or hours, I'm not ready.

One of the coyotes wanders close, head low, and Liv reaches mechanically toward her gray muzzle. It's a shock to see Liv so unafraid when normally she'd avoid a close encounter like this. The coyote sniffs her fingers before settling beside Liv and giving me a look that requires no work to interpret: *Calm the fuck down.*

The whole pack has closed in, forming a protective circle around us. A second pack patrols beyond. River shoves her nose into my palm again but this time it's not a game. She wants me to help Liv. So I squat beside her, take her face in my hands, make her focus on me. She puts her hands over mine, gives me a weak smile. I sit with her while she moves between the world I share with her and the one only mothers know. There's nothing to do except sit, but I can't just sit. I need to do something. I can't just sit here and watch this happen to her.

The coyote Liv befriended growls at me when I stand. River butts my leg with her head. This is stupid and starting to piss me off. Liv should be home, in bed. She should be at the clinic. I could try to carry her, but she'd have to be willing. She could walk part of the way, and I could—

The coyote barrier parts, and Trib bursts through, Tara behind him with a backpack slung over her shoulder and a bag in each hand.

"You knew about this," I say as Máthair steps through the trees behind her with an armful of blankets.

Tara doesn't look at me. "We had an idea." She sets her backpack on the rock next to Liv and hands her a water bottle.

From the looks of this, they're about to get as comfy out here as Liv. "Are you both crazy?"

"Give it a rest. You and I were born in the woods." She starts unloading the backpack and hands me an object I don't bother to look at.

"You left the kids alone?" This whole situation is a disaster waiting to happen.

"No, I left them with Shawn. Are you going to calm down, or am I going to have to send you away?"

"Did you forget what Shawn—"

"Fearghus." Máthair takes my arm, steers me away from Tara. "This is where your daughter chooses to be born, in the elements like we all do. Like you did. You should know this."

"Liv isn't one of us."

"She is. She's the mother of your child."

A coyote calls from deep in the woods, other voices passing the call inward until the whole group is riled up. Several of them peel away from the gathering, a thunder of paws moving away from us. A threat has been detected— what, they're not sure. Something encroaching, something not right. I unholster my SIG and follow. This I can do.

River dashes to my side to help me follow the coyotes' trail. We sweep the woods. I signal the birds to search from the sky. Several times I talk myself out of telling the coyotes to leave the final kill to me. That's the sick part of me I can no longer feed, the twisted pleasure I need to train myself to abstain from. Now, if I'm the one to find him first, that's another story.

Light drains from the woods with each new section we explore. My reliance on River's eyesight becomes too involved. We're in tree-thick territory now, any and all light from the night sky blocked by the pines. I don't know how many hours it's been but it's time for me to head back, at least to check on Liv. Finding nothing has raised my guard, not lowered it. Passing into a thinner grove of trees, I get a sense of Tara nearby. She calls to me, a dark shape in the distance that gains a wide bright smile when we draw near.

"Fearghus," she whispers like she's afraid to disturb the forest now that it's settled for night. "Perfect timing. Are you ready to see your little one?"

She turns and leads me down the hill. It's an endless decline, a ridiculous stumble in the dark as I try to gain control of legs that are intent on breaking my neck. I thought I wasn't ready for our daughter to be born but that's changed. It's spun so hard the opposite way that my brain is jarred from the impact against my skull. I traveled too far away in my patrol, we'll never make it back, and then I see the glimmer of water over rock far ahead and I'm running, tripping over logs, branches smacking my face. When I smell the burning oil from the torches they lit, I know we're close. I stop at the sight of Liv ahead of me, sitting on the ground, wrapped in blankets with a bundle in her arms.

Something climbs into my throat ready to choke me. Torch fire flickers around her, casting a warm glow on the spot where so much blood was spilled. Where I almost died. And where I sold myself to black magic not long ago. She's brought life to this place of death. Replaced the darkness with light. It's so apparent now, what she's doing, a little at a time: replacing all the death around me with life.

"Trey," Liv gasps, reaching a hand for me.

On numb legs I go to her, shocked by the magic of it all.

"Look—can you believe it? It's really her!" Her cheeks are wet with tears.

I fall to my knees next to her. She seems to think I should know, but she's the only one who's met her before. This is my first time.

Liv lowers the blanket. I see a tiny face, a tuft of dark hair. I swallow down the choke it brings. Liv's shrugging the blanket off her shoulders, raising the bundle of our daughter toward me. Then she's in my hands—so light, so fragile. A calypso orchid. A baby bird. I will make her stronger than me. Someday, she will be stronger than all of us put together.

"She's a little different, though," Liv says. "Now she's … right. She wasn't right without you."

She struggles to find comfort in my rough hands, so I hand her back to Liv. Snuggled against Liv's chest, she finds her place, one tiny hand reaching, fingers splayed. I capture that little hand, and she wraps her fingers around my thumb, her skin softer than an orchid petal. The tenderness of it hurts, opens up a new terror in me. She's here in the world now, my sick world.

Tara is kneeling behind Liv, braiding her hair away from her face and off her neck. "I need to go home and talk to Shawn." She glances up at me, measuring my reaction. "Explain some things. Apologize."

She can tell him whatever the hell she wants. I don't care about anything right now but these tiny fingers clasping my thumb, Liv's cheek against our baby's soft hair, her drowsy contentment. The grief she carried after this same baby's recent death—gone, like smoke dispersing in the air. This was the baby she thought was dead, and we brought her back. I know the relief of that. I lived for a long time thinking my own child was dead, and her face shows the end of that grief I imagined so many times.

"I could go to sleep right here," Liv says.

"No," I begin, but my words slip through my fingers. She can do whatever she wants for the rest of her life.

A prickling in my ears has me on my feet fast. I meet Máthair's eye from where she's packing up their bags. Several coyotes behind her turn their heads toward a sound on the other side of the mountain. A siren of angry magic, far away, but getting closer. I'm running toward it before I form the thought. It wants me, and that's what it's going to get. The baby's here and unprotected by the spell Máthair and I created. If I don't offer myself it will go for her. I vaguely hear Tara screaming at me, telling me they cast a protective spell over the area. All the more reason for me to get outside of that protection so it won't need to be tested.

River and Trib are barking at the sky. I yell at them to get back, go back to the women. The siren gains on us and I stop, making myself an easier target. The air is so charged I can barely think or breathe. The anticipation of the impact slows my heart, and I brace myself, but the sound dies, the electric charge dissipates, and I take a breath, listening, hearing nothing.

The dogs peer at me like I made it go away. River's one floppy ear twitches, picking up sound in the distance. We wait, but all we hear is the swish of the trees in the wind.

I go back to Tara's running mouth. I let her have her way—I'm not arguing with her tonight. I don't care what protection they're using. I'm not going to test it against my daughter's life. I drop down next to Liv. If I'm this exhausted, I can't imagine how she feels. Máthair picks up the remaining bags, stopping in the middle of the clearing with a sharp look in my direction.

"Fearghus?" Instead of waiting for me to answer, she turns on her heel to gaze into the trees I just came through. Where River and Trib still stand, looking backward in the same direction. "Do you have a visitor?"

I unholster my SIG and chamber a round. Máthair stops me, a hand on my arm.

"I'm not sure it's someone malicious."

But there's no one there. The prickle hits my ears again but this time, it travels down my spine and I take off again in a sprint, putting as much distance between them and me as I can. The dogs are on my heels; a small group of coyotes rush like wind through the trees beside me. They need to get back. When that pulse hits, I don't know how far its payload will reach. I stop to send them away and that's when I see a figure ahead standing on a swell of rocky ground, arms raised high. Shiny metal on her jacket, glint of belt buckle in the dark. Inis.

It's too late to call out. The black magic is roaring in my ears then hits hard around me, jarring the earth, its pulse traveling up my bones. It's a blast of white, all my senses knocked out, leaving me alone in my head—no grounding of earth, no stars above, no pines standing straight around me. I'm blind, my ears ring. I'm stuck in a blip of time. All the senses I take for granted now so apparent in their absence.

Everything rushes back. I'm down, my face against the ground. Awake enough to feel the pine needles against my forehead, the rock that cut my lip. I'm not KO if I can taste my own blood. This is when I get up, when I sink that last surprise hook and watch the crowd lose their shit.

I'm on my feet. I see her again, her arms only halfway up this time. The roar builds—it's circling, on its way back. It knows it found me but missed me at the last second. Inis loses her footing, goes down on one knee. I watch her struggle back up, raise her arms, the metal buckles on her leather jacket catching the moonlight as the black magic swoops down. A silver streak of light hits her outstretched hands. The crash so loud, it's the sound of being thrust underwater, the only noise the ringing in my ears. Inis wavers, crumples to the ground in a heavy thud against earth.

CHAPTER 16

LIV

THE FIRST SHUDDER in the ground brings me to my feet, the exhaustion of birth forgotten. I'm the only one who can go into the trees after Trey, the only one not targeted by whatever he unleashed. Tara takes hold of my arm. I jerk away before realizing she's not trying to stop me—she wants to take the baby. I hand her over and gather the blanket up and away from my legs. A second blast hits, harder than the first. Tara and I flinch. I expect the baby to cry, but she's sound and still, as content as can be. She's too new to the world to recognize the danger she'll someday face. "Knife?"

Sloane hands me one from her bag. I pass into the trees, my legs wobbly, my breath short. It reminds me I just gave birth, a truth that settles like a hard slap due to one important detail: I can't help Trey now. The immortality granted by the Bevans passed from him to our daughter, not to me. If she's no longer inside me, my blood won't save him unless she's left behind some residual effect.

I have to try. I head in the direction he ran, the blanket snagging on branches and underbrush. The struggle to see my way under the heavy canopy forces my progress to slow. I need my shoes, but it's too late to go back. I can't waste the time. I hear a shuffling of pine needles ahead but with so little light, I can't see what's moving toward me. A dark mass. Upright, but too wide to be human. River and Trib run from behind it and that's when I can make out Trey carrying a limp person. Someone he killed? But he's never brought them back before. Then I see the long hair spilling over his arm, the shiny buckles on the biker boots.

I push ahead, forgetting I can't see the sharp things I'm stepping on or the logs in my path. If he hurt Inis, I have first aid to perform and a man to murder. But when he draws near I get a good look at his face in the dim light. His lip is cut and bleeding, but there's no killer there. I've seen that instinct take him over before, and it's not here now. "Is she okay?"

"Not sure." He keeps moving, clearly powering through his own exhaustion made worse by her weight.

Herded by the line of coyotes behind us, I follow in his footsteps until we reach the clearing. He lays Inis on the ground. She rolls her head when I'm taking her pulse, so I put a steadying hand on her shoulder so she doesn't panic when she wakes up in a new place. "Inis, it's Liv—"

"*Seo dhuit.*" She raises a fist. I open my palm underneath it to accept a tiny decorative glass bottle, corked, and full of a thick black vapor that's tinged purple when exposed to the moonlight.

"What is—"

"Farrelly's mess. Don't open …" Her head falls to the side, her body once again limp. Unconscious. I slip the bottle into my pocket.

"We need to get her back to the house." I find my boots in the torchlight and pull one on, nearly falling over. Trey comes to help. While he's tying the laces, Sloane wraps the blanket around me like a shawl and tucks baby Sloane inside. She's a sweet weight against me, a little beating heart. Trey straightens just in time to witness her open her eyes. The grin that lights his face is one I rarely see. It's visible proof of that unreachable part of him buried under all the anger and hate and grief. Unreachable no longer. I place my hand on his cheek, memorizing that lift of lips, the way it shines in his eyes.

He kisses my hand before heaving Inis over his back, and we all walk back, weary and silent, only awake enough to put one foot in front of the other and not walk into a tree trunk. My endorphins are so depleted my only fuel is the need to be home. Trey sends the dogs and half the coyotes to escort Tara and Sloane to their house. He starts to put Inis on our couch, but I nudge him toward the bed where he drops her, his strength seeming to fail at the last moment. She hits the mattress ungracefully but doesn't wake up. Her breathing and pulse are normal. With sleep, she'll improve. I hope.

We leave her and fall onto the couch, his arm around me, me leaning against him with the baby still swaddled in the blanket-shawl. I'm not sure how much later I awake to him straightening me out across the cushions. I turn on my side, baby nestled between me and the back of the couch. He lies down on the floor, and I'm drifting back asleep before I can demand he join us where it's comfortable despite there being no room.

I'm up and down all night feeding baby Sloane. It's a cycle I remember easily: she fusses, I wake and latch her on, then we both drift asleep as her belly fills. One time I wake to the trickle of rain in the gutters, the stimulation just enough to get me upright. I toe Trey in the ribs, and he sits up fast, on guard. I tilt my head toward the couch. He won't take it until I settle in the armchair and tell him I can't sleep. It's not a lie to try to get him more comfortable; it's true. The night has turned everything surreal. My dead baby has been given a new life and returned to my arms. I ran from an empty life, hoping to find peace and solitude but found chaos and companionship instead. The kind of man I'd never expect to fall for but love with an intensity that might cross into mental illness. A place in his family designed just for me. Now here's Inis, a surprise member of the biological family I thought I'd never find, a mystery solved, a new door that could open into more chaos I don't need.

I have enough to handle right now. Like how much longer I'll last before the compulsion to see Dillon has me behind the wheel and driving straight for him again. When I first settled in Black River it wasn't just sleeping pills I was addicted to, it was also him. It's still him.

Blinking awake, I see Trey crossing the room. He opens the front door. Daylight spills in, along with the rumble of a departing motorcycle engine that must've woken us both. Baby Sloane remains undisturbed, one hand free from the blanket, fingers spread against her cheek like she was searching for something but fell asleep before she could find it.

Trey closes the door. "Did she say anything?"

So it was Inis leaving. "I didn't see her leave."

His gaze lowers and whatever he was going to say lifts away. The dreamlike quality of our night has no doubt become very real for him, as it has for me. I get up to hand her over. There's a slight delay before he steps back. It's such an innocent, subconscious reflex I can't control my laugh. My fearless Trey. Violent brute. Serial murderer. The first hint of fear I've ever seen on him, due to holding his own child.

I push her closer so he has no option but to take her. It's an awkward exchange but once her weight has settled on his arm, I slide away and take a much needed bathroom break, leaving him alone with her so I'm not hovering over them. With her birth I've experienced a release of pressure. Trey's mamó told me I'd have her back, and his mother concurred. It's only natural I'd doubt the truth of it even though I've witnessed the magic they perform. But now she's here, again, and I've been released from the grief, the fear, the doubt, and all that pressure it added up to. For Trey, though, I can see it's backward. She wasn't his before. She only became his now. And the pressure is on from another direction: to keep her safe from the Moores, and now from the black magic he summoned that's contained in the glass bottle in my pocket.

In the bathroom, I lift that bottle out and hold it up to the light. The vapor undulates in the bottle like a living thing, black with a purple sheen. Its movement is almost sentient, testing the glass that contains it almost like a creature would in a cage. I'm overcome by sympathy for the thing, whatever it is. I don't like seeing anything in captivity, even a poisonous black magic on a quest to suck the life from the people I love. For a brief moment I consider keeping it a secret from Trey—but I can't keep secrets from him. I tried to a long time ago, and I won't do it again.

I freshen up and change. When I return to Trey, he's taken over my armchair and figured out how to properly cradle a baby. And she's awake, her eyes locked on his, trying to coo each time he taps her fingertips against his stubbly cheek. Still too new to even coo, all she can manage is a short breath out, but it's too sweet for words. I sneak through to the kitchen, glad to be up and working off the post-birth soreness. I'll go back to resting once I get some blood to my muscles.

I have breakfast half made when he comes in the room with a now very fussy baby. We switch spots and I latch her on, eyeing the hard wooden kitchen chair and deciding the armchair to be the better option. Once she's satisfied, I drag the little bassinet from the bedroom into the living room, swaddle her, and lay her inside. I bring a cushion with me to the kitchen.

"She erased her number," he says, turning the inside of his forearm toward me. Inis' phone number brand is gone. He seems more disappointed than he should be.

"I'd think you'd be glad to see it gone."

"Not when I know why she erased it." He glances at me, seeing I don't follow. "Because I can't get rid of her now after what she did for us."

I go in the other room to retrieve the bottle. When I set it on the kitchen table, he steps closer for a better look. "Aw shit."

"It had to go somewhere. Better it's in our possession and not hers."

He stares at it, nodding. He knows I'm right. He also knows the existence of such a thing puts his newborn daughter in even worse danger. As well as his sister, his mother, his niece, nephew, and every Bevan he's met. Even those he hasn't.

"We need to thank her," I say. "I just don't know how. She saved your life."

"We're indebted to her now." He drops another string of curses under his breath. "She already wanted a piece of the baby. Now she'll think she's entitled."

She already was entitled. If it's true, she and I are related, then my child is as much a part of her family as she is a part of Trey's, and it's not fair of him to think otherwise. All my life I've wanted a family, and now that I've found them, I'm not going to cast them away before I get to know them. There could be others who diverted from the magic, like my mother did. Maybe I want a relationship with them; maybe I want my daughter to know them. I'm so tired of explaining what's fair to him. He's going to have to figure it out on his own.

He returns from a trip downstairs and puts the glass bottle inside a mason jar and tightly secures the lid. Then he steps back and stares at the thing like he's just made a new enemy, one he can't kill. And I wonder if this is just step one of Inis' plan, if she'll be back later to snuff out what's in there, or turn it into something else.

After breakfast he retreats to the basement. I retire to the armchair to snuggle a baby, to admire her soft hair, her strong spindly fingers, her curled toes. She admires me back, her fingers against my face almost as if she's missing her dad. I wonder if she remembers me, or anything of her first brief life. I remember it all, details that used to drag me into a dark hole. Now I'm free to think them. I've been unbound.

Trey passes through carrying dried herbs in from the eaves outside. He brings a box and a pillow for a makeshift ottoman, helps me put my legs up. Tara and Sloane bring the kids. Everyone takes turns holding the baby. Tara disappears downstairs, and I expect to hear raised voices but all is calm. They make food and we eat, luring Trey upstairs for the meal; he's back downstairs as soon as the dishes are cleared. I consider asking Tara what he's up to, but I decide against it. I already know, and I don't want such a special day spent with my newborn and her family once again soiled by thoughts of the danger we're all in. I don't know how he's going to neutralize the black magic in that glass bottle but if I don't let him get every attempt out of his system, he's going to obsess about it until he does.

Night descends and everyone leaves. Baby Sloane is sleeping again, her tiny snores the only sound in the room. I decide to call Inis to see if she's okay, but when I scroll through my phone, it's Dillon's name I end up on.

I could transfer the baby to the bassinet. Slip outside to the porch. Just for five minutes, just to make sure he got his car back. He made it home. He's okay.

The phone rings in my hand; I scramble to silence it before it wakes Sloane. But she's as peaceful as ever, unaffected by the startling sound so close to her face. I see the name on the display: Christian.

"Hi," I whisper.

"No one's gonna call me with the news? What's that bullshit?"

"If no one called then how do you know?" I watch Sloane's face to make sure my voice won't wake her. She won't sleep this soundly forever. I need to enjoy this while I can.

"Tell that man of yours he's a—"

"Selfish asshole? It's lost on him. Sorry, Christian. I was going to call you. You just beat me to it."

"I'm coming out there later this week. Just booked a flight. I need to see this infamous baby destined to destroy my whole bloodline. And what's all this about a black witch?"

"We'll fill you in when you get here. Maybe you can meet her."

"Is she good lookin'?" He does a very solid Virginia accent. He switches back to normal and speaks to someone in the room with him, the distortion making it clear he's covered up his phone. "Okay. I've gotta go. Send me a picture of my baby niece for fuck's sake." He hangs up.

I manage to transfer Sloane to the bassinet without disturbing her. While I'm in the kitchen throwing together a quick meal, Tara's cat appears at the back door looking like she wants in. Living with Trey has taught me to trust what animals appear to be telling me, so I open the door. She streaks through the kitchen and thumps down the stairs.

Trey comes up not much later.

"I hope it's okay I let her in."

He washes his hands. "It is now. I treated her fleas."

"Tara told me she's not her cat."

He nudges me away from the stove. I watch him cook, noting the rigid slant of his shoulders, his tight jaw. He's worried again, about Inis, about the Moores, about what they'll do. It's never going to end and stressing won't help a thing. I don't know how to explain this to him, how to shovel off the anger and anxiety and help him be happy while we can.

"What are you working on down there?"

"Something that's going to help us."

Two more days of Trey holed up in the basement finally has me worried enough to go downstairs. After settling Sloane in her bassinet, I descend the steps. Trey's workbench is cluttered with so much stuff there's barely an inch of table visible. Beakers, flasks, jars of herbs both opened and unopened. Books, stirring rods, and scribbled notes. A metal frame has been built over the Bunsen burner which is lit, the flame tight and blue. He's copying something out of a book when I approach, the cat sitting on the table at his arm.

"You're starting to freak me out again."

His concentration takes a moment to break. "I just got the final piece … just need to combine …" He sifts through the pages of scribbled notes.

"Can I help?"

He finds it, flattens the page in front of him. "Don't need to. I'm done." He looks up at me then, his face softening as if realizing for the first time how reclusive he's been. His eyes linger on mine, and I get a glimpse of that light I saw in the woods the day Sloane was born. "Will you call Tara, ask if she'll babysit?"

"Why?"

"I need you alone for about an hour."

"For …?"

"To walk with me to the bluffs."

When I arrive at Tara's, she and Sloane hover in the doorway, not letting me in. They watch me like they both took an oath not to question me no matter how suspicious they are.

"I don't know what he's going to do," I answer their silent faces. "He said an hour. We're walking to the bluffs." I give Tara two bags of my frozen milk and hand Sloane the baby. "It's going to be confusing now, with you and her having the same name."

Sloane kisses baby Sloane on the forehead. "Call me Máthair. This little one is more deserving of her name than me."

They're still standing there when I back my Civic away from the house. Halfway to the road I get a call from Inis. I stop on the gravel decline, the pine branches making a tunnel around me. She launches right in, like a day hasn't passed since our last conversation. "I found a great place for you in Phoenix, next door to our cousin who has two little girls."

"Inis, I can't move away from Trey."

"He's not going to let you raise her as an O'Dowd. I thought we already sussed that out."

"We did, but—"

"The only way she'll get the teachings from both sides is away from him. Don't worry about her earth magic side. I can find an earth witch willing to help."

I know a guy born into earth magic who'd love to help. I'm not sure how he feels about black magic, but I'm sure the jerk would be willing to overlook anything for the chance of getting me back. "I'd like to know more about my parents before I decide anything, and even then, I won't leave Trey."

"I'm working on that." She exhales into the phone. "Really, though. I don't know what you see in him."

"I love him."

"Sounds like a problem. Is there a treatment for that?"

I drive home slowly, dragging out the miles to give myself time to think. I don't know anything about the O'Dowds. Yes, I believe I'm one of them. But having just learned this, with no idea who they are, what they stand for, it's an impossible decision to make. How much do I want them in my life? In my daughter's life? They could be as bad as the Moores. They could be worse. They practice black magic for god's sake. Not the gentle magic practiced by the Bevans and even the Moores.

Trey's extracting a thorn from a coyote's paw when I park at home. The poor thing won't hold still—it's a big thorn and looks painful. My presence is only making him jumpier, so I go inside and gear up—hiking boots, ponytail, Ruger. Trey's cat is stretched across the kitchen floor, furry belly facing upward and paws curled.

"Does your cat have a name?" I ask when I join him outside. He's watching the coyote disappear into the trees.

He pockets the tweezers and stoops to tie his loose boot laces. "Not yet. Go ahead, pick something."

"Does she have to be named after a body of water?"

He looks up from his boots, the reference hitting home for him just as it does for me. That night we named Trib, Trey took me to the bluffs and joined his mind to mine. He taught me how to fight, how to shoot. How to trust, after my trust had been so broken by Dillon. How to love someone based only on what I knew of his soul because everything else was such a mystery. He showed me the peace he felt while in his element, how happy he could be. He taught me how to be happy again.

I'm wiping my eyes when he stands. Post-partum hormones—that's what it is. Making me cry over a memory that had no emotional impact until now. I remember laughing that night with him. Wanting to kiss him. I don't remember this bittersweet pain in my gut. It wasn't there.

He tugs my ponytail down, forcing me to look up at him. His face is a replay of everything we've been through—things that have rewritten those simple memories with the intensity of emotion I now feel looking into his eyes. It's a swirling mixture of triumphs and mistakes, both mine and his. And I wonder if that range of experiences has built a more resilient, hard-proven love, or a fractured one.

Still holding onto my ponytail, he kisses me, no contact but his lips. My arms are folded behind my back and I stay that way, savoring the single point of touch. It's perfect, how he kisses me sometimes. Like he reads my thoughts in my eyes and gives me just what I need.

He straightens up, smearing the tears from under my eyes. "The body of water thing only applies to the canine."

"Who made that rule?"

He thumbs his chest. "Me. I make all the rules."

I laugh. He grins stupidly.

By the time we reach the bluffs, we haven't settled on a name for his cat. His choice is Alley because that's where he found her. When I explain it could be a bit crude, depending on the state of the namesake alley, he comes up with something new: Dumpster. And then he holds that damn stoic face of his for so long I'm convinced he's actually serious. The laugh he finally releases echoes off the bluffs, and I punch him so hard I regret it for the sore arm I'll have tomorrow.

We make it to the top in good time despite my easy post-birth pace. Cool air rushes up from the river below, sifting the warm air around us. He takes something out of his pocket and hands it to me.

"Ali, spelled A-L-I. That's a nice name, if you don't tell people she's named after an alley." I look at what he's given me: a small square package, brown paper tied with a string. The emotional upheaval that had me crying earlier hits me like a floodwater. We've gone back in time. All the things we've been through, and here we are again, on this bluff, with a mind-altering chewable magic tablet he created in his basement lab. It doesn't matter if our love is resilient or fractured. It's as constant as the river far below us, as solid and real as the cliff we stand on.

"This is different," he says, "from anything I've ever made."

"Is there one for you?"

"No, just you. It's the most powerful cleansing we know. Made more powerful by the element I've tied it to once its magic is released."

"What element?"

"Water." He looks down at the river. "It will purge all past magic from you. Strip it all. What Dillon's done, what Kate did." He looks back at me. "What my ancestors did. What they put in the stars."

The tablet slips through my fingers. He catches it before it hits the ground. He starts to hand it back, but I don't want it. I can't take that. What his ancestors put in the stars is what brought the two of us together. If he's suggesting we remove that—

He takes my hand, uncurls my fingers to open my palm. "You'll have to learn to love me again."

"You said our Alignment wasn't a love spell."

"It's not."

I point to the tablet. "That's going to cause me to hate you again."

"Not hate. Dislike, maybe. The magic of my ancestors is powerful, not just a simple spell that can be stripped away. It can't be neutralized by anything I can do. It will be weakened, how much I'm not sure. My hope is you'll be neutral toward me."

"I might be sick to my stomach around you again."

"I'll take the risk."

"*You'll* take the risk? I think you have that backwards."

"Liv, it's the only foolproof way to kill Dillon's magic."

I'm shaking my head because I'd rather be a slave to Dillon's magic for the rest of my life than chance losing anything I feel for Trey. "There has to be another way."

He takes my shoulders. An embrace, not an act of control. "There isn't. Trust me."

Trust him. To erase whatever brought us together and know that I'll learn to love him again without it. It's a big risk to take. He's not an easy guy to love.

But he is an easy guy to trust. He always has been, from that unfortunate first meeting between us.

"You won't forget what you know about me, or anything we've been through," he says.

"That's part of the problem."

He sets his jaw. Maybe it was a low blow, but he needs to understand where I'm coming from. There are too many things I forgive because of how I love him. Too many things I choose to accept. Without the deeply ingrained love that struck me from the stars that night, I'm not sure how easy those things will be to live with.

"It might change nothing," he says. "Or everything. But it doesn't matter. I'll make you love me again." He takes my hand and presses the wrapped tablet into my palm, not once breaking eye contact. In those eyes I see the force of his will, his internal promise to himself, his promise to me.

"You promise?"

"I promise."

My fingers close around the tablet. I trust his promises like I trust in the rising sun to warm the day. I have to hold onto that. I trusted him before our Alignment, when he was a real ass, when I hated him—I'll surely trust him after I'm cleansed. If it's the only emotion I have for him it's a big step toward love, and a solid platform on which love can be built.

I wiggle the string off the wrapping. "Do we sit?"

"No, we jump." He walks to the edge of the bluff and looks down.

I join him and get a good look at the water, reflecting blue sky and dazzling in the afternoon sun. Crests of small waves shimmer. The darkest blue surrounds the bluff wall, extending out toward the faster current nearer the shore where branches bob on their trek downstream. If the fall doesn't kill me, the terror of it will.

"Water's deep enough right now we won't hit the bottom." He squats to untie his boots.

Well, that's reassuring—not hitting a rocky riverbed after a forty-foot fall. "How deep?"

He pulls off a boot and sets it aside. "Deep enough."

"I think I already hate you."

"Has to be done. It's part of the magic." He strips off both socks, sticks his SIG in his boot, and goes for my boot laces.

I raise my legs automatically so he can pull them off. I can't be going along with this. It's one of many deathtraps I've walked into with him. We survived all the others, but one of us was carrying the Bevan immortality for every one of those times. Until now.

I unholster my Ruger and stick it in my boot. He takes the tablet from my hand, unwraps it, and holds it in front of my lips. "Trust me."

I open my mouth. He places the silky cube on my tongue and starts to speak the spell words in Irish, too fast for me to follow along. The tablet generates its own warmth, a hot spot on my tongue, melting into liquid that tastes of citrus and a grassy flavor I recognize more by smell. I swallow, the heat of it crawling down my esophagus and into my belly like sunlight filling a cave.

A final swallow gives me a jolt. Pieces of me are peeling away, and I can sense it like a realization of something lost—a reach for your phone but it's not there and you remember you left it on the train. A notice someone else received the promotion, not you. That jab of feeling things lost, possibilities missed, cascading over me one by one and it's not right, can't be right. He's done something wrong.

"Trey—"

He takes my hand, turns me toward the open air. "It's okay. Count of three." He counts.

And then we're in freefall, the air rushing past me too fast to think.

TREY

THE IMPACT OF the water severs our joined hands. My feet touch the slimy bottom, and I push off, the cold almost unbearable in the way that makes me feel alive. The surface appears to be a mile away, and then I'm breaking through it, gasping for something warm to fill my lungs.

No Liv.

I tread water, breathing myself out of a panic. She's lighter than me, probably didn't sink low enough to push off. I turn, check the shore, check behind me. I'm about to dive down when she crashes through about fifteen feet away. I swim toward her, stop before her, face to face.

Drops of water run down her nose, fall off her eyelashes like tears. Her bangs are plastered to her forehead. She gazes at me, catching her breath. Water surges around us, the current tugging at my clothes. I'm a live wire in water, prepared to electrocute all life around me. The discharge of magic seems to have brought on more ready power, but I have no outlet. No immediate need for it. Yesterday, her guarded scrutiny would've been a red flag I've screwed up in some way. Today, it's proof I've finally done something right.

She kicks away, toward the shore. I follow her, rising in the shallows to walk with her to dry ground. She wrings out her hair. Sits on a large rock on the pebble beach. I approach. Still those guarded eyes.

Her teeth chatter. She trembles all over. If this did work, my arm around her might not be a welcome move. So I sit beside her on the lower part of the rock. It's already warm from the sun, but I discharge some of that unspent magic and make it warm enough to radiate. A group of coyotes arrive with our boots. I give them all a good ear scratch for the favor. I'm far too aware of Liv's eyes on me. I wish I knew what the hell to say.

She goes to work putting on her socks and boots. "I don't like it. At all."

"I'll make it right." I'm dying to know the degree of her newfound dislike of me, to know how far I have to work back. I can't muster the words to ask.

"You might be disappointed, but I don't hate Dillon." She says it nonchalantly while cinching her boots tight. She doesn't seem to give a shit if it proves I wasted my time.

The familiar build of pressure has blood drumming in my temples. I created nine tablets before the one I gave to her—it was sound. But apparently impotent against the work of Dillon Moore. Putting my fist through the nearest tree trunk isn't going to score any points for winning her back. It's even harder to restrain now that I realize I've removed her love for me and failed to remove him. All she has is him. Nothing of me to counteract it. I've made this shit worse.

"I feel sorry for him," she continues. "I see everything so clearly now. What he had to do for them, how he had to drop his life to marry me. And then what happened … well, it's all a bit … sick."

She stands, faces me. I'm aware there's an angry look plastered on my face, but I'm not sure how severe it is. I should respond to what she said, but I don't remember it anymore—I'm back in my basement with my texts, flipping through them by memory to search for another spell that might have some chance against what he did to her. I go exactly where I can't go: *Dubhealaín.*

Black magic against earth magic. Destruction is black magic's specialty. If my native magic can't annihilate Dillon's, then black magic can. It may have no effect on Liv, but it will affect the magic Dillon planted inside her.

"… or are you not hearing me at all?"

"What?"

"You can wipe the murder off your face. It worked, Trey. The sympathy I have for him is no different from what I'd have for any random jerk who takes advantage of me. I don't love him, can't believe I ever did. The whole thing feels like a dream. It's embarrassing, actually, to be fooled like that for so long."

I guess I'm another random jerk to her now too, minus her sympathy. I'll take it. I pull on socks and boots while she watches the water, absorbed in whatever's been rearranged in her head. I'm on my best behavior now. I have to remember that. No drinking. No aggression. No black magic no matter what the need. I'm a perfect gentleman. If Christian can do it, so can I.

And I have a time limit to win her back because this act won't last long.

When Christian texts to tell me he's landed and about to pick up his rental it's a relief I shouldn't admit. A couple days of good behavior and I'm already about to lose it. I need to witness him in action. I need to copy his ways. It's messed up, but true.

Then he's on my porch with his kid beside him—his half-Moore, half-Kate kid who shot Liv with an arrow nine months ago and only failed in killing her because I was there to undo that fatal wound. I shove my fist in my pocket so it won't be in his face for bringing that kid to my house with no fucking warning.

"You've met Aaron," Christian says.

Their smiles are identical. And sick. And both need to be punched. I don't care if one of them belongs to a fifteen-year-old.

"Christian?" Liv says behind me.

I remember the manners I'm supposed to have. The woman I'm supposed to be wooing. Christian holds up a six-pack of Brunehaut Amber. I take one, go in the kitchen, and pry it open. Three gulps later I remember I'm not supposed to be drinking. Well, guess what: I earned this. I've been sober how long? Long enough to earn one damn beer.

Christian's got the baby when I return to the living room. Aaron shrugs off his backpack and it hits the floor with a thud. It's decorated with a shitload of dangling crap that could account for the weight, but I'm also wondering what's inside. It needs to be searched.

Liv pries the baby away from an unwilling Christian, and I see where she's going next.

"Do you want to hold her?" she asks Aaron. She remembers he tried to kill her. She forgives way too easily.

"I'll snap your neck if you so much as look at her funny."

The kid faces me. "You should just snap my neck now and get it over with. I look at a lot of things funny." Another one of Christian's smart-ass grins. "Sorry about my arrow."

"You're lucky I didn't kill you that day."

"You didn't kill anyone that day. We were all so bummed. I think you've made up for it though."

Christian gives him a look I know well—I got it from my father many times. The shut-up-if-you-value-your-life look. Funny that Christian spawned another mouth as bad as his, and now he's on the receiving end.

"You should've been sterilized at birth," I say to him.

"Me? He gets all that lip from your ex-wife."

I look at the kid again but fail to see any Kate in him. He's a grubbier version of Christian. Ripped jeans and

T-shirt instead of Christian's typical preppy look, hair shaggy around the ears. Big black headphones hanging around his neck. He actually looks like a normal kid if I squint away the Christian in him and forget he's a spoiled rich kid with an overactive mouth and enough Moore magic to be a danger to my household. He's crossed his arms and backed away from Liv and the baby. At least he knows what's good for him.

Leaving him alone with Liv isn't an idea I like, but I need to talk to Christian now before I lose the impulse. I tap his shoulder and jerk my head toward the front door. He follows, leaving it open behind us. I close it.

He's eyeing me hard. "Oh shit. What now?"

"I'm sorry I killed your father."

He exhales, turning to face the driveway instead of look at me. Avoidance. Proof it's a sore spot. He doesn't want to discuss this. He wants to knock out my teeth.

"I wasn't thinking," I add. Not an excuse. An explanation.

"That's not new for you."

"I know. I'm sorry."

He looks at his feet. Rubs his face. "I can't be mad. He treated me like crap. Had it coming, like you said." He faces me, watches me a long time without speaking, and I sure as hell don't know what to say. "He killed my mother. I should be thanking you."

"Don't thank me."

"I won't. Because it was a dick move. Really, dude. A new low for you."

There have been newer lows. A series of them I'd rather not explain now. "So are we good?"

He laughs, punching me in the arm. "I wouldn't be here if we weren't. And I know it wasn't your intent, but the chaos it caused at home probably saved your baby. The power's been disrupted. Too much reorganization going on to come after you. So that's a good thing."

A motorcycle engine rumbles on the road, slowing as it nears where my driveway begins. We can't see it through the trees but I don't need to—the distinctive sound of that Honda engine has become familiar. And Christian's perked up like a coyote catching a scent of trouble on the wind. "What the fu—"

I start walking down the driveway to meet her before she reaches the house. She'd be too interested in why two Moores are welcome in my house, and I'm not willing to disclose anything else to an enemy who already knows too much. She salutes me, riding on past without stopping. She won't hear my cursing, but it's better that way. *Liv's cousin*, I remind myself. *Liv's only known family*. I have to respect her. For Liv. Inis is only an enemy on paper. I need to start seeing the gray areas in situations like these. Stop being so damn black and white.

She's already dismounted when I return to the yard, and Christian has a smile on his face that's more about my failed act of keeping her from the house than having a new woman to chat up. She hands him her helmet, starts removing her gloves.

"You must be Trey's black witch," he says, updating that smile specifically for her.

"Interesting perspective," she says, stone-faced and unaffected. "Especially considering who owes whom a very big favor."

He glances at me, smile widening even more. "Trading favors? Do tell."

She smacks her gloves against his chest. He takes them by reflex, too focused on me to see she's already got him whipped. She opens a saddlebag and removes a small pouch—mint, if my intuition is right. I need to figure out how her people use it, what she's gaining over me when she chews it.

"Black witch in black leather," Christian says, still holding onto her helmet and gloves. "You're a bit of a walking cliché."

"Says the Cadillac-driving rich guy in his Dolce & Gabbana polo."

"That's a rental."

"What's your daily driver?"

"Depends on the day, sweetie."

"Do you like to annoy people?"

"Only black witches." He gives her his woman-melting smile.

She holds his gaze, her stony expression still in place, and *I'm* annoyed to see she and I have something in common: the ongoing need to punch Christian Moore in the mouth. Then she's heading in the house with me on her heels like a stray puppy. Inis goes to the kitchen and helps herself to a glass of water. Liv comes in with the baby, frowning at me before greeting Inis. Liv's cousin. Saved our daughter. Not our enemy. I try to fix my face.

Inis produces a folded piece of paper from her back pocket and hands it to Liv. "Your mother."

Liv hands me the baby. She sits at the table, slowly unfolds the paper. Inis opens the fridge and takes out the pot of potato soup I made yesterday. Opens the lid. Sniffs it. I shift Sloane to one arm and take the pot, put it on the stove, and get a bowl out of the cabinet because that's what a nice guy would do. Inis removes her jacket and sits across from Liv.

Liv looks up from the paper. "So, murdered. I was two years old. Anything on my father?"

"Nothing I could find in writing. But if you're willing to trust what our family says, he was murdered at the same time. Someone did them both in."

"Where was I?"

"No clue. I don't think our people knew about you. Your mother was the daughter of a deserter who ran away, broke all ties with us. Maybe you were there at the killing, maybe you were with a nanny. Doesn't matter. You ended up at the children's home with no known family to speak of."

"But they knew my name."

"Someone did."

Liv turns in her seat to look at me, her eyes sliding past me toward Christian who's materialized in the doorway.

"Soup? I'll have soup." He takes Sloane from me, kissing her forehead.

"Who would want to kill my parents?" Liv says to the room.

Inis hooks a boot on an empty chair, pulling it out to rest her feet. "Easy. The same family who tried to snuff Farrelly out before he was born."

"Which Farrelly?" Christian asks. "Be more specific. There's a million of those fuckers."

Inis points at me.

What's dawning on Christian's face is the same thing dawning in me. He backs into the wall. "But he's not … he's a Bevan now. The Farrellys are … shit, dude, they killed your father and Liv's parents too? That's—" He looks down at Sloane reaching toward his mouth with her slow little fingers.

I'll ask him later what his problem is with Farrellys. And what he was going to say before he censored himself. Because right now I've got Liv looking at me with unguarded eyes for the first time since we jumped off the bluff, and it's unsettling to see the suspicion that lurks there. Before I say something stupid, I need to think. She's pissed. She thinks I withheld this from her. All I have is the truth, and my word might not be enough.

I force myself to look into those accusing eyes. "I didn't know."

"How could you not know?"

How could I not know? For the same reason I didn't know anything about my real family for forty-five years. Why I thought that punk kid in the other room was mine, and that he was dead, along with his mother for fifteen of those years. Why I didn't know the man who raised me wasn't my real father, that my real father was in a grave not far from my real birthplace. That my mother was a prisoner in the home I grew up in. Liv knows how many lies I was raised on, how much truth was dropped on me in the last nine months. And she's going to assume I knew this about her parents, and kept it from her?

A cold flush rushes down my spine when I hear Christian bark my name and realize I've moved forward, a fist on the table beside her. This is what I'm not supposed to do. This is the person I must stop being if I want her to stay with me. I'm about to back away when I recognize her disappointment at almost being attacked, again. Her hurt.

I squat before her instead, slide a hand onto her knee. "I didn't know. You know how much they kept from me."

She lays a hand on my cheek. Her breath catches like she's just remembered something she forgot. Her eyes roam my face, and I know I'm supposed to say something else but there's nothing there, nothing I have ready. Then she covers my hand with her own. "I trust you."

Sloane fusses. Christian hands her to Liv, forcing a break to the first act of intimacy between us. I dish up some soup for Inis and Christian. He calls Aaron so I get out a third bowl.

Liv finishes feeding Sloane but declines my offer of soup. "I need to get going to her newborn check-up. Inis, can we talk when I get back?"

Inis waves. "I'll be here."

I grab my keys but she stops me.

"It's very routine. There's no reason we both have to go. Stay here and catch up with Christian."

This is where I should back down, let her go on her own. Not demand to drive her. Not be overbearing. I help her get Sloane's baby seat in the car and watch her drive away, everything grating against me even though I know giving her space is the right thing to do. I go inside and open another bottle of the beer Christian brought. The wrong thing to do, but I drink it anyway. I catch Inis' eyes on me when I finish it, give her the finger. All it does is make her smirk more.

"What's with you two?" Christian asks.

"He's not supposed to be drinking," Inis says.

"The hell he's not." He looks at me. "For real?"

I thumb toward the AA flyer that's still tacked to the fridge. He covers his mouth like someone just died.

"I'm only having one."

Inis takes a pinch of her mint. "You mean two."

I have no idea how she could know that.

"I smelled it on you when I got here. And Liv can too, if you're trying to be sneaky. We're not stupid."

"Why are you in my house?"

"To visit my cousin."

"Who's her cousin?" Christian asks.

I go outside. Let Inis fill him in. I'm sick of thinking about it.

I've weeded a good portion of the garden when I spot Aaron on the back porch, watching me. He takes my extended eye contact as an invitation to come down, lowering his headphones to hang around his neck as he draws near. I held him as a baby. Thought he was mine. Gave him his name. Then killed a house full of people to avenge his staged death. If that's not screwed up, I don't know what is. "Your family is evil. You know that, right?"

He shrugs.

"Your dad is the only one you can trust."

"And you. And Grandma Sloane."

"Your dad tell you that?"

"Yeah."

He shouldn't trust me, but he's not my kid to teach. "You're welcome in my house, but if you pull any shit, you're dead. If you pass anything you see or learn here back to your family, you're also dead. Got it?"

He gives me a thumbs-up. So much like Christian it's scary.

"Did your dad drag you out here or was it your idea to come?"

"His idea. He doesn't want me at the house when my mom and Dillon are having one of their epic warlord fights."

I laugh. I shouldn't, but I do. Kid has a way with words. It's comforting to hear Dillon's made it home safe, hilarious to hear he's on the warpath. Can't imagine what set him off.

"Did you really cut off my mom's finger?"

I have to retrace the steps in my last visit before I can answer. "Yes."

"Sometimes I wonder if the stuff they say about you is true. It's all so psycho. You should be in solitary."

He's right. I am psycho. Especially since I forgot all about that finger. "So should your mother."

He widens his eyes in a *don't-I-know-it*. The expression is such a mimic of Christian at that age I'm pulled straight into the past, into that house, trying to survive those people, busting my ass to shield Christian from as much as I can. "You living in that house?"

"Not really. My dad's gonna buy a place in the city so I don't have to move back there with my mom. She moved everything out of our city house."

"You tell your dad to get on that." Better yet, I will.

He turns away to face the pines. "Yeah. But I think I should move back. Be there for my baby brother. Ya know?" He looks at me like I'm some source of advice.

My advice involves some high-caliber firearms from my basement that Christian would surely veto. There's nothing Aaron could do to undo the work the Moores will put into his little brother. He's a baby now, but at one time, so was I. They created me. Rex Moore will be worse. He'll have my training and their blood. Without my mother to counteract it all.

"Your baby brother is a lost cause."

"No way."

Tires on gravel. Must be Liv. "You want to finish this up for me?" I gesture toward the garden.

He laughs, raising his headphones back to his ears. Probably hasn't done a second of work in his life. He seems normal. Happy, even. He's lucky Kate had to keep him away from the estate so news of them wouldn't get back to me. Fifteen years of me thinking they'd been killed was worth it so he didn't have to grow up there.

I meet Liv on the driveway and lift Sloane's baby seat out of the car. She's throwing fists and kicking, wanting out like she's glad to see me. I don't know what I've done to deserve this. It's all too good.

"She failed her hearing test," Liv says.

It's like a kick to the gut—the backward force, the sickening ache, the urge to buckle.

"It happens sometimes with newborns. I made an appointment with an audiologist. Nothing to be concern—Trey?"

I can't look at her. Can't acknowledge what I've done. Those calls to black magic knocked me flat on my back. I don't know what it did to Liv when it found her, but I know

I'm right: it left permanent damage. Practicing non-native magic is risky—I knew that and did it anyway. Sloane's outward appearance of health had me fooled, and I let it fool me until now.

CHAPTER 18

LIV

THE GRIEF ON Trey's face awakens something inside me that I haven't felt since our plummet off the bluff. I can see how a failed newborn hearing test would worry someone who hasn't seen countless babies fail only to pass later like I have. But what I see is more than that. It's guilt, an emotion not often expressed by a man who does whatever the hell he wants and dares people to complain.

Now there's a tiny bulb lit in my brain and a quiver in my belly. It's not just sympathy, it's that raw ache from seeing a loved one in pain. He was right. I will learn to love him. And if this is a seedling of that, I'm going to build a bulletproof wall around it and flood it with sunlight.

"I did a bad thing," he says.

"You've done a lot of bad things. You know I don't hold them against you."

He looks at me, stricken, his lips parted like he wants to explain but the words won't come. A flock of birds swoops in from above, landing in the pine tree that hangs over the house. They hop and chirp in the branches, feisty and agitated. It's the kind of behavior that precedes some kind of Moore attack, but Trey is too lost in his head to notice them.

"Let's get inside before we get sniped." I go for the handle of Sloane's carrier. Prodded back to reality, he carries it inside.

Christian and Inis are still camped out at the kitchen table. The tone has lifted, probably Christian's doing. He could lighten an apocalypse. By the time I've put down my bag and shed my shoes, Trey has freed Sloane from her carrier and taken her out to the back porch.

"We've finished off the beer so Mister AA won't be tempted," Christian tells me.

"Thanks." I include Inis as well. She didn't come here to hang out and drink beer. She came here to exchange information about my parents for my decision, which I've made, but she's not going to like it. The dogs thunder onto the porch and start barking. First the birds, now the dogs? Hopefully Trey's paying attention now. I clear the empty bottles from the table and tie the trash bag closed. Remove the evidence, remove some of the temptation. I've been addicted to enough different things lately to know it's only a small help.

Trey yanks open the door. "She can't hear a fucking thing."

"Trey, it's impossible to test a newborn at home. She's not deaf."

"She doesn't react when the dogs bark."

"She's been hearing dogs bark from the womb for months. She's used to it." Even though I say it, and believe it, I get a dark stab of foreboding. Some newborns who fail the test really are deaf.

Inis slides the mason jar imprisoning the bottle of black magic toward her, peering inside. I owe her my answer, and there's no reason to postpone it. "Inis, can we talk somewhere?"

"I'm good with here if you are."

I meet Trey's eye. I didn't envision telling her while he was present but it seems better this way. He'll know where I stand at the same time she does. Aaron comes in the door behind Trey, his headphones around his neck. Now I'm not sure if this much audience is a good idea, and Christian's picked up on my awkward silence because he's gotten to his feet, pointing Aaron toward the door.

"He can stay," Trey says.

Aaron surveys all the faces, not too sure about what he just walked in on. "Nah, I can go on back out—"

"Stay," Trey says. "Just remember what I told you." Then his eyes are back on me. He can't know what Inis and I discussed, or what decision she wants from me. But from the way he's waiting for me to speak, he knows something is about to change our lives.

But it's not—that's what I've decided.

"I've decided to raise Sloane without O'Dowd magic. I'm sorry, Inis, but I have to respect the decision of my mother, or my grandmother, or whoever decided to abandon your ways."

Inis shifts forward in her seat. Whatever light mood Christian had established is now gone. Inis doesn't just look disappointed. She looks pissed. "You need to reconsider."

"I might—someday. But for now, that's what I want. I hope we can stay friends—"

Inis stands, two palms on the table, leaning toward me. "Friends? That's an insult to the blood we share. O'Dowds aren't just *friends*."

In the brief moment it takes her to release those words, Sloane has been passed from Trey to Christian to Aaron who's been pushed from the room. Now Christian's at my shoulder, and Trey's filling the space between Inis and me. I want to yell at them to stand down. She's not going to hurt us. She's disappointed and angry, but she's not a monster. Everything doesn't have to turn into a damn confrontation.

Inis places a finger on the mason jar holding the bottle of black magic. It shatters. She plucks the still intact bottle from the debris. "I'll be keeping this."

Trey extends an open hand toward her. The threat's in his eyes. He doesn't need to ask.

She laughs at him. He lunges. Christian's body covers mine, pinning me against the fridge as a pulse hits the air— so much like the one that shot from the sky and knocked me across that parking lot. Christian hisses, spitting out a string of f-bombs that are lost in the ruckus of toppling chairs and dishes hitting the floor. Christian turns around to assess the damage. I get a view of his back—sliced fabric and wounds weeping through. I slip from behind him. Trey's arms are cut all over, just starting to bleed. The two of them make eye contact before rushing to the front door. I run after them.

Outside, Inis faces the pack of coyotes standing in line between her and her motorcycle. More are joining at the sides, closing her in. She turns around, holds the bottle of black magic high in the air. "Call your animals off."

Trey looks over his shoulder at me. I nod. He turns forward again, makes the slightest jerk of his head. The coyotes part and disperse, settling in formation on both sides of us. Inis tucks the bottle into her inner jacket pocket. She aims a pinched look my way; the slight pensiveness packed in with all that firepower gives me an opportunity—now missed, by Trey taking a step forward. Christian throws out an arm to hold him back. We watch Inis mount her motorcycle, strap on her helmet, put on her gloves. Then she tears away in a cloud of exhaust, digging a rut in the gravel.

I drop to a squat, my face in my hands. I need to go back in time, redo that scene. It wasn't supposed to go like that. The only blood relative I know, and now she's gone, along with a bottle of magic that's programmed to seek and destroy all the people I love. If it gets released, I'll be as broken and alone as I was when I first moved to this town.

A shadow falls over me. I lower my hands, see Christian's shoes. Trey stands far behind him like he's too afraid to come near me. He knows this scene would have played out differently if he hadn't been in the room. Shame has rooted him in place.

Christian extends a hand. "I think I need medical attention."

I take his hand and he ushers me inside. A quick check of Aaron and Sloane shows baby fast asleep in boy's arms. He's poking his phone with his free hand, so I consider him content as babysitter. The kitchen is as wrecked as my relationship with Inis. I right the chairs, and Christian gets to work on the floor. When I see what a mess his back is, I make him take off his shirt and sit. "What did she do?"

"Some black magic bullshit. Happened too fast for us to do anything. It's not good to have them as enemies."

"I tried—"

"Yeah, I know you did." He looks like he needs to hit something. I offer the sting of soapy gauze on his lacerated back as a distraction. "So talk me out of blaming Trey for all that, because I'm having a real hard time—" He turns his ear toward the sound of a motorcycle engine starting up.

I hand him the gauze and sprint outside, catching sight of Trey just as he bursts away leaving ruts of his own. No car we own could catch up to that thing. And that's a plus, because whether it was Christian or me behind the wheel, catching it wouldn't end up well for Trey.

When I return to the house, Christian and I share a look so thick with understanding he cracks under the depth of it and starts laughing, high-pitched and hysterical. I point to the kitchen. He gets a quick grip of himself once the cold gauze hits his wounded skin again.

"I'm thinking I should go with Inis, let her teach Sloane after all. Seems like something she could use against your kind."

"Maybe. But don't think it's an end-all. If Trey had wanted to kill her, he'd have killed her. He might get a little scratched up, but no flavor of magic is going to stop that guy."

"So he didn't just leave to go kill her?"

"Nah. I'm sure he's only after a polite conversation."

My phone dings with an incoming text. Christian grabs it off the table. "Tara. 'Winnie wants us to leave. Heading over.'"

"Text her back and tell her to be careful." I upgrade to trauma center pace, slapping on bandages with less grace and waking up Christian's colorful mouth. When I'm finished, I jab him in the arm. "Done. Now go downstairs and grab a gun for both of us."

"Why—oh crap. Now?" He goes downstairs.

I slide the door open and peek outside. The wind curls against my face, hissing in the nearby trees. No dogs or coyotes to be seen. Birds are quiet. Christian returns and we load guns at the table in silence until he says, "This shit has to stop. I'm the man now, right? I'm putting an end to this stupidity."

He watches the yard from the front door, and I watch the back. I join him when I hear tires on the driveway. He runs outside to help Tara, Máthair, and the kids out of the car while I cover them. All I hear is the wind. Too quiet is usually as bad a sign as a whole flock of birds chattering at Trey. Even though I can't hear or see them, I can sense their watchful eyes on me.

"How long until they get here?" Christian's asking Tara when they reach the door.

Tara stoops to help both kids remove their shoes. "She doesn't yet have much concept of time."

"Great."

Máthair lifts Sloane away from Aaron and sits beside him, her presence nudging him back into reality. He removes his headphones and scans the room. "Did somebody die?"

Winnie takes Will's hand and looks at the ceiling. If our attackers aren't on the roof now, they will be soon.

Christian curses under his breath. He looks at me. It turns into a stare-off. He doesn't like killing people; neither do I. Whether he admits it or not, I know it's true and as much as I don't want to pull the trigger and end someone's life, I also don't want to make him do it. They're not after him.

I go in the bedroom for my hooded cloak, the one Tara affected to blend with its surroundings. As I raise the hood and tuck my hair in, I imagine why the attackers are here: to steal or kill my baby. To kill Trey. These guys volunteer to come here. I'm only protecting my family. All those things are true, but they don't take the wrongness of this away.

Máthair's standing in the middle of the living room when I walk back through. She's handed Sloane off to Tara. "Is this how Fearghus normally handles their men? There are other ways."

"Yeah, but are those ways as fun as this?" Christian holds up his rifle.

"He …" *Murders a lot of people*, I want to say. But it doesn't seem right. He's only defending himself. Now he's defending all of us. "He's had to do this a lot."

"And his coyotes?"

"They help, but not every time." Time presses against me. The more I stall, the closer they'll get, the harder they'll be to take down safely. "How many?" I ask Tara.

She holds up two fingers. I head for the door, but Christian and Máthair seem to be locked in a wordless exchange. Christian finally looks away, throwing a resigned sweep of the hand toward the door. Máthair accepts the invitation and is already on the porch before I think to stop her.

I shoot a glare at Christian. He holds up a hand. "Not my idea. And I don't argue with female Bevans."

Since he's not wearing a shirt to grab, I drag him by a belt loop out the door. Máthair's barefoot in the middle of the yard, her arms raised to the sky. There's a shifting all around us, a heave to the air. I grip the rifle tight, holding it lengthwise against my chest so it's not sucked from my hands. Pandemonium interrupts the unnatural quiet, the sky invaded by a swarming dark mass. It takes a moment to recognize its individual parts darting all around yet moving together as a whole.

"Holy oak, that's a lot of bats," Christian says beside me.

We've unconsciously retreated, our backs against the house.

With one roll of Máthair's wrist, the bats turn as one creature and dive behind the house. Máthair follows on foot, and so do we. Christian takes the lead, his rifle raised. As soon as we round the corner of the house, we see what the bats have found. The swarm has forced a man from the woods and continues to mob him, dive-bombing from all angles. I know bats don't bite humans but it sure looks like they're trying to devour him.

Máthair doesn't raise her voice beyond normal speaking level. "Drop your weapons and I'll call them off."

Two daggers and a handgun are ejected from the chaotic mass. I see a flash of hands in the air before they're overrun by hundreds of tiny bodies and flapping wings.

"Okay," Máthair says. As one, the bats rise and lift away like a puff of smoke from a smokestack.

The man's on his knees, hands on his head like he knows exactly what to do. He thinks he's a soldier, but he's too young to give up his life for a cause he knows nothing about. To the Moores he's just another disposable recruit. Christian yanks the guy's black sock hat off, exposing shaggy brown hair too boyish for this job. The guy focuses his hard-set eyes beyond us. He knows he's about to die. He's trying to do it with dignity.

I don't care what he came here to do. I can't do this.

I lower the hood of my cloak to break the magic and take a step back. The guy raises his eyes, settling them on mine. Then his gaze darts past me, and I turn just in time to see a figure scale the roof. My intake of breath is all it takes for Christian to swing his aim from the guy's head to the house. He shoots fast; the roof attacker flinches but doesn't go down. The bullet grazed him. And now he's reached the peak, lifting a leg over to descend the other side where he'll drop down at the front door and walk right in. Christian's reloading. It's not fast enough.

I raise my rifle and squeeze the trigger.

With my ringing ears comes a cold, debilitating grief that rushes in and takes hold. I lock my knees so the weakness in my legs doesn't take me to the ground. My chest goes raw, but I breathe it down. No use crying over the irreversible. And there'd be no way to swallow the pain I'd feel if he'd gotten in the house to the people I love. To my baby given a second chance.

"Next," Christian says, swinging his rifle toward our captive. A hard shell has slid over Christian's features. Blue eyes now icy cold, mouth set hard in a way I never see. He's now the Christian I don't know. The one who takes over when options are limited and horrible things must be done.

"Wait," I say, but I'm not sure why. I have no way to salvage this.

But then Máthair drops to her knees in front of the guy, taking his face in her hands and forcing him to look at her. "You have someone who loves you, somewhere. Find that person and leave this behind. Stow it where you'll never find it." She moves one hand to his forehead. His eyes roll into his head then close.

She releases him. He shakes himself off like an animal waking from a nap and looks around, blinking and con-fused. Máthair stands, offers a hand to help him up. He glances between Christian and me, scratching his head.

Christian's still aiming the rifle at the guy's head as he cuts across the lawn toward the forest. He seems to know where he's going. It would be a bit awkward to offer him a ride.

"Is that really going to work?" I ask Máthair.

"Of course." She measures my expression before start-ing back up the hill. "Just because Fearghus chose to hone other methods doesn't mean he lacks the ways of peace-ful resolution."

This is what my daughter will learn. She doesn't have to be a killer. She will right wrongs. She'll mend the rift between two families, not destroy one to save the other.

She'll be a healer. Not a killer.

Christian shoots at the ground where the man disappeared into the trees. When he lowers his rifle, the Christian I know has returned, all tension released with that one pointless round. "Can't blame the guy for preferring cold-blooded murder."

I run toward Sloane, joining her side. "Every time they come, I'm going to think they're kidnappers instead of murderers. I don't know which is worse."

"Kidnappers don't sneak up like this. They come straight through the front door."

It doesn't hit me until we're back in the kitchen that she's speaking from experience. I poke Christian and point at the front of the house—there's a body out there that needs to be dragged away before the kids see it. Winnie catches him before he can go. "Aunt Liv has a special gun that sends the bad guys home to their mom."

Christian exhales out a laugh and tries to match Winnie's matter-of-fact tone. "Does she really? That's harsh. You think they'll get in trouble?"

"Five minute time-out," she says.

"Six minutes," Will corrects.

I check my phone and see a new text from Trey: *At AA. Be home later.*

Christian peers over my shoulder. "Wow, only took him an hour to tell you where he was going."

But at least he told me. Yeah, my standards are low. You have to start somewhere.

CHAPTER 19

TREY

Only two days since the last AA meeting and I can't remember a damn thing from it that could help me right now. Instead what I'm thinking is I'm alone in this house. Liv will be gone awhile at Sloane's second hearing test. Christian and Aaron are on their way back to Virginia. If I mounted the Ninja now, I could be to the liquor store and back in fifteen minutes with a little bottle to calm me down. No one would know.

Only thing to smother that plan is I'm not lying to Liv. So I could leave the bottle on the counter because all I need is one drink. There's not a fucking thing wrong with one drink.

I grab my keys and go out to the garage. Mount my bike, stare at the helmet in my hands. Because if it goes on, the next thing to do is start the engine. I close my eyes and browse the store in my head. I'll get something cheap, something I won't like. That will help me stick to one drink. Or I could get the most expensive scotch they sell so I'll drink it slowly, to savor the money spent. No, I'll get a six-pack of beer. Drink one, put the rest away for Christian the next time he visits.

When I hear Liv's Civic descending the driveway toward me, I know I've been sitting a long time. I get off the Ninja, shake out my stiff legs. I've lost my chance, and I hate myself for it. Not as much as I'd hate myself if I'd taken it.

Liv has parked and killed the engine, but she hasn't gotten out. She's sitting still, her gaze fixed straight ahead like she's still driving. I open her door then open the back door to get Sloane's carrier. Sloane's breathy baby noises are the only sound. The quiet in the car is like a tangible force, made stranger by Liv's unmoving posture. Her stiff silence.

Instead of unbuckling Sloane, I go back to Liv. She looks at me then. Wet, red eyes, lines of tears on both cheeks. I lose my mindset for a moment, do a mental rewind, search my memory for where she was, what she was just doing that could have caused this upset.

"She's deaf, Trey. Profoundly deaf. There are more tests, but the audiologist said … she and Dr. Wu said—" She covers her mouth, heaves with a single sob that stabs through me. She swallows it down and gathers a breath. "How is she ever going to protect herself if she—"

"She's not deaf!" I don't know why I say it, why I yell it, why my fist has come down so hard on the Civic's roof because I knew this. I caused it. I didn't need proof. My outburst earns me two arms full of Liv, her face pressing against my chest like I'm any comfort at all. I hold her as she holds onto me. Through the open car door, Sloane's tiny feet kick inside her carrier. I've fought while deaf from close-fired gunshots. The disorientation almost got me killed.

"We have to learn ASL," she says, powering ahead, her ignorance giving her that strength.

"ASL?"

"Sign language. We have to start signing to her right away. And keep talking to her, treat her like a normal baby." She pushes away from me, smears away the tears with her fingertips. "Please don't clam up. Tell me what you're thinking."

I don't know what the fuck I'm thinking. Deafness—it's a vulnerability my daughter can't have. It's too important a sense. On her own, she'll be dead when they send their first guy. She won't hear River's warning howl. The call of the birds. The snap of a branch under an assassin's foot. The shuffle of leaves. Sometimes it's the silence that warns me. If she really is profoundly deaf, she lives in silence. She'll never know when the silence isn't right. Once she finds out her own father's reckless actions are the reason for her deafness, she'll run too far away for me to protect her. And if I tell Liv I'm at fault, it'll kill her forward momentum. She'll lose that strength. She'll hate me. I can't give her another reason to leave me.

Liv shakes my arm. "Trey?"

"I have to—" I clear the tightness from my throat. Take a step back. Force myself to look her in the eyes. I owe her that, after all the shit I've done. I owe her the truth.

"The black magic I used when you were pregnant—it's why she's deaf."

"What do you—"

"It hurt Sloane inside you."

"But she inherited your healing ability. If something hurt her, she'd heal."

She's right. But even when the healing was within me, it had its limits. If someone put a bullet in my brain I couldn't heal from that. "There are limits to what it can fix."

"Inis said I'm immune to black magic. And Sloane too."

"Immune to *her* black magic. Not mine. I summoned it to find you, sent a locator out, and got a return."

Her lips part, her eyes cast away from me like she's just remembered something. "That was *you*?"

"I didn't know it would hurt her. Hurt you. I didn't think. It's my fault she's deaf." The words tear me up on their way out, but it feels right. For once, finally, I'm doing something right.

Her breathing increases like she's trying to hold in a reaction. Her eyes glint with new tears. But the look in them isn't sadness. It's anger, blue-hot and unbridled. She closes the space between us, takes two rough fistfuls of my shirt. "You knocked me across a parking lot into a brick wall. You—I thought it was Dillon, and it was you!"

She shoves me back. The power in it proves a hate as potent as the one she should have for Dillon.

"I'm sorry. I—"

"Sorry?! Sorry doesn't cut it, not this time." She has more to say but she withdraws instead, toward the car to unbuckle Sloane and carry her into the house. When she closes the door it's apparent I'm no longer welcome there, and I hope I've got it right because that means she's not going to leave.

I get on the Ninja. Then I'm buying the first bottle of scotch I touch. I can't recall the miles it took to get there. I don't remember the burn in my throat or the wash of calm that follows the first drink so I take another. It's a salve, a medicine I've been hurting for. There's too much commotion on the street. I ride to the edge of town to an unused gravel lot. The sun tucks itself behind the mountains as the bottle gets lighter in my hand. My eyelids are getting heavy, but I have to get home. Can't leave Liv and the baby unguarded. I start the Ninja. Put on my helmet. The lurch of engine seems far away. Unconnected. The tires on pavement a distant hum.

There's something in the road ahead. Looks like gravel. Could be—

Some asshole won't stop shouting my name. If I could move my arms I'd shove him away. Then I get a signal from my arm that I wish I hadn't—it's so alive with searing pain I growl out a curse I can't hold back.

"Good. That's good. Hang tight, man, I'm calling an ambulance."

"No ambulance."

The guy shifts back so his face is lit by a shaft of horizontal light. Orange hair blazes. Shawn.

"No ambulance? You're outta your mind. Just stay still. You might've broken your neck."

I get my elbows under me; my vision swirls blacker than the space beyond the shaft of light. I shake my head to clear it. He's pulled out his phone, but I need to get it from him before he makes that call. It lights up in his hand, ringing. He answers it.

"I found him. He crashed his bike. I'm going to—yeah, he's alive. I need to call an ambulance. I'm hanging—what?"

He grips my shoulder, trying to keep me down. I knock his arm away and sit up—too fast. I almost lose it. A wave of hot pain rolls up and down one side of my body. I grit my teeth and push myself up. I have to get out of here before he calls anyone. I don't have the power to deal with cops and paramedics right now.

"You people are insane. He's—wait, he's getting up. I have to—" He drops his phone to make a grab for me.

I've got my second leg under me. I blink in the light, notice the truck it's coming from. The intensity of it batters my skull. He's got a hold of me again. I shove him away so hard I stagger, go down on one knee. He stoops, hoists my arm over his shoulders, and helps me up. Fine, I'll take it.

"Where's my bike?"

"Wrapped around a tree somewhere. I think my truck is your better bet."

Anything that gets me off my feet before I plummet headfirst and take him down with me.

"You're going to bleed all over my seats."

He closes me in the cab, and I slump against the door. I watch him sprint back into the path of the headlights, retrieve his phone. He's on another call when he takes the driver's seat; the words don't make sense to me and my head is too heavy to hold up. It bangs against the glass with every bump in the road, but I'm too screwed up in other places to care.

Then the door's opening again and I'm falling out onto the street. Shawn catches me by the arm, throwing it over his shoulders again. He's talking like he's been talking for a long time, but I didn't hear shit before this.

"—figured since my place was closer and—"

I miss everything after that due to the effort it takes to put one foot in front of the other. He shoves the door open with his foot and makes me lean on a counter while he finds a cover for his couch. Unloading my own weight onto the cushions is a welcome reprieve until the signal from its contact with my skin hits my brain. The million points of hell blend together as one, sending everything in my stomach upward. I manage to choke it down.

"Dude, if you barf in my living room …"

"I'm good."

"You're definitely not good. I think that jacket is melted to your skin."

I start to shrug out of it. Decide against it.

"How much have you had to drink?"

"Too fucking much."

"Your sister's pissed."

"Not her business."

He laughs. It throbs in my head, pounding in the backs of my eyes.

"She's gonna tell Liv you're okay, but leave the details for you to tell. We've been looking for you for hours. I'd offer you my couch for the night, but all that…" he swirls a finger at the bloody wreck that is the left side of my body "…should probably be addressed by a medical professional."

Meaning Liv. For her to clean up my mess again. It's all she ever does. It's the position I keep putting her in when I'm supposed to be the guy who's worthy of her love. The higher the stakes are, the worse I fail.

"You need a few minutes to sober up if you want me to take you to the clinic so someone can pick those little pieces of road out of your skin."

I don't know why he's trying to save me from getting busted. With the cops, or with Liv. He owes me nothing. I lean forward, my face in my hands. I can't stay here. I can't go home—I have to go home. That's where I was headed because Liv and the baby are alone right now. The Moores could crash in any minute.

He hands me a bottle of ibuprofen and a glass of water. I drain the glass. The water dislodges gritty dirt from inside my mouth, and I spit into the cup.

"That's all I can offer. I do work with Liv, but I'm just the delivery guy. The blood and guts is above my pay grade." He sits on the other end of the couch. "What are you doing, man? You have a new baby at home."

"She's deaf."

"So what? She seems like a happy, healthy baby. There's nothing wrong with being deaf." He looks at me straight-on, baiting me for information. For the reason why deafness is such a problem to me.

I don't know how much Tara told him, but I'm not giving him anything. "You're a Moore."

He leans back, just out of easy punching range. "Okay, that's random. Did you get a head injury?"

I watch him, waiting for the slightest tic. A shuffle of feet. A quickly averted gaze. Anything to prove his loyalty lies with them instead of Tara. Instead of us. He gives me nothing.

"I don't know anything about those people," he says.

"They prey upon the weak."

"She's a newborn baby. Being deaf doesn't make her any more weak. She's already as weak as she could be. And I wouldn't worry about it until she's old enough to throw a punch or pull a trigger. Then, bonus, she won't need ear protection." He stands abruptly and puts some space between us. "Whoa, okay. Don't kill me. I'm just trying to point out the positives."

"Drive me home." I stand, get an upsurge of stomach bile again. Contain it.

"The clinic is closer …"

Hiding from Liv will only make this worse. "Home."

Liv walks barefoot in the gravel to meet us. Sloane is wrapped snugly against her chest. She stands there in the light from the headlights, her face alarmingly neutral. The unwavering gaze dares me to get out of the truck. Shawn whistles low under his breath and turns off the key. He helps me into the house, dumps me on the couch, and bails. I can't blame him. Liv's offish stance has turned the room so cold I can almost see my breath.

"So you punish me by abusing yourself. It's pretty manipulative. I can't decide if you're doing it maliciously, or if you don't know you're doing it and you're just that messed up."

"I'm that messed up."

"Understatement." She approaches. Sizes up my injuries. "That's some serious road rash. I don't really have the setup to treat you here. Can you get that jacket off?"

I don't want to. I do it for her. She watches me struggle and offers no help. If we were at the clinic, they'd be cutting it off.

"How much did you drink?"

"I don't remember."

"Don't hang your head. Look at me. The only way to beat this is to own up to it. Every time."

I look at her. The hard line of her lips, the fiery disappointment. And the tuft of Sloane's dark hair poking from the top of the baby wrap. She can't know what a fuckup her father is. I have to stop this. "I don't remember what I bought or how much I drank of it."

"Where's the bottle?"

Probably should be in my jacket, but I'd rather not move my arm to check. She follows my gaze and checks for me. Not there. Was probably too big to fit in the pocket.

"Tara's going to have your motorcycle towed so no one finds it out there and calls the police. You're lucky you didn't kill yourself." She walks the room flipping on all the lights. "Lie down on the couch with your left side out."

I do. She leaves and returns with instruments she lays out on the coffee table before pulling the table close enough to use as a stool. "This is going to hurt like hell."

She starts picking at me. From the way she's going at it, I assume she's used to dealing with patients who are anesthetized against cold metal digging into open raw wounds. Or maybe this is her way of making me pay. Half-finished, she has to stop to feed Sloane. I try to doze but the pain is too distracting, the stomach bile too much effort to keep down. When she returns to her work, I involuntarily cringe. She now has a flashlight tucked under her chin like she's moved onto the more difficult pieces.

I turn my face against the couch cushion and pray to the elements I suffocate to death.

A hundred years later she leaves me bandaged on the couch to sleep. I listen as the mattress creaks under her weight in the bedroom. The windows lighten gradually until they glow with the sun. I determine what needs to happen for me to keep them safe. And I make a new oath to Liv. To our daughter. To myself.

CHAPTER 20

LIV

FOR THREE DAYS Trey has left the house early and stayed gone until late afternoon. He's not working. AA meetings aren't that long. He's not at Tara's. He did load his wrecked motorcycle into the back of his truck and drive off one day, but every other departure hasn't had a noticeable reason. I'd ask, but I shouldn't have to. He's my equal, not my charge. When he finally does return home each day, it's to either work in the garden or exercise. Then he lets me check his bandages while looking wistfully at Sloane kicking her blanket on the floor like she's a prize he's not worthy to touch. And every time I open my mouth to demand he explain what's going on in his head, I'm struck silent by the unfairness of it all.

It's a ridiculous, emotionally draining routine. I know what he's doing—avoiding us. He no longer has alcohol to dull whatever regret or failure he feels toward us. I push Sloane into his arms after checking his bandages one night, and he takes her, his eyes on mine like I must grant some kind of verbal contract. Like he thinks I don't trust him not to hurt her again. When I walk through the room later, they're both asleep, her little body flat on his chest. I sit and watch them, returning to every recent event in my head. He must not realize I'm also to blame for her deafness. I'm the one who left. If I'd stayed, he wouldn't have needed to send that horrible pulse of black magic looking for me.

I spend the days he's absent with Tara, Máthair, and the kids. Máthair holds Sloane so I can wash my hair and do some laundry and run around with Winnie and Will, and Tara pretends she isn't dying to badmouth Trey. When I said, "I don't want to talk about him," she accepted it as law. She's a great friend and an even better sister.

I try not to think about what I lost with Inis. And the destructive magic she has in that bottle that's eager to escape and attack the people I care about. The shield potion Máthair and Trey prepared can't last forever. And it can't protect everyone: Sloane's too young to take it, and Trey's too stubborn—and too busy trying to be a martyr.

When Trey leaves for the fourth day in a row, I call out to him, but I'm too late. The door has closed my voice inside. My bond with him was the only solid thing we had before all this. We were being hunted and attacked. We were learning life-changing news. We got through it together due to that bond. Now it seems everything else has settled, but that bond that carried us through it is fraying.

I spend the morning snuggling with Sloane on the couch and catching up on missed sleep. After lunch we take a walk through the garden and into the woods. The dogs are our only protectors for once—the coyotes must have the day off. I squat to let Sloane bury her clumsy fingers in River's mane. She coos, earning an excited whine from River, but it's a sound she'll never hear. She kicks, wanting closer, pining for the tactile sensation, as if making up for her missing sense. Deafness or not, I couldn't love her more. I see her father in her eyes, and I feel my love for her expanding toward him.

We sit on the pine needle floor and watch the light play with the shadows on the ground. She's mesmerized by where it's coming from. I point above us. She watches the branches wiggle in the breeze, cooing with each large gust. I kiss her silky cheek, whisper in her ear that I love her. She doesn't need to hear. She'll know.

Tires crunch on the gravel driveway on our return to the house. I quicken my stride to the back door because there's no knowing who it is. Trey's new pattern hasn't been bringing him home this early. I slip in the back as the front door opens. It is Trey, closing the door and looking at me like he needs to say something. Instead, he raises a hand and signs, *I'm sorry.*

It catches me so off guard I'm speechless. He hasn't touched the ASL book I bought, but here he is signing to me. 'I'm sorry' was going to be the first one I taught him since it seems to be the only thing he says to me lately.

He goes again: *I love my family.*

It's a confirmation that the basics I've learned are sticking. It's hope that we can do this, that he's going to do this with me. He's taken it upon himself to start learning to sign, to move forward in righting the wrong we both caused. His effort turns my chest raw. I've had no time to prepare for such a flip in his behavior. What I saw as avoidance was his tunnel-vision determination to prove himself to me. But there's no way the jerk is going to make me cry.

Then he signs something I don't know. A slightly bent, upward-facing palm sweeping from upper chest to waist. Two loose upward-facing palms.

I swallow to steady my voice. "I don't know that one."

"I'm *here*," he says.

He's not going to get tears from me, but he is going to get a hug because I've already rushed forward and can't stop myself. I can't squeeze him as hard as I want to with Sloane wrapped on my chest. He bends down to me, his frame as solid as I remember it.

"Where did you learn all that?"

"The library."

I pull back to look at him and give Sloane some space to breathe. That's where he's been spending his time? "You look like you want me to kiss you."

"I do."

"I'm not sure you deserve it."

"I will. I promise I will."

"So, a loan?"

He nods. His eyes are a sad, muted version of his daughter's. Dimmed by heartbreak. I put a hand on his stubbly cheek and dig out the memory of when I first kissed him—

that frantic, unstoppable need, the shocking swell in my chest, the crippling, inexplicable love I was afraid to feel for a guy I didn't know. The love might not be so feral now but it's very real and no longer inexplicable. I love him for what we've been through. For what we've built. For the daughter we'll raise and teach to speak with hands instead of voice. And for the strides he's taken to fix his flaws. No matter how often or how badly he fails, he gets back up and tries again, and I love him for that.

I wrap my arms around his neck and draw him down. His mouth is warm, gentle, apprehensive. So I tighten my hold and kiss him harder, hoping the next time he's so overwhelmed that his only solution is a bottle of scotch maybe he'll remember this and come home to me instead.

He joins me in bed that night, his arm warm and innocent around me until I give him a nip on the neck that makes his hands bold and his mouth bolder. He knows where he can't go and it only makes him more creative. And I'm cursing those post-birth limitations because I've never wanted him more.

"Is it a bad time for a person to say 'I love you' during sex?" I ask when his hand is tangled in my hair and his mouth is on my neck.

He stops to look at me in the moonlight flooding through the window. "Not if the person means it."

"What if she means it, but she's not sure he'll believe her?"

He withdraws his hand from my hair, and I fear I've killed the mood.

"I love you, Trey."

He ducks his head, resting it against my shoulder so he doesn't have to look at me. He didn't expect me to say it. Whether he believes me or not, he doesn't think he deserves it.

"I'll always love you. No magic can strip it away from me. All it did was expose what we built naturally, without the help from the stars. It's the real thing and was always there and always will be."

He exhales against my skin, cooling it so chills run the length of my back and arms.

"You're too good for me," he says. "For my sick world."

"Your world isn't what it used to be."

That gets his eyes back on mine. He takes my face in his hands. "Then it's me. I'm a blight. I no longer fit. I'm trying to fix that, but …" He shakes his head.

"I think you see your world differently than I do. I think you see your*self* differently."

He presses his lips against my neck again, ready to dump this conversation and return to business. He doesn't want to acknowledge that I love him, that he's worthy of love. He's believed too long that he's not. It's the source of what's broken in him and until he accepts it as truth, he'll continue thinking he's an ill-fitting piece to his new world.

I end up leaden beside him, sated and content after being kissed to fulfillment. He's a dead weight next to me, too languid to fix the sheets and the mess we made. All the things I wanted to say to him have been subdued, smoothed by the sex and the moonlight and the warmth of his body in a bed that's been cold without him for too long.

Sloane wakes and fusses. Trey finds the power to rise from our shared coma, scoop her from her bassinet, and lay her between us. I latch her on. He props up on his elbow to gaze at us. He fingerspells her name. I fingerspell his. He fingerspells *You are a good fuck*. I laugh. Sloane unlatches due to my movement and lets out a hearty cry.

I resituate her and he runs a finger against the unruly fluff of her hair that never seems to want to stay down. "I bought a new ZX-14."

"A new motorcycle?"

"It's in the garage."

"You won't walk away a second time. You got so lucky—"

"I know. I promise I won't do what I did again. You don't have to worry."

I become aware of how hard I've locked my gaze on his, how thickly my pulse is pounding in my head. Those hours I waited at home while Shawn and Tara searched—I refuse to be that scared again. "We need you."

He kisses my forehead then kisses Sloane's head against that fluff of hair. The promise in his eyes is enough to quiet me. He turns over to his back and closes his eyes.

"Trey?"

"Yeah?"

"I'm going to get in touch with Inis. I have to get that bottle back."

Inis is only willing to see me—and only me—on her turf. She no longer trusts Trey, and she hung up on me twice before I got through to her that Trey isn't involved in this.

Trey doesn't approve and if he wasn't trying so hard to change, he'd be doing all he could to stop me. Then he'd hunt down Inis on his own, kill her, and take the bottle. Which he still might do if I fail.

She's on the road and won't commit to a meeting spot where she'll be stationary for a few days, so I have no choice but to wait until early winter when she's settled for the season in Sedona, Arizona. I book a plane ticket and a car and put it out of my mind all summer and fall. Trey isn't happy, especially when I tell him I'm bringing Sloane. But he continues his AA meetings and sticks to one drink a week and puts all his energy into Winnie and Will's ongoing training and learning ASL.

We're all learning it. Tara and Máthair bring home books from the library and have turned it into a game with the kids. Even Shawn's joined in—he has a deaf cousin who taught him a few signs as a child, and he always regretted not learning more. And Trey's been strangely mild around Shawn since that night he dragged him home.

My tiny, snuggly infant grows into a smiling, grabby baby who wants to touch and feel and put everything in her mouth. She's most sedate on walks in the woods, hoisted high on Trey's chest so she can see over his shoulder, her bright little face tilted up toward the highest branches of the pines. Bundled against the cold, she watches Trey's face like his moving lips are a puzzle she's learning to untangle. She touches her own lips, wondering how she can get hers to work the same.

When the date of my flight to Arizona arrives, I almost don't want to go. With Christian running the Moore household in Richmond, things have never been more pleasant and safe at home. I fear my meeting with Inis will awaken trouble that's been in hibernation, but I have to get that bottle back. It's too dangerous out of our hands. When we do get it back, we're going to encase it in concrete and bury it in the mountains.

CHAPTER 21

TREY

T HE BUSTLE OF the airport is making me twitchy. Liv agreed to allow me to walk her in, as far as they'll let me go without a ticket. Convincing them I have one so I can take her to the gate would do nothing but waste good magic and break part of my oath to her. To be less of an asshole is a brutal toil. I was born one and was taught by the best of them.

Now I'm standing by the windows inside the main entrance while she feeds Sloane on a bench. A cold gust of wind blows in each time the doors open. Scanning people for threats is a neurosis I could only turn off with a drink. Or fooling around with Liv. I'll have neither of those options when she's gone. I'm going to lose my mind.

She toes the bag she's going to check. "You finished the thing?"

The Discretion effect. To hide the Glock and knife I stashed in her bag. I sign back '*no*,' because I have to see her smile again before she leaves.

I get my reward. Plus a kick in the shin. Then she hands me Sloane, a dribble of milk running down her chin. I wipe it with my shirt then hold her close, breathing in her milky baby smell. I'm crazy for letting them leave, for not buying a ticket right now and going with them. My presence wouldn't just ruin our chances of getting the bottle back; it'd blow this test of what I promised to Liv. More trust. Less controlling asshole. I get it. And I'm going through with it even if it kills me. Doesn't change how much I hate it.

We walk to security screening. To my disappointment there's no line. So I take her hard against me, hold her close. Kiss her, kiss Sloane.

"Please don't drink," she says.

I sign, *Okay*.

She signs, *I love you*.

I kiss her again. She goes through the metal detectors. She's several steps beyond the screening area before she turns around, probably because she knows I'm watching.

I sign, *You have a good ass*, because I don't know the sign for 'nice.'

She fingerspells, *You too*.

I show her the sign for 'same.' She mimics it and blows me a kiss. I watch her until she's out of sight.

Back in my truck, I pop the steering wheel because there's nothing suitable to punch. It's brittle in the cold and doesn't come close to human flesh and bones. The third way to calm my neurosis is a good fight. Could easily get myself one of those in the nearest bar but there's no way in hell I'm stupid enough to go into a bar right now. I text Christian: *Send one of your family's guys. I need to kill someone.*

My phone rings when I'm descending my driveway at home. Not Christian. An unknown number. There's an unsettling tingle in the back of my head. I answer the call.

"Cousin."

Can't decide if it's Jared or Dillon Moore. Those assholes sound the same.

"Let's meet. I have some business to settle with you."

I'm not sure how I know it's Jared, or how he got my number. "Didn't we settle up when I left you bleeding on your brother's kitchen floor?"

"Liv's flight just left. She's connecting in Denver, right? I just happen to be in Denver right now."

I go cold in the gut. My phone creaks against my ear. I relax my grip before I shatter the phone I'll need to call Liv and warn her. It doesn't matter how they found out. All that matters is they know.

"In fact, I have a ticket in my hand. I'm flying to Arizona too. Maybe I'll get lucky and get to sit next to her."

"You want TSA all up in your ass? You Moores were never that bright." It's a challenge to keep my voice cool.

"She wouldn't say a thing to start trouble. But if you want to meet, I'll cancel my trip to Arizona and head straight there. Missoula? Spokane? You name the city. Make it a big one, though, where I can get a decent hotel."

It couldn't be anything but a setup but what the hell am I supposed to do? Even if he's lying about being there, he knows her itinerary. He's butt-hurt over what I did to him and wants a second go. The threat to Liv is the only way he'll get my attention. I knew this trip of hers was a test of my trust of her—and of my overbearing grip on her—but damn, the stakes on this test are far too high. She won't be able to put a bullet between his eyes in the middle of the Denver airport.

If I go to meet him, I'll get my fight. With one of the most tempting opponents I could name.

I give him the name of a bar in Missoula and we set the day and time. I go into the house and stare at the single bottle of scotch I own, the one that empties by exactly four ounces each week. I think about Liv's lips against mine, Sloane's gummy smile. Then I go to the closet for a heavier coat and a sock hat and go outside. The recent dusting of snow hasn't yet melted from parts of the forest floor. It's gone slushy from the day's warmth. It will freeze again once night hits.

Liv already knows to keep an eye out for Moores. If I text her now to remind her, that's me being overbearing. Jared knowing her itinerary doesn't change anything. We knew it could happen, and she's already on guard. It would do nothing to suppress my insane need to hop on a sportbike in a Montana winter and break every speed limit between here and Denver. I'd be twelve hours too late no matter how fast I rode.

So I increase my pace and choose the steepest route. Shove everything out of my brain except the sound of my boots squishing against wet ground. I walk until I'm so far away I can't possibly make it home before nightfall without running. Navigating in the dark sucks my remaining stamina so when I do reach the house, I can fall into bed and sleep.

I get a text from Liv in the middle of the night: *Flight was delayed but we finally made it. It's still warm here, feels like a different country. Going to bed. Love you.*

It's my chance to tell her. *Jared knows where you are.* In the quiet of night it seems like an invasion, an attack. So I simply say, *Give her a kiss for me.* And I go back to sleep, sick with helplessness, breathing down the familiar stirring of rage without her body beside me to calm it.

I spend the entire morning in a teeth-grinding stupor doing exactly what I pledged I wouldn't do: dwell on my paranoia. Another walk in the woods tempers it, only for it to return once I'm back indoors. A workout only riles me up worse, so I pick up my phone and dial the number for the American Sign Language expert I found in Kalispell. She's busy and very booked. I set up a meeting at her earliest availability—if Liv and I are going to be Sloane's first exposure to sign language, we need to do it right. She recommends some books; I jot the info down and head to the library. Then I haul my ass over to Tara's to spend the rest of the day with the kids. They keep me busy enough to tame what's going on in my head, and the look Tara gives me when I leave keeps me far away from the scotch that night.

She has the nerve to text me around midnight and ask if I'm home. I let her babysit me all day—the least she could do is pretend I'm capable of being home alone at night. When I fire back, she calls instead of texting again. It's probably more satisfying to chew me out over the phone.

"Settle down," she says. "I'm not trying to harass you."

"That's a first."

"I thought you might be out with Shawn."

I laugh—she's gotten much too optimistic lately.

"Well, never mind, then. Go to bed."

I pick up on an uncertain tone to her voice. Involvement in her relationship with Shawn is the last thing I want, but I'd love to have a reason to start hating the guy again. "What's up?"

"Nothing. Just haven't heard from him for a while. Go to bed, Fearghus. I'm hanging up."

It's all too vague to be anything but an excuse to harass me. I can probably expect this every night until Liv gets home.

I don't sense any oncoming snow so I take the Camaro to my meet-up with Jared. Not that the gained horsepower over my truck matters. I'm not going to need to chase the guy. If he wants to die, he'll get it quickly, before he can back out. Voluntary death hasn't ever weighed on my conscience, and I'm not about to start letting it anytime soon. The Camaro's trunk will be handy for his corpse; it's not as easy to conceal in the open bed of a pickup.

It's much later on the road that I remember why I didn't kill him the first time: to honor Liv's plea not to kill. To make an attempt to be a good man for her. I've been a shit guy for too long to live without exceptions, though, and I just don't see how this is avoidable. Maybe she'll understand that.

The bar is tucked behind a truck stop on the outskirts of Missoula. The cluster of buildings is like an afterthought on the back lot, the bar anchoring it to the pavement so it doesn't slip into the pine forest behind it. I arrive several hours early—a good excuse to scope it out. I holster my SIG under my arm and shrug on my jacket in the parking lot before entering. The lights inside are bright for the lunch crowd, giving it more cheer than a truck stop bar should have. I eat a greasy lunch at the bar and wash it down with ice water while watching the bartender pop tops on beers like I'm a man dying of thirst. When he asks if he can get me anything else, I actually stutter. I pay and get the hell out of there.

After backing the Camaro to the rear of the lot in the shadow of a grove of young ponderosa pine, I sit and watch the road. I imagine Liv in her meeting with Inis. Her calm logic and trusting eyes winning over that black witch. The illusion continues with Liv boarding her plane, Sloane on her hip and that bottle in her pocket. It's so real in my head I wonder if I can see visions like Máthair and Winnie because I'm not that fucking optimistic on my own. Twilight turns the sky orange and violet. A chill creeps into the car. When my ass falls asleep for the third time, I get sick of waiting in the car and go back inside.

The lights are now dim. Low music plays—something mellow and folksy. And Jared's somehow slipped past my surveillance because if that's not him throwing back a shot at the bar then he has a twin. I survey the room for more of them. See nothing but regulars. No fighter's builds. No one who looks to be in Moore employment, biding their time. I know their look like I know my own face.

I walk up behind him.

He turns around. Smiles. Raises a hand for a hand-shake—the chest-high, overfriendly, casual kind. I stare at him long enough for him to give up. He throws back his second shot, tosses some cash on the bar. We walk past the restrooms, out the back door of the bar and into the alley. When the door slams closed, I shove him into the dump-ster before he has a chance to speak. I don't mean to do it. It just feels good. Then I back up and let the prick get his feet back under him. I don't know why I always rush these things. I live for them. Seems more useful to drag it out. Fully experience it.

He smears a hand across the gash on his forehead opened by the corner of the dumpster. "Tara—"

I go for him again. He counters this time, slowing me enough to get a rational thought through my brain. None of them have ever mentioned Tara. I'm not stupid enough to think they don't know about her but if he's calling her by name, it's something I need to pay attention to. I back off, vaguely aware that he's landed a solid punch on my eye that's now affecting my vision. "Tara what?"

He staggers back a step, braces a hand on the dumpster. I've bloodied his nose real great already. He coughs out a good deal of blood. I might have pounded a few ribs—

another premature move that's going to end this too fast. I take my knife out of my pocket and open it. If he doesn't want to answer, I'll carve out his tongue before I kill him. A quick spell at home will wring out what he was going to say, and more.

"We're here to talk about Liv." He grins at me with bloody teeth. "And Sloane."

If he's trying to fuck with me he's succeeding, because now I'm second-guessing what I heard him say. Their names don't even sound alike. "So talk."

"Right about now my brother is—" He crumples under a full-body shudder, falling backward against the dumpster and sliding along its side to the end where he slams into the bar's brick wall.

I grab him by the collar and heave him up. Slam him against the brick again because I like the sound it makes. He goes so quickly slack that I yank him up again, disappointed he's knocked out so fast. But he's not. He's looking at me like he's not sure who I am, is surprised by what I'm doing.

"Tara," he gasps. "Winnie. Will."

Enough. The tongue's coming out, then I'm going to poke a hole in his jugular and let him bleed out while I go get my car for the body. I release him. He slumps to the ground at the same moment there's a tug in my head so powerful I have to take a defensive step back in case he attacks. It feels like Winnie, but it's so strong it has me shaking my head to fling it off. Now's not the time. The vision comes anyway, despite my attempts to block her. It's a third-person view of this alley. Me with my swollen eye, my blood-sprayed shirt, my knife in my hand as I haul Jared to his feet.

Not Jared. Similar build. Very different hair and face. Not Jared but Shawn.

I stumble backward into the side of a parked SUV. Drop my knife. I need earth, exposed earth. I find a crack in the pavement, send a probe in and underneath, through earth to the forest past the parking lot and take a pull of magic that flushes through me. Everything goes vibrant with color all at once so I dial it back, focus it all on Jared.

Shawn.

He's put both hands up in front of him as if shielding me off. I go to my knees, brace forward on my hands. They affected him. So I saw what I expected to see instead of who he was. So I heard what I expected to hear. They know I don't fight with magic. They knew I wouldn't uncover it until it was too late. The guy who searched for me, who dragged me off the side of the road half-dead, who got me home and didn't say a damn thing about it. And I was moments away from killing him.

I get up. I clear my throat. Nothing to say. There's never been anything more fucked up. I offer him a hand and can't blame him for not taking it.

"A mistake," I say. More than a mistake.

"Holy shit, Trey." He's still got this hands in the air. Was probably trying to surrender the whole time and I couldn't see it.

"I thought you were someone else."

"Who the hell did you think I was?!"

My phone's ringing in my pocket. I think it has been for a while. "I couldn't see, couldn't hear you. I didn't—"

He eases himself to his feet, eyes on me, one hand on his knee for support, the other against his bloody nose. I pick up my knife and put it back in my pocket.

"Hey, maybe give that to me."

I hand it to him. There's no other way to prove I'm not going to go crazy again and use it. "Tara can explain."

"That her trying to call you?"

I answer the phone. She's screaming. I'm not even sure in what language, the distortion is so bad.

"What I said about you before?" Shawn says. "A danger to others? Doesn't come close." He holds his ribs. Winces. Shuffles toward me, his hand open for the phone. He puts it to his ear then draws it away, deafened. "Tara, I'm okay. Yeah, I'm okay. He's—yeah." He looks around us, takes in the alley, the building, the parking lot. "I don't know how I got here. Don't even see my truck. Guess I'll hitch a ride home with the guy who just assaulted me. Sounds solid, right?"

She's quiet when I get the phone back. "Tell Winnie I owe her."

"You can tell her yourself. Just get him home. I swear to every element, Fearghus. You keep doing this stuff alone and this is what happens. What you bring on …" She spits out a few curses then the line goes dead.

I go back into the bar and pay the bartender twenty bucks for a bag of ice and a couple clean towels. Shawn's examining his nose in the Camaro's side mirror when I return. I give him the ice and towels, and we get in the car. We circle the lot and the truck stop. His pickup is nowhere in sight. He must've been dumped here by Jared or one of the Moores' guys and he doesn't remember it.

He loads some ice into a towel and holds it against his face. "I knew something was wrong when you were responding to me like you were in a completely different conversation. And how you walked up behind me? No 'hey what are you doing here?' or anything like that. I took you outside so you wouldn't make a scene and get us both thrown in jail. Not so you could break my nose."

"It's not broken."

"That's pure luck, man. God, this headache is kicking my ass." He leans forward in the seat, bleeding into my floorboard.

"You want me to stop somewhere—"

"No, just book it back to Black River. I'd like to get home before you mistake me for someone else again."

CHAPTER 22

LIV

I'M HEADED DOWN the road toward Cathedral Rock, searching the shoulder for a cairn. Only there's no shoulder. It's asphalt then a dirt ditch then scrub, or whatever the people who live here call the prickly green plants that grow out of walls of red rock and encroach on the road. Winter hasn't seemed to touch this place. Inis assured me I wouldn't pass her cairn, and something in her voice made me think she affected it to call out to me as I drove by.

It's hard to keep my eyes on the road, much worse the shoulder, with the magnificence of Cathedral Rock hovering in the distance. And Sloane's been sucking her fingers for a good fifteen minutes. She's not going to last much longer without a meal. When she bleats with frustration, I finally see something that could pass for an actual shoulder. I pull over and park. I go around the red dust-covered rental car and climb into the back seat to feed her. She starts kicking and reaching as soon as she spots me. Driving by myself with her is not my favorite thing. Without being able to hear my voice, she must think I left her alone. It's not easy to drive with one arm twisted behind me so she can hold my hand.

A few minutes later I see the cairn, several feet into the scrub and built with the same red rocks that crumble from the rock walls beside the road. I'd have never spotted it from a moving car.

"Thank you," I say to Sloane, making sure she can see my lips. "You're my smart girl."

She smiles, breaking her latch. I lift her up so she can see outside. The strangeness of the landscape is a surprise to her all over again. She rests her little hand on the window, her eyes wide. She moves her mouth but no sound comes out. She's mimicking something she read on someone's lips. I wish I knew what she was trying to say.

I unload my backpack into the trunk and reload it with bottled water, diapers, and snacks. Both the Glock and the dagger sit there in the pile of things I'm not taking. Then there's the packs of portable magic prepared by Tara: one plastic zipper bag containing a waxy ball I'm supposed to light with a match, another bag with a cluster of dry herbs I'm supposed to squeeze in my fist then hurl at the ground. Staring at all these weapons doesn't make the decision easier. I'm the one who called this meeting. If I show up armed, it will turn this peaceful rendezvous into the confrontation I'm trying to avoid.

I wrap my baby carrier around me and put on a jacket. With Sloane's furry head gently bouncing against me, I head into the vegetation, keeping an eye out for snakes and scorpions. I have no idea if they're out at this time of year, but I'd rather spot them before they spot me. I don't have a pack of coyotes looking out for me here.

When I encounter Inis' motorcycle behind a large cluster of rocks, I know I'm heading the right direction. I stop there beside a set of twisty juniper trunks growing out of cracks they don't seem to fit in, wondering if I should stay and wait for her.

"Hi."

I turn around. She's on the path behind me, hands clasped behind her back.

"Hi. Thanks for meeting me. You were right about the cairn." I wish I could see her hands.

"You're alone?"

"Yes, just Sloane and me."

"Where's Farrelly?"

"At home."

She bends to lift her jeans at the ankle. The sun glints off a blade she holsters above her boot. I wish I could tell her he wouldn't hurt her, but I can't be sure that's the truth. He's been unpredictable lately. It's a relief to see she's comfortable enough around me to not need the knife.

"Caged at home—a very fitting place for him. All of them, really."

"They're not all like him."

"I always wondered why our kind never got along with their kind. I get it now. All that earthy magic turns them into animals."

Sloane is sagging in the carrier, so I lift her higher and tighten the knot. I didn't come here to argue with Inis about the Bevans, or why I've chosen them over her, over my own blood. She's still bitter. I get that. I hope she can put that aside for me.

"Which is why your daughter has so much potential, if only you'd see it."

"I do see it."

"Her dual lines of magic? So you've changed your mind?"

"Do you have the bottle?"

She withdraws it from her jacket pocket and holds it up. With the tiny neck of the bottle pinched between her fingers, it dangles above the rocky ground. Either it's a threat, or she has a sick sense of humor. Everyone at home took a dose of Máthair's shield spell—I made sure of that before I left—except for two. The two who are most important to me.

"It's yours," she says, wrapping her fingers around the bottle for a more secure hold, "if you stay with me and raise her as an O'Dowd."

"I'm not leaving Black River. But if you give me the bottle, I'll be open to visits, maybe lessons, as long as you tell me what you plan to teach her."

"You stay with Farrelly and he'll veto that."

"Trey isn't involved in this. If you and I make a deal, I'll handle him."

Inis spins on her heel toward the road. "You brought someone."

"No, I didn't. I told you—"

"Then why do I sense earth magic? Don't you feel that?" She backs up to a large rock and places a hand on it. "If you lied about Farrelly, I'm going to cut out his heart and convert all his power into mine."

I get a stab of fear that Trey is here, that he followed without telling me. That he's going to sabotage this meeting I've had planned for months. It's our only chance to get the bottle back. Our last chance. If he's here I'll cut out his heart for her.

"Incoming," she says. "Two o'clock."

A man comes around the cluster of rocks and it's Trey I see. I trusted he'd stay put. Not once did I consider having a hard talk with him. Threatening him. After all the shit he's pulled lately, I'm crazy to trust him.

I take a big breath and get a grip. It's not Trey I see at all. It's Dillon. Blond hair lit by the slant of early winter sun, he's smiling like a hunter who just found his trap full of not one victim but two.

"If you're smart, you'll stop there," Inis says.

He stops and puts his hands in the air, grinning like he's playing a game. "What's that?" He cocks his head toward the bottle in Inis' hand.

She's already ignoring him, though, she's so intent on me. Her eyes are pinched in the same way they were that day she tore Trey and Christian up in our kitchen. I'm reliving the scene in the driveway, my split-second chance to stop her, to tell everyone to back down and let Inis and me handle this ourselves. To step away from Trey and Christian, distance myself from the Bevans' world. To join hers.

"Inis—"

"You set me up?" She's dropped to a squat to draw the knife from her ankle, the bottle palmed but still not safe.

"I didn't. He must've followed me here."

She takes her eyes off him to look at me, and I see what her next words are. *So you do know him.*

I don't have to reply. She sees my words too—the short answer, the one that tells a story she's not going to like. Yes, I know him, and so does Trey. It looks exactly like we set her up. She stabs her dagger toward Dillon. A narrow disruption in the air makes a quick beeline toward his leg, and he throws a hand to block it. Too late, by the way his leg buckles and he goes down on one knee, hissing out curses at her. When he looks up the wind shifts. A hard gust shoves me toward Inis, but she's moved away from the rock it would have banged her up against.

She aims her dagger at me. I instinctively wrap my arms around Sloane, even though she said her magic can't hurt us. She may have prepared for that, affected that knife in some way so it could. I can't fight a magic knife. I can only hope it's harmless to our O'Dowd blood or rendered impotent by my amulet. This wasn't supposed to go this way, not a second time, not when I left Trey a thousand miles behind me so he couldn't start a fight. Not in the middle of a state where the Moores never set foot.

"I didn't set you up, Inis. He's after me. I have no idea how he knew I'd be here."

She backs away, leveling her blade between Dillon and me. He's too busy trying to stop his bleeding to do anything else to her. If she hit the femoral artery, he's in trouble. As much as I hate everything he and his family have done, I can't stand here and watch him die.

"Inis—"

She's retreated to her motorcycle. I watch her put on her helmet and gloves just like that day she left the house. Something moves in my peripheral vision: a slinking figure, low to the ground, but with more mass than the scrubby evergreens trembling in the wind. I spare a glance away from Inis and spot a coyote moving in. Another behind it. I turn; more coyotes to my left. The motorcycle engine fires up and she's riding away, leaving an absence that's now being smoothly and quietly filled by at least twenty coyotes. Dillon and I are surrounded, and I don't know whose side they're on.

Dillon is knotting his jacket around his leg for a tourniquet. I don't know how much blood volume he lost. When it's a stain soaked into the dry desert ground, it's hard to tell how thick the puddle is. He attempts to stand. Shakes his head as if staving off unconsciousness. Lowers himself back to the ground. "Liv?"

Knowing I'd be crazy to help him, I take my chances with the coyotes. They part for me and fill my wake with a line of furry bodies and upright ears, assuring me it's my side they're on, and they're building a wall between me and him. Back at the car I drag a large dead branch into the middle of the road. I call 911 and tell the operator there's a man bleeding to death just off the road heading toward Cathedral Rock, his position marked by a branch in the road.

With Sloane strapped into her seat in the back I make a U-turn, but I don't make it a minute down the road before I've turned around again and parked in the same spot by the cairn. I shove my little first aid kit that's useless for a wound like his into my backpack. Sloane giggles against her fist on our run back to Dillon, thinking I'm playing the game where I bounce her around the yard just to hear that rare giggle. When I throw my jacket on the ground and lay her on it, she squeals at the sky. I push his hands away from the tourniquet he's still trying to adjust and undo the knot. He's positioned it wrong anyway. I rip open the hole in his pants for a better view of his leg. "Not the femoral."

"Is that good?"

"Yes." I take a bottle of water from my backpack and dump it over the wound to wash out the dirt he's already gotten in it. He hisses and pounds the ground. "Stop moving." It's a relief to see a slow weep of new blood instead of a firehose. If it had been the femoral he'd already be dead.

"Don't you know any Bevan healing spells?"

I rip open a package of gauze and cover the worst of the wound. "Direct pressure. Here, like this." I take his hand and position it. "No tourniquet. And don't remove the gauze. Just keep holding pressure."

A glance at Sloane shows coyotes closing in again. I hand him the pain reliever out of my first aid kit and what remains of the bottle of water. "Stay here. Help is on the way. You should probably start thinking of a good story, one that doesn't involve me or..." I pick up Sloane and shake out my jacket to cover the pause "...my friend."

"Friend?"

"And if you tell anyone I helped you, I'll deny it."

"Seeing you with her—" His face softens and he reaches for Sloane. I stand and step back, out of his reach. He lowers his hand and stares at the ground. "It reminds me of good times. Our lives were good, Liv, and I wish ..."

I turn and walk away from him, blocking his voice like the poison it is.

Sloane mouths silent words on my walk back to the car, watching my lips to see if I'll do it back. I can't look at her, not while the weight of what I just did is crashing down so hard. Dillon followed me here to do what? Take Sloane? Hurt her? Hurt me? And knowing this, I just tried to save his life anyway.

I return to the car and drive back to the highway, my focus on the horizon, tears welling but wiped away before they can run. I'd prepared for failure on this trip; I knew there was a chance I wouldn't get the bottle back. But I never could have imagined my coming here would alert the Moores of its presence and make its danger to us so much worse. I can't decide if my help—my oblivious, insane, and undeserved kindness—will cause him to choose to forget what he just saw. Will spare us. Or if it simply proves my failure to protect my daughter from the people who want her dead.

Catching sight of Trey in the airport at home sets my feet running, and I collide with him and hold on, my bag slipping from my shoulder and hitting the floor at my feet. His breath warms a spot against my hair that spreads through me, into that heart of his he claims lives inside me, shocking it back into rhythm. Sloane squeals and paws at him; he peels her from the baby wrap holding her against me.

I watch him talking to her. She pats his face, over and over, looking from him to me like he's a found person. A person we'd lost. He fingerspells her name. She starts patting his hand. He breaks into a smile, but it looks more earned than spontaneous. And very pained. Our absence was hard on him, and it was all for nothing. My trip has put us in a worse position, not a better one.

During the plane ride home I decided there's no way to head off the Moores. They're the proactive ones, the side who chooses to continue this fight. Unless we decide to commit to the war as heartily as they have, we'll never overpower them. A good defense is what we should perfect, and staying together, working together, is the only way to achieve it.

He drapes an arm around me, drawing me close for a kiss. I don't realize how long it's lasted until he's broken it and started grinning again. "We're in public, woman."

"That was all you."

"Getting me in trouble with state troopers is one thing. Now the TSA?"

"Oh my god, really? You're the one who parked in that abandoned lot. Not me."

"You made me do it."

I give him a promise-of-pain glare as I pick up my bag. The airport is not the ideal place to make him take those words back. Or prove how true they are, and how much I can make him do.

He shifts Sloane to his opposite arm so he can hold my hand as we walk to the exit. He doesn't ask any details about my trip, and I don't offer them—just like I didn't offer anything specific that day when I called him to say I didn't get the bottle and I was coming home, defeated, finished. I've put the need to recover that bottle behind me along with Inis herself and the family I've longed to learn more about. The more I try to mold that missing family into my life, the less it fits. If I'm meant to know more about my birth family, the truth will find me and I'll be ready and open to it. Until then, I'm a Gilchrist, but I'm no longer in the void I've lived most of my life in. I'm also a Bevan, fighting alongside them until this war is over. I've found my place and there's nowhere I'd rather be.

That night in bed he takes a fistful of my hair like he's been starved of me, as impatient and frantic as he was that first night so long ago when he kissed me in the kitchen after we shared a carton of ice cream and he killed someone in his front yard. I kiss him back until neither of us can catch our breath. Then he moves down my cheek to my ear, my neck, my chest, his lips hot over my heart. If his heart lives inside me, it's trained mine to respond to him, beating in rhythm of his lips on my skin.

I get a flash of an image so out of context I grab his head to stop him: Dillon, spotting that bottle in Inis' hand. Trey has to know the new danger we're in so he's prepared. I have to tell him.

He's gone up on his arms, holding his weight off me to study my face. "What?"

"I have some bad news."

"Can it wait?"

"Dillon ambushed Inis and me. We met in the middle of the desert, and he somehow knew how to find us. He saw the bottle. He knows about it."

He's still looking into my eyes but his have gone unfocused, and I wonder if being trapped underneath him and caged between two pillars of his arms is a good place to deliver this news. I lay a hand on his chest; he flinches, jolted back to reality. I could speak to fill the roaring silence but there's nothing else to say. He created the danger in that bottle; I lured our enemy to it. Our blame of each other is neutralized by our blame of ourselves.

He rolls off me and sits on the edge of the bed. "I had a chance to kill him and I didn't take it."

"So did I."

"It's not your job." He looks up, toward the door, his intention as obvious as if it's playing out before us.

"You're not going back there. Don't even think about it."

"I have some bad news too."

My stomach sinks into the mattress. I sit up. Alcoholism, black magic, murder—there can't be anything worse than all the bad habits he's recently tamed. Unless he's fallen off one of those wagons while I was gone. I can't decide which would be worst.

"I beat the shit out of Shawn. Almost killed him."

He doesn't look at me. I grab his arm to make him. I have to see what's on his face because his words are too flat to tell if he's exaggerating. He dips his head, closes his eyes. I jerk his arm to get his attention, but he's unresponsive, just a rigid statue absorbing my demands.

"The Moores affected him. I saw him as Jared. I didn't know he was Shawn until ..."

"Until what? Is he okay?"

He nods, wiping his face down with both hands. I lay a hand on his shoulder and in the next moment he's twisted and snatched it. "Can we finish this?"

With his face inches from mine we stay that way. I don't know what he sees in my eyes that keeps him glued, but I do know what I see in his: a fiery mix of so much hate, vengeance, grief, and defiance that my need to quell it with love is strong enough to shut every thought down but the ones that latch my arms around his neck and crush my mouth on his. He's back on the bed with me, raising my legs around his waist. My head bangs against the headboard; I brace my hands against it to gain some space. He flips me over. Trails a slow finger down my backbone from neck to tailbone then plants a hard kiss on the small of my back. It's a tingly burst of magic up my spine, straight into my brain. A stake of claim. I want to turn over and tell him I'm his, not to feel threatened by any mention of Dillon. But then he kisses the same spot, gentler this time, the fizzle of magic settling where his heart lives inside me, and I realize there's no need to tell him something he already knows. That stake of claim is only a reminder to himself, to plant his feet and right his world when it spirals out of control.

I become aware that he's drawn away, leaving my back exposed to cold air. What's more distracting is the hum in my ears, a vibration that's all around but also inside me. I turn over. He's watching me, expectant, like something's been unveiled and he's waiting for me to respond. Dust motes swarm in the beam of moonlight beside him but they're more like glitter, rainbow-colored and reflective. And that hum—it's now more present outside, and it has a sense of movement to it, a force. Alive.

"Sorry," he says. "That was an accident."

He looks stricken, like he's not sure what I'll do. I reach into the dust motes. The disturbance of air does nothing to alter their movement. I turn my hand, expecting to capture them, but they reflect off my palm like fragments of light. They're not dust motes at all. They're the moonlight itself.

I sit up so fast I almost bang his forehead with mine.

"Sorry," he says again. "It'll stop in a minute."

Those kisses felt like magic because that's exactly what they were.

I slide out of bed and go to the window. That hum is fading and the moonlight is turning normal again. "What's that thing, that vibration outside?"

He doesn't answer until I turn around and look at him. His pupils are huge.

"The elements."

If this force I sense outside like a blanket of life is what he's a part of, I now understand it's more than water and sunlight and wind. It's the pressure of air under the clouds. The movement of every individual creature on land, sky, and water. The slow curl of the river around the house. Every growing tree, every falling leaf. It's more than a few pieces of the puzzle that make up nature. It's the totality of it. The earth. The universe. The awareness of all of that in constant motion, a harmony of perfection. With my feet against the wooden floorboards, I feel the pull of it like a current that's traveling through the floor, into the stone foundation and out into the earth. "This is what you feel?"

"When I tune in."

"And you just tuned me in with you?"

"By accident." He balls the sheet in his fist, watching it happen as if all effort is going into that one motion. "It helps me focus sometimes. Settle my mind."

"Can you do it again?"

He looks up at me, his eyes harsh. "No."

"Why not?"

"It changes you. It's not you."

It's the same thing he said about Sloane when we discussed hearing aids and cochlear implants and schools for the Deaf. He insisted she's perfect, and whatever shortcomings we think she has won't be shortcomings if we learn how to teach her to succeed in our world like we'd teach any child. And I believe him.

CHAPTER 23

TREY

I HIRE A CREW in the spring to tear off the end of the house and build two extra bedrooms. It's a slugfest with Liv when she finds out she's not getting a second bathroom, but I'm not going to run plumbing for another bathroom in a house that holds only three people.

"It's a luxury we don't need," I tell her when she's glaring at me across the breakfast table.

"A tiny second bathroom in a small cabin is a luxury? Not even close. What you were raised in was luxury."

"Which is how I know we don't need it."

Sloane bangs on her highchair tray—one of her many signals to tell us to sign so she's not left out of the conversation. Liv takes a gentle hold of one of her hands to stop her. *Don't bang*, she signs while speaking the words. *Tell us what you want.* Liv looks at me, expecting me to sign, *Okay, I'll build a bathroom.*

Eggs are so good, I sign. *I'm going to be the first one to eat them all.* I take an enthusiastic bite.

Sloane looks at the mess she's made of scrambled eggs on her tray.

"You're a pain in my ass," Liv says to me.

"I aim to please."

"What if I want another baby? That would bring the household up to four."

I burst out laughing. "You're not getting another baby."

Three years later I'm with a team of coyotes sweeping the woods for threats while Tara and Máthair help Liv give birth again. I can't make sense of how I won the bathroom argument but lost the baby one. She clearly didn't want the bathroom badly enough. If she did, we'd have that too. I don't know how the hell she always gets what she wants.

"None of the names we picked fit him," she says when I'm sitting beside her, my head resting against a tree trunk, our new son in her arms.

Tara and Máthair left long ago to relieve Shawn of babysitting the three older kids. Liv and I have stayed for the sunrise. It's now spilling over the mountain, marking the first day of our brand new hell: keeping not one child safe from the Moores, but two. His sister may be the one they want, but they live to destroy the people and things I care about. When they find out I have a son, they'll be ecstatic at the idea of torturing a child so similar to me all over again. These years of peace will be broken, and they'll prove there was no peace on their end. They've been using the time to prepare. Well, so have we.

"Marcas," I say. It wasn't on our list. It was her father's name.

She's quiet for a long time—so long when she speaks she wakes me from a doze.

"He looks like a Marcas."

The summer sun's fully on us now, making me sweat. "Then that's it."

"Marcas Fearghus Bevan."

"That's too much of a mouthful. And Fearghus is a crap name. Too hard to spell."

"It's perfect."

She gets everything she wants. And every day I wish I could give her more.

Marcas passes his hearing test a few days later, and I let out a breath I'd been holding since he was born. Stupid, since Sloane's deafness isn't genetic. It was caused by me. I can't undo it, but I will fix it. My AA meetings have been replaced by one-on-one lessons with Rebecca, the American Sign Language expert in Kalispell who managed to cram Sloane and me into her calendar as soon as I told her what I'd pay her. What Sloane and I learn we teach to everyone else. It's a brain-consuming task that keeps me from thinking too much about all I have that the Moores could take. How long it's been since they've sent someone after me. What they could be planning. The payback I owe

Dillon for killing my father. And the scotch in my cabinet that could dull it all so well.

The only exception from my one drink a week rule are my occasional drinks at the pub with Shawn, a tradition started after I almost beat him to death in an alley. I buy; he makes sure I'm sober before I get behind the wheel. It's a symbiotic relationship, useful for grilling him about his childhood and his mother until he convinced me he's not the kind of Moore who'd be a threat. His mother was taken in by Bevans and has been estranged too long from the Moores to have any power at all. He knows so little because there's so little to tell. I still don't like the guy, but he's growing on me. Like mold.

I'm returning from the pub on a day chilled by the first evidence of fall when I notice headlights in my rearview mirror following me down the driveway. Dusk settles earlier now—I need to start leaving the pub before we lose so much light around the house. I don't want anyone to have an easier time sneaking up when I'm not home. There's nothing stealthy about the car behind me—it's coming with a purpose. At the bend we lose the shadow of the trees long enough for me to take a quick inventory: Audi sedan, Michigan plates, older male driver, no other visible passengers. He must be lost. Hoping for help with directions before night hits.

As we near the house, he hangs back a bit, maybe realizing for the first time he's on someone's private drive and is about to get shot. I consider the SIG stashed under my seat, decide to leave it so the poor guy doesn't piss himself. I park behind Tara's CR-V—looks like she, Máthair, and the kids are over for dinner. And no doubt helping Liv. I don't know who's the bigger handful: the four-year-old or the four-month-old.

The Audi has stopped in the driveway thirty feet behind me when I get out of the truck. I start toward him. A few steps later I halt—my senses lurch from the alcohol-induced calm too fast for my blunted brain to catch up. The ring of common magic is too potent to be coming from someone in the house. In a heartbeat the SIG is in my hand, pointed at the driver now stepping out of the car. He doesn't flinch. He comes toward me, raising one hand in the air. The other arm is unnaturally stiff and still. Molded to an unmoving shape. Prosthetic.

"Killing me once wasn't enough?" he says.

It's a voice that goes with a different face, a face I'm not seeing until I blink and the one I remember fills the face in front of me. The last time I saw it, splattered in blood, contorting as I drove a knife into his shoulder—

Someone speaks behind me. "Paul?"

I turn. Máthair's on the porch, hands covering her mouth. She steps into the grass, walking, gaining speed. His one good arm lowers to reach for her. When they come together, he's forced to step back to absorb her motion. I readjust my aim for his head. I no longer have a clear shot of his chest.

"*Tá brón orm,*" Paul says, "*Tá brón orm,*" over and over as Máthair holds on, her cheek against his chest.

When she finally steps back, she takes his face in her hands, staring, shaking her head at him. He takes a glance at me, raises that one good arm high again. "I think your son wants to finish what he started twenty years ago."

"He's just surprised to see a person come back from the dead." She turns to look at me. "Put it down, Fearghus."

"You need to back away from him."

"I'll do no such thing." She places a hand on the prosthetic arm as if confirming it's true.

"They couldn't save the arm. I told them I could live without it."

"You can't play piano anymore." She takes his good hand with both her own. "I mourned for you, for so long."

"I know. I wished every day I could've called you, but it wasn't safe. For me, for you, or for Trey." He levels a look at me so weighted it has me lowering the gun. As the blood rushes back into my arm, I'm confronted by conflicting images of my past. The times I counted on him, the times he let me down. The poisonous mix of who he was to me, to my mother, to Christian. Our friend one day, our enemy the next. Too many things I can't forgive. And what I did to end it, what I've had to live with, what I accepted as reality, as my unchangeable past.

Fingers pry the SIG from my grip. Liv's beside me, replacing that gun with her hand. She's diluting that poisonous gloom of ever-present death that surrounds me, like she always does.

Now Paul's in front of me, offering a handshake with the arm he has left. I stare at the hand. I stare at him.

"I haven't spent a second in the presence of a Moore since the day you left me dying on the rug."

"You should be dead."

"I would be, if your father hadn't hauled me off to a group of people who thought I was worth saving."

My father couldn't have found him in time before he bled out. "Group of what people?"

He looks at Máthair. "Bevans."

She places a hand on her chest. "No one ever said a thing to me."

"They decided that was best."

"We buried you, Paul."

"You buried a lot of people that day. They might've noticed the old man's body missing, but not mine. Martin fudged it anyway. He made me give him my clothes. I think he had an extra corpse lying around."

"Martin knew you weren't dead?"

"It was his idea for me to disappear." He looks away from us, pulling his hand from Máthair's grip that had found him again when I declined the handshake. "I heard about Martin. I'm sorry, Sloane." Instead of facing her when he turns back around, he focuses on me. "I also heard about Pierce. So if you keep a list of all the Moores you've killed, you can scratch me off."

"What makes you think I'm not going to kill you?"

"You would've done it by now."

He's right, and I don't know why I didn't shoot him and drag his body away the moment I realized who he was. Whatever stopped me is given a jolt of power by Liv squeezing my hand. By her presence beside me. All my work at being a good man for her, of being worthy of her and our kids. Years of it will go to shit if I'd acted on an impulse I'd later regret.

I killed Paul that day because I was high on power and fixed on making them pay for all they'd done. He got it because he was one of them, but if I'd taken the time to think I'd come to realize he was a victim just like me. He didn't deserve it.

"Trey," he says. "It's behind us. I forgive you."

This time it's me who offers the handshake, and it's him who accepts it before pulling me into a hug I return. If this unclenching ball in my gut and dizzy swarm in my head is what forgiveness feels like, it's some twisted shit. Maybe it'd be less intense if it wasn't double-sided.

After our ASL session with Rebecca, I stop in town with Sloane and Winnie to pick up some groceries. Winnie's been joining us for lessons because she's proven to be the quickest learner and the best teacher for Will, who has no attention span for me or Tara but sucks knowledge off Winnie like they share a brain.

While I unbuckle Sloane, Winnie hops from the truck and walks the crack in the pavement to the sidewalk with the grocery list she made for me on the drive. She's too patient for an eight-year-old. Too helpful. I was such a little shit at that age. I don't know why Máthair didn't leave me at the Moore estate and not look back.

I sense a presence and glance up. Winnie's been joined by someone in uniform. The new sheriff, from what I can tell. I set Sloane on her feet and take her hand.

"Saw another fellow in a fancy car heading down to your place yesterday," he says. "Seems you're collecting quite a crowd out there. Not breaking any occupancy codes, are you?"

I'm not going to answer that. Especially since he sounds like he's adding to a conversation I never had with him. It's a power move. A dangle of information above my head like a piece of bait he wants me to bite. He doesn't seem to like my non-reaction because he's swiftly dropped that chummy grin.

"Interesting how you went from recluse to family guy overnight," he continues. "Polygamy isn't legal here, brother."

If I wasn't holding Sloane's little hand, the urge to throat-punch the guy would be too hard to stifle. Then I'd have a real mess on my hands. "You talking about my mother and my sister?"

"Ah, just giving you a hard time." He ruffles Winnie's hair. She frowns up at him, combing it back into place.

Sloane pulls on my arm. I pick her up.

"How's that new truck treating you?"

Sloane starts patting my chest. She wants me to sign so she can follow the conversation. I'm not going to include her in something that's about to turn ugly. "It's four years old."

"It looks like you just drove it off the dealer's lot. I can guess how much it set you back. Lots of folks around here could buy a house with that kind of money. Hell, two houses."

I've had my share of run-ins with law enforcement, just never here in Black River. Looks like that's about to change. For once it won't be my fault.

So I don't do something to make it my fault, I snag Winnie's shirt and she follows me into the grocery store. Every time she glances over her shoulder at the sheriff we left on the sidewalk, I turn her head forward. Keeping her moving is a great distraction to my anger. I won't let it get on top of me. The last time that happened I almost killed Shawn. Before that, I almost killed myself. Nothing good ever comes of it. I set Sloane on her feet, and Winnie hands me her list. "Was that policeman being rude?"

"No, he was being an asshole." I rip a bag off the dispenser and start loading it with apples.

She smacks a hand over her shocked smile.

"Remind me to ask Rebecca to teach us that sign," I say. "It's not fair to leave Sloane out of this stuff."

Winnie giggles and signs to Sloane: *Your dad said a bad word.*

Poop? Sloane asks.

I tie a knot to close my bag of apples and watch them leaning in, their faces close, giddy about the worst word they know. Their innocence is such a conflict to all that's in my head. All I know. All I've done. Moments like these remind me and put a weakness in my bones, a dread in my stomach. It doesn't take long before both feelings are consumed by a surge of anger—their innocence won't be taken by the Moores. I'll train them to fight it off before they'll need to. They'll be ready. My anger will be converted to fuel something good, not something bad.

"Hello, Winifred." A woman has joined us by the apples.

"Hi, Ms. Presler." Winnie fingerspells her name for Sloane, who's shyly shrunk behind her.

"This must be your little cousin. And your …?" The woman turns toward me.

"My Uncle Fearghus," Winnie says.

I offer a hand. "Trey."

"Your niece here is quite a student. She sure surprises me sometimes. She can predict the weather better than any meteorologist. And that tree limb? I just don't know how she knew it would fall. Someone on the playground could've been very hurt if it weren't for her." She reaches to squeeze Winnie's shoulder.

I give Winnie a hard look. She might be a hero, but she's failing at something equally important—keeping us undercover. It's been drilled into all the kids so much I wonder if they've become complacent. We don't need to give that sheriff any more abnormalities to scrutinize. There's nothing around here to keep him occupied. He's trying to nose out trouble.

Winnie opens her mouth, ready to fib. I can imagine what she'll say. *I saw it breaking loose. I heard the wood snapping.* Bullshit, and she knows it. She doesn't need to probe my brain to know it's a bad idea to dig herself any deeper with me, and what she sees on my face has her snapping that mouth closed.

I don't bring it up again until we're back in the truck moving down the road. "Tell me that tree limb would've killed someone so I can let you off the hook."

"It was going to hurt Brian and Joshua."

"Hurt. Not kill?"

She doesn't answer, which is answer enough. We've had this discussion many times. I launch into it again, and she groans, thoroughly annoyed she has to endure it again.

"Say it, Winnie. *I won't use my abilities unless people are dying.*"

She groans again, reciting it mechanically. I catch her eyes in the mirror—resolute, defiant. If she had her way, we'd be offering spells to the public as a community service. She has no idea what a small town would think if they knew the truth about us. That sheriff would love a good reason to pay us a visit and take a close look around. There are plenty of bodies still buried on my property, and I'd rather they stay that way.

"Chill out," Tara says later when I'm dropping Winnie off. "So what if they think Winnie has some psychic gift? There's no way they can prove anything."

"I don't want the attention."

"No one stones witches anymore, Fearghus. No one believes in them either."

"No, but they do believe in murder, and they sure as hell won't have a problem throwing me in jail when they find a ton of corpses on my land."

"Maybe you should stop killing people, then."

My boots crunch the fresh layer of ice back to my truck still running to keep Sloane warm inside. What Tara suggested has already happened. I haven't killed anyone in years, and for the first time in my life, I don't miss it.

CHAPTER 24

LIV

After days on the road, we're parking in the same clearing in the middle of the Illinois woods where we parked so many years ago for Mamó's funeral. I unload Sloane and Marcas from the back seat and wrestle Sloane into her brown robe, made new for this occasion. For Marcas, we brought a blanket in the same fabric. He hasn't yet turned one year old and has a strong dislike of all clothes. He's perfectly content in a diaper and a blanket he can toss away whenever he pleases.

Máthair takes Marcas so I can slide into my own robe. Then we're all on the trail, Trey and Tara in the lead, Sloane riding on Trey's shoulders. Máthair, Marcas, and I are next, with Winnie and Will behind us, running to catch up. Warm patches of sunlight filter through openings in the canopy above. Spring is moving closer to summer here, unlike at home where the ground hasn't yet thawed. We stop to don our oak leaf crowns where they amass under the wide spread of branches of the same grand oak I remember from our last trip here. Winnie drops to a squat, settling her palms beside bare feet as if hungry for a larger bite of whatever power resides here.

Trey swings Sloane to the ground. Her big eyes take in the rise of the oak, following it to its full height before she walks to its trunk and lays a hand against it. Then she reaches for me, hoping to share the experience. Even though I won't feel what she feels, I join her anyway. The smile on her face is experience enough.

We bring a hush to the crowd when we arrive to the gathering. The sea of brown robes stills, all faces turned to us. This is not our special day, but we've stolen the crowd, just as we did the last time we came here. As if sensing why all eyes are on us, Sloane recoils behind Trey's legs. He picks her up, and she buries her face in his neck.

Christian emerges from the crowd dressed in a white tunic with embroidered collar and loose pants. His smile couldn't be more radiant even though we've just stolen his show. "Way to make an entrance," he says, throwing an arm around Trey's shoulders and turning him so he and Sloane fully face the crowd. "Now smile."

The clearing erupts—voices, applause, stomping feet. It's such a storm of noise Marcas covers his ears. And Sloane—she's been roused from her shyness to face her people. They've waited generations to meet her, and now she's here, watching their excitement with silent wonder. Unaware of her fame. Her power.

Christian offers her his arms, and she reaches toward him, her eyes still taking in the throng of faces glued to her. We follow him through the crowd as the noise dies, settling into normal conversation.

"Where's your bride?" Tara asks.

Christian points to a break in the surrounding trees. I hand Marcas off to Trey, and Tara, Máthair, Winnie, and I head that way. Just inside the wall of trees is a small cluster of women. Bethany sits on a blanket in white cotton sheath dress. The neckline and bell sleeves are embroidered with the same pattern as Christian's tunic. Two women braid a crown of miniature daises into her hair.

"Oh!" she says, standing to hug Máthair then Tara. "And Liv," she says. "What a relief to see you. It's hard being the only outsider here."

"You are no outsider," Máthair says.

Bethany takes Máthair's outstretched hand. "And to think Christian and I were going to get married in Vegas. Thank you for changing our minds. I just didn't realize a Bevan wedding was so …"

"Unconventional?" I offer.

She grins. "Earthy."

Years ago, Christian dropped all his family secrets on her in one big intervention just like Trey did to me. He expected her to run. He was wrong.

Máthair links her arm with Bethany's and leads her toward the clearing. The rest of us follow, ushered by the crowd to the front of the wide semicircle of packed bodies all clad in brown where Trey is already waiting with

Marcas and Sloane. The hum of voices quiets as Máthair and Bethany meet Christian in front of the flat stone altar.

The earth itself seems to hush for one drawn-out moment before Christian takes Bethany in his arms and hugs her so long and hard she starts tapping him on the back for release. Máthair takes him by the arm, and he steps quickly back, making a display of straightening and brushing himself off. As usual, his humor is a cover for stronger feelings and now that his attempt to gain solemnity fails due to the smile he can't put away, I'm sure everyone in the clearing can see how wildly he loves this woman. How lucky he feels to have her back after so much heartbreak. He wears the face of a man in a dream hoping he'll never wake up.

I have to look away. I'm tearing up and I don't want to cry. But then I meet Tara's teary gaze and we laugh, her elbowing me and me elbowing her back.

Máthair joins Christian's hand with Bethany's and winds a garland of fern around them, crisscrossing in a pattern that must be magic due to its complexity. Once finished she raises their joined arms and the clearing fills with a cheer louder than the one that greeted our arrival.

A carpet of wild geraniums blooms around Christian and Bethany like an optical illusion. Green stalks rise, purple petals open, and Bethany looks at her feet, taking in the new flowers with disbelief. Trey has gone very still beside me with his hands held straight at his sides and his eyes intent on those flowers coming alive. He breaks his attention, taking a breath he must've been holding.

"Did you just—"

He puts a finger to his lips.

Aaron joins them up front, along with Bethany's son. Two grown men, best friends for years and now brothers. Christian steps forward to scan the crowd for one more: his own brother, the one who reunited him with Bethany, the one responsible for all the good here.

Trey raises his hood and steps backward, blending into the crowd. I catch Christian's eye so I can point him out, but when I turn to locate Trey in hiding he's disappeared completely. I wish it was only humility, but I know it's not. The man still doesn't feel worthy of his own good deeds. He led his family into a triumph against the Moores— they tried to keep Christian and Bethany apart, but Trey broke that down. He pushed for love, helped prove it always wins, and we've gathered to celebrate that win, to absorb it, to allow it to power us for the next fight. It's an accomplishment he's taught himself not to recognize, not to own.

I ask Trey later if there's any significance to the wild geraniums he grew at Christian and Bethany's feet. "Do they hold any meaning?"

"We believe they bring peace."

With this answer I know our victory isn't just a win for love over hate, but also a march toward peace.

Several years after Christian and Bethany's wedding, I'm opening the back door to send Sloane and Marcas outside. Another spring has finally found our low plot of land between the mountains, bringing recently returned birdsong in its warmth. Each winter I never realize so many birds are missing until they return the next year. The silent, near-arctic landscape of winter has been transformed by the birds hopping between limbs, creating rain from the melting ice.

Marcas turns around to wave before tromping down the stairs after Sloane. At four years old, with his square, strong shoulders and long legs he'll hopefully grow into, he's a perfect little version of his dad, even more evident now that Trey's taking him to his barber in town. They come home with matching haircuts and matching smiles—Marcas' lighthearted and effortless, Trey's weighted by the years it took to earn it, the other life it struggled to survive, its rebirth from the dead.

Sloane inherited my small frame and mess of thick hair that won't be tamed. If I didn't know what a sound sleeper she was, I'd think she was tossing and turning and building up static electricity all night for the stuck-her-finger-in-light-socket look she wakes up with every day. We braid it and pin it, and she comes back from playing outside missing all the pins and looking like a feral child. She's a trilingual eight-year-old—she's fluent in ASL and can read and write English and Irish. And she's had more martial arts training than most adults. Both she and her brother are learning everything Trey learned as a child, and they attend special one-on-one lessons with a Chinese martial arts teacher three days a week in Kalispell. Between that and school, sometimes I wonder if she's overburdened.

The little spare time they have is spent roaming the woods. Marcas is finally old enough to reliably follow his very watchful big sister's direction. She can't hear the trouble he might get in, but she doesn't need to. Their animal entourage has better hearing than any human ear. Sloane doesn't need human language to communicate with them. It's all in her head—and theirs. I asked her once how she does it, and she replied, *I just listen.* It's hard to imagine she knows the meaning of the word, but sometimes I think she listens better than all of us, to things we will never hear.

I go downstairs and take a seat at Trey's workbench. He looks up from his scribbled spell words. "What's that look?"

"Before you do a mind share with Sloane, I have to tell you something."

He goes back to paging through one of his texts. "Go."

"Remember when you did one with me and things you probably didn't want to share leaked into my mind?"

He halts his page flipping to glare through the workbench. "Things like what?"

"Memories, impulses … bits of personality that tried to make a home in my head. I didn't let them, but she's so young …"

He sits heavily on the stool next to me, letting the text fall back against the table with a thump.

"I'm not trying to persuade you not to do it, I just wanted to remind you. I don't think I ever told you exactly—"

Ali the cat jumps onto the table, somehow avoiding every beaker and apothecary bottle in the cluster on top.

"You mentioned it. You didn't give any detail."

"The memories aren't something I wanted to bring up."

"Or something I want anywhere near Sloane's head." He shoves the text, knocking down two empty beakers that roll against Ali's haunch. She watches them rotate to a stop, unsurprised, unrattled. "Would've been a handy way to teach her a ton of stuff, but now I see it's not worth it. She'll have to continue learning the normal way."

Which is more hours of training every day without end. No breaks. No excuses. Since it's been going on since before she could remember, she never complained, never questioned it. She has Winnie and Will's level of skill to aspire to, and she's making it there in record time. Because she inherited Trey's healing ability, muscle fatigue heals in hours, allowing her to train more often and harder than a normal child. Nothing would cause her to question something that's such a part of our lives, but I have a hunch something's changed. "Is she burning out?"

"She's asking questions."

Questions we're not ready to answer. So little activity from the Moores has turned our lives almost normal, those answers nearly absurd. If we were under constant attack like we used to be, there would be nothing to explain. She'd be living it; she'd already understand it.

"Are you going to tell her?"

He looks at me but he's far away, wrestling with a decision I'm leaving to him. He's told me how he resented his father for waiting so long to tell him things he wondered as a child. Now he's on the other side—the parent, the protector. He must understand his father a little better now, and the lines in his forehead prove how much it bothers him that these new insights can't be shared with the man who raised him. "Not yet."

I know part of the reason for his wait: he hopes she'll overcome her social phobia. He doesn't want to load any more worries onto her before she's tamed her fear of a world she can't easily communicate in without us.

He bows his head, rubbing the back of his neck. "She can't speak spell words."

It takes a moment for me to realize what a big thing I missed. I've seen Trey cast enough magic to know the spells often involve spoken words—something Sloane is unable to do.

"It's not a deal-breaker to what we do," he says. "It's just another limitation."

I squeeze his arm. "She'll overcome it. She finds ways around limitations."

"It's one more thing he'll have over her."

He meaning Rex Moore. I'd remind him she's destined to win, but all he'll do is remind me that even if she wins there's no prediction she survives. And I'll say there's no prediction she dies either. It's a well-rehearsed routine that never reaches any other conclusion. So I skip all that and slide my arms around him instead. He leans into me, his rough cheek against my forehead.

"I'll talk to Winnie," he says, pressing me against him. "She'll have to teach Sloane to project her mind."

"Will it work?"

"It fucking has to."

I go upstairs and find Marcas on the back porch by himself.

"Where's your sister?"

"She told me to go home and wait for her." He always signs as he speaks, even when Sloane isn't around. We've all asked him why and his answer is always the same: *She might be watching us.* She hasn't shown any evidence of sharing Winnie's foresight, but if she ever were to see our future selves in a vision, our signing would sure make things easier.

I walk to the porch railing to see if I can spot her. "What's she doing?"

He joins my side and shrugs. "Don't know. I'm hungry."

Thirty minutes later Sloane still hasn't returned, and I tell myself thirty minutes is nothing abnormal. It only feels that way because Marcas is usually with her. They've stayed away longer than that several times this week alone. I holler to Trey; he comes upstairs trying very hard to not be alarmed, but he sets right off with Marcas, heading for the trail they took earlier. River and Trib stampede across the yard in their direction.

I text Tara: *Sloane at your house?*

She replies right away: *No, what's up?*

She's been in the woods a while, and Marcas isn't with her. Trey just took Marcas and the dogs to look for her.

Should we come?

No, we're probably overreacting. He'll find her.

I make lunch and text Trey. His phone dings from the other room. I stand on the porch and watch the treetops bending in the breeze. I put lunch away. At the two hour mark, Tara calls. I tell her I know nothing more, that Trey left his phone at home so I can't call him. She and I talk each other out of a panic, and I hang up and go outside looking for coyotes. They'd know where Sloane is. I'm not sure how I'd ask though, or how I'd tell them to go find Trey so they can help with the search.

The sun has heated the yard and burned the fog off the covers of Trey's cold frames. Sprouts he started in the house reach upward from inside. He and Sloane transplanted them a few days ago and they've already doubled in size. Beyond the garden, the land he cleared for sparring ground sits abused, like it withstands stampeding animals every day. It's not just used in good weather. The kids must learn to defend themselves in all kind of conditions. Bad weather is often an incentive to take it outside and up the game. When all four kids come inside shivering and covered in cold mud, I leave the management of the single bathroom and back-to-back scrubbing of the little ones to him. A second bathroom is a luxury, after all.

I do help with the endless cleaning, icing, and bandaging of wounds. On three children, at least. Sloane's are mostly healed by the time she's come inside. She's gaining useful knowledge watching me clean, splint, and bandage every-one else, though, including her dad. He's the volunteer enemy and punching bag, and as they improve he suffers— joyfully and proudly.

I go back inside and find a text from Christian: *This Inis' bike?* Following it, a photo of a motorcycle parked on the circle drive in front of the Moore mansion.

Looks like it, I text back. I don't follow the thought through to where I know it goes. Eight years of worrying about that bottle can't be validated on this day. Not while Sloane is missing. Not when Trey and Marcas are out there searching for her, vulnerable and unreachable.

Then she's here, Christian texts. *I just pulled up. I'll call as soon as I find out what the hell is going on.*

Trey bursts through the back door. "The sheriff has her."

"What?"

He takes off his shirt and wipes the sweat off his face. "From what I can tell. How long has it been since I've killed anyone? Streak ends today." He heads down the hall.

Marcas comes inside. Lines of sweat run through the brown dust on his face. "Dad's really, really mad."

"Let's get you cleaned up." He washes his hands while I wipe his face and neck down with a wet towel. Then I strip him to his underwear and tell him to go find clean clothes. Trey comes through in his own clean shirt before thundering down the basement stairs. The only thing down there he could need is guns. I wait in the kitchen for him. When he emerges he has a look in his eye I haven't seen for years. "Trey, stop and tell me what happened before you do something you'll regret."

He passes me by and is halfway to the front door before he stops. "I don't know what happened. I'm going to find out."

"To the sheriff's office?"

"The coyote pack is trailing the car on the road into town. They sent a female back to find me. The sheriff put Sloane in his car and drove off."

"Why was she all the way to the road?"

"Don't know. But if that sheriff thinks he can take her—" He looks aside like he just remembered something. Then he's handing me the SIG from the back of his waistband. "Take this. Killing him with bare hands will be easier to cover."

He's out the door before I can come up with anything to say. I'm out of practice when it comes to dealing with his anger. It's been too long since it's surfaced like this. I take the SIG back to the gun safe and find Marcas in his room, still undressed, playing with his miniature animal figurines.

"Look at this one's butt." He finishes signing then holds up a horse.

"Didn't I ask you to get dressed?"

"Oh yeah. I forgot." He goes to his drawer and pulls out the first piece of clothing he touches. "Is Sloane going to jail?"

"Kids don't go to jail. The sheriff was probably just worried she was lost. Dad will bring her home."

"Dad said a hundred bad words."

"He's very frustrated right now."

"Is Sloane gonna get in trouble?"

"I'm not sure. Now what about those clothes?"

My phone rings in the kitchen, so I give up on the clothing battle with the four-year-old and rush to answer it.

"Not good," Christian says. "They're negotiating with her for that bottle."

I slump against the wall and slide down it to the floor. "Why would she do that?"

"I could probably explain if I knew what they were offering her."

"After eight years?"

"It sounded like they've been after her for a long time. Sorry, Liv, I'm just not here much anymore. I'm a bit out of the loop. Dillon and Jared's people have completely taken over this house. You can blame that on Trey."

And Trey would blame Christian, for not stepping up when Pierce and Martin were killed. Trey eliminated those with power so Christian could accept a role he never wanted. If Seanmháthair had stayed she'd still be a hidden force there, but she probably left knowing Christian would never be her soldier on the ground. She was the mistress of the house, the matriarch, but with Christian as her only living descendant, her hold was a lost cause. And from what I've been told, she'd always remained disconnected from the politics of the house. "Okay, so what do we do?"

"No fucking clue. I'm not going up against a black witch, I'll tell you that. Trey's going to—" Voices come through in the background. "Hold on."

I sit against the wall, trying to make out what he's saying and what a female voice is saying but the exchange is too far from his phone's microphone. We should've never let that bottle out of our hands. We should have buried it in a hole ten feet deep, filled first with stone, then with dirt, and planted one of Trey's sacred oaks on top of it. Marcas wanders into the kitchen, still wearing only his superhero underwear. I pull him into my lap and hug him tight.

"Okay," Christian says into the phone. "Good news, I think. She wants to trade the bottle for something they'll never give her."

I can't imagine anything she'd want from them. "What?"

"I should've said 'some*one*.' Rex."

Marcas looks at me right at the moment Christian says it, and I see my own stunned eyes reflected in his. I close them, breathing out, telling myself she has some greater plan. She's disabled the magic in that bottle. She's going to trade it, one weapon against us traded for another. But the only one still live is the one she will receive, and she's going to disable him as well, stripping the Moores of all power over us.

It's a perfect plan. But it's a dream. She could just as easily be giving the Moores a Bevan-seeking death ray in exchange for the child trained to kill my daughter. A child she'll train in black magic to make him even more lethal. It's what she wanted to do with Sloane, and what I denied her. "There's no way—"

"Right. There's no way they'll give him to her, so don't worry. They treat that kid like he's their king, and he's got the ego—and name—to prove it. Never thought I'd see a kid trained harder than Trey. You know they wake him up in the middle of the night to train? It's pretty sick, some of the shit Aaron's told me. And he's not here much anymore either now that he's working on his master's."

"You're too young to have a son who's working on a master's."

"I know, babe. Just pretend he's my brother. Sometimes it's easier that way." The way it comes out has me imagining the cockeyed smile he's most likely just produced. Gosh, I miss him. His way of lightening up the dark, of making me smile when there's terror hiding behind every corner.

"So, nothing to worry about." I repeat it, hoping it will settle in.

"Nope. We need to video call so you can see my thumbs-up. We're good. Now go find something to do, like throw some grass seed in Fearghus' garden. He loves to weed. Remember you've gotta keep that guy occupied."

"He's picking up Sloane from the sheriff's office."

"Already? Well, like father like daughter. Make him call me when he gets home. He's gonna love what Inis said about Jared."

CHAPTER 25

TREY

*L*IV MARCAS SLOANE. *Liv Marcas Sloane.* Their names are my mantra so this restraint doesn't slip. So I remember what I could lose, so I keep my hold. Even though my jaw is so clenched the contact of my molars has the nerves sensing cold when there's no cold. It's like I'm clamping down on ice—another good distraction so I don't release the arm that's ready to pop the sheriff's jaw so fast and hard he's down and out before he can finish the sentence. Then it's my boot's turn on his neck and the shithead won't be getting up. Ever.

"That sound about right to you, Mr. Bevan?" he finishes up.

I don't know what he was saying. Some kind of lecture about letting my children get too far away from me. On my own damn land. Where it's none of his fucking business. *Liv Marcas Sloane.* And Sloane's cool little hand slides into mine because she's just been released to me by the deputy and must realize I'm about to pounce.

I look at her face, normally so expressive, but she's as blank as can be. Her hand trembles in mine—a nervous reaction to being stuck with a stranger, unable to communicate. Without us or her interpreter provided by the school, she's all alone in a town where no one speaks her language.

One more glance at the sheriff has him backing up a step, dropping his hand closer to his side arm. And I turn and pull Sloane out the door.

"What were you thinking?" I say to her once we're enclosed in the cab of the truck. I don't sign. She can read my lips.

She crosses her arms and turns away. Mad because I'm not signing. She has a full-body tremble going now, the result of an adrenaline dump, nerves held taut for too long now releasing. I want to grab her and shake the words out of her. I pop the steering wheel instead. She jumps and looks at me, not because she heard it but because she felt its force carried through the truck. And I feel like a violent monster, an out of control piece of shit father scaring his own child. Throwing around strength and power to invoke fear and obedience. Pierce Moore. My grandfather. I can't be like them.

What were you thinking? I sign.

Her eyes search my face, curious if my change in temperament will stick. Then she huffs a breath, realizing she's not going to get out of this easily. But she can't get control of that tremble. Her anxiety around strangers, without us, is too severe—and not getting any better no matter how much we socialize her. It's getting worse, and I don't know how to help her.

I tried to tell him where my house was. I showed him I wanted paper to write, but he wouldn't give me any.

Of course not. He set this up. He wanted me here, in his domain, enduring a lecture from him to get her back. I sign: *You should not have gone so far from the house.*

I didn't know I was gone so long. Her teeth are chattering with those damn nerves.

"Hours, Sloane." I know she can lip-read that, but I sign anyway: *Hours.*

I never get to do anything I want to do.

I turn fully toward her so she can clearly see my face. "Sloane. You were missing for *hours*."

She shrugs, remaining that way, eyes big. Shaking her head like I'm the one being ridiculous. Sassy, just like her mom. Well, it's her mom she'll have to deal with. I start the truck.

She turns on the radio and cranks the bass like she likes it. It pulses in the seats, vibrates my rearview mirror. I turn it off. She glares. When Liv's done ripping her apart, I'm going to take her to Tara's and let Tara have a go. I'm useless here, and I know it. She doesn't listen to me. She knows I love her too much.

River wakes me that night. I get a rush like I used to, when the Moores' men were a regular occurrence. River's warning howl is off, though, and I wonder if she's just messed it up. She's getting old. The bark is frantic, demanding. Liv sits up next to me. "Wha—"

I cover her mouth with my hand. Point to the trapdoor in the closet with the gun safe, the loose floorboard across the room where the ammo is. Point to the kids' rooms. She's up and moving, and I'm pulling on jeans and sneaking down the hall. I grope the top of the fridge for the sheathed dagger I left there—find it. I take it outside. River's out of breath and almost hoarse, like she's been barking all the way home from the edge of the property. I can't get anything from her until she shuts up. Trib's nowhere around. A few coyotes stalk through the garden. They wouldn't be here if men were here.

"Trey!" Liv calls from inside. Then she's bursting out the door. "Sloane's not in her room!"

I take her by the shoulders. If we lose our shit, we won't ever find her. "Go back to Marcas. I'll get her." I close her back inside so she doesn't see what I'm about to do. It's too dark to find her on foot and I'm not stupid enough to think I don't need help this time. I leap down the stairs and crouch on the ground. Unsheath the dagger. Split my palm wide, wait until the blood is really running and press against earth. It's bitterly cold, a spring night in the mountains as frigid as winter. But I press down and tap in. The elements unite around my call for kin and an electric-blue blast lights the path from my spilled blood in three directions: One toward the house for Marcas. One across the river toward Tara's house. And one due north into the forest. I follow it with my eyes until it disappears among the pines. At that moment a figure emerges, trudging as if burdened by weight. She stops, my path of magic just as visible to her, bridging the land as if we were face to face. I see into her eyes, and she looks back. Caught, but still determined. Taking a step forward despite her fear.

I was wrong earlier. I don't love her too much to punish her. I'd just never been pushed far enough.

When I start crossing the yard toward her, she goes to her knees, settling her load against them but keeping her chin up, her eyes on me. The child has some real nerve, and she has no idea what unimaginable punishments I've learned in my life. Ones I've experienced firsthand. As I draw near, she circles protective arms around her burden—a fawn. So weak it can barely hold its head up. Matted fur. Injured, by the unnatural slant of its rear leg.

My anger seethes, my head hot. It's coming from that place I sealed off years ago. I stop a few steps away, just to be sure. I can't trust myself.

She releases the fawn to sign: *I'm sorry, Dad.*

I can't speak, certainly can't sign. I look to the stars, press fists against temples, squeezing blood from my slashed palm. Reaching for some kind of sanity, some force that will stop the violent monster, the Pierce Moore, my grandfather. I gather a breath and hold it. *Liv Marcas Sloane.* Funny how a portion of my mantra is the reason I need it now.

"Sowwy," she says.

Her deaf voice. Rebecca has done so much speech training with her, and she's had such a hard time. Never uses that sweet voice. It embarrasses her. I've seen how people look at her when she tries, and I understand why she stopped trying. Her rare voice is a lead blanket on my anger, a fissure in my heart. I crouch before her. "You can't do this."

She watches my lips then signs, *I know. I'm sorry.*

Why?

She lifts her chin. *You always say to leave nature alone. I thought if I brought her closer, you'd let me help her. You can't ignore her when she's here.*

I stand and turn my back on her. Stare at the dark house. Think of Liv hunkered in a bedroom with Marcas, terrified the Moores finally came and took our daughter. Sloane doesn't see the gravity of our protection of her because she doesn't know what's at stake. Who's hunting her. Who's destined to fight her, hoping to kill her. All my family has endured, all the hope my ancestors have loaded onto her. She doesn't know what could be on her trail while she's casually tracking an injured animal through the forest.

I have to tell her. Not just the basics. I have to tell her everything.

I couldn't get her earlier because the dogs and coyotes wouldn't leave my side, she signs when I turn around.

They're not supposed to.

Dad, we have to help her. The animals are my only friends. Only they understand me.

I'm yanked straight into the past, into the forest surrounding the Moore estate. Sycamore, maple, and oak reigning over young pines. Floors carpeted with green moss. Fallen logs rotted through. Wildflowers dotting the paths carved by deer. Only animals as my friends. Only animals to understand me. Until Christian was old enough to be my friend, the isolation was like a hungry predator, eating me day after day, each bite bigger than the last.

I scoop up the fawn and head for the house, Sloane following behind. The fawn's breath is ragged, its bones sharp against me. I make eye contact with a nearby coyote, send the pack away. We go through the back door. Liv meets us in the kitchen, Marcas on her hip, his head on her shoulder, asleep. I pause to look at her. She doesn't need to ask.

Sloane and I mend the fawn in the basement and build her a bed in the corner. And then I tell her everything.

When she goes to bed, I close her curtains against the rising sun. I avoid the creaky spots in her floor for Liv and Marcas' sake, not for Sloane who won't hear them. She slipped out of this house in the night without a sound. I hear every creak in this house. Every shuffle of sock against wood floor. Every out-of-place breath. She used what I taught her against me. I'm more proud than angry—teaching a deaf child to be quiet with her movements is no simple task. But it's a skill she must have to survive what lies in her future. A small weight lifts off my shoulders, knowing she's mastered it so young. If she can sneak past me, she can sneak past anyone.

I go outside and lean on the porch railing, looking over the yard. Marcas' red wagon full of his stick collection. Sloane's river-stone cairns standing tall, balanced with patience and care. Liv's bed of pansies with their faces turned toward the rising sun. The trampled earth of our sparring ground, the smear in the mud where Will went down, two marks beside it where Winnie knelt to see if he was okay.

I didn't just bring one child into this. I brought two. I moved my sister and her children here. Our mother. Years ago this land was my solitary confinement, my hell.

I managed it alone, with only myself to protect. Now I must protect them all, and I'm failing. I'm not doing enough. There's a countdown somewhere I can't see, and I don't know what to do to stop it.

Sloane asks to see Grandma Sloane when she wakes up. Liv offers to drive her, but she wants to walk. I stifle the urge to say no. I won't restrict her freedom. I sign: *Take River with you.*

Liv pours me a second cup of coffee, and we stare at each other instead of our daughter leaving through the door. It's a battle of who will break first, who'll be the one to go to the door and watch her cross the yard, confirm she has River with her. Then Liv gives me a smile, and we get up together. Coyotes are spilling from the trees to join girl and dog.

Liv returns to her coffee at the table. A second cup for her too. She didn't sleep much either. "Were you outside all night?"

"No, just went out after Sloane went to bed." I made no progress toward what to do about that countdown, but I did make a decision Liv isn't going to like. "I'm teaching her *dubhealaín.*"

She sets her mug down hard. "No."

"It's our only advantage over the Moores. They don't know it, couldn't ever learn it. They don't have the texts."

"Inis was there. She could be teaching them."

"She won't. Her people only teach their own kind."

She puts her face in her hands. I know she's thinking about what my black magic did to Sloane, about what a danger it could be to Sloane herself.

"She's part O'Dowd," I say. "She'll be a native practitioner. And she's not as stupid as me."

"But she's only eight years old."

"And has more common sense than I'll ever have."

That gets a laugh out of Liv. It brightens her face, bringing to my attention how somber it'd been a moment ago. She feels the countdown too; she's as helpless as me. We're teaching our children everything we can, but it still won't make Sloane evenly matched against Rex Moore. He has his hearing. They'll teach him to use that against her. With black magic, Sloane will have an advantage they'll never expect. Even if they do, there's no way for them to train against it. It's a mystery to them without the texts. They don't encounter black witches often enough to be familiar with it.

"I'm saying no, Trey."

"I'm not asking."

She pulls back. Studies my face, determines I'm not screwing around. The look I get in return isn't what I wanted, but it makes no difference.

"Don't do this," she says. It's an attempt to give me one final chance to back down, to give her a say in the matter.

If she's not going to agree, I can't give her a say. She hasn't been fighting them her whole life. She doesn't know what I know. This is the only way.

I get up and leave the room so I don't have to endure those eyes working to undo me. I check on Sloane's fawn in her bed of towels in the basement. She's no longer suspicious of me—bad news. She's too young to have encountered other humans and won't realize they're all not like Sloane. We've saved her only so she can die another way.

Sloane was saved too. She died once, and Liv and I brought her back. I won't allow her to die another way. The Moores are professional abusers, but they won't take a child's life. I was fifteen when they stopped treating me like a child. To put an age on that countdown would apply a goal, a thin layer of sanity. It's as good a guess as any. In seven years Sloane must be comfortable killing a man. She must know Bevan magic well enough to wield without a voice or help from our texts. And now there's something new on that list—I have seven years to teach her *dubhealaín*. She must know it like she knows our magic. Like a second nature. A second skin.

I slide the text from the shelf and look at the worn rust-red velvet cover of the only text not marked by our bronze medallion. It's not our native magic, but we preserved it anyway. I think I finally know why.

I undo the tie holding it closed, flashing back to the last time I opened this text. The last time I bulldozed ahead, leaving Liv and her wishes in my rubble. The catastrophe that resulted. I climb the stairs. Liv's still at the table, staring out the window yet unconnected to the scene outside. Focused on something in her own head.

She turns around when I sit across from her. I take her hand. I explain why our daughter must know black magic, how it's the key that might save her, how I promise to teach her what I failed to learn myself: restraint. And I don't stop until I get Liv's blessing, and with it, another small step toward becoming the man I promised her I'd be. Toward finally doing something right.

Upon Sloane's return to our side of the river I meet her in the yard and press my amulet into her hand. I've delayed giving it to her until she can understand the weight of its protection. Now she knows what hunts her, what hunts all of us. I tell her it saved her mother's life and someday it might save hers.

She holds it against her heart and signs, *I hear it.*

Hear what? I ask.

Singing. It sings with magic.

CHAPTER 26

LIV

Four years of trying to interest Sloane in activities with other deaf children has resulted in nothing but her spending more time alone in the woods. At twelve, her only friends are her cousins. Every specialist who's worked with her at school has encouraged us to involve her in the local Deaf community. As the only deaf child at school, she's missing out on important interaction with other children.

Trey and I understand. And we've tried. We've struggled along with her, prying her loose from our legs for preschool. And kindergarten. And first grade. Even with an interpreter, she's the odd one, unable to follow group conversations, lost in her silent world on the playground. As she grew, she abandoned the leg death-grip and moved onto the hand, forcing us to twist one hand away only for her to grasp the other. We learned new sneaky ways to physically sever ourselves from her so she could learn to mentally sever herself from us. The separation routine only improved because her social awareness and embarrassment grew. She still wanted to cling, but the shame of it overpowered her. I could see the hard swallow of tears and the quiver of the chin every time, and once back in my car I would do the crying for her. It went on much longer with her than her peers. Marcas learned to separate from us years before she did.

Deaf community events, we thought, would be different. She'd be surrounded by people she could understand, people who could understand her. But every day camp and barbecue and playdate we've driven her to has done nothing but prove how different she is. With the hearing children at school, she's the 'Deaf Girl,' and with the Deaf children at day camp, she's the girl who's more interested in the wildflowers she could gather and dry than the game of tag.

I can't tell these specialists about her magic blood, or that most of her spare time is spent training with her father so she will someday be able to defend herself against an army set loose to kill her. Being deaf isn't the only thing between her and her peers at school. Her teachers would probably be more insistent about better socialization if her grades weren't so good.

It's Marcas' grades we worry about. All the hours of training and practice of magic seem to help Sloane focus, but for Marcas, they're an unconquerable distraction. Trey wakes him up early now to train before school, hoping to wear him out so he'll sit still at his desk. At three months into third grade, he's only been to the principal's office twice. It's a record.

Unlike his sister, Marcas has no trouble making friends. But that's a situation we have to watch closely. He knows the secrets we must keep, but his mouth sometimes runs ahead of his good sense. And he's often blindsiding us—what's so clearly off limits for public conversation isn't so off limits to him.

"No, Marcas, it's not okay to practice chokeholds on your friends at school."

"We do them at home all the time!"

"Most families don't."

He drops his head back and groans. "Can I have a notebook?"

I pull one out of the kitchen cabinet. He sits at the table and writes "Famly Secrits" on the cover, turns to the first page and looks up at me. "How do you spell 'chokeholds?'"

Sloane's phone dings on the table. I go to the light switch on the basement stairs and blink the light while spelling 'chokeholds' for Marcas. She comes up a few minutes later.

Phone, I sign.

She's made and kept more friends since we got her that phone than any activity we had to force her to do. After a conversation with her school principal, she became the only student allowed to use a phone all day. She can communicate with anyone—all they do is speak and the phone displays their words to her. She types a response, the phone recites it aloud. And outside of school there's plenty of texting.

I'm fingerspelling 'coyotes' to Marcas when Sloane asks if I can drive her to a friend's house. I check the clock, sign: *It's too late for a school night.*

I only need fifteen minutes. I just need to help her cat.

Your dad says no more fixing pets.

She sighs heavily. *Please? Just one more. Her mom is going to get rid of him if I don't fix him.*

Trey and Tara had a bite-each-other's-head off argument the other day about Sloane's new reputation around town as the pet fixer. One visit from Sloane and a pet's behavior problem is cured—dogs stop bringing home dead animal 'presents,' cats stop tearing up furniture and urinating in the house. Trey says it draws too much attention; Tara says there's no harm in something no one can prove. I can't take a side—it's too hard to weigh Sloane's good heart and her urge to help against preserving our facade of normalcy. It's also hard to discourage her from an activity that gets her around new people. So what if she has a way with animals? But sometimes people have a problem with things they can't explain, and they start to look closer. Trey's rivalry with the sheriff doesn't help.

Sloane's biting her lip, watching me for my response. She twists her one long lock of hair around her finger. A couple weeks ago she got her hair bobbed to shoulder length but left that one piece—her lucky piece—long. It gives her always-busy hands something to do when she's at her desk at school and those hands must stay idle.

I grab my keys and tell Marcas to take his notebook downstairs with his dad.

"Is Dad's stuff in the basement a family secret?" he asks on his way down.

"Yes." Hell yes.

Only a week into November and winter has fallen upon us. I brush the dusting of snow off the windshield with the wipers. It's too dry to stick. Flurries swirl around the car on our way through town. While stopped at a red light, I take my hands off the wheel to ask Sloane if she told her friend we're coming. Through her window I see a car angle-parked at the curb. A BMW M5. Newer than the one Dillon drove me out of town in. But no one in Black River drives a BMW, much less an M5. A horn honks—I return my eyes to the road and see the light is now green.

We cross two streets before I take a right and circle the block to pass that car again. Sloane's telling me it's the wrong turn, and I nod at her. She asks where I'm going and I hold up a finger, make the final right turn and pull up beside that car and stop. Virginia plates.

Another horn honks. Sloane's patting my leg because I'm not answering her. The car behind me goes around, and I follow because it's a bad idea to be sitting there in the street beside that car. He could be watching us. He could be in it.

"*Mom*," Sloane says in the voice she never uses.

I look at her and say, "It's okay."

She settles back, not rattled enough to pull out her phone and make me explain now. I'm grateful the wait will give me a few minutes to come up with what to tell her. I can't lie to her. I can't tell her the truth. I need to come up with something in the middle.

That car looked like one of the Moores' cars, I sign when we park in front of her friend's house.

Because it's from Virginia? she asks. She notices everything. The visual world is her main source of perception, and she sucks in every detail.

Yes, and the model. I'm sure it's a coincidence. Do you want me to come inside?

She looks at the house, taking in a shaky breath. It's a dead giveaway to her anxiety she doesn't hear. She wipes her palms on her jeans over and over—a nervous tic she's recently developed whenever confronted with a social situation without a human interpreter. I don't automatically go with her anymore. And I worry there's more to it than being deaf, that her fear is mutating into a more serious form of social anxiety.

I want to reach for her hand, but I don't. She sets her jaw, straightens her spine, and gets out of the car. I keep telling Trey these little visits with people are good for her. They're not just helping her work past her fear, they're also building her confidence, making her brave, giving her the tools she'll need to deal with hearing people without us standing beside her ready to help. She needs to learn to navigate the hearing world without us; the more experience she has now, the better equipped she'll be when we can't be waiting in the driveway for her.

Trey never voices what's written on his face when I say these things: that she won't live long enough for it to matter. It's what we're both thinking, what we both refuse to speak aloud for fear it will make it true.

I'm still thinking about that BMW when a porch light flips on ahead of me and Sloane hops out the open door. Her friend carries a small orange cat. Sloane types into her phone and holds it up so her friend can hear; her friend nods an animated and gleeful understanding. A woman appears behind them and waves to me. I wave back.

Everything work out? I ask Sloane when she's back in the car.

I back out of the driveway. She's too giddy to wait for us to stop so I can sign. She uses her phone to interpret. I listen to what she did and respond, but only half my brain is into it. The other half is thinking about that car and whether I should forget about it or tell Trey.

As soon as we get home, I text Christian to ask if Dillon's still driving an M5. He responds right away: *Haven't been to the house in a while but that fucker is always driving an M5.* I wish I'd snapped a picture of it to send him to confirm. I'm sure there's someone at the estate he can safely ask. Or maybe not. The whole property has been taken over by Dillon and Jared's side of the family.

I sit on the basement stairs and watch Trey and our children work magic until their bedtime. Marcas begs to look at the black magic text, but Trey says no after a glance my way—he keeps those spells tight between the three of them. I'm not sure why. He knows he has my permission. Perhaps it's a tender spot for him, a reminder he doesn't want brought up in my presence even though I forgive what he did to Sloane and me. He doesn't involve Tara either, after she declined his offer of teaching Winnie and Will. The only person he's ever discussed the teaching of black magic with is his mother, who came to him not long after I gave him my permission. She told him Pierce Moore knew black magic. She'd seen him use it. She wasn't sure how he learned, or who else in the Moore family knows. Trey was glad to have that information, but he wasn't swayed— he still believes it's critical for Sloane and Marcas to learn. Especially Sloane. And that the black magic text ended up in his basement for a reason. Tara's collection doesn't include one.

The flurries have turned to sleet, tinkling against the window panes while I tuck the kids in bed. When I return to the kitchen in search of Trey, I see Ali sitting at the back door staring through the glass, her tail swishing against the floor. I get a muscle-memory urge to duck before I remember Trey, Tara, and Máthair collectively charged Sloane's amulet with some kind of joined power that creates a protection around the house. They swear it's strong enough to shield us from snipers, although I wouldn't want to have to test that out.

I go closer to the glass and peer out. Trey's on the porch, shading his face from the sleet, surveying the sky. I slide the door open a crack. He comes inside, his hair sparkly with ice he brushes into the sink.

"When you go outside in a sleet storm, you worry your cat."

"Nah, she's not worried." He bends to scratch her head. "She's just glad it's me out there and not her." He hands me my mug of tea—his mother's recipe for contraception. "Drink up. I need to do some things to you."

"You get more romantic by the day. What's outside?"

He shakes his head like I shouldn't be bothered. Then he pauses as if reconsidering. "I might be a little out of it tomorrow."

"Out of it?"

"Not myself. I think I might crash at Shawn's so I don't upset the kids."

I set down my mug. Something must be serious for him to want to crash at Shawn's. "What's going on?"

"Lunar eclipse. They mess with my head."

"How?"

He shrugs. "Bad migraine that knocks me on my ass. I have a way of managing it, but it's not an option anymore."

Intuition tells me he's minimizing the symptoms. "What do you normally do?"

"Get passed-out drunk. I'm not doing it this time."

I'm surprised this hasn't come up in the time we've been together. I'm not sure how often lunar eclipses happen, but I know he's never had any migraines bad enough to upset the kids. It would explain those random twenty-four hour relapses he's had through the years. Would've been nice to know the reason for those at the time, so I didn't have to go to sleep alone, terrified his hard-earned sobriety had been snatched away. And two little kids could've been told their dad was sleeping so late on the couch simply because he had a migraine, instead of whatever white lie I came up with.

"I can drop the kids at Tara's for the night. I'll stay here and help you."

"No," he says automatically, like he always does. He never wants help. Demands to suffer alone. Over a decade later and he's still raising that shield. If he doesn't admit people care about him and want to help him, he won't expect it. And won't be let down if no one does.

"Don't be an idiot." I slide my arms around his midsection and hug tight. "And it's been so long since I've tortured you while incapacitated."

He peels me off him. "I know. Zero Moore activity for way too long. And we have no one there who can tell us anything." He goes to the back door, puts a hand on the glass. "Remember the ten guys who attacked us in the woods? That was nothing. They've had over ten years now. They'll send a hundred."

"There's no way they could get a group like that out here without someone seeing."

"Sure there is."

River comes into view on the porch. She has a stiff way of walking now, with some days it turning to a full limp. Her fur is dry, only covered by a light layer of sleet. She must've taken cover in her shelter. Trey goes outside with her. They go to the railing, peering into the night side by side. Discussing surveillance? Battle strategy? He gives her a good ear scratch before he comes back inside.

"There's a BMW with Virginia plates parked in town."

He stops dead. "Where?"

"Fifth and Main."

He snatches his keys off the counter, and I take hold of his arm. "Trey, stop and think. If he's here, you need to stay with us."

He props a hand against the countertop and bows his head. Closes his eyes. Breathes. Then he looks up at me and says, "Okay."

And he takes me against him so fast and hard it's like he's overpowering some other emotion, one that used to rule him but no longer does. When the crush of his arms lessens enough for me to move, I tilt my face up at him, curious. He closes his eyes and kisses me, holding on even tighter, pressing air from my lungs as he steals breath with his lips.

I manage to get out of his grasp, but then I notice the look in his eye. He makes a grab and I dodge. Another grab, and I shuffle around him. Now there's a little smirk playing on his lips. Pursuit. He likes it too much. "You're sick," I say but ruin it with a laugh I can't hold back.

He snags my belt loop too fast to counter and tugs me against him, undoing my pants as I latch my arms around his neck and kiss him hard like I know he wants it. Like I want it. It isn't until we're tangled in the sheets that I remember what we were talking about before this: Dillon in town. The Moores. Impending violence and death encroaching faster each day. It puts a stutter in our love-making that makes him pull back to look at me. "What?"

"Nothing. I just remembered—but forget it. Don't stop." I wrap my legs around him because they'd fallen away. I tilt my hips to force him deeper, a move that could get him to focus even if one of the Moores' men had just leapt through the window. He's still looking at me though, torn, unde-cided. And it's my turn to say, "What?"

He takes my face in his hands. Presses his forehead against mine. And like that night he tapped into the magic of the earth and accidently brought me with him, I'm pulled into the same realm where the tinkle of sleet against the window pane is music, the wind is a voice that speaks a language I know deep within, the dome of cloudy sky is a presence above me even with the roof between, and the warmth of his seed is like the sun heating me through, baking the earth I'm now such a part of, promising life, and love, and everything that proves we will win.

I'm not sure how much time passes before either of us can speak. The magic has shed off in layers so I'm no longer connected to anything but the sheets twisted around my ankles and his skin glued to my side.

"Sorry," he says. "I couldn't help myself."

"You better not have gotten me pregnant."

He chuckles, sounding very pleased with himself. "I'll make you some tea."

Sloane runs to the car the next day after school to ask if she can go with a group of friends to the ice cream shop in town. I get out to talk to the mother who's driving them—the same mother who waved to me from her porch the night before. Then I watch Sloane climb into the SUV and try to get a grip on the panic. I'm thankful to Marcas for talking my ear off all the way home. It was the right thing to do. She needs a normal childhood. But with Dillon possibly loose in town, how could I let her out of my sight?

At the entrance to our driveway, Trey's laying a line of stones etched with the design from my amulet. It's another layer of protection, another way to know if his territory has been breached by an enemy presence. Marcas unbuckles himself, and I stop the car so he can get out to help. An hour later I leave them to pick up Sloane in town. She comes right out when she sees the car. Her movements are rigid, and she rubs her palms on her jeans several times as soon as she's in the seat.

Did you have a good time?

It was okay. She turns completely away from me to look out the window. It's an act. She doesn't want me to see her face. What she doesn't realize is I can hear the shudder in her breathing as she tries to hold back tears.

She lets me take her hand and hold it for a long time while we sit there. When she finally looks at me, her eyes are wet.

Everyone was talking at once. I couldn't understand anything and my phone couldn't either. Everyone ignored me.

I pull her against me. Kiss her head. As good a lip-reader as she is, multiple speakers talking over one another make the difficult task impossible. She presses her cheek against my chest, and I hum to her like I did when she was a baby. At one time the vibration was the only thing that would calm her in the night when she was upset and unable to tell me why. She lets out a long breath. That's when I smell the spearmint.

I hold her away from me and point to her mouth. She opens it, showing me the source of the fragrance: gum.

I never buy that flavor. Never even want it around me. *Did your friend give you that?*

She shakes her head. *A nice man. He talked into my phone. He said he has a deaf daughter, and that it was okay to feel alone.*

What did he look like?

She returns her attention to the ice cream shop lit up in front of us and signs: *Weird. I don't remember.*

I pull a tissue out of the glove box and hand it to her because I don't want her chewing that gum. She spits it into the tissue, looking at it curiously.

That's weird. I didn't know I was chewing gum.

In that moment I know it was Dillon. He found her, he interacted with her, and he took her memory of it so I would never know.

TREY

I WAKE BEFORE THE sun and slip out of bed without disturbing Liv. After throwing on a shirt, jeans, and a coat, I go out to my truck and start it up, praying to the elements she doesn't hear. I have to do this, but I won't be able to if she begs me not to leave. All the animals are on high alert even though the chances of Dillon paying us a visit this early are slim. He wouldn't miss sleep for that. He'll come when he's well rested and well fed.

A thorough search of town gives me nothing. Either he's left or he's laying low. Or it wasn't him in the first place. I'll come back around lunchtime, drive past all the local places to eat. He has to come out of his hole at some point.

I go to Shawn's and knock on the door. He takes forever to answer, rubbing his face and squinting at me like his eyes haven't had time to adjust to light.

"You ready to replace that faucet?"

"Aw, man, right now? You know how early it is?"

He's been on my ass to help him do this for months. Now's the time if he wants my help. "I'll put some coffee on."

We're finished after lunch. This time my search of town pays off: BMW M5 with Virginia plates parked right on Main. I pull in beside it and get out, recognizing magic blood nearby even before I make a conscious effort to skim the vicinity for it. Those fifteen years living on my own had dulled that sense but now it's more acute than ever. Voices carry from across the street despite the traffic moving by, and I see him standing in front of the police station. Talking to my best friend the sheriff.

I lean against my truck's tailgate and cross my arms. He meets my gaze from across the street. The stare-off proves what I suspected—he's pissed I caught on before he finished whatever duty he's here to perform. He didn't expect me to interrupt him. He planned offense, not defense. I watch him wrap up his conversation with the sheriff and head toward me. This public location isn't going to do me any favors.

"It's been too long, cousin," he says, nearing me. "How's Liv?"

He stops in front of me. Traffic moves by steadily. I keep my arms crossed, hands wedged tightly underneath them. If I didn't, they'd be grabbing him by the collar so I could head butt him in the fucking face.

"Okay, so not talking. Well I need to talk to you. You want to grab a beer somewhere?"

"I don't drink."

He snorts, surprised. "Ah, a boy scout now. How about I buy you a Kool-Aid?"

Here's where the old me would've grabbed him by the neck, popped him in the nose with an elbow then slammed his face into my knee. Right in the middle of a busy street with a dozen eyewitnesses I'd have to steal memories from.

I'm not so easily baited anymore and from the way he's dropped that smirk, I can tell he's not pleased.

"How about you and I walk a few blocks that way…" I point northwest "…so I can cut your throat and leave your body for the coyotes?"

He clicks his tongue. "Words before actions, sobriety … Fatherhood has changed you, cousin."

That's when I grab him by the collar. "Get in your car and drive out of this town."

He isn't exactly limp, but he's not resisting either. "I came here to warn you."

As if I could trust any warning that came out of his mouth.

"I care about Liv, and I don't want her hurt. I care about Sloane. You forget she was mine once."

Two hands on his collar, I slam him against his car. Now he's resisting, so I tighten my grip and slam him again. I'm about to send a fist into his gut when I notice the audience. The sheriff who's come back out of the police station across the street. The cars in the road, full of faces, crawling past. People who would be long gone before I could wipe their minds of this. I can't destroy my family's life in this town. I'm not alone anymore. I can't pick up and move whenever I need to because of something I've done.

I let him go. He slides a bit down the car before he rights himself.

"I knew you had it in you."

"You heard what I said. Get in the car and drive." Both my ears pop, sending a wave of nausea that releases a payload of pressure in my head. It's a familiar feeling that normally has me headed to the nearest liquor store to stock up for a long night. My ears ring but it subsides fast so I can once again hear my surroundings.

"Not before I say this. My family has something that—" He tilts his head, looking at me funny. "I didn't even hit you and you've got a bloody nose."

Crap. Already? I need to get home before that lunar eclipse hits full-on—but not before I follow this shithead out of town. A trickle of blood runs down my upper lip now. I stand there and stare at him anyway. He seems to have lost his train of thought to something new, something he's working out in his head as I watch. More lies, for sure. I'll spare him from it. I shove him backward so he's on the driver's side of his car. "Get in."

"You won't win against them, man. You need to pack up and leave. Take Liv and Sloane somewhere safe. Put an ocean between you and them."

"I follow you until Casper. When I turn around you're going to keep driving and never fucking set foot here again."

"Rex is—"

I grab him again but I'm torn away by several guys who had simply been bystanders a moment ago. Shouts of "easy, guys" and "break it up" cut through the ringing in my ears that's returned, and I have to shove away to get some air, pressing my temples to dial it back. This is bad. Worse than I remember.

When I straighten, there's a body in between Dillon and me, and Dillon's watching me like he just had an epiphany. It doesn't matter what bullshit he feeds me. He's not trying to save Sloane and Liv. He's trying to save his son from us. We're the ones who win—in their version of the prophecy, and in ours.

Someone's gotten Dillon in his car, so I get in my truck and wait for him to back out. I know I said Casper, but I keep following him an hour past it because I can't get an image out of my head. It's like a slow motion video on repeat: Him facing me. Pulling a gun. Aiming it at my father. Firing. I try to think ahead, to bring on the image that would be playing a month from now if I cut his throat and left his body at the side of the road. All I see is a void, a black nothingness. An unknown that could destroy all I've worked so hard to build. Now the lunar eclipse is almost on me and I have a long drive home, so I turn the hell around and don't look back.

I arrive home half-blind from the pressure in my head. I can't see to park my truck, so I leave it in the driveway and fall out of the door. Through the fog of the migraine, I get a hard nudge of awareness—someone unfriendly has just crossed my sacred stones. I wipe my bloody nose on my shirt and try to blink away the blackness. Then I grope for the SIG under the driver's seat of my truck and take off up the driveway, hoping to head them off before they get too close to the house.

The rack of lights on top of the car has me cursing aloud. His headlights are agony to my brain. He stops the car and gets out. I stick the SIG in the back on my pants.

"I'd rather you drop it, Mr. Bevan."

Footsteps hit gravel behind me—a runner's pace. "Dad!"

"Go back to the house, Marcas."

But he keeps coming. And so does the sheriff. With his gun drawn but aimed at the ground.

"Mom was worried—"

"You should be at Tara's."

"Mom didn't take us because you didn't come home. She was worried because you didn't answer your phone."

When I don't answer or look at Marcas, he turns to face what has all my attention. He makes a quick grab for my hand, shifting his weight behind me.

"You gonna holster your gun, sheriff, with a kid this close?"

He does. Marcas starts talking again, so I take his shoulders, turn him toward the house, and give him a gentle shove. "Go."

Running footsteps retreat as I take a breath and face the sheriff, trying my best not to look completely strung out. "I have a killer migraine, so if this can wait—"

"I'll be brief, Mr. Bevan. That display in town today had me wondering if I should remind you this is a quiet town. We don't tolerate that kind of trouble. It looks like you took it out of town, but there's no town nearby that wants it either."

I salute him—a better use of my hands than giving him the finger.

"I also planned to drop by and warn you there's been a grizzly sighting nearby. Causing a bit of trouble, wandering close to homes."

"I'm not worried about grizzlies."

"That's fine. But you might want to discuss wildlife safety with your daughter. She seems to have some unorthodox views about wild animals that the law enforcement of this town doesn't agree with."

Unorthodox views, huh? "So this is a witch hunt?" Fitting. "Get off my property."

He watches me while my nose bleeds onto my shirt for so long I'm afraid I might collapse in the driveway right in front of him. He'd have a field day with that. Then he's in his car, backing up my driveway toward the road. River and Trib emerge from the cover of the woods. They're feeling their age and know when to lie low even though they're still driven to help me. I stumble to the house. Liv runs out just in time to catch me before I fall to my knees.

"Take the kids—"

"It's too late. I can't leave you like this."

"Tell Tara to come—"

"Shh."

I make a reach for the couch, but she steers me away to the bedroom, I'm sure, but I surrender to the agony of my liquefied brain before I see where I land.

I'm in and out of it all night. I know I'm not truly unconscious because the pressure in my skull never subsides; I never reach any level of relief. The unsteady vibration courses through me like I'm a tiny boat in an ocean storm. The climb and fall, wave after wave of it, never finding a rhythm I can hold onto.

There is a constant in the chaos that takes on three forms. One is Liv, dabbing my face, offering me drinks, telling me it's almost over. The others are my children: Marcas reading to me from his books about mythological sea creatures as I weave in and out of the fog, and Sloane, who does nothing but sit and hold my hand. She's the one who remains the longest. Her pacific silence like an anchor, she watches the window, patient for the moon's light to return and drop me back into the elements where I belong.

All I've endured has led me to this house filled by the three of them. I wouldn't change any step of the way for fear it'd reach a different place than this one right now. I'd live it all again if I had to. Suffer it on repeat. The grief I've known, the regret I've had, it's all been made right by the boy reading me his stories, the silent girl mooring me with her small hand, and the woman who's healed me in more ways than I can name.

We have a war to fight, and I don't know when it will begin, or when it will end, but I know we will win. I've come too far to lose what I have, and I won't ever give it up.

"I'm very glad Sloane and Marcas aren't affected by it," Liv tells me in the morning when I'm mostly back to my normal self. "I had no idea it was so severe."

The clarity of the white light in the room after suffering that disorienting blindness all night has me so revived I go outside just to get it full in the face. The clouds have moved out, leaving a sky so clean and blue I gesture Liv to come out and look. She stands next to me, rubbing her arms. "Why does that happen to you?"

I shake my head. It's not something I ever figured out.

"Every lunar eclipse."

"Yep."

"Have you searched your texts?"

"Many times. It's never mentioned."

"Have you asked your mother? Because it seems so … out of sync with everything else about you. A lunar eclipse is a natural process of the earth, the solar system. You're so much in tune with everything else, I don't see why it would be such a huge exception."

I see her point, but it's the same, every time without fail. It's too regular to be wrong.

She lifts my arm and snuggles against me. "It just doesn't fit. Almost like it's an accident. Like …"

She doesn't need to finish because I know what she's thinking. It's like what happened to Sloane. Misused magic and the damaging consequence that often goes along with that. Changing her for life. Irreversible.

But sometimes there isn't an explanation, no matter how hard Liv tries to find one. She doesn't want to treat the symptoms, she wants to know the underlying cause. She wants a cure. Magic isn't that scientific.

She's gone all goose-fleshed due to the chilly November morning I've dragged her out in, so I drag her back inside.

That weekend I take Sloane and Marcas on a walk in the woods before dinner. We swing by Tara's and pick up Winnie and Will. About a quarter mile from the house, I make them drop their coats, gloves, and hats. They know what's up, but they don't know this time, I'm going back to the house. They're on their own.

Marcas starts running in place to keep himself warm before the chill settles in. I rub his little buzzed head.

"You've got a long night ahead of you, bud. You might want to save that energy."

I don't bother signing because Sloane has her back to us, gazing into the forest.

"Night?" Winnie says. "Worst uncle *ever*." But she's grinning like hell, and she surrenders her phone before I have to ask.

Will has a few texts to get out before he hands over his. Sloane watches him and follows suit. Once her eyes are on me, I sign the usual ground rules: *No splitting up. No returning to the house before sunrise unless someone's dying. Find a place to make camp, build a shelter, find food or fast. Only use magic if there are no other options. And everyone must build their own weapons.*

Will fist pumps the air after that last order. The kid has some serious skill building spears and arrows. I wish Sloane was as good—but he has years on her. She will be as good someday.

"And I'm not staying," I say and sign.

Will yells, "Yes!" as everyone else's eyes go wide. Then he fakes a cough and signs while he says, "Um, I mean, please, Uncle Fearghus. Don't leave us out here with no parental supervision." He's so monotone and unconvincing I have to laugh. I don't remember when he grew into such a little shit. I think it might come with being fifteen in this family. At sixteen, he's had a year of practice.

"Questions?"

Sloane comes forward to give me a hug. She lets me hold her a long time, almost as if she knows how important this is for her future. For her safety. For her survival. How important it is to me that she's strong enough to survive a cold November night in the woods without warm clothing, food, and water. Without me.

"I'll send some coyotes to ambush you. Be mindful of the younger ones. They aren't as familiar with the game."

Marcas is already on the hunt for good sticks for his weapons, so I call him back over for a hug and to tell him to listen to his sister. I've already put some targets in the woods on the trail. When the coyotes attack, it's the targets the kids must aim for. Winnie and Will are practically out of sight, jabbering on, making plans. Sloane pops Marcas on the shoulder and they follow. Before she disappears from view she turns around. *Don't let Mom worry.*

I sign, *Okay.*

She signs, *I love you.* And I sign it back.

When I return to the house, I call for River but she doesn't come. I walk around the front of the house and call again. Trib comes out of their shelter, and all I have to see are his eyes to know. Old age has finally defeated River. She's been having trouble walking for weeks, and I knew this day wasn't far off. I go to the shelter and look in. She lifts her head, too weak to do anything else. It splinters through me. Punches out a piece I never knew was so big. She's been with me longer than Liv. There was a time she was my only friend.

I carry her inside and sit with her all night. For once in his life Trib comes inside too, his head on my knee as I doze against the wall. By the time the kids march out of the woods the next morning, River's gone.

Trib follows a week later. The kids help me dig a second grave next to River's while the coyotes gather at the sidelines. Marcas repeats *"it's not fair, it's not fair,"* over and over until Liv takes him inside, leaving Sloane and me watching the graves like there's something we can do to change it.

A few weeks later Liv tells me she can't bear the sadness in the house, or how lonely it is without the two of them around. So I take the kids to the pound and they pick out two new dogs: a furry six-year-old shepherd-mix that could easily pass for River's brother, and a female hound-dog puppy with giant paws, floppy ears, and a coat that will be no help to her this winter. I see another project in my near future: adding heat to the dog shelter.

We let the kids name the dogs—a bit of bad luck for the mutts. River's lookalike becomes Buzzy due to the bands of brown in his coat that look like stripes on a bee, and the hound gets the name Snickerdoodle. It mutates into Snickers then Nicky, which Sloane says isn't so long to fingerspell and fits her better anyway. Then Marcas updates Buzzy to Buzz, and we have two respectable names for two dogs that will never be River and Trib. But they'll find their place— if they survive the coyotes' hazing.

CHAPTER 28

LIV

W E'VE DECIDED TO make Sloane's fourteenth birthday a surprise. When we asked her what she wanted to do and got a "nothing" back, we decided to make it really something. Winnie's on a stepstool, hanging streamers across the kitchen ceiling. She's so tall she could do it on tiptoes. Máthair and Marcas are icing cupcakes at the table. We sent Will on a run for Chinese food, and Shawn's due to arrive any minute.

Tara and I move to the other room to wrap presents. I open the window to let the breeze in. It's cool for July, almost springlike. When Trey and Sloane set off early this morning to do some training, she had to run back for a heavier jacket. She caught me red-handed with the cupcake pans. When she came back through the kitchen, I made sure to have a box of blueberry muffin mix in my hand. She either doesn't suspect a thing, or she does, and she's humoring me.

"One month," Tara says. That's how long she has until her babies leave for college. "All I'll do is worry. All day, every day."

"They'll be together. It's a much better deal than most mothers get."

"True." She peeks into the box I'm about to wrap. "What's that?"

I hand her the silver hair fastener I bought for Sloane. It's some kind of elastic material covered in flakes of real silver. It's more like a piece of jewelry than a hair band. Tara stretches it, raising her brows. "It's amazing the silver stays on. How do they do that?"

"No idea. I thought she could use it on her braid." Sloane's been growing that lock of hair out for years. Even when braided it hangs several inches past her hair, which is already long itself.

I'm bringing the presents into the kitchen when Trey and Sloane appear on the back porch, earlier than expected. Our ruined surprise is quickly forgotten once I spot her teary eyes and the brutal gash on Trey's forearm.

"Sorry," he says. "There was no good excuse that could've kept us out there with this." He holds up his arm. He's bleeding all over the floor.

Máthair moves the cupcakes to the counter and puts an arm around Sloane, who gives in to the sobs she must've been holding back for how hard they come on.

I pull a chair out for Trey, pull another over for me. "What happened?"

"Your daughter got through my defenses. She's too good for her old man."

Sloane obviously got the words off his lips because it makes her cry harder.

It's okay, I sign. *Your dad has a lot of experience with wounds much worse than this one.*

Will comes in the doorway with bags of food, stopping short when he sees the birthday girl back early. Then he spots the gory wound I'm holding pressure on and does a double take. "Guess I missed all the fun." He sets down the bags, hooks Sloane around the neck for a sideways hug. "You okay?"

She nods, wipes her eyes.

He signs, *You're not allowed to cry on your birthday. Even if you maim someone.*

Winnie gets me the suture. I face Sloane so she can see my lips. "Do you want to do it?" It would be great practice and might make her feel better.

She looks at Trey. He waves her over. I guide her at the beginning, but then I let her do the rest on her own. She does a great job, and so does Trey. Not a flinch, and he kisses her forehead when she's finished and fingerspells with his good arm. *Next time we bring a first aid kit with us.*

She nods enthusiastically. Trey's eyes catch mine. He knows what I'm thinking: that she's a walking first aid kit. Her blood is rich with healing. She could've healed him with her blood and they'd still be out there as if nothing happened. We've told her the history of that power, where it came from, and how it protects her, but we've never told her how she can use it to save others. We can't decide if she's old enough to know.

Later that night after the kids have gone to bed, I find Trey missing from the house. I open the front door to check the driveway. A soft breeze toys with my hair, still wet from my bath. A tinge of purple spreads from the western sky into deep blue, and stars twinkle lazily in the east. My check reveals all the cars still in place. Instead of going inside, I close the door and step off the porch in my house slippers. All at once I'm seeing myself standing here, many years ago, after waking up in Trey's bedroom as if in a trance, driven out here by an ethereal purpose to find him unconscious on the ground. Wounded and bloody, he needed my help, and I did all I could to save him, completely unaware how much he'd stolen my heart.

I follow my footsteps that day and when I reach the spot where he fell, I continue walking down the slope to the rear of the house as if tugged by an invisible string. Then I see him, sitting on the ground between the rows of the garden, facing the woods. Buzz and Nicky sit still beside him. It could be a painting with the early night sky above them, the pitch of night fading to indigo, framed by the black silhouettes of the tall pine trees in the distance. The final light of the sky casts an eerie glow on the vegetables and herbs, twisty limbs climbing high out of their cold frames, thick leaves spreading wide across the ground.

The dogs turn to look at me when I near, but Trey remains fixated on the woods before him. I sit at his side. The breeze explores me. There's a rustle in the woods and the dogs take off, Nicky stopping to bay halfway there, losing her lead.

"I've fucked up," Trey says.

"With what?"

"Sloane."

It's an outrageous thought. She couldn't be more perfect; he couldn't be a better father. I won't deny he worried me sometimes, but he's made good on every mistake. He's turned into the father I always knew he could be—even if he didn't believe me. I'm not sure how to respond.

There's a hard line between his brows. "I know why the Moores did what they did to me. You can't create a killer without hardening him from a young age."

"They didn't harden you. They abused you."

"Same thing. Same outcome. Without it, they'd have created a killer who couldn't kill. That's a failure. She has the training, but she also has sympathy. Optimism. A sense of hope. She'll never be able to do it."

"Do what?"

"Kill."

I reach for his hand, my fingers instead met by the bandage on his forearm covering the wound Sloane sutured this morning. It all clicks into place. He's bothered that she cared she hurt him.

"She has too much sympathy and no hate," he says. "No anger."

"I don't want our daughter to have anger."

He turns to me. "Anger for the people who are planning her death? Have been slaughtering her ancestors for centuries?"

"Why does she need that? You've taught her to protect herself—"

"It's not enough. I haven't taught her to kill. Not like I've been taught. Not like Rex Moore has."

"She was upset this morning because she hurt someone she loves. That's it. If you were an attacker, it would've been different." After I say it, I do see his point. How different would it have been? She doesn't have a hurtful bone in her body. And being deaf and often misunderstood by hearing people has taught her many lessons in patience and understanding. All her life she's had to work very hard to be understood and to understand others—two sides of one ingredient that builds compassion. When confronted by an enemy, her first impulse would be to try to see where they're coming from, to try to reach a middle ground where she could understand them with something deeper than words. She must always reach further. Her connections with others must delve deeper.

I look into the western sky, no longer indigo but a midnight blue. I see his point, but there's no reason to obsess over it. We're not going to do to her what the Moores did to him. Even if it wasn't too late, it would be out of the question.

"I need to go to Virginia and stir them up so they start sending men again."

"No, Trey. That's crazy."

"She has to see what they do to us. She needs to be motivated by more than self-preservation. She needs more than that to win."

"There are other ways to win than by killing people."

"Not against them."

"I don't think—"

"I should take her there. She'll see exactly how they are. We could ambush them. I could help her. There's no reason to wait for them to come to us."

I'm not sure what kind of visit he has in mind, but the mention of ambush gives me an idea. I could remind him he's tried that. Twice. Neither time giving him the results he expected. He's forgetting the advice Máthair gives him every time he gets the idea to go back. It's not meant for him. It's not his job. His job is here, with his family, and it's all their ancestors have asked him to do.

"There is a way Sloane can see it all," he says. "See what they did to me, to Christian and Máthair. To you. I can let her into my head." He still glares into the distance, not turning to look at me, like he's asking but not asking. The old Trey. Imperious and hardheaded. Oblivious to the needs of others and to common sense.

Unease settles hard onto me. I'm out of practice for this kind of fight. He's been too reasonable for too long, and I feel like I'm the one being ambushed, not the Moores. "I don't want that for her."

His eyes don't move out of their hard stare. "Without it she'll have no frame of reference. She won't fight them like they need to be fought."

I say nothing, hoping he hears his words hanging in the air like I do. The only person who knows how the Moores need to be fought is Sloane. She might not know yet—she's only fourteen. And it's not up to us to tell her what to do. It's something she must figure out on her own, and when she does, she'll know.

"I need to visit Christian anyway. It's been too long since I've seen him."

Damn him, he can't seriously be considering this. The porch light blinks—it must be Sloane. I get up, climb the hill to the house, and find her standing in the kitchen watching Trey through the glass door.

What's Dad doing?

Just sitting with me. Talking. I take her shoulders and turn her in the direction of her bedroom. She doesn't budge.

Are you talking about me?

We're always talking about you. Marcas, too. I take her face and kiss her forehead.

She takes another lingering glance at her dad before moving toward her bedroom.

I lower her window shade and sit next to her on the edge of her bed. I brush her bangs off her forehead and she gives me this weak, all-knowing smile. Captures my hand with hers.

"Do you want to talk?"

She watches my mouth then shakes her head. Just like when she was a little girl, she wants me to sit and share her silence. So I tug the band off the end of her braid and comb the long lock of hair with my fingers. I start a fresh braid, and she relaxes into the bed, closing her eyes. I know she can't hear the hiss of wind through the pines outside or the creak of Marcas' bed through the wall, but I'm certain there are things she hears with other senses that I don't hear at all. Perhaps that's what brought her out of bed.

By the time I finish the braid, her breathing has already deepened in light sleep. I let myself out of her room. Back in the kitchen I go to the window to look out at Trey still sitting in the same position, no doubt contemplating his ridiculous trip to Virginia. All I need is a rifle with a scope and I could shoot him.

A ghostlike figure appears at the edge of the forest, moving toward Trey. I go out on the porch and recognize Máthair's small frame, slightly hunched with age. She must've predicted I needed her. Sometimes I forget I'm surrounded by witches. I turn to go inside and leave them— if she knew to come, she surely knows what help I need. But before I close the door behind me there's a tickle on the breeze in my ear that turns into a tiny voice. Her voice. *Please join us.*

They're seated on the ground when I do: Trey still glaring into the woods, Máthair reaching for my hand. The night is in full force now, stars in varying sizes and intensity in unending layers above us. Wispy clouds swim below them, looking close enough to touch.

"It's such a walk for you, and so late."

She squeezes my hand. "I walk every night. Longer distances than I did to get here."

"You shouldn't," Trey snaps.

"I'm cloaked," she says.

"And they could be affected to see through it."

"You underestimate me, Fearghus."

"You underestimate them."

If he doesn't stop arguing with his mother, I'm going to clock him. "Trey's in a foul mood because he thinks Sloane isn't angry or hateful enough to fight the Moores."

She looks at him, her gaze cool and patient despite how irritating he is. He remains as closed off as ever. And when he speaks, I'm as surprised as she appears to be. We're not used to this being easy. We usually have to drag the words out of him.

"She needs to know everything I know." He turns his face toward the woods again, the hard line deepening between his brows. "All of it."

Máthair studies him, taking her time to form her response. "If the end she's destined to bring required everything you know, our ancestors would have appointed you. There's a reason they chose Sloane. They knew she'd be isolated from all you and I know. We need to trust they knew she was the one." She pauses, waiting until he looks at her. "*Is treascairt na tragóide é an crann greamaithe.*"

A destiny embraced is a tragedy overcome. They're the words from the note Mamó left him before she died.

"And think it through, Fearghus. If you show her everything you know of the Moores, all those hateful, despicable things, how would that change her perception of her duty? Of why you're training her?"

Trey swears under his breath, giving words to the jarring jolt of my own realization. Máthair has thought of something we missed. If Sloane learns everything Trey endured, she'll no longer be cast as the heroine in her future. She'll see her role as something else, a repeat of history, a child trained for a specific use just like the Moores tried to do to Trey. She won't see herself as someone who can end a war. She'll believe she was created as a tool for revenge. Used, by her own family.

Trey shoves himself up and walks a few paces away before dropping to a squat, hanging his head. "She can't ever think that. It's not true."

"It's not," I echo, only to add my voice. We all know it's not true. If there was a way to get her out of all this, we would. We've discussed every option and all of them come to the same conclusion: the Moores will always find her, either by human means or magical ones, and they'll hunt her like prey. If she's destined for this fight, she must face it head on. She's not their prey.

"Then may I suggest letting Sloane be Sloane and not burdening her with images that will do nothing but harm her vision of her place in all this."

If the weight lifting off me is also lifting off Trey, it doesn't show in his face when he turns around. The slump of his shoulders and hard lines around his eyes show he's more haunted than ever. "I feel it coming."

Máthair takes a breath, twisting to take in the house, her gaze remaining on Sloane's curtained window as if dedicating this moment to memory. "So do I. And I think she does too."

CHAPTER 29

TREY

L IV AND I are seated in the high school principal's office to talk about Sloane. Her deafness is the reason we're on a first-name basis with every teacher and principal she's had. Until today, all discussions have revolved around how to best equip her in a hearing classroom. Her academic performance. Her socialization. This is the first time Liv and I have been called for a meeting due to Sloane's behavior. A fight. Initiated by her. I'm having a hard time suppressing a sick smile until I recall the image of Sloane's traumatized face as she and her interpreter were led into the counselor's office three doors down.

"So this other boy—he's a sophomore too?" Liv asks.

This principal, Camille, is prim and no-nonsense. She's as to-the-point in person as she is on the phone. She doesn't waste our time discussing philosophical crap that isn't functional. I like her.

"He's a junior. And very familiar with our strict no bullying policy." Camille spins in her chair to retrieve a printed handbook on the shelf behind her. "Be assured I'm working with Jared's parents as well."

"Jared?" Liv says.

I let out a breath, and on it: "You've gotta be fu—"

Liv sends her heel into the top of my boot and gives me a look of death. I shut up.

"Yes," Camille says. "Jared Larson."

Larson? The first name is a nice coincidence, but the last name? No fucking way. "He related to the sheriff at all?"

"He's Sheriff Larson's son."

I'm about to spring from the seat but thankfully Liv has a bruising grip on my arm before I can move.

"Which makes the decision to report this incident to law enforcement easy for me. School policy defines two types of assaults. The first one is defined as an attempt to harm another person. The second, an attempt to seriously injure or kill. Knowing your daughter, I'd file hers under the first. But knowing the seriousness of Jared's injury … to be honest it gives me pause." She glances between the two of us. Censoring herself. She wants to ask how the hell sweet Sloane Bevan could KO a kid.

"It's irrelevant though," she continues. "Since this is the sheriff's son, law enforcement is involved whether I report it or not. This is your daughter's first offense. With her clean record and academic performance, and if we agree it falls under minor assault, I'd recommend in-school suspension. But I've never had a student knock another unconscious."

"The kid has a concussion," I say. "He's fine." Sloane could have done much worse.

"He's in the hospital, Mr. Bevan."

I'm 'Mr. Bevan' now. Great.

Camille shifts her attention back to the school handbook, tapping her pen against it. "It's so hard to believe this is Sloane."

"She was being tormented for being deaf, Camille. She was reacting to bullying, not just assaulting a random kid," Liv says.

"Students with disabilities are disciplined in accordance with policy just like other students. We do not believe in double standards. There are limitations under federal law but they don't apply here."

Liv glances at me because we're thinking the same thing: deafness is not a disability. But to a hearing school, it is. It's something we've always fought, and it's our damn fault for staying in Black River where our only option was a regular public school.

Camille closes the handbook and sets down her pen. "Three-day suspension and after-school counseling for minor assault. I won't be forwarding this to the school board. But if I'm challenged it will go there. What are your questions?"

"None," I say and get up.

Camille stands to shake my hand. "No more incidents, Trey. Your daughter is too bright for this."

"There won't be."

Liv and I get in the car and sit in the parking lot. They're keeping Sloane in the counselor's office until school dismisses in fifteen minutes, giving Liv enough time to rant before Sloane comes out. I have nothing to say. The punishment is suitable. Sloane won't do it again after I talk to her. And she got to break that little shit's nose and teach him the lesson he needed. All is good.

"What I want to know," Liv says, "is how long the bullying was going on. Why didn't she tell us?"

"Maybe it wasn't. Maybe this is how Sloane handles people picking on her." Sounds good to me.

"I don't believe this is the first time someone has picked on her."

"Doesn't matter. No one will ever pick on her again. Not at this school."

The bell rings and bodies pour out. Sloane comes out in a cluster of kids, all trying to talk to her at once like she's some kind of celebrity, and she of course can't make sense of any of it. I start the Camaro, earning some attention from nearby boys impressed by the exhaust. One of them nudges Sloane on the shoulder and points. She nods at him and heads our way. Good—it's usually Liv who picks her up, and I figured she'd be looking for her car. It saves Liv and me from having to wade through teenagers to get her.

Upon learning her sentence, Sloane lifts her chin and signs, *Okay.* But watching her in the rearview mirror, I see her eyes go reflective with tears.

Can we talk at home? Liv asks her.

She nods and looks quickly out the window.

"Dibs," I say to Liv.

"Fine." She points at me. "But she can't do this again. She's to report bullying, not handle it herself."

We unload from the car at home, and I catch Sloane's eye and tilt my head toward the woods. She drops her backpack on the porch and follows me to the bank of the river where we each take a seat on neighboring flat stones. She picks at the bandages on the knuckles of her right hand. She must've spent some time with the school nurse today too.

I take her left arm and stretch it out. She stifles a wince when I twist, exposing the purple bruise on her elbow. That must be how she knocked the kid out.

Good work, I sign.

Her eyes fill with tears again, but she doesn't look away from me. She skims my face, trying to figure me out. She expects me to be angry and she's prepared to take it like an adult, but my last comment has thrown her off.

If you're going to shut some asshole down, don't do it at school.

Her eyes go so wide a tear sneaks out of each one. I wipe them with my thumbs.

Your principal went easy on you, and she shouldn't have. She has rules to follow too. Next time, you'll be expelled. There will not be a next time. You understand?

She nods, tears in full effect now. She smears them off but they keep on running.

Was he the only one giving you a hard time?

She turns away. I've never had to worry that she'd be dishonest with me, but I see a fib about to materialize. I tap her on the arm and sign, *Truth.*

She lifts her bandaged hand—it's left her unable to sign. I dig out my phone and point to her pocket for her to dig out hers. All she needs is two thumbs for that. I sign, *Tell me.*

I watch the river water playing over the rock while she jabs out a big block of text. What I get on my phone is an unpunctuated run-on sentence that explains how he wasn't the only one, but he's the one who started it. He spread news that I'm an ex-con and we all worship demons—I work hard to stifle a chuckle. I keep reading. She couldn't understand the other kids' new behavior around her until a good friend told her what was being spread around, but even then she ignored it, expecting it to die out. But her lack of response only made Jared Larson worse. He started mocking her behind her back—she didn't know he was there and couldn't hear what he was saying. When she'd turn around, he'd stop. All the kids would laugh. Then today she turned around and saw Marcas' name on his lips. And she snapped.

I lower my phone and see she's busy hammering out another text. Buzz has found us. He's nudging his nose under her elbow and messing up her keystrokes. It's softened the frown on her face, so I don't call him off. Moths flutter down from above, one landing on her shoulder, another on her knee. I've allied with the coyotes and birds, but she's befriended every creature in these woods.

Her second text comes in: *He has a little brother in Marcas' grade, and I was afraid he'd give him trouble too, at least I think that's why I hit him. I didn't really have a chance to think about it, it happened so fast.*

I sign, *I don't think he's going to give you or Marcas any trouble ever again.*

If there's ever a time for a high five it would be now, only I'm not the high-fiving type.

She sends another text: *And after he was down, I took a pull of black magic and made him mute when around me. I'm sorry, Dad. So sorry.*

When I look up from the screen she's squared her shoulders, her breath coming hard like her heart is beating out of control, prepping to get her the hell away from a father who's going to kill her. Too bad I think I've just become the high-fiving type, because my hand is in the air and she's staring at it like it's some alien creature. She drops black magic on the kid after she knocks him out? Who raised this girl? Someone way more awesome than me.

Her hand raises slowly to meet mine with something too soft to be a high five. I close my hand over hers. Poke her in the forehead with my other hand. And laugh my ass off. It's bad, I know, but I can't help it. She moves from her rock to mine, scooting beside me. I put my arm around her and hug tight, kissing the top of her head that's so high I barely have to bend down. She's fifteen and I don't know where the years have gone, but I do know one thing: the Moores are not taking her away from me.

Back at the house Sloane goes straight to Liv and gives her a long hug that has Liv looking at me like I worked magic. I wait until Sloane drags her backpack into her bedroom then I say, "I told her to kill him next time."

Liv lets out a single burst of a laugh. "Things are so simple in your world."

Looking into Liv's eyes, my world comes down around me. Sloane may be trained to take down a guy twice her size, but now I'm all too aware of something new. She's not trained to turn off the emotion. To just handle it. After one harmless knockout, she's rattled and upset and worried about consequences. When I was fifteen I'd have killed without mercy. Without remorse. Hell, I tried, and I was punished for it, and it only made me want to do it more.

She's not prepared, and I have no time and no idea how to prepare her.

Liv straddles me in bed, dragging her fingers down the sides of my face to press circles in the tense spots in my jaw. "Temporomandibular joint," she says.

"I love it when you talk dirty." I'm rock hard and ready to go but now that she's started this, I feel my eyes roll back in my head and my backbone surrender its form. "Keep that up and you'll have to fall asleep unsatisfied."

She bends to kiss me, her mouth soft, just a little tongue. Like stoking a fire. She doesn't want me to go out.

I cross my arms behind my head to prop up and look at her. Another kiss would be nice. More tongue would be better, but she's glaring at my arm then snatching it and yanking it out from under my head. I can't even get out a *what the hell* before she's saying the same thing to me. I look where she's looking. My forearm, scrawled with Inis' number.

"Why is that back?" she asks.

I sit up against her. She slides back on my thighs as I scrub a hand over it. It's as distinct as it was the day Inis put it there, and Liv's narrowed eyes prove she remembers exactly how this works—the number remains on my skin until I stop thinking of the person who put it there. So if it's back, I can guess why Liv's looking like she's about to slap me—and with this kind of evidence it's pointless to argue. I'm going to hunt Inis down and show her what I think about her timing.

Liv scoots off me to kneel on her side of the bed. "Trey?"

"I've no idea why it's there. Haven't thought about that woman for years." I keep my eyes on hers because her sensors will pick up any shifty move and be a nail in my coffin.

"You sure about that?"

"Yeah, pretty fucking sure." A clammy heat crawls up my body, restoring the pressure in my jaw that had just relaxed under Liv's expert touch. She's pushing for answers because, shit, I'd be pushing hard too if I were her. So there's no need to lose my cool.

"Okay," she says. "So then why is it back?"

I try to kick free of the sheet which has twisted around my ankles and is very close to pissing me off.

"Easy." She lays a hand on my chest. "I'm not upset. I believe you."

"Then get back on me and let's finish this." I snag her by the hips and haul her back on top of me. She's compliant until I slide my hands under her shirt.

Her quick grip on my forearms isn't strong enough to stop me, but I do stop because I know that's what she wants. I'm being too forward after an interruption that soured the mood. This may have been going differently before but now that the air has changed I can't just lie here and relax. I need my hands on her. I need her under me. I need to bury myself inside her until all the heat in my head has unfurled into my blood, diffused, cooled.

"I'd rather you calmed down first," she says.

I flip us so I'm on top. Kiss her hard on the mouth. "So calm me down."

Her breathing has gone rapid, her eyes heavy-lidded. She snakes a leg around mine. I kiss her again, seeking out the tongue I wanted earlier. I give her more of my weight. She squirms in the tight space underneath me, so I break the kiss to make sure I haven't crushed any vital organs.

"Forget what I said," she says breathlessly, "about you calming down first."

So I strip her down and plunge inside and with my face buried in her neck and the binding of her arms, I'm gone from the world. It's just me and her surrounded by a perfect void. Her grip is an anchor, without it I'd be sucked away. She nuzzles my cheek so I turn and kiss her, capturing both her wrists above her head. The taste of her mouth, the clench of her body on mine—it makes me want to—

"Stop," she says. "Wait, just feel it for a second, just—"

I feel it all right. Joined bodies, heartbeats, breath. I release her arms. She rests a hand against my chest. Her pulse becomes a force, a power I could tap into, and I sense mine syncing even further, drawing upon something both new and familiar so I go deeper. I'm chasing it down, gaining on it, a dribble of magic coming into me, mingling with my own. Now together I see the contrast of the two: my earth magic, her—

She jerks her hand away and looks at it before turning shocked eyes on me.

"Shh," I say, a finger to her mouth. She's about to analyze this, and we need to let it be or it will slip away; we'll never reach it again. I put my lips to her ear. "*Is trí na dúile a shínim. Is leis na dúile a aimsím. Is tú mo chuisle. Leatsa mé. Sín amach, is ceanglaímis."*

The pocket of magic in her is real now, like a seed, dry and ungerminated. I drill deeper, tracing it to its foundation. Its root. Something once alive but now in stasis—unwatered, unfertilized. Waiting.

She whispers my name on an outward breath. It's filled with so much ecstasy I lose connection to everything but the physical—her soft skin against my mouth, her body entwined with mine. But it's too damn good to care about that other connection I lost and when she binds her arms around my neck again, I let it all go.

I roll off her and catch my breath. She gets hold of my hand. We lie there as I try to gather what just happened, to determine if I just made some irreversible mistake. Or if I should figure out what initiated it so I can someday try again.

"What were you saying, when you … I couldn't make sense of the Irish with all the other things going on."

"It was …" I rub my face to think. The words were automatic, coming from some primitive part of me. Millennia of magic passed down from ancient generations. Magic that resides in me, magic I never allow out of the confinement I built for it. I have to think myself back to that moment, rehear the words I spoke.

"Through the elements I reach," she prompts. *"With the elements I find…"*

She seems to have lost the rest so I finish it for her. *"You are my pulse. I am yours. Stretch out and let us connect."*

"Damn, Trey. That's … something. And what it opened in me—" She shudders, reaches for the sheet to draw over herself. "I'm not sure what to say."

"Say you'll try it again with me sometime."

"I would, if I knew what it was."

"It was your black magic blood. Found—somehow— and waking up."

If I could open something in her like the world she's opened for me, my worth might have a chance of someday reaching hers.

LIV

WEEKS PASS WITH Inis' number embedded on Trey's arm, long enough for me to decide why it's really there. She's demanding that he contact her, but he's too stubborn to consider it. He won't do something when forced. And I have a hunch she knows this, and it's a play of power between them. She has something to say that might be of use to him, but only if he'll bow to her will. They're both too old to be acting like children.

"I'm going to call Inis," I tell him over dinner one dark winter evening. It's just the two of us. We never see Sloane anymore—she spends her rare free time with her grandmother, learning things Trey can't teach. Marcas followed her there tonight so Winnie could help him with his home-work. She's home from college and the only one he'll take help from because she claims she has visions of his good grades. Whether the visions actually come to her isn't something we'll ever know; it's her optimism that makes them come true in real life. That's all that matters.

"You should call her," he says.

I look up at him in surprise. I expected this to be a fight. As if realizing what he just said, he turns away, frowning.

"I thought you'd try to talk me out of it."

He scratches his eyebrow. "Me too." He shrugs, shoot-ing a boyish smile at me. Who is this man? And why have I never noticed the smile lines by his eyes, or how the perma-nent crease between his brows seems dull in comparison?

There was a time he considered Inis to be as untrust-worthy as the Moores, as deserving of his hate. As her rel-ative it was hard not to be troubled by that. He blamed the practitioners of the type of magic that deafened our daugh-ter as much as he blamed himself for drawing upon it. But he never treated me any differently for being descended from them. He never loved me less. He taught his chil-dren black magic and sought out the strain of it in me. His own actions, working toward an acceptance of some-thing he hated.

"What?" he asks. Because I've got tears in my eyes now, from something I should have recognized long ago.

"I didn't think I could fall harder in love with you."

He chokes on the water he just took a gulp of. "What'd I do now?"

I dial Inis' number. She picks up after several rings. "Cousin."

"Hi, Inis."

There's an awkward pause in which I feel guilt for not calling her sooner, followed by frustration she revived the number on Trey's arm instead of call me like a human being.

"Strange to be hearing from you."

"We thought you might be trying to get in touch with us."

She laughs—joyful or patronizing, it's hard to tell over the phone. "I was."

Another block of silence gives me time to remember our last conversation in the Arizona desert where Dillon crashed our meeting and she fled, thinking I'd betrayed her. I left her several messages after that, explaining, apologizing, swearing my innocence before I gave up. I was never certain she got them or believed them. "I have no hard feelings for you, Inis, and I hope you have none for me."

"Then listen when I tell you this. The Moores have nothing over you."

Unless she's visited every one of their properties and analyzed all their operations she couldn't possibly know what the Moores have over us. "What do you mean?"

"That's all I can say."

I exhale hard and look at Trey. Vague statements do nothing to help us. Neither do these games. He raises his forearm toward me to show the number has been erased. All that build-up, for this? "Inis, your number's been on Trey's arm for a long time. If that's all—"

"That *is* all. They have *nothing*. Remember that. I'm gagged against saying more. I'm—" She's coughing with deep, choking coughs that go on so long I wonder if someone's there to help her. When she speaks again, her voice is weak. "See what I mean? Goodbye, Liv. Find power in night. Tell Sloane. And good luck." She hangs up.

Trey takes the phone away from me and sets it on the table. I must've been staring at the display for a while. "That was too vague to be useful."

I tell him anyway, hoping he can glean some meaning out of it. All he does is curse and land a fist on the table. He's been living with her number on his arm for no reason other than her display of command over him. "I don't know how she's related to me. She's so different."

He snorts in agreement.

All my life I longed to find my biological family, assuming once I did I'd finally have people who understood me, who I could connect to on a natural level without barriers. Without these games and confusing intentions. I imagined what it would be like to be on the same wavelength with someone. To just click.

It was a romanticized idea that ignored the other part that makes a person up: her life experiences, her upbringing. The situations in life that mold her. And how taking the left fork in the road when your biological stock takes the right can lead you in a direction so opposite you won't recognize one another should you ever meet up again.

When my mother—or grandmother, or great-grandmother, I'm not sure who—took that opposite fork, she did so for a reason. She made a hard decision—a brave decision—to run from her family and start a new line that didn't pass magic to the new generation. I'll never know her reason, but the trust I feel for it is rooted deep and spread so wide it's undeniable. It's a truth I know is right for me, more right than that strange strain of magic Trey discovered inside me.

"Trey, the magic in me … I think we should let it be."

He reaches across the table for my hand. "If it scares you—"

"It doesn't scare me. Well, maybe a little. It feeds off hate and anger and death—I know all that is a natural part of the world, just like your magic, but I don't want any part of it."

"You learn to manage it. There's a balance—"

"I just know it's not right for me. It's the opposite of where I stand in the world. And even if you revive it, I won't use it. I don't want to use it."

He takes a good, long look into my eyes. He squeezes my hand then withdraws, returning all attention to the food on his plate. "Okay."

My first reaction is to ask him to repeat that because there's no way he backed down that easily. "Okay?"

"Yeah, but I can't promise not to go poking around for it. It's too tempting. Just blows my mind that it's there."

"As long as you don't do anything with it."

"That I can promise." Then he's looking into my eyes again, so intent it steals my breath. "We could be so powerful together."

"We already are."

He smiles. It reaches his whole face, his whole being. It's the smile that only Marcas used to wring out of him—the spontaneous one that was completely free of worry, lacking all burden and high on spirit. Every time I see it, I look for some stationary object to hold onto before the earth shifts.

Spring arrives with another lunar eclipse that leaves Trey too weak to do anything but groan curses into the mattress. His eyes won't roll down out of his head, and he starts talking gibberish. I consider going to town to buy him some liquor so he can get through it like he used to, but there's always the chance he'll pick up the drinking exactly where he left off so many years ago. It's just not worth it.

So I call Tara instead and ask if she can drive my kids to school so I can stay with Trey. Once they're gone the silent house seems to help, and I finally get him sitting up. He drinks a glass of water and asks for coffee. His eyelids are slow to blink. After a night like that, he needs rest, not caffeine, but I'd like to get his nose to stop bleeding first.

I leave him in bed to answer my phone in the kitchen. It's Sloane's principal, Camille.

"I'm sorry to call with bad news, Liv, but Sloane's been in some trouble again with Jared Larson. We're holding them in the counselor's office. I'd like to speak with you and Trey in person."

"Is she okay?"

"Yes, both children are okay. There was nothing physical this time, but Jared has an unusual complaint about your daughter that we need to address. He claims she took his voice. I don't know if this is a joke between the two of them, but it's causing a disruption in school. I need to speak with you as soon as possible."

I check on Trey, telling him to call Tara if he needs help. Then I head to the school with a tightening in my chest that's foreign to me. I can normally find Zen in stressful situations. It's a skill I've always had that seems to be missing now. I can't separate myself from this situation

Sloane is in. It's my fault—Trey's too. We kept Sloane in a hearing school knowing her differences, her struggles. We chose this for her.

Camille and Sheriff Larson are standing outside the front doors of the school when I arrive. It seems odd, and gets even odder, when beside them I see Sloane's interpreter who's rarely without Sloane. Camille scans the parking lot while Sheriff Larson speaks forcefully into the radio on his shoulder as if he's calling in a crime.

"Sloane is missing," Camille says as I approach. "She somehow escaped from the counselor's office. She had to walk past several people to get out of the front office, but no one saw her leave."

The tightening in my chest drops into my stomach. It's stupid—Sloane's gone off on her own before. It's hardly surprising. Something tells me today, this is not a determined trek on the heels of a woodland creature all the way to the road. It isn't curiosity propelling her legs further than her common sense would allow. It's not wandering too far; it's running away. Today she has a motive. I text her: *We're worried. Where are you?*

She often turns her phone off during class. She doesn't need it when her interpreter is present, and the teachers prefer it not being a distraction. I hope she's turned it back on.

"I'll start a sweep of town," the sheriff says. "If you'll check any places your daughter would likely go, we'll find her before lunchtime. This town isn't big enough for a girl to hide in for long." He looks out at the road with a hunter's gaze I don't like at all. It's not the town's square footage we need to consider but the miles of surrounding mountainous forest that need to be searched by foot. And even then, if Sloane doesn't want to be found—

"Liv?"

"I'm on it," I say to Camille. "I'll call as soon as I find her."

I get back in the car. Press my forehead against the steering wheel. Try not to think about the useless black magic buried within me that could surely help right now. Trey's magic isn't any more useful than mine today—he's too weakened from the eclipse last night. Before I drive away I call Tara.

"Location spell," she says. "Easy. I'll call you back."

The drive to her house takes me through town. It's not the way Sloane would take on foot if she was going to Tara's or going home but it's my only option. I'd only get lost on foot in these woods if I attempted to follow her. Trey's taught me a lot, but it's no substitute for the knowledge of the earth they share. The forest is a second home to them. A first home, really. An original home. Even though they no longer live in nature, it's a part of their subconscious they'll never forget.

Shadows darken in the car while I'm waiting at a red light. Cloud cover has moved in. I watch the sun being obscured when an abnormal object on the road catches my eye. A large black utility van. Windowless. Followed by another. Then another. They're crossing the intersection in front of me in a caravan and my red light lingers much longer than it should. They stream by in an unending line. Ten. Twenty. The red light remains, and I look in my mirror at the unconcerned driver behind me, waiting patiently as if this light isn't five minutes long. On the sidewalk, people go about their business. No one's noticing the suspicious SWAT team vans cruising by. No one cares.

A police car has pulled up to the light on the opposite side—Sheriff Larson's car. He's on the hunt for Sloane, but he's going to sit here and wait for this train of strange vans to roll through his town without question? I go back to counting vans, a lull taking hold. But I've seen these before. A long time ago. Chicago. Parked in the alley behind Tara's house.

We can't fight this. We need to flee like we did that night at Tara's.

I spin the wheel and floor it, squealing through a U-turn in the direction of Marcas' school. The pungent smell of burned rubber fills the car. I come up behind a car going the speed limit and pass it on the shoulder, kicking gravel, its honking horn long behind me. I fly into the school parking lot and screech to a stop at the front door. People call out to me as I run past the front office, but I keep going, straight to Marcas' class where I burst through the door.

His teacher jumps back against the wall.

"I need Marcas. An emergency. I'm sorry." I've already got him by the arm.

"Did you sign him out in the—"

I drag him through the door. He's trying to jerk away, demanding to know what's wrong.

"Marcas, we have to run!"

If there's one thing he's good at, it's running. We race down the hall, past the principal who's trying to stop us. Slam through the heavy metal door. I thank Trey for the years of hard training because Marcas and I hop in the car and buckle up with perfect accuracy and more running power in us had we needed it.

"What the heck, Mom?"

"Your sister's missing. Your dad's sick at home. And there are about thirty vans filled with the Moores' men heading toward our house right now."

He gapes at me out of the corner of my eye. I'd look at him and take his hand for reassurance, but I can't take my eyes off the road or hands off the wheel. The car's engine is making sounds I've never heard. I don't think I've ever pushed it this hard.

"Wrong turn!" he yells.

"We're going to Tara's."

"But they're going to our house. We have to help Dad!"

"I'm helping him by making you safe."

He pounds the seat with both hands as if needing to divert energy before he explodes. Tara's house might not be safe but there's no other way. Those vans were all headed in the same direction. If another group was sent to Tara's, it's a risk I'll have to take. Being with Máthair is the safest place for him right now. She has some kind of immunity against the Moores' evil. They've never harmed her.

Tara meets us in the driveway. "All signs point to her being very close to your house."

No. I get out of the car, taking Marcas' hand and putting it in Tara's. "Don't let him out of your sight."

"What—why? What's going on?"

"Black vans headed to our house, at least thirty of them. Just like the ones that unloaded behind your Chicago house that night. Get everyone in the car and start driving. I have to go help Trey."

"Liv—"

"I'm not staying here!" Marcas screams.

I go inside for the gun safe, loading my waistband and pockets before sprinting into the woods toward the footbridge across the river. A pulse of light hits somewhere behind me, illuminating the trees that streak by on both sides. The trail that's become short with familiarity stretches by miles. Rounding a bend, I spot a moving object—Buzz running at his full speed with his ears folded back. We nearly collide then he circles me and leads the way. I wish I could communicate with him like Trey and Sloane do. Am I too late? Are they already dead?

We slow our pace at the edge of the woods. I draw a nine millimeter. The spring air is cold in my overheated lungs, dry in my throat. The wind shifts through the trees—the only sound aside from my rapid breath and Buzz's panting. He swallows hard, looking up at me with big brown eyes. I wish I could ask him what to do. *What the hell do I do?* I'm blind to what's happening. I'm walking into this without cover. As soon as I emerge from the trees, I'll be an easy target. One person facing an army.

Buzz perks his ears, facing behind us. He raises his nose to sniff the air then starts wagging his tail. Marcas pops into the scenery, running so fast I grab for his arm but I only get empty air. Screaming at him would alert them to our location. It's too late anyway—he's leapt from the cover of the trees and is cutting up the side of the house so I have no choice but to follow.

What we encounter in the front yard takes a moment to register. Dappled sunlight on the empty driveway, clouds breaking up in the sky above. There's no way we beat them here. They already came. Trey's dead inside, and Sloane is gone. I cover my mouth to keep from scaring Marcas with whatever sound is climbing up my throat, but it doesn't matter. Soon he'll be as ripped in half as me.

He runs up the driveway and stops in a patch of sunlight, his hand shading his eyes so he can peer ahead. His jacket billows in the breeze. Then he jumps at the same time I do—a thump from inside the house. I make it to the front door before him and hold him back to stick my head inside and listen. Another hard thump on the floor, sounds of struggle. I aim the nine millimeter and creep around the doorjamb and along the wall into the hall. With Marcas close behind me, I whisper for him to cover his ears. Then I kick my bedroom door open. Trey looks up at me before delivering a final blow to a guy's temple with the hilt of a knife. The guy goes limp. Trey kneels on his attacker's back and takes hold of his head—I push Marcas from the doorway just before the snap of vertebrae.

I press Marcas against the wall. "Don't move."

The bedroom has been painted with blood. Trey falls to hands and knees beside the guy, shaking his head hard as if trying to stay conscious. There's a dark stain on his jeans just below his hip, too saturated to be from anyone's wounds but his. I help him onto the bed. "Knife wound?"

He nods. I grab a towel off the ground, still wet from his shower. "Hold pressure. Here." I press his hand against the wound. His idea of pressure isn't good enough, and I know it's because he's still feeling the effect of the lunar eclipse. The fight he just finished drained him of any strength he had. "Are any more of them in the house?"

"Not sure."

"There are thirty vans headed here. They should be here by now."

"Start the car. I can't fight like this."

"Sloane is missing."

He grabs my wrist. "What?"

"Mom," Marcas says from the hall. "I think there's a—" His voice is abruptly muffled.

I pluck the nine millimeter off the bed and aim out the bedroom doorway, firing a round into the forehead of a guy who's clamped a hand over Marcas' mouth. The body falls away and Marcas screams, rushing to bury his face against my side.

"*A mhic*," Trey says, reaching a hand toward him.

I let Marcas go. Trey releases the pressure on his wound to take Marcas' head in his hands, two thumbs on his forehead. When Marcas blinks rapidly I know that last memory was just taken, and if we don't get Marcas out of this house there will be too many bad memories for Trey to erase. I wipe Trey's blood off Marcas' face with my sleeve and move him closer to the headboard so the other dead body is out of sight. Then I step over it to check the yard outside the window. "If we stay in here I can handle them one at a time."

"They won't keep coming one at a time. We need to move."

Trey shouldn't be going anywhere with a wound like that. But if they start coming in groups, we'll have no chance at all. I rip the sheet off the bed and use the knife Trey dropped on the floor beside the body to slice long strips that I hand to Marcas to hold. Then I take the towel away from Trey and cut the clean end off, fold it, and bind it to him with the strips of sheet. He grunts when I tighten the knot. Marcas lays a sympathetic hand on his arm. "Toughen up, Dad."

"Is there any magic the two of you can use against them?"

"They'll be shielded against our magic. There are things we can do but they take time."

"What about—" A heavy weight lands on the roof above us and we all look up.

Trey reaches for a boot. I help him into it, Marcas tying laces as I shove the other foot into the second one. Trey uses me for leverage to stand and it just about brings me to the floor. But once he's up I can handle enough of his weight to get us moving. Marcas trails behind us with a firm grip on my jacket. We make it to the front door, then onto the porch. Halfway across the yard to the truck, we stop.

A black wall emerges from the forest on both sides, merging together to form a semicircle around us. A hundred bodies—two hundred. Muscled. Well-armed. Dead in the eyes. Soldiers.

The wind shifts, sucking upward in a surge that fills with a throng of birds so great they block out the sky. Trey raises a hand and they settle in the trees, screeching and raucous as if denied a fight they crave. One man has stepped forward from the wall to assess the flock. Trey slips a spare pistol from the back of my pants and aims one-handed from around my shoulder while addressing the one who came forward. "I wouldn't."

I plug the ear on that side with my finger and look at Marcas. He covers his ears, his eyes so wide I see the pines reflected in them.

"Then call them off," the man says, stepping closer.

Marcas waves a hand in front of us. Fire leaps from the ground in a curved line, protecting us from everything but bullets. He could probably send a wave of fire toward the enemy line and end this quickly, but that might set his beloved forest on fire. I see now why Trey never fights with magic. He's too afraid of what he'll do.

The man takes the conjured fire in stride. His attention shifts over to the corner of the house where Tara and Máthair come into view. And behind them, Shawn, carrying my Mossberg. If he's surprised, he doesn't show it—his glare is as fierce as Tara's. And for once Máthair's composure has been broken. She's wearing a wicked serenity that's complemented by the wind kicking up behind her, the angry sway of the one-hundred-foot-tall pines. If one of those comes down, we will all be dead.

Maybe Sloane's safe, wherever she is. If we all die here, she'll know to go straight to Winnie and Will. They'll help her get to the Bevans in Chicago, who will hide her better than we did. She'll survive.

Trey slumps, losing his legs just for a second before he rights himself again with a heavy breath that doesn't go unnoticed by the leader of the army. Shawn steps over to take my place, getting stronger, taller shoulders under Trey's arm. I hug Marcas' lanky frame against me and wonder if we have any bargaining power. If they'll hear a plea to save him, if they'll allow a child to walk away.

"We came for the girl," the leader says.

"She's not here," I say.

A black utility van speeds backward down the gravel, coming to a sliding halt as the back doors fly open. Two men hop out, dragging with them a young man and woman, their wrists bound, black sleeves running from forearm to hand: tar—and on their feet too. Just like Trey told me they did to him. Tara gasps beside me as Winnie and Will lift their eyes to us. Shawn shifts away from Trey to raise the Mossberg, biting out a string of curses.

"Who sent you?" Trey takes an impossibly steady step forward. The fire's hot from where I stand. From his new position, it must be scorching. "Jared? Tell that coward fucker he's dead."

With this distraction Winnie and Will spring into action. Winnie bursts upward from her knees, slamming the top of her skull into her handler's chin as Will swings a leg to knock down his. Trey's firing, I'm firing, and it's enough cover to get Winnie and Will through the flames and onto our side. It's good to know Marcas' fire won't hurt his kind. I'm not so sure if that includes me.

Trey and I reload and the black-clothed men drag away their wounded. The leader is speaking low into a radio. I start counting the remaining soldiers but give up when I find it's still too many. They could start shooting us as easily as we're shooting them. Once they find out Sloane really isn't here and we have no idea where she is, there will be no need for them to keep us alive.

I hand Tara a dagger to cut the ropes from Winnie and Will's wrists. There's a rumble in the clouds and I look up, catching a splatter of cold rain on the cheek. Máthair is unusually still, her vicious calm a force of its own. She's waiting for something. A power to build. If we can stall them enough, there might be a chance—

A black Cadillac cruises down the driveway. It stops behind the van that held Winnie and Will. Trey walks through the wall of Marcas' flame too fast for both me and Shawn to grab him and keep him safe on our side. His legs are solid but his arms quiver, and I know this time it isn't weakness but adrenaline-fueled rage.

"Trey!" My voice has called him out of it before, but this time I'm not sure if anything will.

Dillon exits the backseat of the car in no hurry. He takes a slow look around. Raises an eyebrow, brushes off his slacks. Then he reaches into his pocket and out comes the bottle of toxic black magic, the one I tried to get back from Inis, but failed. "Look familiar?" Dillon asks.

I glance at Tara. She knows what I'm asking: are any of them shielded against it? She gives the subtlest shake of her head. It's been too long, too much out of our minds. That bottle has lost its threat, and the shield she and Máthair created when it was a current danger to us has been forgotten. Everyone but me and Shawn will be its victim if that bottle is opened. Even Sloane, wherever she's hiding, will be drained dry. The magic in that bottle has been held against its will for so many years it will be insatiable.

Trey aims at Dillon's forehead.

"You shoot me, Bevan, and this thing will smash open on the ground."

A shimmer of color has everyone looking at the edge of the woods not guarded by black-clothed men. Sloane steps from inside a cloak, becoming visible to us now that she's revealed herself. As she removes it from her shoulders it scatters into a thousand moths carried away by the wind.

She signs to Trey: *I'll go.*

He shakes his head at her. Jerks his chin toward our group behind the fire.

I have to, she signs. *It's time.*

"No," Marcas chokes. He finds my hand. This is a memory that will weigh heavy in his heart. Trey can't take it from him. I feel another hand settle on my shoulder: Máthair.

Sloane walks toward Dillon and stands before him, waiting. Her frame is small but her silent presence is mighty. He pockets the bottle, keeping his eyes on her the whole time, not trusting her peaceful composure. He tells her, "Raise your arms," and she reads the words on his lips, lifting both arms like a caught criminal. He pats her down, finds a knife he hands to a soldier nearby. Then he finds her phone, her only method to communicate in the hearing world. He drops it to the ground and grinds it into the gravel with his heel.

Sloane doesn't watch—her eyes remain on his until she turns around to look at us, the wall of flame dying with the sweep of her eyes. Stripped of weapons and communication, she appears unafraid. Nothing like the little girl who feared being alone in the hearing world without us. My cheeks are wet with tears, my heart skewered. I put a hand over it to make sure it's still beating because it feels like it's stopped, cutting off blood and breath. I know we expected this, we prepared her for it, but no, it's not happening. It can't happen, not this way. We were supposed to get out of it.

"Sloane," Trey says, even though she can't hear him.

She signs, *I love you.*

Marcas whimpers with his face against me. I wish I could hold him and cry but that's not what Sloane needs to see right now. So I take his hand and we join Trey's side. The sound of footfalls in gravel tell me everyone else has come to stand behind us. We are just a small portion of the family who stands behind her, the centuries of people who passed their magic and power to one girl who was chosen to shoulder it because she's the only one strong enough to bear it. She's the only one with the answer to this war that's taken so many lives. This she knows, and she knows her destiny is to win.

Warrior, Trey signs to her.

She nods once. Dillon opens the Cadillac's door and she slides inside, unflinching and collected as ever. He gets in behind her and the door shuts, the dark tint sealing her away.

Our warrior will return. It's in the stars, and the stars have never let us down.

SLOANE

Y FAMILY STANDS frozen in time. The only motion bold enough to move in this moment is the roll of tears down my mother's cheeks. I slide on the leather seat with the force of the car pulling away and crane my neck, the mural of my family growing smaller. I know they can't see me through the tinted windows, but I wish I could tell my mother I'm not scared, and she shouldn't be scared while I'm gone. I will come home, and when I do we won't ever be scared again.

I wish I could tell Marcas I slipped my amulet into my boot to hide it just like he showed me, with it nestled in the arch of my foot so it's easier to walk on. His sneaky ways

I've criticized for their dishonesty are now serving me and might just save my life.

Before I turn away, I look into the eyes of my father, whose gaze tears through metal, plastic, fabric, and foam to spring hot and bright in my head. Like a puzzle solved, it's there. Rooted. Permanent. He doesn't simply believe in me as any father would. He believes I will defeat an entire family of killers who've been hunting my people forever hoping to cut off my bloodline. I only wish I could ask him how.

DEAR READER,

THANKS SO MUCH for reading *The Catalyst*! Sloane's story continues in the final book of the series, *The Warrior*. Subscribe to kaycamden.com to receive updates on my writing progress and other news.

If you liked this book—or even if you didn't—please consider leaving a review. All reviews help, and indie readers count on them because we don't have big publishers promoting our work. And please tell your friends! All my ebooks are lendable, so pass them along!

Are you on Goodreads? Send me a friend request!

I love to hear from readers! Email me at kay@kaycamden.com

Again, thank you for reading. Our time is valuable and finite and there are far too many good books to read. Thank you for choosing mine!

—Kay

ACKNOWLEDGMENTS

My thanks go to—

My fourth grade teacher, Darlys Presler, who read chapter books aloud in class—fun books, the ones kids wanted to read.

Dr. Bill and his website lifeprint.com and ASL University.

Authors of books that helped in my research of Deafness: Thomas Spradley, Brandi Rarus, Marc Marschark, Peter Hauser, Oliver Sacks.

Elsa S. Henry and K. Tempest Bradford and the *Writing the Other* class series.

Countless online resources for Deafness that I wasn't diligent enough to make note of.

The ILF, again.

My readers, reviewers, and raters. Thank you for your time, your focus, your thoughtful feedback. Thank you for every review and rating, both good and bad. Thank you for getting as angry at these characters as I do. And thank you for loving them too.

the
ALIGNMENT SERIES

www.ingramcontent.com/pod-product-compliance
Lightning Source LLC
Chambersburg PA
CBHW031930110726
47902CB00001B/116